"N. K. Jemisin has captured the living, breathing soul of New York City in a way that only a writer of her skill can. *The City We Became* is a masterpiece that plays by no rules—beautiful, musical, joyfully weird, and as impossibly fantastical as it is deeply true"

Peng Shepherd, author of *The Book of M*

"Thrillingly expansive without ever becoming abstract or highflown" *Los Angeles Times*

"A wonderfully inventive love letter to New York City that spans the multiverse. A big middle finger to Lovecraft with a lot of heart, creativity, smarts, and humor. A timely and audacious allegorical tale for our times. This book is all these things and more"

Rebecca Roanhorse, author of *Trail of Lightning*

"Jemisin's writing is visionary and immersive ... A sciencefiction/fantasy GOAT" *GQ*

"Jemisin's fantastical stories are anchored in complex societal systems and fully-imagined new worlds—all with fault lines lying in wait—that aim to help us better understand our own" *Time*

"Three consecutive Hugo Awards and a cover blurb from Neil Gaiman—yes, it's time for you to pick up a novel by Jemisin, whose speculative fiction has a degree of inclusivity rare in the science-fiction world" *Washington Post*

By N. K. Jemisin

The Inheritance Trilogy

The Hundred Thousand Kingdoms
The Broken Kingdom
The Kingdom of Gods
The Awakened Kingdom (*novella*)

The Inheritance Trilogy (*omnibus*)

Dreamblood

The Killing Moon
The Shadowed Sun

The Broken Earth

The Fifth Season
The Obelisk Gate
The Stone Sky

How Long 'til Black Future Month?
(*short story collection*)

The Great Cities Trilogy

The City We Became

THE CITY
WE
BECAME

THE GREAT CITIES TRILOGY:
BOOK ONE

N. K. JEMISIN

orbitbooks.net

ORBIT

First published in Great Britain in 2020 by Orbit

1 3 5 7 9 10 8 6 4 2

Map by Lauren Panepinto

Equation on pp. 176–77 from Weisstein, Eric W. "Sphere with Tunnel."
From MathWorld—A Wolfram Web Resource.
http://mathworld.wolfram.com/SpherewithTunnel.html

Excerpt from *The Bone Shard Daughter* by Andrea Stewart
Copyright © 2020 by Andrea Stewart

A CIP catalogue record for this book is available from the British Library.

ISBN 978-0-356-51268-6

Printed and bound in Great Britain by Clays Ltd, Elcograf S.p.A.

Papers used by Orbit are from well-managed forests
and other responsible sources.

MIX
Paper from
responsible sources
FSC® C104740

Orbit
An imprint of
Little, Brown Book Group
Carmelite House
50 Victoria Embankment
London EC4Y 0DZ

An Hachette UK Company
www.hachette.co.uk

www.orbitbooks.net

"One belongs to New York instantly, one belongs to it as much in five minutes as in five years."

—Thomas Wolfe

NEW JERSEY
UPSTATE
WESTCHESTER
YONKERS
THE BRONX
INWOOD HILL PARK
shorakkopoch
FORDHAM HTS.
MANNY +BEL
BRONX ART CENTER
BRONX ZOO
BRONCA
THROGS NECK
HIGHBRIDGE
HARLEM
MANHATTAN
Port Authority
TIMES SQ.
Penn Station
FDR DRIVE
WILLIAMSBURG BRIDGE
MANHATTAN BRIDGE
BKLYN BRIDGE
CITY HALL
HOBOKEN
JERSEY CITY
RIKERS
LGA
COLLEGE POINT
ASTORIA
L.I.C.
JACKSON HEIGHTS
THE QUEEN
FLUSHING
QUEENS
JAMAICA
VINTAGE NEW YORK CITY
CHECKER CABS
(212) 816-7469
CHECKER CAB DREAM WEDDINGS
Prosperity & Progress
BETTER NEW YORK FOUNDATION
A SUBSIDIARY OF TMW, INC.
NEW YORK • CHICAGO • MIAMI • HAVANA • RIO DE JANEIRO • SYDNEY • NAIROBI • BEIJING • ISTANBUL

RED HOOK
BED STUY
Bed Stuy do or die
Crown Heights stand up
Flatbush represent!
JFK
S.I. FERRY
BROOKLYN "MCFREE"
FLATBUSH
BAY RIDGE
ST. GEORGE
BROOKLYN
BENSONHURST
AISLYN
COLLEGE OF S.I.
HEARTLAND VILLAGE
VERRAZZANO BRIDGE
STATEN ISLAND
CONEY ISLAND
the Rockaways
S.I. MALL
FRESH KILLS
LONG ISLAND
HERE THERE BE DRAGONS
SÃO PAULO
LAGOS
PARIS
CAIRO
HONG KONG
LONDON
~~NEW ORLEANS~~
~~PORT AU PRINCE~~

PROLOGUE

See, What Had Happened Was

I sing the city.

Fucking city. I stand on the rooftop of a building I don't live in and spread my arms and tighten my middle and yell nonsense ululations at the construction site that blocks my view. I'm really singing to the cityscape beyond. The city'll figure it out.

It's dawn. The damp of it makes my jeans feel slimy, or maybe that's 'cause they haven't been washed in weeks. Got change for a wash-and-dry, just not another pair of pants to wear till they're done. Maybe I'll spend it on more pants at the Goodwill down the street instead...but not yet. Not till I've finished going *AAAAaaaaAAAAaaaa* (breath) *aaaaAAAAaaaaaaa* and listening to the syllable echo back at me from every nearby building face. In my head, there's an orchestra playing "Ode to Joy" with a Busta Rhymes backbeat. My voice is just tying it all together.

Shut your fucking mouth! someone yells, so I take a bow and exit the stage.

But with my hand on the knob of the rooftop door, I stop and turn back and frown and listen, 'cause for a moment I hear something both distant and intimate singing back at me, basso-deep. Sort of coy.

And from even farther, I hear something else: a dissonant, gathering growl. Or maybe those are the rumblers of police sirens? Nothing I like the sound of, either way. I leave.

"There's a way these things are supposed to work," says Paulo. He's smoking again, nasty bastard. I've never seen him eat. All he uses his mouth for is smoking, drinking coffee, and talking. Shame; it's a nice mouth otherwise.

We're sitting in a café. I'm sitting with him because he bought me breakfast. The people in the café are eyeballing him because he's something not-white by their standards, but they can't tell what. They're eyeballing me because I'm definitely Black, and because the holes in my clothes aren't the fashionable kind. I don't stink, but these people can smell anybody without a trust fund from a mile away.

"Right," I say, biting into the egg sandwich and damn near wetting myself. Actual egg! Swiss cheese! It's so much better than that McDonald's shit.

Guy likes hearing himself talk. I like his accent; it's sort of nasal and sibilant, nothing like a Spanish speaker's. His eyes are huge, and I think, *I could get away with so much shit if I had permanent puppy eyes like that.* But he seems older than he looks—way, way older. There's only a tinge of gray at his temples, nice and distinguished, but he feels, like, a hundred.

He's also eyeballing me, and not in the way I'm used to. "Are you listening?" he asks. "This is important."

"Yeah," I say, and take another bite of my sandwich.

He sits forward. "I didn't believe it either, at first. Hong had to drag me to one of the sewers, down into the reeking dark, and show me the growing roots, the budding teeth. I'd been hearing breathing all my life. I thought everyone could." He pauses. "Have you heard it yet?"

"Heard what?" I ask, which is the wrong answer. It isn't that I'm not listening. I just don't give a shit.

He sighs. "Listen."

"I *am* listening!"

"No. I mean, listen, but not to me." He gets up, tosses a twenty onto the table—which isn't necessary, because he paid for the sandwich and the coffee at the counter, and this café doesn't do table service. "Meet me back here on Thursday."

I pick up the twenty, finger it, pocket it. Would've done him for the sandwich, or because I like his eyes, but whatever. "You got a place?"

He blinks, then actually looks annoyed. "*Listen,*" he commands again, and leaves.

I sit there for as long as I can, making the sandwich last, sipping his leftover coffee, savoring the fantasy of being normal. I people-watch, judge other patrons' appearances; on the fly I make up a poem about being a rich white girl who notices a poor Black boy in her coffee shop and has an existential crisis. I imagine Paulo being impressed by my sophistication and admiring me, instead of thinking I'm just some dumb street kid who doesn't listen. I visualize myself going back to a nice apartment with a soft bed, and a fridge stuffed full of food.

Then a cop comes in, fat florid guy buying hipster joe for himself and his partner in the car, and his flat eyes skim the shop. I imagine mirrors around my head, a rotating cylinder of them that causes his gaze to bounce away. There's no real power in this—it's just something I do to try to make myself less afraid when the monsters are near. For the first time, though, it sort of works: The cop looks around, but doesn't ping on the lone Black face. Lucky. I escape.

I paint the city. Back when I was in school, there was an artist who came in on Fridays to give us free lessons in perspective and lighting and other shit that white people go to art school to learn. Except this guy had done that, and he was Black. I'd never seen a Black artist before. For a minute I thought I could maybe be one, too.

I can be, sometimes. Deep in the night, on a rooftop in Chinatown, with a spray can for each hand and a bucket of drywall paint that somebody left outside after doing up their living room in lilac, I move in scuttling, crablike swirls. The drywall stuff I can't use too much of; it'll start flaking off after a couple of rains. Spray paint's better for everything, but I like the contrast of the two textures—liquid black on rough lilac, red edging the black. I'm painting a hole. It's like a throat that doesn't start with a mouth or end in lungs; a thing that breathes and swallows endlessly, never filling. No one will see it except people in planes angling toward LaGuardia from the southwest, a few tourists who take helicopter tours, and NYPD aerial surveillance. I don't care what they see. It's not for them.

It's real late. I didn't have anywhere to sleep for the night, so this is what I'm doing to stay awake. If it wasn't the end of the month, I'd get on the subway, but the cops who haven't met their quota would fuck with me. Gotta be careful here; there's a lot of dumb-fuck Chinese kids west of Chrystie Street who wanna pretend to be a gang, protecting their territory, so I keep low. I'm skinny, dark; that helps, too. All I want to do is paint, man, because it's in me and I need to get it out. I need to open up this throat. I need to, I need to . . . yeah. Yeah.

There's a soft, strange sound as I lay down the last streak of black. I pause and look around, confused for a moment—and then the throat sighs behind me. A big, heavy gust of moist air tickles the hairs on my skin. I'm not scared. This is why I did it, though I didn't realize that when I started. Not sure how I know now. But when I turn back, it's still just paint on a rooftop.

Paulo wasn't shitting me. Huh. Or maybe my mama was right, and I ain't never been right in the head.

I jump into the air and whoop for joy, and I don't even know why.

I spend the next two days going all over the city, drawing breathing-holes everywhere, till my paint runs out.

I'm so tired on the day I meet Paulo again that I stumble and nearly fall through the café's plate-glass window. He catches my elbow and drags me over to a bench meant for customers. "You're hearing it," he says. He sounds pleased.

"I'm hearing coffee," I suggest, not bothering to stifle a yawn. A cop car rolls by. I'm not too tired to imagine myself as nothing, beneath notice, not even worth beating for pleasure. It works again; they roll on.

Paulo ignores my suggestion. He sits down beside me and his gaze goes strange and unfocused for a moment. "Yes. The city is breathing easier," he says. "You're doing a good job, even without training."

"I try."

He looks amused. "I can't tell if you don't believe me, or if you just don't care."

I shrug. "I believe you." I also don't care, not much, because I'm hungry. My stomach growls. I've still got that twenty he gave me, but I'll take it to that church-plate sale I heard about over on Prospect, get chicken and rice and greens and cornbread for less than the cost of a free-trade small-batch-roasted latte.

He glances down at my stomach when it growls. Huh. I pretend to stretch and scratch above my abs, making sure to pull up my shirt a little. The artist guy brought a model for us to draw once, and pointed to this little ridge of muscle above the hips called Apollo's Belt. Paulo's gaze goes right to it. *Come on, come on, fishy fishy. I need somewhere to sleep.*

Then his eyes narrow and focus on mine again. "I had forgotten," he says, in a faint wondering tone. "I almost... It's been so long. Once, though, I was a boy of the favelas."

"Not a lot of Mexican food in New York," I reply.

He blinks and looks amused again. Then he sobers. "This city will die," he says. He doesn't raise his voice, but he doesn't have to. I'm paying attention now. Food, living: These things have meaning to me. "If you do not learn the things I have to teach you. If you do not help. The time will come and you will fail, and this city will join Pompeii and Atlantis and a dozen others whose names no one remembers, even though hundreds of thousands of people died with them. Or perhaps there will be a stillbirth—the shell of the city surviving to possibly grow again in the future but its vital spark snuffed for now, like New Orleans—but that will still kill *you*, either way. You are the catalyst, whether of strength or destruction."

He's been talking like this since he showed up—places that never were, things that can't be, omens and portents. I figure it's bullshit because he's telling it to *me*, a kid whose own mama kicked him out and prays for him to die every day and probably hates me. *God* hates me. And I fucking hate God back, so why would he choose me for anything? But that's really why I start paying attention: because of God. I don't have to believe in something for it to fuck up my life.

"Tell me what to do," I say.

Paulo nods, looking smug. Thinks he's got my number. "Ah. You don't want to die."

I stand up, stretch, feel the streets around me grow longer and more pliable in the rising heat of day. (Is that really happening, or am I imagining it, or is it happening *and* I'm imagining that it's connected to me somehow?) "Fuck you. That ain't it."

"Then you don't even care about that." He makes it a question with the tone of his voice.

"Ain't about being alive." I'll starve to death someday, or freeze some winter night, or catch something that rots me away until the hospitals have to take me, even without money or an address. But I'll sing and paint and dance and fuck and cry the city before I'm done, because it's mine. It's fucking *mine*. That's why.

"It's about *living*," I finish. And then I turn to glare at him. He can kiss my ass if he doesn't understand. "Tell me what to do."

Something changes in Paulo's face. He's listening, now. To me. So he gets to his feet and leads me away for my first real lesson.

This is the lesson: Great cities are like any other living things, being born and maturing and wearying and dying in their turn.

Duh, right? Everyone who's visited a real city feels that, one way or another. All those rural people who hate cities are afraid of something legit; cities really are *different*. They make a weight on the world, a tear in the fabric of reality, like . . . like black holes, maybe. Yeah. (I go to museums sometimes. They're cool inside, and Neil deGrasse Tyson is hot.) As more and more people come in and deposit their strangeness and leave and get replaced by others, the tear widens. Eventually it gets so deep that it forms a pocket, connected only by the thinnest thread of ... something to ... something. Whatever cities are made of.

But the separation starts a process, and in that pocket the many parts of the city begin to multiply and differentiate. Its sewers extend into places where there is no need for water. Its slums grow teeth; its art centers, claws. Ordinary things within it, traffic and construction and stuff like that, start to have a rhythm like a heartbeat, if you record their sounds and play them back fast. The city ... quickens.

Not all cities make it this far. There used to be a couple of great cities on this continent, but that was before Columbus fucked the Indians' shit up, so we had to start over. New Orleans failed, like Paulo said, but it survived, and that's something. It can try again. Mexico City's well on its way. But New York is the first American city to reach this point.

The gestation can take twenty years or two hundred or two thousand, but eventually the time will come. The cord is cut and the city becomes a thing of its own, able to stand on wobbly legs and do ... well, whatever the fuck a living, thinking entity shaped like a big-ass city wants to do.

And just as in any other part of nature, there are things lying in wait for this moment, hoping to chase down the sweet new life and swallow its guts while it screams.

That's why Paulo's here to teach me. That's why I can clear the city's breathing and stretch and massage its asphalt limbs. I'm the midwife, see.

* * *

I run the city. I run it every fucking day.

Paulo takes me home. It's just somebody's summer sublet in the Lower East Side, but it feels like a home. I use his shower and eat some of the food in his fridge without asking, just to see what he'll do. He doesn't do shit except smoke a cigarette, I think to piss me off. I can hear sirens on the streets of the neighborhood— frequent, close. I wonder, for some reason, if they're looking for me. I don't say it aloud, but Paulo sees me twitching. He says, "The harbingers of the Enemy will hide among the city's parasites. Beware of them."

He's always saying cryptic shit like this. Some of it makes sense, like when he speculates that maybe there's a *purpose* to all of it, some reason for the great cities and the process that makes them. What the Enemy has been doing—attacking at the moment of vulnerability, crimes of opportunity—might just be the warm-up for something bigger. But Paulo's full of shit, too, like when he says I should consider meditation to better attune myself to the city's needs. Like I'mma get through this on white girl yoga.

"White girl yoga," Paulo says, nodding. "Indian man yoga. Stockbroker racquetball and schoolboy handball, ballet and merengue, union halls and SoHo galleries. You will embody a city of millions. You need not *be* them, but know that they are part of you."

I laugh. "Racquetball? That shit ain't no part of me, chico."

"The city chose you, out of all," Paulo says. "Their lives depend on you."

Maybe. But I'm still hungry and tired all the time, scared all the time, never safe. What good does it do to be valuable, if nobody values you?

He can tell I don't wanna talk anymore, so he gets up and goes to bed. I flop on the couch and I'm dead to the world. Dead.

Dreaming, dead dreaming, of a dark place beneath heavy cold waves where something stirs with a slithery sound and uncoils and turns toward the mouth of the Hudson, where it empties into the sea. Toward *me*. And I am too weak, too helpless, too immobilized by fear, to do anything but twitch beneath its predatory gaze.

Something comes from far to the south, somehow. (None of this is quite real. Everything rides along the thin tether that connects the city's reality to that of the world. The *effect* happens in the world, Paulo has said. The *cause* centers around me.) It moves between me, wherever I am, and the uncurling thing, wherever it is. An immensity protects me, just this once, just in this place— though from a great distance I feel others hemming and grumbling and raising themselves to readiness. Warning the Enemy that it must adhere to the rules of engagement that have always governed this ancient battle. It's not allowed to come at me too soon.

My protector, in this unreal space of dream, is a sprawling jewel with filth-crusted facets, a thing that stinks of dark coffee and the bruised grass of a futebol pitch and traffic noise and familiar cigarette smoke. Its threat display of saber-shaped girders lasts for only a moment, but that is enough. The uncurling thing flinches back into its cold cave, resentfully. But it will be back. That, too, is tradition.

I wake with sunlight warming half my face. Just a dream? I stumble into the room where Paulo is sleeping. "*São* Paulo," I whisper, but he does not wake. I wiggle under his covers. When he wakes, he doesn't reach for me, but he doesn't push me away either. I let him know I'm grateful and give him a reason to let me back in later. The rest'll have to wait till I get condoms and he brushes his ashy-ass mouth. After that, I use his shower again, put on the clothes I washed in his sink, and head out while he's still snoring.

Libraries are safe places. They're warm in the winter. Nobody cares if you stay all day as long as you're not eyeballing the kids' corner or trying to hit up porn on the computers. The one at Forty-second—the one with the lions—isn't that kind of library. It doesn't lend out books. Still, it has a library's safety, so I sit in a corner and read everything within reach: municipal tax law, *Birds of the Hudson Valley*, *What to Expect When You're Expecting a City Baby: NYC Edition*. See, Paulo? I told you I was listening.

It gets close to noon and I head outside. People cover the steps, laughing, chatting, mugging with selfie sticks. There're cops in body armor over by the subway entrance, showing off their guns to the tourists so they'll feel safe from New York. I get a Polish sausage and eat it at the feet of one of the lions. Fortitude, not Patience. I know my strengths.

I'm full of meat and relaxed and thinking about stuff that ain't actually important—like how long Paulo will let me stay and whether I can use his address to apply for stuff—so I'm not watching the street. Until cold prickles skitter over my side. I know what it is before I react, but I'm careless again because I *turn to look* ... Stupid, stupid, I fucking know better; cops down in Baltimore broke a man's spine for making eye contact. But as I spot these two on the corner opposite the library steps—short pale man and tall dark woman both in blue like black—I notice something that actually breaks my fear because it's so strange.

It's a bright, clear day, not a cloud in the sky. People walking past the cops leave short, stark afternoon shadows, barely there at all. But around these two, the shadows pool and curl as if they stand beneath their own private, roiling thundercloud. And as I watch, the shorter one begins to . . . *stretch*, sort of, his shape warping ever so slightly, until one eye is twice the circumference of the other. His right shoulder slowly develops a bulge that suggests a dislocated joint. His companion doesn't seem to notice.

Yooooo, nope. I get up and start picking my way through the crowd on the steps. I'm doing that thing I do, trying to shunt off their gaze—but it feels different this time. Sticky, sort of, threads of cheap-shit gum fucking up my mirrors. I *feel* them start following me, something immense and wrong shifting in my direction.

Even then I'm not sure—a lot of real cops drip and pulse sadism in the same way—but I ain't taking chances. My city is helpless, unborn as yet, and Paulo ain't here to protect me. I gotta look out for self, same as always.

I play casual till I reach the corner and book it, or try. Fucking tourists! They idle along the wrong side of the sidewalk, stopping to look at maps and take pictures of shit nobody else gives a fuck about. I'm so busy cussing them out in my head that I forget they can also be dangerous: Somebody yells and grabs my arm as I Heisman past, and I hear a man yell out, "He tried to take her purse!" as I wrench away. *Bitch, I ain't took shit*, I think, but it's too late. I see another tourist reaching for her phone to call 911. Every cop in the area will be gunning for every Black male aged whatever now.

I gotta get out of the area.

Grand Central's right there, sweet subway promise, but I see three cops hanging out in the entrance, so I swerve right to take Forty-first. The crowds thin out past Lex, but where can I go? I sprint across Third despite the traffic; there are enough gaps. But I'm getting tired, 'cause I'm a scrawny dude who doesn't get enough to eat, not a track star.

I keep going, though, even through the burn in my side. I can feel *those* cops, the *harbingers of the Enemy*, not far behind me. The ground shakes with their lumpen footfalls.

I hear a siren about a block away, closing. Shit, the UN's coming up; I don't need the Secret Service or whatever on me, too. I jag left through an alley and trip over a wooden pallet. Lucky again— a cop car rolls by the alley entrance just as I go down, and they don't see me. I stay down and try to catch my breath till I hear the car's engine fading into the distance. Then, when I think it's safe, I push up. Look back, because the city is squirming around me, the concrete is jittering and heaving, everything from the bedrock to the rooftop bars is trying its damnedest to tell me to go. Go. *Go.*

Crowding the alley behind me is . . . is . . . the shit? I don't have words for it. Too many arms, too many legs, too many eyes, and all of them fixed on me. Somewhere in the mass I glimpse curls of dark hair and a scalp of pale blond, and I understand suddenly that these are—this is—my two cops. One real monstrosity. The walls of the alley crack as it oozes its way into the narrow space.

"Oh. Fuck. No," I gasp.

I claw my way to my feet and haul ass. A patrol car comes around the corner from Second Avenue and I don't see it in time to duck out of sight. The car's loudspeaker blares something unintelligible, probably *I'm gonna kill you*, and I'm actually amazed. Do they not see the thing behind me? Or do they just not give a shit because they can't shake it down for city revenue? Let them fucking shoot me. Better than whatever that thing will do.

I hook left onto Second Avenue. The cop car can't come after me against the traffic, but it's not like that'll stop some doubled-cop monster. Forty-fifth. Forty-seventh and my legs are molten granite. Fiftieth and I think I'm going to die. Heart attack far too young; poor kid, should've eaten more organic; should've taken it easy and not been so angry; the world can't hurt you if you just ignore everything that's wrong with it; well, not until it kills you anyway.

I cross the street and risk a look back and see something roll onto the sidewalk on at least eight legs, using three or four arms to push itself off a building as it careens a little . . . before coming straight after me again. It's the Mega Cop, and it's gaining. *Oh shit oh shit oh shit please no.*

Only one choice.

Swing right. Fifty-third, against the traffic. An old folks' home, a park, a promenade . . . fuck those. Pedestrian bridge? Fuck that. I head straight for the six lanes of utter batshittery and potholes that is FDR Drive, do not pass Go, do not try to cross on foot unless you want to be smeared halfway to Brooklyn. Beyond it? The East River, if I survive. I'm even freaked out enough to try swimming in that fucking sewage. But I'm probably gonna collapse in the third lane and get run over fifty times before anybody thinks to put on brakes.

Behind me, the Mega Cop utters a wet, tumid *hough*, like it's clearing its throat for swallowing. I go

over the barrier and through the grass into fucking hell I go one lane silver car two lanes horns horns horns three lanes SEMI WHAT'S A FUCKING SEMI DOING ON THE FDR IT'S TOO TALL YOU STUPID UPSTATE HICK screaming four lanes GREEN TAXI screaming Smart Car hahaha cute five lanes moving truck six lanes and the blue Lexus actually brushes up against my clothes as it blares past screaming screaming screaming

screaming

screaming metal and tires as reality stretches, and nothing stops for the Mega Cop; it does not belong here and the FDR is an artery, vital with the movement of nutrients and strength and attitude and adrenaline, the cars are white blood cells and the thing is an irritant, an infection, an invader to whom the city gives no consideration and no quarter

screaming, as the Mega Cop is torn to pieces by the semi and the taxi and the Lexus and even that adorable Smart Car, which actually swerves a little to run over an extra-wiggly piece. I collapse onto a square of grass, breathless, shaking, wheezing, and can only stare as a dozen limbs are crushed, two dozen eyes squashed flat, a mouth that is mostly gums riven from jaw to palate. The pieces flicker like a monitor with an AV cable short, translucent to solid and back again—but FDR don't stop for shit except a presidential motorcade or a Knicks game, and this thing sure as hell ain't Carmelo Anthony. Pretty soon there's nothing left of it but half-real smears on the asphalt.

I'm alive. Oh, God.

I cry for a little while. Mama's boyfriend ain't here to slap me and say I'm not a man for it. Daddy would've said it was okay— tears mean you're alive—but Daddy's dead. And I'm alive.

With limbs burning and weak, I drag myself up, then fall again. Everything hurts. Is this that heart attack? I feel sick. Everything is shaking, blurring. Maybe it's a stroke. You don't have to be old for that to happen, do you? I stumble over to a garbage can and think about throwing up into it. There's an old guy lying on the bench—me in twenty years, if I make it that far. He opens one eye as I stand there gagging and purses his lips in a judgy way, like he could do better dry-heaves in his sleep.

He says, "It's time," and rolls over to put his back to me.

Time. Suddenly I have to move. Sick or not, exhausted or not, something is...pulling me. West, toward the city's center. I push away from the can and hug myself as I shiver and stumble toward the pedestrian bridge. As I walk over the lanes I previously ran across, I look down onto flickering fragments of the dead Mega Cop, now ground into the asphalt by a hundred car wheels. Some globules of it are still twitching, and I don't like that. Infection, intrusion. I want it gone.

We want it gone. Yes. It's time.

I blink and suddenly I'm in Central Park. How the fuck did I get here? Disoriented, I realize only as I see their black shoes that I'm passing another pair of cops, but these two don't bother me. They should—skinny kid shivering like he's cold on a June day; even if all they do is drag me off somewhere to shove a plunger up my ass, they should *react* to me. Instead, it's like I'm not there. Miracles exist, Ralph Ellison was right, any NYPD you can walk away from, hallelujah.

The Lake. Bow Bridge: a place of transition. I stop here, stand here, and I know...everything.

Everything Paulo's told me: It's true. Somewhere beyond the city, the Enemy is awakening. It sent forth its harbingers and they have failed, but its taint is in the city now, spreading with every car that passes over every now-microscopic iota of the Mega Cop's substance, and this creates a foothold. The Enemy uses this anchor to drag itself up from the dark toward the world, toward the warmth and light, toward the defiance that is *me*, toward the burgeoning wholeness that is *my city*. This attack is not all of it, of course. What comes is only the smallest fraction of the Enemy's old, old evil—but that should be more than enough to slaughter one lowly, worn-out kid who doesn't even have a real city to protect him.

Not yet. It's time. *In* time? We'll see.

On Second, Sixth, and Eighth Avenues, my water breaks. Mains, I mean. Water mains. Terrible mess, gonna fuck up the evening commute. I shut my eyes and I am seeing what no one else sees. I am feeling the flex and rhythm of reality, the contractions of possibility. I reach out and grip the railing of the bridge before me and feel the steady, strong pulse that runs through it. *You're doing good, baby. Doing great.*

Something begins to shift. I grow bigger, encompassing. I feel myself upon the firmament, heavy as the foundations of a city. There are others here with me, looming, watching—my ancestors' bones under Wall Street, my predecessors' blood ground into the benches of Christopher Park. No, *new* others, of my new people, heavy imprints upon the fabric of time and space. São Paulo squats nearest, its roots stretching all the way to the bones of dead Machu Picchu, watching sagely and twitching a little with the memory of its own relatively recent traumatic birth. Paris observes with distant disinterest, mildly offended that any city of our tasteless upstart land has managed this transition; Lagos exults to see a new fellow who knows the hustle, the hype, the fight. And more, many more, all of them watching, waiting to see if their numbers increase. Or not. If nothing else, they will bear witness that I, we, were great for one shining moment.

"We'll make it," I say, squeezing the railing and feeling the city contract. All over the city, people's ears pop, and they look around in confusion. "Just a little more. Come on." I'm scared, but there's no rushing this. *Lo que pasa, pasa*—damn, now that song is in my head, *in me* like the rest of New York. It's all here, just like Paulo said. There's no gap between me and the city anymore.

And as the firmament ripples, slides, tears, the Enemy writhes up from the deeps with a reality-bridging roar—

But it is too late. The tether is cut and we are here. We become! We stand, whole and hale and independent, and our legs don't even wobble. We got this. Don't sleep on the city that never sleeps, son, and don't fucking bring your squamous eldritch bullshit here.

I raise my arms and avenues leap. (It's real but it's not. The ground jolts and people think, *Huh, subway's really shaky today.*) I brace my feet and they are girders, anchors, bedrock. The beast of the deeps shrieks and I laugh, giddy with postpartum endorphins. *Bring it.* And when it comes at me, I hip-check it with the BQE, backhand it with Inwood Hill Park, drop the South Bronx on it like an elbow. (On the evening news that night, ten construction sites will report wrecking-ball collapses. City safety regulations are so lax; terrible, terrible.) The Enemy tries some kind of fucked-up wiggly shit—it's all tentacles—and I snarl and bite into it 'cause New Yorkers eat damn near as much sushi as Tokyo, mercury and all.

Oh, now you're crying! Now you wanna run? Nah, son. You came to the wrong town. I curb stomp it with the full might of Queens and something inside the beast breaks and bleeds iridescence all over creation. This is a shock, for it has not been truly hurt in centuries. It lashes back in a fury, faster than I can block, and from a place that most of the city cannot see, a skyscraper-long tentacle curls out of nowhere to smash into New York Harbor. I scream and fall, I can *hear* my ribs crack, and—no!—a major earthquake shakes Brooklyn for the first time in decades. The Williamsburg Bridge twists and snaps apart like kindling; the Manhattan groans and splinters, though thankfully it does not give way. I feel every death as if it is my own.

Fucking kill you for that, bitch, I'm not-thinking. The fury and grief have driven me into a vengeful fugue. The pain is nothing; this ain't my first rodeo. Through the groan of my ribs I drag myself upright and brace my legs in a pissing-off-the-platform stance. Then I shower the Enemy with a one-two punch of Long Island radiation and Gowanus toxic waste, which burn it like acid. It screams again in pain and disgust, but *Fuck you, you don't belong here, this city is mine, get out!* To drive this lesson home, I cut the bitch with LIRR traffic, long vicious honking lines; and to stretch out its pain, I salt these wounds with the memory of a bus ride to LaGuardia and back.

And just to add insult to injury? I backhand its ass with Hoboken, raining the drunk rage of ten thousand dudebros down on it like the hammer of God. Port Authority makes it honorary New York, motherfucker; you just got Jerseyed.

The Enemy is as quintessential to nature as any city. We cannot be stopped from becoming, and the Enemy cannot be made to end. I hurt only a small part of it—but I know damn well I sent that part back broken. Good. Time ever comes for that final confrontation, it'll think twice about taking me on again.

Me. *Us.* Yes.

When I relax my hands and open my eyes to see Paulo striding along the bridge toward me with another goddamned cigarette between his lips, I fleetingly see him for what he is again: the sprawling thing from my dream, all sparkling spires and reeking slums and stolen rhythms made over with genteel cruelty. I know that he glimpses what I am, too, all the bright light and bluster of me. Maybe he's always seen it, but there is *admiration* in his gaze now, and I like it. He comes to help support me with his shoulder, and he says, "Congratulations," and I grin.

I live the city. It thrives and it is mine. I am its worthy avatar, and together? We will

never be

afr—

oh shit

something's wrong.

INTERRUPTION

The avatar collapses, sagging onto the thick old hardwood of the bridge despite São Paulo's efforts to catch him. And amid its triumph, the newborn city of New York shudders.

Paulo, crouched beside the unconscious boy who embodies and speaks for and fights for New York, frowns up at the sky as it flickers. First it is the hazy midday blue of northeastern skies in June, then something dimmer, redder, evocative of sunset. As he watches, eyes narrowed, the trees of Central Park flicker as well—as does the water, and the very air. Bright, then shadowed, then bright again; rippling, then nearly still, sudden new rippling; humid with a light breeze, still but with a hint of acrid smoke, back to humid. A moment later, the avatar vanishes from Paulo's hands. This is a variation on something he's seen happen before, and for a moment he grows still with fear—but no, the city has not died, thank God. Paulo can feel the presence and aliveness of the entity around him . . . but that presence is much, much weaker than it should be. Not a stillbirth, but not a sign of health and ease, either. There have been postpartum complications.

Paulo pulls out his phone and makes an international call. After one ring, the person he's calling picks up, sighing into the phone. "Exactly what I was afraid of."

"Like London, then," says Paulo.

"Hard to be sure. But yes, so far, like London."

"How many, do you think? The greater metropolitan area crosses three states—"

"Don't make assumptions. Just 'more,' as far as you're concerned. Find one. They'll track down their own." A pause. "The city is still vulnerable, you realize. That's why it took him away, for safekeeping."

"I know." Paulo gets to his feet because a jogging couple is about to pass. A biker follows them, even though the path is supposed to be pedestrians-only. Three cars pass on the road nearby, even though that particular section of Central Park is supposed to be pedestrians-and-bikes-only. The city continues to spite itself, despite itself. Paulo finds himself watching for signs of danger in the people around him: warping flesh, those standing too still or watching too intently. Nothing so far.

"The Enemy was routed," he says into the phone absently. "The battle was . . . decisive."

"Watch your back anyway." The voice pauses for a rough smog-cough. "The city *is* alive, so it isn't helpless. It certainly won't help you, but it knows its own. Make them work fast. Never good to have a city stuck halfway like this."

"I'll be careful," Paulo says, still scanning his surroundings. "I suppose it's good to know you care." The reply is a cynical snort, which nevertheless makes Paulo smile. "Any suggestions for where to begin?"

"Manhattan would seem a good start."

Paulo pinches the bridge of his nose. "That covers a lot of territory."

"Then you had best get started, hadn't you?" The connection clicks silent. With an annoyed sigh, Paulo turns to begin his task anew.

CHAPTER ONE

Starting with Manhattan, and the Battle of FDR Drive

He forgets his own name somewhere in the tunnel to Penn Station.

He doesn't notice, at first. Too busy with all the stuff people usually do when they're about to reach their train stop: cleaning up the pretzel bags and plastic bottles of breakfast, stuffing his loose laptop power cord into a pocket of his messenger bag, making sure he's gotten his suitcase down from the rack, then having a momentary panic attack before remembering that he's only got one suitcase. The other was shipped ahead and will be waiting for him at his apartment up in Inwood, where his roommate already is, having arrived a few weeks before. They're both going to be grad students at—

—at, uh—

—huh. He's forgotten his school's name. Anyway, orientation is on Thursday, which gives him five days to get settled into his new life in New York.

He's really going to need those days, too, sounds like. As the train slows to a halt, people are murmuring and whispering, peer-ing intently at their phones and tablets with worried looks on their faces. Something about a bridge accident, terrorism, just like 9/11? He'll be living and working uptown, so it shouldn't impact him too much—but still, it's maybe not the best time to move here.

But when is it ever a good time to make a new life in New York City? He'll cope.

He'll more than cope. The train stops and he's first through the door. He's excited but trying to play it cool. In the city he will be completely on his own, free to sink or swim. He has colleagues and family members who think of this as exile, abandonment—

—although, in the flurry of the moment, he cannot remember any of those people's names or faces—

—but that doesn't matter, because they can't understand. They know him as he was, and maybe who he is now. New York is his future.

It's hot on the platform and crowded on the escalator, but he feels fine. Which is why it's so weird when he reaches the top of the escalator, and suddenly—the instant his foot touches the polished-concrete flooring—the whole world inverts. Everything in his vision seems to tilt, and the ugly ceiling fluorescents turn stark and the floor kind of...heaves? It happens fast. The world pulls inside out and his stomach drops and his ears fill with a titanic, many-voiced roar. It's a familiar sound, to a degree; any-one who's been to a stadium during a big game has heard some-thing similar. Madison Square Garden sits on top of Penn Station, so maybe that's it? This sound is bigger, though. *Millions* of people instead of thousands, and all of those voices doubled back on each other and swelling and shifting into layers beyond sound, into color and shaking and emotion, until he claps his hands over his ears and shuts his eyes but it just keeps coming—

But amid all of the cacophony, there is a through line, a repeated motif of sound and word and idea. One voice, screaming fury.

Fuck you, you don't belong here, this city is mine, get out!

And the young man wonders, in confused horror, *Me? Am... am I the one that doesn't belong?* There is no answer, and the doubt within him becomes an unignorable backbeat of its own.

All at once the roar is gone. A new roar, closer and echoing and indescribably smaller, has replaced it. Some of it is recorded, blaring from PA speakers overhead: *"New Jersey Transit train, southbound, stopping at Newark Airport, now boarding on track five."* The rest is the sound of a gigantic space full of people going about their business. He remembers then, as it resolves around him: Penn Station. He does not remember how he ended up on one knee beneath a train-schedules sign, with a shaking hand plastered over his face. Wasn't he on an escalator? He also doesn't remember ever before seeing the two people who are crouched in front of him.

He frowns at them. "Did you just tell me to get out of the city?"

"No. I said, 'Do you want me to call 911?'" says the woman. She's offering water. She looks more skeptical than worried, like maybe he's faking whatever weird faint or fit that's apparently made him fall over in the middle of Penn Station.

"I...no." He shakes his head, trying to focus. Neither water nor the police will fix weird voices in his head, or hallucinations caused by train exhaust, or whatever he's experiencing. "What happened?"

"You just kinda went sideways," says the man bent over him.

He's a portly, middle-aged, pale-skinned Latino. Heavy New York accent, kindly tone. "We caught you and pulled you over here."

"Oh." Everything's still weird. The world isn't spinning anymore, but that terrible, layered roar is still in his head—just muted now, and overlaid by the local and perpetual cacophony that is Penn Station. "I . . . think I'm fine?"

"Yeah, you don't sound too sure," the man says.

That's because he's not. He shakes his head, then shakes it again when the woman pushes the water bottle forward. "I just had some on the train."

"Low blood sugar, maybe?" She takes the water bottle away and looks thoughtful. There's a little girl crouched beside her, he notices belatedly, and the two of them are nearly mirrors of each other: both black-haired, freckled, frank-faced Asian people. "When was the last time you ate?"

"Like, twenty minutes ago?" He doesn't feel dizzy or weak, either. He feels . . . "New," he murmurs, without thinking. "I feel . . . new."

The portly man and frank-faced woman look at each other, while the little girl throws him a judgy look, complete with lifted eyebrow. "*Are* you new here?" asks the portly man.

"Yeah?" Oh, no. "My bags!" But they're right there; the Good Samaritans have kindly pulled them off the escalator, too, and positioned them nearby out of the flow of traffic. There's a kind of surreality to the moment as he finally realizes he's having this blackout or delusion or whatever it is in the middle of a crowd of thousands. Nobody seems to notice, except these three people. He feels alone in the city. He is seen and cared for in the city. The contrast is going to take some getting used to.

"You must have gotten your hands on some of the really good

drugs," the woman says. She's grinning, though. That's okay, isn't it? That's what'll keep her from calling 911. He remembers reading somewhere that New York's got an involuntary commitment law that can hold people for weeks, so it's probably a good idea to reassure his would-be rescuers as to his clarity of mind.

"Sorry about this," he says, pushing to his feet. "Maybe I didn't eat *enough*, or something. I'll . . . go to an urgent care clinic."

Then it happens again. The station lurches beneath his feet—and suddenly it is in ruins. There's no one around. A cardboard book display in front of the convenience store has fallen over, spilling Stephen King hardcovers everywhere. He hears girders in the surrounding structure groan, dust and pebbles falling to the floor as something in the ceiling cracks. The fluorescent lights flicker and jerk, one of the overhead fixtures threatening to fall from the ceiling. He inhales to cry a warning.

Blink: everything is fine again. None of the people around him react. He stares at the ceiling for a moment, then back at the man and woman. They're still staring at him. They saw him react to whatever he was seeing, but they did not see the ruined station themselves. The portly guy has a hand on his arm, because he apparently swayed a little. Psychotic breaks must be hell on inner ear balance.

"You want to carry bananas," the portly guy suggests. "Potassium. Good for you."

"Or at least eat some real food," the woman agrees, nodding. "You probably just ate chips, right? I don't like that overpriced crap from the train dining car, either, but at least it'll keep you from falling over."

"I like the hot dogs," the girl says.

"They're crap, baby, but I'm glad you like them." She takes the little girl's hand. "We've got to go. You good?"

"Yeah," he says. "But seriously, thanks for helping me. You hear all kinds of stuff about how rude New Yorkers are, but... thanks."

"Eh, we're only assholes to people who are assholes first," she says, but she smiles as she says it. Then she and the little girl wander off.

The portly man claps him on the shoulder. "Well, you don't look like you're gonna chuck. Want me to go get you something to eat or some juice or something? Or a banana?" He adds the latter pointedly.

"No, thanks. I'm feeling better, really."

The portly man looks skeptical, then blinks as something new occurs to him. "It's okay, you know, if you don't got money. I'll spot you."

"Oh. Oh, no, I'm good." He hefts his messenger bag, which he remembers costing almost $1,600. Portly Guy looks at it blankly. Whoops. "Um, there's probably sugar in this—" There's a plastic Starbucks tumbler in the bag, sloshing faintly. He drinks from it to reassure Portly Guy. The coffee is cold and disgusting. He belatedly remembers refilling it sometime yesterday, before he got on the train back home in—

—in—

That's when he realizes he can't remember where he came from.

And he tries, but he still can't remember the school he's here to attend.

And this is when it finally hits him that *he doesn't know his own name*.

As he stands there, floored by this triple epiphany of nothingness, the portly guy is turning up his nose at the tumbler. "Get some real coffee while you're here," he says. "From a good

Boricua shop, yeah? Get some home food while you're at it. Anyway, what's your name?"

"Oh, uh . . ." He rubs his neck and pretends to have a desperate need to stretch—while, quietly panicking, he looks around and tries to think of something. He can't believe this is happening. Who the hell forgets their own name? All he can come up with as fake names go are generic ones like Bob or Jimmy. He's about to say *Jimmy*, arbitrarily—but then, in his visual flailing, his eyes snag on something.

"I'm, uh . . . Manny," he blurts. "You?"

"Douglas." Portly Guy has his hands on his hips, obviously considering something. Finally he pulls out his wallet and hands over a business card. DOUGLAS ACEVEDO, PLUMBER.

"Oh, sorry, I don't have a card, haven't started my new job yet—"

"S'okay," Douglas says. He still looks thoughtful. "Look, a lot of us were new here, once. You need anything, you let me know, okay? Seriously, it's fine. Place to crash, real food, a good church, whatever."

It's unbelievably kind. "Manny" doesn't bother to hide his surprise. "Whoa. I— Wow, man. You don't know me from Adam. I could be a serial killer or something."

Douglas chuckles. "Yeah, somehow I'm not figuring you for the violent type. You look . . ." He falters, and then his expression softens a little. "You look like my son. I'm just doing for you what I'd want somebody doing for him. Right?"

Somehow Manny knows: Douglas's son is dead.

"Right," Manny says softly. "Thanks again."

"Está bien, mano, no te preocupes." He waves off then, and heads in the direction of the A/C/E train.

Manny watches him go, pocketing the card and thinking about three things. The first is the belated realization that the guy thought he was Puerto Rican. The second is that he might have to take Douglas up on that offer of a place to crash, especially if he doesn't remember the address of his apartment in the next few minutes.

The third thing makes him look up at the Arrivals/Departures board, where he found the word that just became his new name. He didn't tell Douglas the full name because these days only white women can have given names like that without getting laughed at. But even in modified form, this word—this *identity*—feels more true than anything else he's ever claimed in his life. It is what he has been, without realizing. It is who he is. It is everything he's ever needed to be.

The full word is *Manhattan*.

In the bathroom, under the sodium lights, he meets himself for the first time.

It's a good face. He pretends to be extra meticulous about washing his hands—not a bad thing to be in a smelly Penn Station public bathroom—and turns his face from side to side, checking himself out from all angles. It's clear why the dude figured him for Puerto Rican: his skin is yellowy brown, his hair kinky but loose-coiled enough that if he let it grow out, it might dangle. He could pass for Douglas's son, maybe. (He's not Puerto Rican, though. He remembers that much.) He's dressed preppy: khakis, a button-down with rolled-up sleeves, and there's a sports jacket draped over his bag, for when the AC is too high maybe since it's summertime and probably ninety degrees outside. He looks like he's somewhere in that ageless yawn between "not a kid anymore" and thirty, though probably toward the latter end of it to judge by a couple of random gray threads peppered along his hairline. Brown eyes behind dark-brown-rimmed glasses. The glasses make him look professorial. Sharp cheekbones, strong even features, smile lines developing around his mouth. He's a good-looking guy. Generic all-American boy (nonwhite version), nicely nondescript.

Convenient, he thinks. Wondering why he thinks this makes him pause in mid-hand-wash, frowning.

Okay, no. He's got enough weirdness to deal with right now. He grabs his suitcase to leave the bathroom. An older guy at the urinal stares at him all the way out.

At the top of the next escalator—this one leading up to Seventh Avenue—it happens a third time. This episode is better in some ways and worse in others. Because Manny feels the wave of... whatever it is... coming on as he reaches the top of the escalator, he has enough time to take his suitcase and get himself over to some kind of digital information kiosk so he'll be out of the way while he leans against it and shudders. This time he doesn't hallucinate—not at first—but he *hurts*, all of a sudden. It's an awful, sick feeling, a spreading chill starting from a point low on his left flank. The sensation is familiar. He remembers it from the last time he got stabbed.

(Wait, he got *stabbed*?)

Frantically he pulls up his shirttail and looks at the place where the pain is worst, but there's no blood. There's nothing. The wound is all in his head. Or... somewhere else.

As if this is a summons, abruptly the New York that everyone sees flickers into the New York that only he can see. Actually, they're both present, one lightly superpositioned over the other, and they flick back and forth a little before finally settling into a peculiar dual-boot of reality. Before Manny lie two Seventh Avenues. They're easy to distinguish because they have different palettes and moods. In one, there are hundreds of people within view and dozens of cars and at least six chain stores that he recognizes. Normal New York. In the other, there are no people, and some unfathomable disaster has taken place. He doesn't see bodies or anything ominous; there's just no one around. It's not clear anyone ever existed in this place. Maybe the buildings here just appeared, sprung forth fully formed from their foundations, instead of being built. Ditto the streets, which are empty and badly cracked. A traffic light dangles loose from an overhead fixture, swinging on its cable but switching from red to green in perfect tandem with its other version. The sky is dimmer, almost as if it's nearly sunset and not just post-noon, and the wind is faster. Clouds boil and churn across the sky like they're late for the cloud revival meeting.

"Cool," Manny murmurs. This whole episode probably represents some kind of psychotic break on his part, but he cannot deny that what he sees is gorgeous and terrifying. *Weird* New York. He likes it, regardless.

But something is wrong with it. He must go somewhere, do something, or all of the bifurcated beauty that he sees will die. He knows this, suddenly, more surely than instinct.

"I have to go," he murmurs to himself in surprise. His voice sounds strange—tinny and sort of stretched out. Maybe he's slurring? Maybe it's the peculiar echo of his voice from the walls of two different Penn Station entryway walls in two different Penn Stations.

"Hey," says a guy in a neon-green button-down nearby. Manny

blinks at him; Normal New York abruptly resumes, Weird New York vanishing for the moment. (It's still somewhere nearby, though.) The button-down is part of a uniform. The guy is carrying a sign hawking bike rentals at tourists. He faces Manny with open hostility. "Puke your drunk ass off somewhere else."

Manny tries to straighten, but he knows he's still a little diagonal. "I'm not drunk." He's just seeing juxtaposed multiple realities while being plagued by inexplicable compulsions and phantom sensations.

"Well, then, take your high ass somewhere else."

"Yes." That's a good idea. He needs to go . . . east. He turns in that direction, following instincts he never had before a few minutes ago. "What's thataway?" he asks Bike Guy.

"My left nut," Bike Guy says.

"That's south!" laughs another bike rental hawker nearby. Bike Guy rolls his eyes and grabs his crotch at her in the iconic New York Sign Language gesture of suck-my-dick.

The attitude's starting to grate. Manny says, "If I rent a bike, will you tell me what's in that direction?"

Bike Guy's suddenly all smiles. "Sure—"

"No, sir," says Bike Woman, serious now as she comes over. "Sir, I'm sorry, but we cannot rent a bike to someone who appears to be intoxicated or ill. Company policy. Do you need me to call 911?"

People in New York sure like to call 911. "No, I can walk. I need to get to—" FDR Drive. "—FDR Drive."

The woman's expression turns skeptical. "You wanna walk to *FDR Drive*? What the hell kind of tourist are you? Sir."

"He ain't no tourist," says he of the southern left nut, as he chin-points at Manny. "Look at him."

Manny's never been to New York before, at least as far as he knows. "I just need to get there. Fast."

"Take a cab, then," says the woman. "Taxi stand's right there. Need me to grab one for you?"

Manny shivers a little, feeling the rise of something new within himself. Not sickness this time—or rather, not just sickness, since that terrible stabbish ache hasn't faded. What comes instead is a shift in perception. Beneath his hand, which rests on the kiosk, he hears a soft rattle of decades' worth of flyers. (The kiosk has nothing on it. There's a sign: DO NOT POST BILLS. He hears what used to be there.) Traffic's flying past on Seventh, hurrying to get through the light before a million pedestrians start trying to get to Macy's or K-Town karaoke and barbecue. All these things belong; they are rightness. But his eyes stutter over a TGI Fridays and he twitches a little, lip curling in involuntary distaste. Something about its facade feels foreign, intrusive, jarring. A tiny, cluttered shoe-repair shop next to it does not elicit the same feeling, nor does a vape shop next door. Just the chain stores that Manny sees—a Foot Locker, a Sbarro, all the sorts of stores one normally finds at a low-end suburban mall. Except these mall stores are here, in the heart of Manhattan, and their presence is . . . not truly harmful, but irritating. Like paper cuts, or little quick slaps to the face.

The subway sign, though, feels right and real. The billboards, too, no matter what's on them. The cabs, and flow of cars and people—all these things soothe the irritants, somehow. He draws in a deep breath that reeks of hot garbage and acrid steam belching from a manhole cover nearby, and it's foul but it's *right*. More than right. Suddenly he's better. The sick feeling recedes a little, and his side dulls from stabbing pain into cold prickles that only hurt when he moves.

"Thanks," he says to Bike Woman, straightening and grabbing his roller bag. "But my ride's coming." Wait. How does he know that?

The woman shrugs. Both of them turn away to resume hawking bikes. Manny walks toward the area where people are waiting for Lyfts or Ubers. He has both apps on his phone, but he hasn't used them. There should be nothing here for him.

However, a moment later, a cab rolls to a stop right in front of him.

It's like a cab out of an old movie: smooth and bulbous and huge, with a black-and-white checkered strip along its near flank. Bike Guy does a double take, then whistles. "A Checker! Haven't seen one of those since I was a kid."

"It's for me," Manny says unnecessarily, and reaches for the door.

It's locked. *I need this open*, he thinks. The door lock clicks open. So, that's new, but he'll process it later.

"What the—" says the woman inside as Manny tosses his bag onto the back seat and climbs in after it. She's a very young white woman, so young that she doesn't look old enough to drive, who has twisted around to stare at him. But she's mostly indignant rather than scared, which seems a good starting place for their future relationship. "Hey. *Dude*. This isn't a real cab. It's just an antique—a prop. People rent it for weddings."

Manny pulls the door shut. "FDR, please," he says, and flashes his most charming smile.

It shouldn't work. She should be screaming her head off and trying to get the nearest cop to shoot him. But something else has occurred between them, helping to keep the woman calm. Manny has followed to the letter the ritual of getting-in-a-cab, introducing enough plausible deniability that she thinks he's deluded rather than a potential threat. However, there's power in what he's done that goes beyond just psychology. He's felt it before, hasn't he? Just a moment ago, when he somehow drew strength from the chaos of Seventh Avenue to ease the pain in his side. He can actually hear some of that power whispering to her, *Maybe he's an actor. He looks like That Guy whose name you can't remember, from That Musical you like. So maybe don't freak out yet?* Because New Yorkers don't freak out around famous people.

And how does he know all this? Because he does, that's how. He's trying to keep up.

So he adds, after a breath passes and she just stares, "You're going that way anyway, aren't you?"

She narrows her eyes at him. They're at a red light, but the walk sign nearby is blinking. He's got maybe ten more seconds. "How the hell did you know that?"

Because the cab wouldn't have stopped if you weren't, he doesn't say, and reaches for his wallet. "Here," he says, handing her a hundred-dollar bill.

She stares at it, then her lip curls. "Right, a fake."

"I have twenties, if you'd prefer." There's more power in twenties anyway. A lot of businesses in the city won't take hundreds, also for fear of counterfeit bills. With twenties, Manny will be able to compel her to take him where he needs to go, whether she wants to or not. He'd rather persuade, though. Force is...he doesn't want to use force.

"Tourists *do* carry a lot of cash," she murmurs while frowning, as if reasoning with her better instincts. "And you don't *look* like a serial killer..."

"Most serial killers take care to look like ordinary people," he points out.

"Not helping your case with the mansplaining, guy."

"Good point. Sorry."

That seems to decide her. "Well. Assholes don't say sorry." She considers for a moment longer. "Make that two Benjies, and okay."

He offers the twenties, although he does have another hundred-dollar bill in his wallet. There's no need to use the bills for power anymore, however. She has completed the ritual by accepting his directions, then performed the orthogonal ritual of haggling for more money. All the stars have aligned. She's on board. As she's pocketing the money, the traffic light changes and a car immediately honks behind her. She casually flips that driver off and then wrenches the wheel to drag the cab across four active lanes as if she's done this, or driven the Daytona 500, all her life.

And that's that. Even Manny is amazed at how well this strange power works as he hangs on to the door handle and the ancient lap-only seat belt and tries not to look alarmed by her driving. He has some inkling of *why* it works. Money talks and bullshit walks in New York. In a lot of cities, probably—but here, the nation's shrine to unrestricted predatory capitalism, money has nearly talismanic power. Which means that he can use it as a talisman.

The traffic lights miraculously stay in their favor for several blocks, which is fortunate because the young woman is likely to break the sound barrier at this rate. Then she curses and slams on the brakes as a light ahead makes a fast switch to red. Too fast; amazing that she doesn't run the light. He smells a waft of burnt rubber through the open window as he leans forward to squint at the light. "Busted light?"

"Must be," she says, tapping her fingertips rapidly on the wheel. This, Manny knows, is a gesture required by the ritual of hurry-up-damn-it, but it doesn't work, because that ritual never works. "They usually line up better than this. Just one light out of sequence can start a traffic jam."

Manny presses his hand against the cold, spreading ache in his side that is beginning to throb again. Something about the traffic light has pinged his new sense of wrongness—and the wrongness is enough to erode whatever anesthetic effect he's managed to summon. He opens his mouth to suggest that she run the light, which is risky. The wrongness has probably weakened his influence on her, too, and now there's nothing to stop her from thinking twice about the strange Black dude in her antique cab. But whatever is happening on the east side of the island—FDR Drive—is growing urgent. He can't risk getting kicked out of the cab until he gets there.

Before Manny can speak, however, a BMW passes through the intersection ahead. There are long, feathery white tendrils growing from its wheel wells.

He watches it go past in utter shock. The driver sees it, too; her mouth falls open. *Feathery* doesn't quite fit what they're seeing. It's more like an anemone's fronds, or the tendrils of certain jellyfish. As the car rolls by, gliding along behind a slower driver, they see one of the tendrils seem to ... inhale. It opens itself out a little, revealing a thickened stalk that tapers as it stretches away from the wheels, up to slightly darkened tips. All of it is translucent. Not all of it is *here*—in this world, that is. Manny sees at once that it is like the dual city: here, but also in that other place where the sky is wild and people are a never-thought.

All of that is academic, though, because in the next moment,

Manny notices something that makes the little hairs on the back of his neck stand up. The tendrils twitch as the BMW thumps over a pothole—but it's not the pothole that they're reacting to. They're longer, see. Turning, like some kind of wiggly, wormlike radio antennas. Stretching toward the Checker cab as if they sense Manny inside, and smell his fear.

After the BMW moves on, its driver apparently oblivious, it takes a moment for Manny's skin to stop crawling.

"So, you saw that, too, right?" asks the driver. The traffic light has finally changed; they speed toward FDR again. "Nobody else was staring, but you..." Her eyes meet his in the rearview.

"Yeah," he says. "Yeah, I saw it. I don't... yeah." It occurs to him, belatedly, that she might need more explanation than this, if he doesn't want to get kicked out of the cab. "You're not crazy. Or at least, if you are, you're not the only one."

"Oh, well, that's comforting." She licks her lips. "Why couldn't anyone else see it?"

"I wish I knew." But when she shakes her head, he feels compelled to add, "We're going to destroy the thing that's causing it." He means it to reassure, but he also realizes, as he says it, that it's true. He doesn't let himself think further about how he knows it's true. He doesn't ask whom the *we* in his statement refers to. They're too far into this now. If he starts doubting himself here, that will weaken the power—and, more importantly, he'll start questioning his own sanity. Then they're back to involuntary commitment.

"Destroy... what?" She's frowning as she looks at him in the rearview this time.

He doesn't want to admit that he doesn't know. "Just get me to FDR, and I'll handle it."

Much to his relief, she relaxes and flashes a lopsided smile over her shoulder. "Weird, but okay. The grandkids are gonna love this story. If I, you know, have grandkids." She drives on.

Then at last they're on FDR, moving faster toward that vague-but-rapidly-sharpening sense of wrongness. Manny is clinging to the old-fashioned leather handle sewn into the seat back before him because she's still doing the race-car-driver act, whipping around slower cars and cresting hills with enough speed that it feels a little like riding

the Cyclone? what is

a roller coaster. But they're getting closer to the source of all the trouble. There's a knot of small aircraft over and boats crowding along the nearby East River, all of them generally centering on something farther south. All Manny can see from here is smoke. Maybe it has to do with that bridge incident he heard about on the train? Must be; they've begun to pass signs warning of delays, detours, and police activity below Houston Street.

But it's also clear that they're much closer to the *wrongness* than to the bridge disaster. Now they're passing more cars, over on the uptown side of FDR, that seem to be infested with the weird white tendrils. Most are growing from the wheels, same as on the Beemer they saw before. It's as if the cars have rolled over something noxious that's allowed a kind of metaphysically opportunistic infection at the site of the damage. A few vehicles have it in their front grilles or curling up from their undercarriages. One car, a newish Beetle, has the tendrils in a spray up one door and crawling over the driver's window. The driver doesn't notice. What will happen if it touches her when she opens the door? Nothing good.

Then the traffic slows sharply . . . and the city's second, unseen disaster comes into range.

His first thought is that it's like an explosion, kind of. Imagine a fountain bursting up from the asphalt and flaring twenty or thirty feet into the sky, and *wiggling*. In lieu of water, the fountain flares with tendrils—dozens of them, anemoneic and enormous. Some writhe together in a way that is both mesmerizing and vaguely phallic as they tower above the roofs of the cars. Manny can tell that the root of the . . . growth . . . is located somewhere up ahead on the downtown side, probably in the fast lane, which must be how it's getting so many cars on the uptown-going side despite the median barrier. He sees a shiny new SUV with Pennsylvania plates pass that is so covered in the tendrils that it looks like a spectral hedgehog. Good thing the driver can't see them, or his vision would be too occluded to allow driving. But an ancient, rusty Ford Escort with missing hubcaps and peeling paint comes right behind it, and the tendrils haven't touched it at all. What's the pattern? He can't begin to guess.

This explosion of ick is what's causing the traffic jam, Manny sees, as the flow of cars slows to a crawl and the Checker comes to a near halt. Although most people can't see the flare of tendrils, they're still somehow reacting to its presence. Drivers in the fast lane keep trying to pull into the middle lane to get around the thing, drivers in the middle are trying to get into the right-hand lane to get around them, and drivers in the right-hand lane aren't budging. It's as if there's an invisible accident up ahead that everyone's trying to avoid. Thank God it's not rush hour or the traffic wouldn't be moving at all.

They've stopped for the moment, so Manny opens the rear passenger-side door to get out. A few of the cars behind them immediately set up a banshee chorus of horns, protesting even the possibility that he might slow things down more, but he ignores these and leans over to speak into the window when the driver rolls it down. (She has to lean across the seat and turn a manual crank to do this. For a moment he stares in fascination, then focuses.) "You got emergency flares?" he asks. "Triangle reflectors, stuff like that?"

"In the trunk." She puts the car in park and gets out herself—there are more horns at this—but she's glancing over at the tower of tendrils. Its tips wave above the pedestrian bridge that crosses this part of the FDR. "So that's what this is all about?"

"Yep." Manny pulls out the emergency kit when she opens the trunk. He's keeping most of his attention on the thing, though. If any of those tendrils come at them ... well, hopefully they won't.

"You better hurry and do whatever you're going to do. Cops are probably already on the way to deal with the, uh, obstruction. I don't know if they'll see it—nobody else seems to, or a lot more people would be getting out of their cars and walking—but they're not gonna help much."

He grimaces in agreement. Then he notices the way she's glaring at the fountain of tendrils. He has a tiny epiphany, beginning to understand. "You from here?"

She blinks. "Yeah. Born and raised right over in Chelsea, two moms and everything. Why?"

"Just a guess." Manny hesitates. He's feeling strange again. There are things happening around him, to him—a rise in tension and power and meaning, all of it pulling toward a moment of truth that he's not sure he wants to confront. Beneath his feet there is a vibration, a pulse like wheels clacking steadily over track segments that thrums in time with his pulse. Why? Because it does. Because, somehow, everything on this road and under it and around it *is* him. The pain in his side is awful, but ignorable because somehow *the city* is keeping him functioning, feeding him strength. Even the idling of the traffic-bound cars feeds him, pent energy just waiting for its chance to leap ahead. He looks around at the drivers in the nearby cars, and sees that most are glaring at the tendril thing, too. Do they see it? Not really. But they know *something* is there, blocking the flow of the city, and they hate it for that alone.

This is how it works, he realizes in wonder. This is what he needs to defeat the tendrils. These total strangers are his allies. Their anger, their need for a return to normalcy, rises from them like heat waves. This is the weapon he needs, if he can figure out how to harness it.

"I'm Manny," he says to the cabdriver, on impulse. "You?"

She looks surprised, then grins. "Madison," she says. "I know. But Number One Mom says I got conceived via IVF in a clinic just off Madison Ave, so . . ."

Too Much Information. Manny chuckles anyway, because he's all nerves and could use a laugh. "Okay, here's the plan," he says. Then he lays it out for her.

She stares at him like he's crazy, but she'll help. He can see that in her face. "Fine," she says at last, but it's just a show of reluctance. Maybe New Yorkers don't like to be seen as too helpful.

They lay out the flares and triangle markers to encourage people to go around the fast lane. Because the cab isn't moving, angry commuters glare and honk as they pass, assuming that the cab is somehow making the traffic worse. It probably is. One guy starts screaming at Manny loudly enough to spray the inside of his door window with spittle, though fortunately he's also too angry to remember to roll the window down first. It's a measure of how much everyone is picking up on the weirdness, though, that no one veers back into the fast lane even after they pass the parked Checker cab.

The mass of tendrils is growing as Manny watches. There is a low, crumbly sound that he can hear from that direction, now and again when the wind carries it to him: probably the sound of roots digging into asphalt, and probably into the rebar within the asphalt, and maybe into the bedrock that's under the road. He can hear the tendrils, too, now that they're close enough: a choppy, broken groan, stuttering and occasionally clicking like a corrupted music file. He can smell it—a thicker, much-fishier brine scent than that of the nearby East River.

Trimethylamine oxide, he thinks out of the blue. *The scent of the deep, cold, crushing ocean depths.*

"What now?" Madison asks.

"I need to hit it."

"Uh…"

Manny looks around before spotting exactly what he needs—there, in a convertible sports car's open back seat. The Indian woman driving it stares at him in blatant curiosity. He steps toward her quickly and blurts, "Hey, can I have that umbrella?"

"How about pepper spray?" she suggests.

He holds up his hands to try to look less threatening, though he's still a six-foot-tall not-white guy, and some people are just never going to be okay with that. "If you loan it to me, I can clear this traffic jam."

At this, she actually looks intrigued. "Huh. Well, for that I guess I can give up an umbrella. It's my sister's, anyway. I just like to hit people with it." She grabs the umbrella and hands it to him, pointy tip first.

"Thanks!" He grabs it and trots back to the cab. "Okay, we're golden."

Madison frowns at him, then at the tendril flare, as she opens the cab's driver-side door to get back in. "I can't see what's beyond that thing," she says. "If there are cars, and I can't brake in time—"

"Yeah. I know." Manny vaults up onto the Checker's hood, then its roof. Madison stares while he turns and arranges himself to sit straddling the roof, one hand gripping the OFF DUTY sign. Fortunately, Checkers are high and long, narrow-built for city streets. He can get enough of a grip with his legs to hold on, though it's still going to be dicey. "Okay. Ready."

"I am so texting my weed man as soon as this is over," Madison says, shaking her head as she gets into the cab.

The umbrella is key. Manny doesn't know why, but he's okay with accepting what he can't quite understand, for now. What's really bothering him is that he's not sure *how* to use it. Given that everything in him cries out that the forest of tendrils is dangerous—deadly if it so much as touches him, maybe because the tendrils look like anemones, which sting their prey to death— he needs to figure it out fast. As Madison starts up the cab, he experimentally lifts the umbrella, metal tip pointing toward the tendril mass like a jouster's lance. It's wrong. The right idea, but the wrong implementation; weak, somehow. The umbrella's an automatic, so he unsnaps its closure and presses the button. It pops open at once, and it's huge. A golf umbrella—a nice one, with no hint of a rattle or wobble as Madison accelerates and the wind pulls at the umbrella. But still wrong.

The tendril mass looms, ethereal and pale, more frightening as the cab accelerates. There is a beauty to it, he must admit—like some haunting, bioluminescent deep-sea organism dragged to the surface. It is an alien beauty, however, meant for some other environment, some other aether, and here in New York its presence is a contaminant. The very air around it has turned gray, and now that they're closer, he can hear the air hissing as if the tendrils are somehow hurting the molecules of nitrogen and oxygen they touch. Manny's been in New York for less than an hour and yet he knows, he *knows*, that cities are organic, dynamic systems. They are built to incorporate newness. But some new things become part of a city, helping it grow and strengthen—while some new things can tear it apart.

They're speeding now, doing at least fifty. The tendrils shadow the sky and the air has turned cold and the smell of lightless oceans has grown nauseating and it's getting hard to hold on to the cab's roof. He hangs on anyway and half shuts his eyes against the wind and the burning salt of the thing's scent and *what is he doing?* Pushing out the interloper. But he's an interloper, too, isn't he? And if he doesn't do this exactly the right way, then only one of the interlopers here is going to walk away from this confrontation intact, and *the umbrella isn't strong enough.*

Then, when the Checker is only feet away, close enough that Manny can see the slick, pore-flecked skin of the tendrils, and his side screams with agony like someone's jabbed an ice-cold pike through him—

—he remembers the words of the woman who gave him the umbrella. *I just like to hit people with it,* she'd said.

Manny lets go of the OFF DUTY sign. Immediately he starts to slide back on the cab's roof because they're going so fast that he can barely hold on with his legs alone. But he might survive falling off the cab; he *won't* survive contact with the nest of tendrils if he doesn't get this umbrella *up*. He needs both hands for that, wrestling against the wind and his own fear, but in the welter of seconds that he has, he manages to lift the open umbrella above his head. Now he might die, but at least his hair won't get wet in any sudden rain shower.

Suddenly there is energy around him, *in* him, blazing rusty red and tarnished silver and greened bronze and a thousand colors more. It has become a sheath around the whole cab—a sphere of pure energy brightening enough to compete with the June midday sunlight—and in its suddenly loud song Manny hears the horns of a thousand cars trapped on the FDR. The hissing air is eclipsed by the shouted road rage of hundreds of mouths. As he opens his mouth to shout with them, his cry is delight and the ecstasy of suddenly knowing that he *isn't* an interloper. The city needs newcomers! He belongs here as much as anyone born and bred to its streets, because anyone who wants to be of New York can be! He is no tourist, exploiting and gawking and giving nothing but money back. He *lives here* now. That makes all the difference in the world.

So as Manny laughs, giddy with this realization and the power that now suffuses him, they strike the tendril mass. The sheath of energy surrounding the cab burns through it like a checkered missile. Of course, the cab is part of the power; this is why the city sent it to him. Manny feels the umbrella snag on something and he clings tighter to it, rudely not lifting it or moving it aside because *I'm walking here, I have the right of way* and he's playing metaphysical sidewalk chicken with this violent, invasive *tourist*—

Then they're through.

Manny hears Madison yell from inside the cab as they get through the mass and see that there's a line of stopped cars dead ahead. She slams the brakes. Manny loses his grip on the umbrella as he frantically grabs for the OFF DUTY sign, catching it even as his whole body flips onto the windshield and hood. The cab spins out as Madison throws the wheel; now, instead of flying forward, he's being thrown around by centrifugal force. In his panic, he loses his grip on the sign and doesn't know how he finds the strength to grab for the edge of the hood below the wipers, even as his legs come loose and most of his body flies free in the direction of the stopped traffic. If the cab flips, he's dead. If he loses his grip and gets tossed onto the hatchback up ahead, he's dead. If he falls off the cab and under the wheels—

But the cab finally skids to a halt, a bare inch away from the stopped car up ahead. Manny's feet thump onto the hatchback's trunk, not entirely of his own volition. It's okay. Just nice to have something solid under his feet again.

"Get your feet off my fucking car!" someone inside shouts. He ignores them.

"Holy shit!" Madison sticks her head out the window, her face panicky, like how he feels. "Holy— Are you okay?"

"Yeah?" Manny's honestly not sure. But he musters the where-withal to sit up, and look back down the fast lane.

Behind them, the tendril forest has gone wild, its fronds whipping and flailing like a dying thing. It *is* dying. Where they punched through its thicket of roots, there is a Checker cab cutout like something from a kids' cartoon—complete with an umbrella-shaped hole on top of its roof, and a hunched human silhouette underneath. The edges of the cutout glow as if hot, and the fire rapidly eats its way outward and upward, fast as a circle of flame burning through a piece of paper. Within seconds this burn has eaten its way through the base of the tendrils, then starts burning all the way up. No ash or residue remains in the wake of this process. Manny knows this is because the tendrils aren't really there, aren't really *real* in any way that makes sense.

The destruction is real, however. Once the last of the tendrils has burned away, a hovering, brightly colored knot of energy—the remnant of the sheath that surrounded the cab, now a wild, seething thing of its own—dissipates in a miniature explosion that ripples concentrically outward. Manny shudders as the wave of light and color and heat passes through him. He knows it won't hurt, but he's surprised when it warms the place on his side that hurt so badly before. All better now. More dramatically, tendrils that have attached themselves to the nearby cars wither away the instant the energy hits them. He feels the power roll onward out of sight as it passes beyond the nearest buildings and into the East River.

It's done.

And as Manny climbs off the cab's hood and settles back onto the ground, once again he feels something waft through him, from the soles of his shoes to the roots of his hair. It's the same energy, he realizes, that suffused the cab when it torpedoed through the tendril mass—and which soothed him at Penn Station, and which guided him from there to here. That energy is the city, he understands somehow, and it is part of him, filling him up and driving out anything unnecessary to make room for itself. That's why his name is gone.

The energy begins to fade. Will his memory come back when it's done? No way to know. Though Manny feels he should be frightened by this realization, he . . . isn't. It doesn't make sense. Amnesia, even if it's temporary, can't be a good thing. He might have a brain bleed, some kind of hidden injury; he should go to a hospital. But instead of being frightened, he is actually comforted by the presence of the city within him. He shouldn't be. He has an inkling that he just had a near-death experience. But he is.

The East River churns at his back. He looks up at the towering breadth of Manhattan: endless high-rise co-ops, repurposed banks, cramped housing projects sandwiched between ancient theater houses and soulless corporate headquarters. Nearly two million people. He's been here one hour, but already he feels like he has never lived anywhere else. And even if he doesn't know who he was . . . he knows who he is.

"I am Manhattan," he murmurs softly.

And the city replies, without words, right into his heart: *Welcome to New York.*

CHAPTER TWO

Showdown in the Last Forest

Madison drops Manny off up in Inwood. "It's way out of my way," she says as he hauls his bag out of the car, "but there's a great empanada place around here that I like. Anyway, I think my cab likes you." She strokes its broad old real-leather dash, as if petting a horse. "This thing's engine is gas-guzzling shit, but it ran smoother on the way up here than it ever has before. Maybe running over semi-visible sea monsters is good for the spark plugs, or something."

Manny laughs at her through the open passenger window. "Well, I'll be sure to call you and your cab to help next time, too," he says. Because there's going to be a next time, he feels certain.

"Ugh, thanks, no, pass," she says. Then she tilts her head to the side and gives him a once-over so frank that Manny finds himself blushing. It ends with her grin and wink. "You, uh, ever want to consider a different kind of ride, though, call Checker Cab Dream Weddings and ask for me."

Manny can't help chuckling, though it's awkward. He doesn't think he's used to such aggressive flirting. She's pretty, and he's interested, but something makes him reluctant to take her up on the offer. What? He's not sure. Maybe it's just the fact that he seems to be transforming into the living embodiment of a major metropolitan area, and that's not an ideal time to start dating anyone. So he tries to make it kind as brush-offs go, because it's not her, it's him. "I'll, uh, keep that in mind."

She grins, taking the rejection in stride, which makes him like her that much more. Then she pulls away from the curb, and there he is alone in front of his new home.

It's one of the older apartment buildings of Inwood, sprawling over half a block and with an actual garden out front, he notes as he walks through the wrought-iron gates. Someone in the building has planted poppies and, he thinks, echinaceas. In the foyer, which is huge, there are black-and-white tiles on the floor and fancy cornices in marble along the walls. The ceiling is embossed tin buried beneath so many layers of paint that it looks lumpy. No doorman, but this isn't that kind of neighborhood.

None of it feels familiar. The address was in his phone, thankfully, on a sticky app marked with *New addy!!!* followed by barely legible finger-scrawled information. But he does not remember ever visiting New York before.

(*What kind of person abbreviates "address" to "addy"?* he wonders. What kind of person is three exclamation points' worth of excited about having a new address? Is that the sort of person who would rent an apartment and pick a roommate sight unseen?)

The sluggish, ancient elevator is the kind with an inner gate that must be pulled shut before the whole thing will move. On the top floor, the elevator doors open to reveal a hallway lit murkily by ancient fluorescents and stretching away into a distance that shouldn't be possible given the length of New York city blocks. From within the elevator, it's eerie, like something out of a survival horror video game. As Manny steps out, however, something seems to swipe its way across his perception. When he blinks, the hallway light is brighter, its shadows reduced, its contrasts softened, and its faint scents—lingering food smells from someone's dinner, dust, paint, a whiff of cat piss—sharpened. Now it's just a hallway...but it feels safer, somehow, than it did a moment before.

Weird. Okay, then.

4J is the apartment number in his phone. Manny's got a key tagged with the same number, but he knocks just to be polite. There's a thump of hurried feet from beyond and then the door opens, held by a lanky Asian guy who's got sleep lines all over one side of his face. But he brightens and spreads his arms at once. "Hey, roomie!" he says in a heavy British accent. "You made it!"

"Yeah," Manny says, grinning awkwardly. He has no idea who this man is. "Had some, uh, some trouble on the FDR."

"The FDR? Isn't that on the east side of the island? Why would your cab go that way from Penn? Was the traffic that bad, after that horror show at the Williamsburg?" But the man ignores his own question in the next instant, stepping forward and grabbing Manny's suitcase. "Here, let me. Your boxes and other suitcase all got here a few days ago."

It's all so normal. Inside, the apartment is enormous, with a full-sized kitchen and two bedrooms that are nicely spaced from each other—one just past the living room, the other farther down the hall, past the bathroom and a storage closet. His roommate has claimed the closer one, so Manny heads to the far end of the apartment to find a spacious room that features a full suite of bedroom furniture. Apparently pre-amnesia Manny wanted a furnished space. There aren't any sheets on the bed, and there are dust bunnies in the corners, but it's nice. The window displays a great view of a commercial parking lot. He loves it.

"See? Yeah?" says the roommate, watching him take it all in. "It's a great flat, yeah? Just like the pictures I sent you."

Pictures. He's the kind of guy who signs a lease based on pictures. "Yeah, perfect." But he can't keep calling his roommate "you." "Uh, this is embarrassing, sorry, but your name—"

The man blinks, then laughs. "Bel. Bel Nguyen? PhD candidate in political theory at Columbia, just like you? What, was the train ride that bad?"

"No. Uh—" It's a useful excuse. He evaluates its potential benefits and decides to deploy it. "Well, yeah. I had, I don't know, a fainting spell? When I was getting off the train. And my head's feeling a little . . ." He waggles his fingers, hoping to convey confusion rather than delusion.

"Oh. Shit." Bel looks honestly concerned for him. "You need anything? I could, uh— Maybe some good tea? I brought some from home."

"No, no, I'm okay," Manny says quickly, although all at once he's not entirely sure of that. Here in this so-ordinary place, as he thinks about what happened on FDR Drive, it seems less and less possible. If he's got amnesia, then maybe there's something genuinely wrong with him. Maybe he's been hit in the head. Maybe he's got early-onset dementia. "I mean, I feel okay. But there are things I'm having trouble remembering clearly."

"Like my name?"

Manny considers replying, *No, like mine*, but decides against it. Discovering that one's roommate is actively undergoing a break with reality is high on the scale of "things one wants to learn *before* signing the lease." "Among other things. So, uh, sorry in advance if I ask about things you've already told me. Or if I tell you things you already know. Like, uh, my nickname. Call me Manny."

He's braced for pushback, but Bel only shrugs. "Manny it is. You want to change your name every week, mate, whatever, as long as the rent checks clear." He laughs at his own joke, then shakes his head and lets go of Manny's suitcase. "Sure you don't want that tea? It's not a bother. Or—huh. I was thinking about going for a walk, to get the lay of the land, so to speak. Join me, yeah? Fresh air might do you good."

It's eminently sensible. Manny nods, and after a pause to dump his jacket and change into fresh jeans—he's just noticed the streaks on his khakis from sitting on the taxi's roof—they head out.

The apartment building is only a few blocks from Inwood Hill Park. The park is gigantic, Manny remembers seeing on a map somewhere. (He seems to have no trouble remembering general facts, he notes clinically. Only things specific to his own life elude him.) It's also the last untouched bit of an old-growth forest that once covered the entire island of Manhattan. It mostly looks like any other park on first impression—paved pathways, ironwork fences, benches, tennis courts, and the occasional dog walker complete with leashed, yapping coterie. Surprisingly empty, although that's likely a factor of it being the middle of the day on a weekday, when most people are at work or school. Past the mani- cured bit of mowed lawn and decorative trees, Manny beholds a forested hill rising above all, covered in a dense tangle of trees and shrubs that clearly have never seen a backhoe or road grader. He stares at this, astounded that it exists less than five miles from the lights and bluster of Broadway, while Bel inhales, his eyes shut in palpable bliss.

"Ah, this is why I wanted to live up here—well, that and the fact that I couldn't afford anywhere else on the island." He grins at Manny and resumes walking down the path; Manny does, too, turning to take in the sights. "Worse than London proper, this place. But then I read about this, a forest in the middle of the bloody city, and knew it was right for me. Spent a couple of summers up at Hackfall Wood in North Yorkshire back when I was a sprog. Near my grandmother's house." His face falls a little, and something in his tone flattens. "Course, she disowned me when I turned out to be a bloke-in-progress instead of a girl, so I haven't been back for ages."

"Sorry to hear that," Manny says, and then he registers more than the pain in the words. He blinks at Bel in his surprise. He's got the sense not to say anything, but Bel catches the glance, and his expression immediately goes neutral.

"Forgot that, too, then? This where you suddenly recall you don't really want to live with a trans fellow after all?"

"I—" Then Manny realizes how his amnesia story must sound. He can't think of anything to offer except honesty. "I did forget. But if I wanted out, I'd have made up a better lie than this one."

Well, way to impress his roommate with his pathological tendencies. But the statement surprises Bel into a laugh, though there's still a bitter edge to it. He does relax, just a little. "Suppose that's true enough. And you do seem *different*, somehow, from the chap I met on Skype last month."

Manny tries not to tense. He focuses on the asphalt beneath their feet as they walk. "Oh?"

"Yeah. Hard to say how." Bel shrugs. "To be honest, I was a bit worried about you. You seemed nice enough, but there was, hmm, an *edge* to you. Back home, a lot of queer cis blokes are just as ready to kick my arse as the straights, yeah? And something about you felt like an arse-kicker extraordinaire. But you said we weren't going to have a problem, and I wasn't spoiled for choice, so..." He sighs.

Oh. "We aren't going to have a problem," Manny says again, as reassuringly as he can. "At least, not about that. You put dirty socks in the fridge, though, and all bets are off."

Bel laughs again, and just like that the air is cleared. "I'll take care with my socks, then. No promises on the hats."

They both fall silent as ambulances race past the entrance of the park. They're pretty far along the walking path by now, but three ambulances in full siren aren't going to be ignorable no matter how thick the blanket of trees surrounding them. It's still Manhattan, after all. Bel grimaces in their wake. "Heard they were calling in emergency personnel from the whole, what do you call it? Tri-state area? for this mess. God, I can't wait to see which entire ethnic group they're going to scapegoat in the wake of this one."

"Maybe it's a white guy. Again."

"A 'lone wolf' with mental health issues, right!" Bel sigh-laughs. "Maybe. *Hopefully*, so they won't use it as an excuse for more hate crimes or new wars or any of that. Fuck, what a thing to hope for."

Manny nods, and there's nothing good either of them can think of to say after this, so they fall into a companionable silence thereafter. It's a soothing walk, Manny finds, though just about anything would be soothing after the past couple of hours. More significantly, the park feels *right*—like the Checker cab, like the people who helped him at Penn Station, like his own inexplicable sense of belonging within this city that feels so strange and alive. His memory loss is weirdly selective. He remembers going to cities that have this same weird vibrancy before. Paris, Cairo,

Tokyo. None of them, however, felt made for him. It is as if every other place he's visited or lived has been a vacation, and only now has he come home.

At one juncture of paths, there's a map. Manny's marveling at the sheer size of the park when his gaze catches on the words *Inwood Park tulip tree*. In the same moment, Bel steps forward and puts a finger to the icon, leaning close to read the nigh-microscopic text nearby. "'According to legend,'" he reads, "'on this site of the principal Manhattan Indian village, Peter Minuit in 1626 purchased Manhattan Island for trinkets and beads then worth about 60 guilders.' And apparently a big tree grew there, too, but it died in 1932. Ah, so this is where your ancestors began the whole business of stealing the country." He chuckles and imitates Eddie Izzard. "'Do you have a flag? No? That'll be one island, then, keep the change, and we'll kick in some free small-pox and syphilis.'"

Manny's skin is a-prickle all over. Why? He doesn't know, but he speaks automatically, unable to take his eyes off the map icon. "I think the apocalyptic plagues actually started a couple of centuries earlier. Columbus."

"Right, right, 1492, sailing the ocean blue." Bel steps back and stretches. "Seems a good break point. Want to go look at this extremely important rock, then head back?"

"Sure," Manny says. He has a feeling it's more important than it sounds.

The extremely important rock isn't far from the park entrance, over near where a vast meadow edges Spuyten Duyvil Creek. As monuments go, it's unassuming, Manny notes as they approach it: just a boulder that's about waist-high, surrounded by a circle of bare dirt and a ring of grimy concrete. It's positioned at a juncture of several paved paths, with a nice view of the creek and a high, narrow bridge that probably leads to the Bronx, or maybe that's Queens. There are a few people around; he can see an old man in the distance, feeding pigeons as he sits on a park bench, and a young couple having a romantic picnic on the overgrown lawn, a good ways off. Otherwise, though, they're alone.

He and Bel stop by the rock for a while, reading the plaque that names the spot Shorakkopoch, after the name of the village that was displaced. Or maybe that's the name of the long-gone tree; the plaque isn't clear. Bel sits on the rock and clowns for a moment by trying to cross his legs and meditate on the "energies," while Manny laughs. The laugh is a little forced because there are definite energies here, strange and palpable as the umbrella became on FDR Drive, and he really has no idea what that means.

Then again, he recalls, the umbrella wasn't the source of the strange power he used—or, at least, not the sole source. The power had come into the umbrella because it was everywhere, floating through the air and flowing along the asphalt of the city, and Manny just used the right combination of things? ideas? to summon it forth. A car, in that place of choking exhaust and whipping curves and potholes; that had been utterly necessary. Movement, too, that had been part of what made the power come. In the city that never sleeps, FDR is the highway that never stops, except for occasional accidents and traffic jams. Is the power dependent on context, then? Manny folds his arms, staring at the rock and wondering what secrets it holds.

"Ow," Bel says as he gets off the rock. "History hurts. Whose bloody idea was it to put a *rock* on this spot? How's that supposed to commemorate anything? Americans like statues. What's wrong with a statue? Someone was being cheap."

Cheap. Manny blinks. There is something in that word, a tickle of a thought. He nods absently when Bel says something about getting dinner, trying to tease out that tickle. But then he catches a sudden sharp note in Bel's voice. "What's this, now?"

It pulls Manny out of introspection, and he turns to see that a woman is walking toward them. She's portly, short, white with a florid complexion, and dressed for office work. Nondescript. There's no reason for Manny or Bel to pay attention to her, in fact, except that she's got a cell phone in one hand, upraised toward them. Its camera light is on.

The woman stops, still filming them. "Gross," she says. "I can't believe you two. Right out in the open. I'm calling the cops."

Bel glances at Manny, who shakes his head in confusion; he has no idea what she's talking about, either. "Oi," Bel says. His accent has shifted, a little less BBC generic and a little more South London—somehow Manny knows this—and his expression has gone hard. "You recording us, love? Without asking? That's a bit rude, innit?"

" 'Rude' is people being perverts in public," the woman replies, doing something on her phone that looks like zooming in. It's pointed at Manny's face as she does this, and he doesn't like it one bit. He resists the urge to turn away or reach for her phone, however, since that seems likely to only incite further rudeness on her part.

He does step forward. "What exactly do you think—"

She reacts as if his single step forward was a full-on bull charge, gasping and mincing back several steps. "Don't touch me! Don't touch me! If you lay a finger on me, I'll scream and the cops will shoot you! You druggies! Druggie perverts!"

"Pervert I'll own, maybe, but druggie?" Bel has shifted to

put a hand on his hip, expression skeptical. "I'll have you know I'm straight-edge. You sure you haven't been overindulging on the Percocet, yourself, love? You're definitely seeing things." He waves a hand in front of her phone. She jerks it back and dances off to one side.

At which point Manny begins to wonder if *he's* seeing things. Because as the woman turns her back toward Manny, he notices that there is something jutting up from the back of her neck through the tangle of her loose bun. It's long and thin, somewhere between the thickness of a hair and a pencil, and as he stares, it moves just a little. Its tip flicks once, fitfully, when there is no wind. Toward Manny, then back up into the air. He narrows his eyes, and it trembles as if the force of his gaze has disturbed it. It flicks again, toward him and away.

Manny goes still, overwhelmed by an epiphany of familiarity. His thoughts are startled word salad, but those words are: *Cordyceps*, *puppet strings*, *drinking straw*, and more coherently, *That thing on FDR Drive!*

He drags his gaze from the white thing sticking out of the woman's neck, to her face. "That's not who you really are," he says. "Show yourself." Bel frowns at him.

The woman turns to him, inhaling and opening her mouth to complain again—and then she goes still. It's the stillness of a bad freeze-frame, catching her mid-inhalation and before the expression on her face can settle into either contempt or anger, leaving it interstitially vacant for the moment. She hasn't put down the camera, but her thumb must have gone slack; the recording light flicks off.

"The fuck," Bel says, now staring at her.

Manny blinks—and in the nanosecond that his eyes are shut,

the woman's clothing turns entirely white. The suit, the shoes, even the pantyhose. Her hair, too, which abruptly makes her look like a cross between a church lady and a female Colonel Sanders. She starts moving again, chuckling at Manny and Bel's obvious discomfiture and then raising her free hand to waggle in a *ta-daaaaa* gesture.

"What a relief!" she declares. Her voice has changed. It's lower now, alto rather than soprano. Around this voice, her smile is all teeth and nearly manic. "It's hard enough to act like one of you people already, but pretending that I didn't know you was getting old. It's good to see you again, São Paulo. Every place feels the same in this universe, your directions twist in and out like holes through cheese, but aren't you a little out of place? I remember the taste of your blood being a little farther south."

She's looking at Bel. "What?" Bel says. He looks at Manny. Manny shakes his head—in denial, not confusion. He gets what's happening, though he doesn't want to get it. That white thing sticking out of her head. *Antenna* is another of the words that have risen to the top of his mind. The white thing is like a receiver, channeling someone else's voice and thoughts and image from elsewhere.

(*How do I know this?* he thinks in a momentary not-quite-panic. *I am Manhattan*, comes the answer, which has its own questionish baggage. He'll ponder it later.)

The woman, meanwhile, is peering narrowly at Bel, as if she's having trouble seeing him, even though he's right there. She glances at the camera as if to confirm what her eyes are seeing, then lowers the camera. "Are you"—and her head tilts—"not who I think you are? Are you something else, underneath that covering?"

Bel stiffens perceptibly. "Who I am is none of your fucking business, woman. You want to move along, or shall I move you?"

"Oh!" The woman inhales. "You're just human. Pardon me, I mistook you for fifteen million other people. *You*, though." She turns her gaze on Manny, and he sees then that her eyes have changed color, too. They were brown, but something has faded them to a brown so pale that they verge on yellow. It's difficult to stare at those eyes and not think of predators like wolves or raptors, but Manny makes himself do so, because predators attack when one shows weakness.

"*You* definitely aren't human," she says to him. Manny manages not to flinch, but she laughs as if she's sensed the aborted nerve impulse. "Well, I knew you had to go to ground somewhere after our battle. Here, though? A forest? Trying to air out the reek of the trash you've slept under?"

"What?" Manny frowns in confusion. The woman blinks, then frowns back, her eyes narrowing.

"Hnh," she murmurs. "I was pretty sure I'd hurt you. Broken some bones. But you seem intact, to the degree that your species can be. And—" Abruptly her head tilts, belligerence giving way to confusion. "You're cleaner than you should be. Even your smell is . . ." She trails off.

She's crazy. But Manny knows, because of that awful white thing jutting from the back of her neck, that "crazy" is an inappropriate, incomplete word for what he's witnessing. It's impossible not to see that thing and understand that, somehow, this woman is affiliated with the giant mass of tendrils on FDR Drive. Maybe this is what happens to the people whose cars picked up tendrils in passing: if they touch a person, that person is then *compromised* in some fundamental, metaphysical, infectious way.

Whatever's speaking to Manny right now, through this woman, is not present—but that means there's something out there broadcasting Tentacle Monster TV, and this woman's got her own direct high-speed cable connection to it.

"So what are you?" Manny decides to ask.

She snorts, though she keeps staring at him. Without blinking; it's creepy. "No small talk, just right to business. No wonder everyone thinks New Yorkers are rude. But no bluster, either, this time? Where has all of your—" She looks away for an instant, her eyes flickering as if scanning some invisible dictionary, and then her gaze returns. "—shit-talking. Yes. Where has your shit-talking gone?"

Manny tries not to use profanity if he can help it. "We've never met."

"Untrue! Untrue!" She raises a hand and points at him, her eyes wide. He has a momentary flashback to his childhood, seeing syndicated repeats of *Invasion of the Body Snatchers* with Donald Sutherland, and it is entirely too easy to envision this woman with staring, alien eyes, screaming at him. But then she frowns again. "You *aren't* injured, though. Has your shape changed? I didn't think your species could do that, except slowly, growing old and such."

"Manny, mate," Bel murmurs, having stepped closer to him while the woman babbled, "this lady is clearly thirteen short of a baker's dozen, and I'm a little freaked out by the instant bleach job—"

"Manny?" the woman blurts before Manny can reply. She looks from Bel to him and back to Bel. "His name is Manny?"

"Shit," Bel says. "Sorry, shouldn't have used your name—"

"Don't worry about it." Manny keeps his gaze on the woman,

so he sees it when she inhales—and all at once her face distorts. For an instant she is *very* not human, her eyes flashing from yellowy brown into glaring white and her cheekbones seeming to shift and multiply under the skin of her face—and then her expression settles into a bright, manic-eyed grin.

"Manhattan," she breathes. He shivers with the pull of it. There is power in the way she speaks his name, power that she seems to know how to use in ways that he does not yet, and this frightens him. So does the avid, greedy malice in her unstable eyes. "You are *Manhattan*, where money talks and bullshit walks! Do you never sleep, young man? I see you aren't wearing silk and satin."

Manny tries not to let the nonsense confuse him. What matters is he faces an adversary who radiates danger. How does one fight spectral alien sea-tentacles in human form? He has no umbrella here, no antique cab...nothing but the Shorakkopoch rock, which he doesn't know how to use.

On FDR, he followed his instincts, and they eventually led him to the solution. *Keep her talking*, his instincts say now, so he obeys again.

"On FDR," he says, meeting the woman's bright-eyed gaze, "I killed your creature with an umbrella. Or..." He amends himself as intuition flutters at the back of his mind. "No, not your creature. You?"

"Just a little bit of me. A toe, to hold." She lifts a foot, which is clad in a simple white-leather ballet flat, and waggles the toe. Her ankles are swollen; too much time sitting at a desk, Manny guesses, and apparently being possessed by monsters from the beyond does nothing for the circulation.

"I'd expected to lose that toehold," the woman continues, with a long-suffering sigh. She turns and starts pacing, clutching the cell phone to her breast with a melodramatic sigh. "We usually do, when you entities actualize, or mature, or whatever you call it—and we did lose it, later. Someone came along and *stubbed* our toe, damn it. Such a vicious little thing he was. Positively thuggish. But after he was done with me and I lay bleeding and hating in the cold depths between, I found that my toe still held. Just a little. Just one toe, in just one place."

"FDR Drive," Manny says. His skin prickles with chill.

"FDR Drive. Until you tore even that toehold loose. *That* was you, wasn't it? You people all look alike to me, but I smell it now. Like him, but not." Her head tilts from one side to the other as she says this. It is a gesture that feels both contemplative and contemptuous. "Too late, of course. Before you ever got there, I'd infected quite a few cars. Now we have hundreds of toes, all over the Tri-state area." She bounces a little on the balls of her feet, then frowns down at herself as if annoyed by her momentary paucity of toes.

In Manny's mind, fountains of tentacles are erupting on highways and bridges throughout a hundred-mile radius. He tries not to let her see how much this idea frightens him. What does it mean? What are they doing? What will they do, once they've infected enough cars and people and—

"What the fuck are you *talking* about?" asks Bel.

She rolls her eyes. "The politics of spacetime fractionality and superpositioning," she snaps, before dismissing Bel again and sighing at Manny. Bel just stares at her. "Well. You're obviously *part* of that other one, which means that you have four more bodies out there somewhere. Four more, oh . . . what do you people call those? Organs?" She stops abruptly, frowning to herself, then rounds on Bel and points west. "You! Human! What is that?"

After a deeply worried glance at Manny, Bel follows her gesture to Spuyten Duyvil Creek. She's pointing past it, actually, at a dramatic-looking cliff beyond which is dotted with houses and condo buildings. "Westchester?" Bel suggests. "Or maybe the Bronx. I wouldn't know, I've only been here a couple of weeks."

"*The Bronx.*" The woman's lip curls. "Yes. That's one. Manhattan is another. The one I fought, *he* is the heart, but you others are the head and limbs and such. He was strong enough to fight us even without you, but not strong enough to stand, after. Not strong enough to push me out now. Thus does the toehold become an entire foot."

In spite of everything, Manny is actually beginning to understand. "Boroughs," he murmurs in wonder. *I am Manhattan.* "You're talking about the boroughs of the city. You're saying I really *am* Manhattan. And"—he inhales—"and you're saying there are others."

The woman stops pacing and turns, too slowly, to study him again. "You didn't know that until just now," she says, her gaze narrowing.

Manny goes still. He knows he's made a mistake by showing his hand, but only time will reveal how bad a mistake it was.

"Five of you," says the woman in white, in satisfaction. (Like that, something in Manny's brain adjusts the designation into capital-letter status. The Woman in White.) She's smiling, and it's cold. "*Five* of you, and only poor São Paulo to look after you all! He's with the one I fought. You're alone. And you don't know what you're doing at all, do you?"

Manny's stomach has knotted with fear. He can tell she's about to do something, and he still has no idea how to fight her. "What do you want?" he asks, to stall her. To buy time to think.

She shakes her head and sighs. "It would probably be sporting to tell you, but there's no sport in this for me. I just have a job to do. Goodbye, Manhattan."

All at once, she's gone. The Woman in White, that is; between one blink and another, the white woman's clothes and hair flicker back into their ordinary tints. She slumps a little, just an ordinary brown-eyed woman again. But after a moment of confusion, the woman's lips tighten and she raises her cell phone again. The camera light goes back on.

But something worse is happening. When the hairs on the back of Manny's neck prickle, he jumps and wheels around, suddenly convinced that someone is coming at him from behind. He sees the forgotten young couple on the lawn, still picnicking, but otherwise there's nothing there—

Wait. No. Rising from cracks and spars in the asphalt of the path . . . are ghostly little white nubs.

Manny grabs Bel and yanks him back just as white nubs rise through a crack he'd been standing on. More wriggle through even the unbroken portions of the asphalt. When Manny sees that no white nubs are rising from the narrow ring of bare soil that surrounds the tulip tree rock, and perhaps another three or four inches beyond that, Manny pulls them both to stand within this apparently protected circle. "What are—" Bel begins. Bel can clearly perceive the white nubs, Manny is relieved to see. At least he doesn't have to explain this, too. Bel backs himself against the rock, looking around in horror as the nubs become inchworms.

"Just disgusting," says the woman. She stands amid an ankle-high lawn of the tendrils now—and the one coming from the back of her neck has fissioned into two, both of them uncannily oriented on Manny. Incredibly, through all this, she's still recording them. Or—not just recording? An instant later a voice crackles from the phone's speaker. Manny can't make it out, but he hears the woman say, "I need the police. There are these two guys in Inwood Hill Park who are, I don't know, menacing people. I think they're drug dealers, and they won't leave. Also, they're having sex."

"Listen, woman, I don't think you know what sex *looks* like—" Bel splutters. In the distance, the young couple giggles, though Manny doesn't think it's because of what Bel said. They're busy making out and haven't noticed what's happening by the rock.

The woman ignores Bel, intent on her conversation. "Yes. I will. I'm recording them. Right, uh-huh." She hesitates, then screws up her face and adds, "*African American*. Or maybe Hispanic? I can't tell."

"I'm obviously British Asian, you stupid bint!" Bel stares at her openmouthed. Meanwhile, however, the tendrils are still growing, and getting long enough that they're going to be able to touch Bel and Manny even if they climb on top of the rock. Which probably isn't going to help, since the rock isn't big enough for two people to stand on.

Which reminds Manny that the rock is *meaningful*. An object of power—somehow. Shorakkopoch, site of the first real estate swindle of the soon-to-be New York. What can he do with that?

Oh. *Ohhhh.*

He pushes at Bel. "Get up on the rock," he says. "I need the room. And give me whatever is in your wallet."

It's a measure of how freaked out Bel is that he complies, scrabbling onto the rock and groping for his back pocket. "Worst mugging ever, mate," he quips with a shaking voice.

Manny has pulled his own wallet out of his pocket. He finds

himself remarkably calm as he opens it and rummages for something that will serve that tickle of an idea in his mind, and a detached, analytical part of him contemplates this lack of fear. He *should* be terrified, after seeing what these tendrils have done to another human being. What will it be like to have his body invaded and his mind overtaken by whatever entity these things serve?

Like dying, he decides. And since some part of him has faced death before—he's aware of that suddenly; it's why he's so calm— Manny also decides that he's not going out like that.

There's not much in his wallet. Some receipts, a five-dollar bill, an Amex card, a debit card, an expired condom. No photos of loved ones, which will strike him as odd only later. An ID—but immediately he tears his eyes away from this, not wanting to see the name he had prior to this morning's train ride. Who he used to be is irrelevant. Right now, he needs to be Manhattan.

The instant his fingers touch one of the credit cards, he feels a flicker of that strange energy and focus that he had on FDR. Yes. "Land has value," he murmurs to himself, distracted from the rising, whipping field of white all around him. "Even public land, like in a park. It's just a concept, land ownership; we don't have to live like this. But this city, in its current form, is built on that concept."

"*Please* tell me you aren't losing it," Bel says from where he's crouched on the rock. "I don't think both of us can afford a psychotic break at the same time. We just signed a lease."

Manny looks up at him—and tosses the fiver to the ground, just beyond the rock's ring. He feels rather than hears a sudden, hollow, high-pitched squealing from where the bill has landed, and he knows without looking what has happened. Where the bill has touched the asphalt, it has *hurt* the tendrils, and caused the ones in that immediate area to withdraw.

Bel stares at this. Frantically he pulls a handful of disordered bills out of his wallet. Some of them are euros, some British pounds, US bills, and a few pesos; clearly Bel travels a lot. He tosses one of the pound notes. It lands not far from the bill Manny threw, but nothing happens.

"I told you to give it to me," Manny says, snatching the wad of bills from Bel's shaking fingers. Doing this strengthens the strange feeling; Manhattan was built not only on land valuation, but stolen value.

"Just trying to help with this *bollocks*," Bel snaps. "God, do whatever nonsense you have to do, they're getting closer!"

Manny starts casting the bills around the edge of the field of white, make-it-rain-style. He quickly sees that the money is having an effect, but not much of one. A five-pound note clears the space underneath it, but no more, and he loses sight of it after a moment amid the surrounding field of tendrils. The euros and pounds work, too, but it seems to depend on their value. A hundred-dollar bill clears not only its own space, but an inch or so around itself. A hundred-euro note clears slightly more—but all of it together adds up to only enough space to keep the nearer tendrils from being able to reach Manny. And if the tendrils keep growing, they'll eventually be able to reach Manny no matter how many additional inches of land he's gained.

That's it. Suddenly, Manny understands: he is effectively *buying* the land around the tulip tree rock. But it costs a lot more than sixty guilders now. "Bel, do you know how much Manhattan real estate runs? Per square foot?"

"Are you actually insane."

One of the taller tendrils whips toward Manny's thigh, and he swats it with a twenty-dollar bill. It squeals and withdraws. "I really need to know, please!"

"How the bloody fuck should I know? I'm a flat renter, not a buyer! Maybe a thousand dollars a foot? Two thousand?"

That's the problem, then, Manny realizes, with a bitter groan. Manhattan real estate is horrifically expensive, and they don't have enough cash to buy their own lives.

In desperation, he tosses his Amex, and that has the biggest effect yet, clearing a rectangular chunk of space the size of a sedan. Apparently he's got good credit. Bel doesn't have any cards, however, and there are tendrils beyond the space he's cleared—and now Manny's only got the debit card left. How much money is in his bank account? He can't remember.

"Okay," says the woman, with satisfaction. Manny is stunned to realize he forgot her for a moment. She smiles at them from amid the thickest knot of gently waving tentacles, her head and shoulders now festooned with at least a dozen. "The police say they're on their way. You people might have been able to get away with doing drugs or blowing each other in broad daylight before, but I didn't move here to put up with stuff like that. We're gonna get you out, one by one."

Manny's consternation about Manhattan real estate prices is eclipsed by sudden dry-mouthed fear. If the police do show up—which isn't a guarantee; even as a newcomer, he can tell Inwood is still too brown a neighborhood for a definitive or quick response, especially during a citywide emergency—they will walk right into the rapidly growing field of white tendrils that now surrounds Manny and Bel. And if one tendril has turned a nosy, racist white woman into a conduit for disembodied existential evil, he doesn't want to see what infected NYPD will become.

He's getting ready to throw the debit card, and hoping desperately that that account just happens to contain a million dollars or so ... when they hear another cell phone.

New York, New York, big city of dreams ...

It's mostly a gabble of tinny sound from this distance. Probably an iPhone. But from the gabble, Manny can make out handclaps over a beat. Electronic drums and ... a record scratch? Like in old-school rap?

Too much ... too many people, too much ...

Manny whips around to see a middle-toned Black woman coming toward them along a path that converges with the Shorakkopoch clearing. She's tall and strong, with an upright carriage and thighs that are nothing but curve, the latter accentuated further by the pencil skirt she's wearing the hell out of. Some of her bearing comes from all this style, plus smart heels and an elegantly texturized, honey-blond-dyed cap of curls—but most of it's just *her*. She's a presence. She looks like either a CEO on her way to an incredibly stylish meeting, or a queen who just happens to be missing her court.

Then Manny sees that she's also holding up a cell phone. Instead of filming, however, she's using this one to blare music. The song is a little before Manny's time, but he's heard it once or twice, and—*ah*. With every tinny beat of the synthesized drums, the field of tendrils that has filled the tulip tree rock clearing begins to twitch en masse. As Manny inhales in relief, the woman steps onto the cobbles, and the tendrils flinch away from the brisk click of her heels. The ones she steps on actually *scream*, in tiny hissing squeaks as they writhe—and then vanish. When she directs the phone downward, the ones that haven't already withdrawn shudder as if each beat is a painful blow. Then they crumble away, leaving no residue or sign that they were ever there. The tendrils are crumbling away *everywhere*.

Too much . . . too many people, too much . . . Yes. The city might welcome newcomers like Manny, but mind-controlling parasitic otherworldly entities are the rudest of tourists.

"Five of us," Manny murmurs. He knows who, or at least what, this woman is.

Bel throws a look at him, then shakes his head. "Friend, I sincerely hope you drink. I'm going to need something potent and extremely fruity after this." Manny laughs, as much to release pent adrenaline as anything else.

By the time the chorus ends, the tendrils are gone, and the clearing is as it was before: trees, grass, asphalt, a lamppost, a rock, and Bel and Manny crouched to defend themselves against (now) nothing. Even the tendrils on the neck and shoulders of the white woman have vanished—and she now stares at all of them, especially the Black woman, with rising alarm. But. She's still filming.

Manny and Bel turn to the Black woman, who stops the music at last and tucks the phone into her tote purse. (A Birkin, Manny notices with some admiration. Apparently he's the kind of man who knows his expensive Birkin bags.) There's something familiar about her, but Manny can't place it. Maybe it's just that she's like him. He stares at her, filled with an inchoate hunger.

"So, I'm guessing y'all haven't figured out how this shit works yet," she says to them. Her gaze rakes Bel, then Manny, and stops there, narrowing a little. "Oh, okay. Just you, then."

Manny nods, swallowing. Another like him. "I, uh, I don't

know anything. Do you?" He knows it sounds inane, but he can't think of anything else to ask.

She raises her eyebrows. "Well, that depends on what you're asking. If you mean have I suddenly started hearing crazy business in my head, and seeing those white pigeon-feather things all over my hood? Yeah. If you want to know why, I don't even know." The woman shakes her head. "I had to kill three patches of them just to get to the 3 train."

"Pigeon-feather things?" But Manny understands that she means the tendrils. To him they look like sea creatures, but he can see the resemblance to feather shafts, too.

"You people really are the worst drug dealers," says the white woman, shaking her head. "Just brazenly talking about your designer drugs." In the distance—Manny can't tell if they're actually approaching or just happenstance—they can hear sirens.

That's it. Manny straightens, setting his jaw.

The Black woman is staring at the white woman now. "You actually called the cops on these men? For what, walking in the park while Black and Asian?" She lets out an incredulous laugh. By the time that laugh has faded, however, Manny's walked over to the white woman and snatched the phone from her hand.

"Whoa," says Bel, more startled than prohibitive. Manny ignores him. The woman yelps and draws breath to scream, but before she can, Manny steps in closer and wraps a hand around the lower half of her face, covering her mouth.

The Black woman utters a swift curse, but then backs up to where she can watch the two paths coming out of the woods. The white woman grabs for Manny's arm rather than trying to wrench away. It's exactly what Manny expected; she's clearly unwilling to back away from someone whom she regards as having no right to exist in public, let alone within her personal space. She isn't scared, not really. She assumed that he would not dare attack her.

Well, then. It's the work of a moment for Manny to switch his grip to the woman's throat instead. Her eyes widen. "Don't scream," he says.

She inhales. In a sharp movement, Manny tightens his hand and turns them around, yanking the woman off-balance and angling his body so that the couple on the grass won't see. (Not that they're paying attention. To judge by their positions and the way they're moving, Manny suspects they're actually filming themselves having sex in public. No reason not to be careful, though.) If they do happen to glance toward the group around the tulip tree rock, it will look like Manny's just standing close to the woman while they have an intimate talk.

The woman freezes, scream taut but unreleased in her throat tendons. Manny loosens his grip as soon as it's clear she's taken the hint. He only wants to keep her quiet, not cut off her air, and he needs to keep his grip gentle or he'll leave finger marks. There's an art to doing this.

(How does he know that? God.)

Once she's still, Manny asks her conversationally, "Don't drug dealers usually kill snitches?"

She inhales a little, her eyes locking onto his. *Now* she's scared. Manny smiles as, with his free hand, he thumbs through her phone. It's all fine and friendly. Just a little shakedown between friends.

"I've always heard that about dealers," Manny continues as he searches through the phone's stored data directory. Got it. Next, active apps. "I mean, we're *not* drug dealers. But if we were, it doesn't make a lot of sense that you just stood there filming us.

That just doesn't sound *safe*, does it? But I think you filmed us because you *didn't* think we were dealers. Because we were just ordinary people going about our own business, and it bothered you to see us comfortable and unafraid. So now you've inserted yourself into something very dangerous. Hold still."

She freezes at the whipcrack of those last two words. This close, he can feel the tension in her body. Easy to tell she was shifting her weight, about to try to lunge away. Satisfied, Manny resumes thumbing through her phone.

"Anyway, let's see...ah, you're on Facebook. Live?" He browses her settings. "Guess not. And you don't have any backup apps logged in..." He glances at the top of her Facebook profile and beams in delight. "Martha! Martha Blemins." The woman makes an unhappy sound around his hand. "That's an incredibly pretty name, Martha. And Blemins is such a unique spelling. I see you work at Event Flight. As a marketplace analyst? That sounds really important."

Martha Blemins is terrified now. Her hands have locked around Manny's wrist, but he can feel them trembling, the palms a little damp. Tears have begun trailing from one eye. She's so visibly on the brink of panic that Manny is honestly surprised when she manages to speak. "Y-you can't hurt me," she says, her voice wavering. "You b-better not."

Manny feels a great wave of sadness come over him. "I *can* hurt you, Martha," he confesses. "I know how, and it wouldn't be the first time I've hurt someone else. I think...I think I've done that a lot."

He knows this is true, suddenly—and he hates that *this*, out of the gray undifferentiated morass that is his past, is the knowledge that's returned to him. Her pulse flutters fast against his palm.

This will have traumatized her, he feels certain; it's a mugging without the mugging. She'll never sleep easily again in New York, never walk to work without looking over her shoulder. He's in her head now, waving at her from the little box of assumptions that she carries about Certain Kinds Of People. The fact that she applied these assumptions preemptively means there's nothing he could've done to change them, but he still hates that he's just confirmed her stereotypes.

The sound of sirens is fading. Either the police passed by on their way something else, or they've parked and are headed this way on foot. Time to go. Manny lets go of Martha's throat, steps back, and—after wiping it carefully against his pants leg and holding only the rough edges of her decorative case—hands her phone back to her. She grabs it and stares at him, mute with shock.

"Have a really nice day, Martha," he says, meaning it. But he has to add one more thing, if they are to be safe from the danger she presents. He has to be more dangerous, in her mind. So he says, "Hopefully we won't ever see each other again."

Then he backs away, down one of the paths that leads away from where they last heard sirens. Bel is staring at him, though he moves to follow Manny after a moment. The Black woman sighs but falls in as well, and Manny turns to head up the hill with them.

Martha stays where Manny's left her, not making a sound, and not turning to watch them leave.

They're almost to the edge of the park—no cops so far—before the Black woman finally says, "I take it you're Manhattan."

He blinks out of melancholy and turns to her. She's pulled some kind of breakfast bar out of her bag and is eating it.

"Yeah. How did you guess?"

"Are you kidding? Dudes like you—smart, charming, well dressed, and cold enough to strangle you in an alley if we had alleys?" She snorts to herself, while Manny tries not to let her see how much this assessment hurts him. "Dime a dozen on Wall Street and at City Hall. Figured you'd be meaner, actually. The kind of dude who didn't stop at just threats."

I haven't always, Manny thinks, in despair.

Bel makes a sound that's somewhere between an audible swallow and a throat-clearing. "So you remembered who you were?" When Manny frowns at him, he smiles. It's rueful and doesn't quite meet his eyes. "I mean, you're back to being the bloke I met before. The one with the edge."

Manny wrestles with several responses before deciding: "No."

"Don't sound too sure there, mate."

He isn't, but he doesn't want to talk about it. To distract himself, he considers the Black woman and guesses, "Queens?" She gives him such a disgusted look that he immediately amends, "Brooklyn."

This seems to mollify her. "Yes. It also has the virtue of being my name. Brooklyn Thomason. Esquire, though I'm not practicing anymore. Went into politics instead."

Her name is actually Brooklyn. And she *remembers* herself. Which means that whatever has happened to make them what they are, memory loss isn't part of the normal process.

"How did you know?" he blurts. "How to find me? How did you know to play music? Why don't *I* know any of this?"

She regards him coolly, despite the sweat that dots her brow after steady uphill walking. They're circling around the park, Manny realizes. His spatial awareness is completely foiled by the trees, but he suspects they're heading south and will emerge from the park somewhere near...Dyckman? He remembers seeing that on his phone's map. "You're not from here, are you?" she asks.

"No." He stares at her, wanting to know how she knew that, too. The bike salespeople at Penn Station seemed to think he was a local.

She sees his confusion and sighs. He gets the fleeting impression that she doesn't like talking to him, though he can't tell why. Maybe it's personal, or maybe she dislikes men who jack up women, on general principle. "I don't know how I knew. I just feel it. That's been my whole day so far—doing and thinking stuff that doesn't make any sense, just 'cause it feels right."

Manny lets out a slow breath to calm himself. "Yeah. Same."

Bel's calmer now, and his regional accent has faded back into generic Britishness. "I'm glad I have no idea what you're talking about. It sounds, ah, fraught."

Brooklyn snorts at this, though she then focuses on Manny again. "I've heard...something...since I was a child," she admits. "Muttering, feelings, images. Felt things, too—little twitches and sighs and touches. All for so long that I don't even really think about it anymore. For a while I talked back. Never told anybody they were love songs to the city, but not everybody needs to know everything."

Her expression has gone flat, and he understands then what she doesn't like—not him, but the fact that she has to speak about something so obviously personal. He nods back, trying to convey that he won't use this against her, but she just shakes her head, annoyed at the situation regardless. That's when something about her scowl hits Manny. He stops in his tracks. She stops after another step or two, then turns back with visible reluctance. There's a held breath in her expression this time, as if she's bracing herself for something. That's his confirmation.

"Oh wow," he says. "You're MC Free."

"Whaaaaaat." Bel stops, too, staring at her. "Oh, shit, you are."

"I'm Brooklyn Thomason," she replies. It's gentle, but firm. "MC Free was my stage name thirty years and thirty pounds ago. These days I'm on the city council. I got a JD and a fourteen-year-old and a side hustle renting out vacation property." Then she sighs, relenting. "But...yeah. That's who I used to be."

"My God," Bel says in a tone of naked reverence. "The greatest of the early female MCs. Lewisham was all *over* you back then. I grew up on your music."

Brooklyn's expression turns faintly sour. "Every time somebody says that to me, I pop another gray hair. You notice I dye it now?"

Bel winces and takes the hint to get over it. "Yyyyyeah, sorry. Shutting up."

They all shut up for a while, because the hill has winded them. On impulse, Manny lifts his eyes to the tree canopy as they walk. It's cooler, here in the forest shadows, than it is on the asphalt streets and concrete sidewalks. Strange to think that there are probably wild animals in this forest, like raccoons and maybe deer or coyotes; he's read that those are making a comeback in some areas of the city. But other kinds of animals abound here, too. How many other people, besides Martha Blemins, have been mugged here? How many beatings, how many stabbings, how many rapes? Whole villages of Lenape were driven away from the city and its immediate vicinity by the Dutch; how many of them died in the process? How much blood and fear has soaked into this old bedrock?

I am Manhattan, he thinks again, this time in a slow upwelling of despair. *Every murderer. Every slave broker. Every slumlord who shut off the heat and froze children to death. Every stockbroker who got rich off war and suffering.*

It's only the truth. He doesn't have to like it, though.

They reach Dyckman after a while. The clotting traffic on the street means that rush hour has started. School's out, sending packs of same-aged children forth to flow along both sides of the street. No one's looking at Manny and company as they emerge from the park. If the police did respond to Martha's call, there's no sign of them anywhere nearby. Then again, given the Williamsburg, they probably didn't bother to come.

"So what now?" Manny asks.

Brooklyn sighs. "No idea. But I'll tell you what: I'm pretty sure there's a reason all of this is happening, all of a sudden." She eyes him. "You know the bridge thing is part of this, right?"

Manny stares at her. Bel looks from one to the other of them, incredulous. "The Williamsburg? What, fell down because of—" He gestures vaguely in the direction of the tulip tree rock. "Those squiggly things, and that *other* woman?"

Brooklyn frowns at him. "Other woman?"

"The one that Mrs. Nosy Parker turned into for a moment. Before you showed up." He shivers a little. "Never seen anything creepier, except those horrid little white things."

Brooklyn shakes her head in confusion, and Manny has to explain. It's actually difficult to find the words for what they saw, though after a few attempts he manages to get across that the woman Brooklyn saw was just temporary housing for someone, or something, else. "She controls those things," he says, gesturing at the back of his neck while Brooklyn digests what he's said. "I'm sure of it. The ones on FDR Drive, too. Anything those tentacles touch."

"Something told me to avoid the FDR today. Not that I usually drive anyway; took the subway." Brooklyn sighs. "That's how I, I don't know, felt you? There was a crisis response meeting for city leaders up in Washington Heights. I was about to head home, but something told me to take the train uptown instead. The, uh, something, got stronger, the closer I got to you. Then there you were, in trouble."

"There are five of us," Manny says. He watches Brooklyn start as she takes his meaning.

"Oh, hell. You think the other three are in trouble, too." She frowns, then shakes her head slowly. "Look, I'm glad I could help you, but . . . I didn't sign on for an extra job. I got a kid, and my father is sick. You want to try and find them, go ahead. I have to get home."

Manny starts to speak, to try to persuade her, and then something catches his attention from the corner of his eye. He follows it and finds himself looking across the street, at a little bodega on the corner. Next to it is a laundromat that's been gracious enough to put a tiny, rickety bench out front. An elderly man sits there with a small dog on a leash. He's busy chatting in Spanish with a woman, who stands in the doorway of the laundromat; they're laughing about something. But the dog is watching Manny and company with a steady, fixed stare that does not at all feel like the gaze of an animal.

Then Manny looks closer. Between its clawed toes, like bits of ghostly grass picked up on its last walk, are half a dozen gently waving white tendrils.

Brooklyn sees it, too. "Are you fucking kidding me."

Staring at the dog, his skin all over prickling, Manny says, "It's what happened on FDR. The tendrils, anything that got close to them . . ."

"Like a goddamn disease," Brooklyn breathes.

Bel is staring at the dog, too. He's squinting a little, as if the tendrils are hard to see, but then he grimaces and visibly shivers. "I saw that old fellow walking his dog earlier, when we were walking. If everybody who was in the park just now is, um, infected, then I imagine it'll be all over the city within a day or two."

They all fall silent for a moment, digesting this.

"The white things came off of that woman when I got rid of the others," Brooklyn says. She's hiding it well, but her confident facade has slipped a little at the sight of the dog. The dog makes this something insidious, and ominous. "She was only marinating in her own evil, nobody else's, by the time we were done."

Manny finds himself thinking about the wave of force that spread outward from FDR in the wake of his little stunt with the cab. He has an idea of what it is now: the city's energy, dissipating outward in a circular wave once Manny no longer needed it in concentrated form. How far did that splash of energy go? He can't guess, but he remembers seeing it kill all the white tendrils that it touched.

A powerful weapon—if Manny can figure out how to use it consistently. Manny turns to Brooklyn. "Look, I can't make you help me, but if I have to do this on my own, I'm going to need a crash course in how to be a New Yorker."

She blinks. Then there is another of those peculiar shifts in which the world doubles—and here in the other, weirder New York, his perspective is suddenly wider, higher. Macro scale instead of micro. And here in this other realm she looms over him, vast and sprawling, wildly patchwork and dense. Not just older but bigger. Stronger in many ways; her arms and core are thick with muscled neighborhoods that each have their own rhythms and reputations. Williamsburg, Hasidim enclave and artist haven turned hipster ground zero. Bed Stuy (do or die). Crown Heights, where now the only riots are over seats at brunch. Her jaw is tight with the stubborn ferocity of Brighton Beach's old mobsters and the Rockaways' working-class holdouts against the brutal inevitability of rising seas. But there are spires at Brooklyn's heart, too—perhaps not as grand as his own, and maybe some of hers are actually the airy, fanciful amusement-park towers of Coney Island—but all are just as shining, just as sharp.

She is Brooklyn, and she is mighty, and in this instant he cannot help but love her, stranger or not. Then she is just a middle-aged woman again, with a shining, sharp grin.

"I guess I could help you with that," she concedes. "I guess I *have* to, if this shit is spreading. But there ain't no one way to be a part of this city." She slips into and out of the vernacular like changing purses, effortless and with ever-perfect fit. Manny soaks it all in, getting a feel for the cadence, trying to keep up. "Takes most people a year, at least, to really feel the city's call."

The city's *caul*, he hears. Her nose moves when she says it, as if there's a *w* in the word. The accent layers extra consonants into words and extra meaning onto thoughts. "I'll give it my all," he replies, deliberately adding a *w* to the last word and testing out its new flavor. It's not quite right. Brooklyn instead of Manhattan. But still better than the Midwestern accent that currently infests his language, and which he now consciously decides to shed. It does not belong here.

"Let me call my family," she says at last, with a sigh. "Tell them I'll be late home. Then let's go find a coffee shop or—"

And then they both feel it. In the other world, Brooklyn and Manhattan step back, to the degree that entities with foundations instead of feet can do so, to make room for the explosive, brilliant skylineburst of another of their number.

In the people world, they look at each other and murmur in unison, both slipping into a perfect South Indian English accent: "Oh, come on. *The shape of the Earth* is non-Euclidean. All that means is that you use different math! Don't get it twisted."

Bel stares at them. "That is the creepiest thing I've seen today, barring the alien-mind-control spaghetti."

"Okay," Brooklyn says. "Crosstown bus, then. There's a stop a few blocks from here."

Manny nods. He knows instinctively that they have to go, though he does not yet have enough of a sense of the city to fully understand what he's feeling. "Where...?"

"Queens," Brooklyn says. "Shit. That was Queens."

Of course. Manny takes a deep breath, then turns to Bel. "I think you'd better head back home. Sorry, but... This is going to get weird. Weirder."

Bel rocks back on his heels and lets out a whistled breath. "And as things have been entirely too weird for me already, yes, I agree. Go with God, and so on." He steps back and waves. "Do try not to get eaten by the spaghetti people, though. Even now, you're not the worst roommate I've ever had."

Manny half smiles and nods farewell, then turns to pace Brooklyn as she heads in the direction of the crosstown bus stop. He waits until they're a block or so away from Bel, and well away from the tendril-infested dog, before saying, "So, is there a reason we aren't taking a cab?"

"Not sure what to tell the cabbie," Brooklyn says. "Queens is huge; we're not gonna just 'feel the Force' at random there. We'll take the crosstown bus to where we can pick up the 7. Mass transit led me to you, so I'm hoping that'll happen again there. Since I'm apparently doing this now. So much for going home." She sighs.

"Okay." It's frustratingly nebulous. But Manny understands precisely why she's walking fast, and why they aren't waiting for these peculiar new instincts of theirs to provide some more specific, concrete direction. The jittering, rapidly rising sense of urgency within him is undeniable. Queens is out there becoming its person, and that person is in danger. If they're going to do her any good at all, they need to hurry.

Except. Well. Manny's pretty sure they're already too late.

CHAPTER THREE

Our Lady of (Staten) Aislyn

It's time.

Aislyn Houlihan is at the St. George Terminal of the Staten Island Ferry, trembling. She's been here for twenty minutes, trembling. There are open seats because it's early enough in the day, just before the start of rush hour, that the ferry won't be anywhere near full—but she's opted to pace in front of the glass window-wall instead of sitting. The better to tremble while she paces.

The terminal is mostly just a big, brightly lit room where a few hundred people can assemble. There's nothing that should be scary about it. Its walls are lined with ads for movies Aislyn isn't planning to see and makeup she probably won't ever wear. The people standing or sitting around her are *hers*, her people; she feels this instinctively even though her mind resists when her gaze skates over Asian faces, or her ears pick up a language that probably isn't Spanish but also definitely isn't English. (*Quechua*, her strange newer senses whisper, but she doesn't want to hear it.) They aren't bothering her, though, and there are plenty of normal people around, so there's no good reason for her to be as terrified as she is. Terror doesn't always happen for a good reason.

There's a garbled announcement over the PA system, and abruptly the big doors along one side of the room open up. Beyond them is an outdoor pier where the 2:30 p.m. ferry is preparing to leave. The hundred or so people cattling around the terminal begin moving toward it, and Aislyn belatedly tries to stumble after them.

From the first step it's wrong. Everything feels wrong. Staten Islanders normally take the ferry *away* in the mornings, leaving the island quieter, emptier. It's afternoon now, though. All over the city—Manhattan is always *the city*—thousands of SI denizens are growing antsy with the end of the workday, shifting in their trendy seats, thinking wistfully of a place where there are still forests and ranches and mostly-unspoiled beaches, and where most families live in discrete houses and own cars like normal people. What Aislyn is doing is *leaving* the island at a time when most want to *return* to it. She is swimming upriver, reversing the polarity. The wrongness of it presses against her skin. Her hair follicles tingle. She tries to keep her feet moving anyway, use the flow of the crowd to counter the wrongness. Through the doors. Outside onto the pier, moving toward the boat. She's choosing her own direction in life! The wrongness is just her imagination.

Or...maybe something else is happening. Maybe it's not the hard gust of wind off the harbor that's making her steps drag; maybe it's her own leaden feet and bedrock legs. Maybe the scalp tingling isn't her hair streaming in the wind. Maybe it's the island—*her island*—pulling at her in warning, in fear, in love.

Or maybe it's an incipient panic attack.

She tries to fight it off, and gets as far as the ramp that leads onto the ferry. *John F. Kennedy* reads the ferry's name, placarded on the wheelhouse; this is the name of her tormentor. Did JFK fear anything before somebody—the mob according to her father, a crazyman according to her mother—shot out his brains? If she gets on this boat, she'll be going to a city where things like that happen on a regular basis. People kill each other on SI, too, all the time, but it's different in the city. Everything is different there.

If she gets on this boat, she will come back different.

Someone nudges her, hard. "Hey, blocking traffic."

If she gets on this boat, will she come back *wrong*?

Someone else puts a hand on her upper arm. It's closely packed enough on the ramp that the person actually jostles her, grunting out a curse as the crowd shoves them forward and causes them to squish Aislyn's right breast. It doesn't hurt, and it's obviously an accident, but when she glances around to see who's touching her, her gaze skates over skin so Black that it's like looking into a Magic 8 Ball before the little plastic thing inside bobs up to say: NOW PANIC.

Her thoughts ignite—*GET AWAY GET OFF ME DON'T TOUCH ME GET ME OUT OF HERE*—and her body contracts without any conscious input. Now she is moving against the flow (with the island's wishes, though, at last), lurching from one stranger's horrifying touch to another and wondering the whole time who's screaming with such an ear-piercing pitch. Only belatedly does she recognize her own voice. People around her freeze or jerk away from the crazy lady, but they're still too close. Crushing her. She writhes around them, already turned toward the glass doors. "Whoa, whoa, whoa!" someone says, and it sounds like they're going to try and stop her. Who is it? She can't let that Black guy touch her again.

It's a white hand that catches her wrist. She doesn't see its owner, but she rakes her nails down flesh before yanking free. Someone else screams and then the crowd parts and finally, finally, she is free. She runs back through the glass doors, through the terminal. There's a cop coming out of the single-stall family bathroom, still fastening his belt and with a folded copy of the *Post* under one arm. He yells after her, and Aislyn knows she should stop. Her father has told her and told her: *Only criminals run.* And she scratched somebody, isn't that assault? She's a criminal now. They'll take her to RIKERS ISLAND, which is a completely different and much worse island than her own. They will make her leave SI, they'll *force* her onto a police boat, and they'll never let her come back—

"But no one can make a city do anything it doesn't want to," says someone close by, in a puzzled tone, and Aislyn looks left to find a woman running beside her.

She's so startled that she stumbles in midrun. The woman quickly puts out a hand to steady her, and they both jog to a halt. She's a little surprised to find herself well outside the terminal, between two of the dozen-odd bus platforms that edge up to it. Passing strangers stare and she flinches away from their gazes, but the breeze has worked to break her out of the cycle of panic. She swallows, beginning to calm.

"There, there," says the woman, who's holding her shoulders now. She smiles comfortingly, and she's comforting to look at: white-blond hair in a pixie cut surrounding a pale, gray-eyed face. She's wearing sandals that clearly don't impede her ability to sprint. Her white jeans are probably stylish; her white blouse definitely is. The woman speaks while Aislyn stares at her in breathless dumbness. "That's better, isn't it? Nothing scary here.

No boats. No water. No illegal immigrants touching you. No peer pressure, trying to make you cross the harbor! I don't blame you at all, by the way. Manhattan is very pretty, but he's full of bees."

The nonsense of this monologue breaks the remnants of Aislyn's panic. Manhattan's an it, isn't it? Not a he. And . . . *bees*? She giggles despite herself.

But before she can process the words further, her phone starts ringing. She jumps violently. The woman pets her shoulder, incongruously—has been petting Aislyn since they met, as if determined to single-handedly replace the memory of all those strangers' touches with just her own—but weirdly, this makes Aislyn feel better. She grabs her phone and sees MATTHEW HOULIHAN (DADDY).

"Where are you?" he asks, when she answers.

"Just out running errands," she says. She's never been good at lying, and her father is excellent at figuring out when she's trying it, so she always makes sure there's some truth in whatever she tells him. She did stop at the grocery store on the way to the ferry station, to buy garlic. "Got something at the grocery store, now shopping a little. Everything okay at work?"

It's always better to get him focused on himself rather than her. He sighs and takes the bait. "Just getting sick of these *immigrants*," he says. He's always careful to use acceptable words when he's on the job, rather than the words he says at home. That's how cops mess up, he has explained to her. They don't know how to keep home words at home and work words at work. "These *people*. Had to arrest a guy this morning—just sitting in his car, right? I figured he was dealing. Didn't find anything, but he's got no ID, right? So I run his tag and tell him we're calling ICE. Just to shake him up, see. He was acting all smooth. He says he's Puerto Rican, they're *citizens*, calls me all kinds of shit, starts talking about getting on that Twitter to complain about profiling." She can practically hear her father's eye roll. "Damn straight I *profiled* him. Right into a cell, for assault."

Making a conversation of his rants is a skill Aislyn has long since perfected. Pick a point in his last sentence, ask a question related to it, tune him out again. Only by doing this has she been able to make space for her own thoughts over the years. "Assault, Daddy? Are you okay?"

He sounds startled, and also pleased, which is good. "Oh—no, Apple. Don't worry about your old man. If he *had* assaulted me, I'd have kicked his ass over his beany head. Nah, I just needed something to run him in on." She can actually hear his shrug. Then he chuckles. "Said he was listening to New Age music on his car radio to relax, if you can believe that! These people."

Aislyn nods absently while he rants, peering around and trying to remember which bus she's supposed to take back home from the ferry. As she does so, though, her eyes catch on the strange woman, who's still standing there with a hand on Aislyn's shoulder. Aislyn can barely feel the hand; her nerves don't seem to register its weight or the warmth that should be there. By contrast, her other arm—the one grabbed by the Black man on the ferry ramp—still tingles. Did he do something to her? Were there maybe drugs on his hands, and are they seeping through her skin? Her father has warned her that some drugs work this way.

But what has caught her attention is what the woman in white clothing is doing, now and again, as she stands beside Aislyn. With her free hand, she's touching other people as they pass on the sidewalk—not all of them, just a person here and a person there, and just a light friendly pat on the shoulder. They don't seem to notice. But when one man stops to tie his shoe, Aislyn sees something odd. Where the woman has touched him, there's a thin, pale nub poking through the cloth of his T-shirt. As Aislyn watches, the nub lengthens and thickens, growing until it wavers above the man's shoulder, six inches long or so and drifting with the breeze. It's white, about the thickness of yarn.

Okay, that's super weird. It's also weird that the woman with the white-blond hair has chosen to remain so close while Aislyn's on what's obviously a private phone call. Maybe she's just trying to make sure Aislyn's okay.

Her father is winding down. But just when Aislyn thinks she's free, he adds, "Anyway, I just heard an alert over the channel and, well, I thought about you." Aislyn tenses. *The channel* is what her father calls police radio. "They said a girl with your description caused a disturbance and assaulted somebody."

This, too, is habit: Aislyn chuckles it off. She knows she sounds nervous. She always sounds nervous. "Aren't there a lot of brown-haired thirty-year-old white girls out there?"

He chuckles, too, and she relaxes. "Yeah. And I can't see you cutting somebody with a knife." (*A knife?* she thinks—but her nails are pretty long.) "Or getting on that ferry."

Inadvertently, Aislyn stiffens. The woman in white pats her shoulder again, murmuring something soothing, but it doesn't help as much this time. "I could get on the ferry," Aislyn blurts. "If I wanted."

His chuckle annoys her now. "You? That city would eat you up, Apple." Then, as if he's heard her affront or cares about it, his voice changes to a more soothing tone. "You're a good girl, Aislyn, and the city isn't a place for good people. What have I always told you?"

She sighs. " 'Everything that happens everywhere else happens here, too, but at least here people *try* to be decent.' "

"Yeah. And what else?"

" 'Stay where you're happy.' "

"Right. The city ever becomes the place where you're happy? Go there. But as long as this is it? Stay home. Nothing wrong with staying home."

Yes. She has told herself this every day of her adult life, to console herself for being a grown woman who still lives at home with her parents. It's a lie. She's lonely and ashamed and she hasn't given up hope for a life of excitement and sophistication, somewhere and sometime. But this is the sort of lie that she needs, especially in the wake of her disastrous attempt to board the ferry.

"Yeah. Thanks, Daddy."

She knows he's smiling. "Tell your mom I'm gonna be home late. An arrest means paperwork. These fucking people." He sighs as if the Puerto Rican man sat around New Aging while brown just to make him late for dinner, and hangs up.

Aislyn puts her phone away, then finally pulls her purse back up to her shoulder to compose herself—or she tries to. The strange woman is still holding Aislyn's shoulder, although she's frowning a little, as if wondering how her hand got there. Aislyn looks at the woman's hand, too. "Uh, is something the matter?"

"What? Oh." The woman finally removes her hand and smiles. It's a little strained. "Everything's fine. I'm just going to have to do this the hard way, apparently." Then her smile broadens, more genuine. "But I know I'm right about you."

For the first time, Aislyn begins to feel uneasy. The woman doesn't look scary, but there's something about her that's a little off. "Right about what?"

"Well, for one thing, I haven't been able to claim you as my own." The woman folds her arms and turns to face away from the ferry station, toward the cluster of tall office buildings and high-rise apartments that dominate this side of the island. "You have the right inclination, but even though the city just rebirthed itself this morning, you're already closely enough bound with the essence of this place to keep me from pulling you in. You even *smell* like a city now, and not an ordinary human being." She shrugs. Aislyn puzzles over all of this, then surreptitiously angles her head to sniff at her pits.

The woman has begun murmuring to herself as she stares at the paltry skyline of St. George. "Haven't had this much trouble since London. Usually it's easier to isolate the vectors. City morphology defies predictability, of course, but there are epigenetic manifestations, metabolic fluxes that should follow through in a perceptible way. It's this city, though." She shakes her head, scowling. "Too *many* New Yorkers are New York. Its acculturation quotient is dangerously high."

Abruptly the woman's head swivels to face Aislyn. (That's what it looks like, a swivel. As if the woman's neck muscles are motors or pulleys or something else mechanical.) She looks thoughtful. "Do you know who you are?"

"Uh, I don't, uh . . ." Aislyn looks around again. Which bus platform was it? There are so many, and they all look alike. Maybe she should just pick one and start walking toward it. Because something about this woman has made Aislyn think she needs an exit strategy. "Sorry, but I don't think . . ."

There is a moment—in retrospect she will recall this with great clarity—when Aislyn feels the woman's attention shift. Before now, the woman in the white outfit has been . . . not quite present.

Underneath her comforting smiles, there has been a distance, and a ... going-through-the-motions-ness, if that is a thing? All at once, however, the woman becomes *here*; she becomes more. Now she looms. She's only a few inches taller than Aislyn, but within those inches, she towers. She smiles, and buried in the woman's shadow, Aislyn feels small and forgotten and terribly, hopelessly alone.

But in almost the same moment, *that other feeling* rises within her. It's the feeling that hit her this morning, while she was in the middle of washing the dishes from breakfast and thinking about *Scotswoman's Secret*, the romance novel she'd been reading the night before. She had been fantasizing a little, maybe, about being a proud, strong-willed noblewoman from the Highlands who decides to start discreetly sleeping with the handsome foreign stable hand, who isn't Black but whose penis nearly is, except for the tip when it gets excited (that part is pink, and Aislyn isn't sure whether it's creative license on the author's part or something that's actually possible).

Then, while scrubbing crusted eggs off a pan and visualizing the previous chapter's sex scene, Aislyn began to hear shouting in her mind. These were crude, vulgar, *angry* shouts—shouts so suffused with rage that had she heard them with her ears, she would never have been able to make out the words. Incoherent anger. In her mind, though, she had not only heard the words, but *known* them, and *felt* them. She'd wanted to fight, as the speaker of those words was fighting, somewhere. Somehow she'd known that. The vicarious aggression had suffused her with a rage so terrible, so overwhelming, that she had to go to her room and destroy a pillow. That wasn't like her, not at all. She never fought back. Yet this morning she had ripped that pillow to shreds, then risen from foamy carnage filled with a powerful compulsion to go to the city. So powerful had she felt in the wake of that rage that for the first time in years, she actually tried it.

Only to fail. Again.

Now, however, Aislyn feels that strange angry strength stirring inside her again. Who is this woman to stand over her so? She doesn't belong here, Aislyn knows. Aislyn might be afraid of the city, but SI is *her* island, and she will not be *loomed over* on her home ground.

But before Aislyn can open her mouth to stammer out some devastating variant of *Please leave before I call the police*, the Woman in White leans down to grin into her face.

"You are Staten Island," she says.

Aislyn starts. It isn't the words that surprise her, but the fact that someone else has said them. The woman laughs softly, eyes flicking back and forth over Aislyn's face as if drinking in her shock. The woman continues: "The forgotten one, and the despised one when they bother to remember. The borough no one, including its own, thinks of as 'real' New York. And yet here you are! Somehow, despite their neglect and contempt, you've developed enough distinctiveness of culture to survive rebirth. And this morning, you heard the rest of the city calling out to you. *Didn't you?*"

Aislyn takes a step back. Just for personal space reasons. "I didn't—" But she did. She *did*. She heard the city's raw, defiant demand, and some part of her tried to respond to it. That's how she ended up at the ferry station. She trails off midsentence because she doesn't actually need to say the words. The Woman in White knows Aislyn as surely as Aislyn knows her island.

"Oh, you poor thing," the Woman says, her expression shifting from avid to tender so quickly that Aislyn's anger vanishes. Now all she feels is a rapidly growing unease in this woman's presence. "You can't help sensing some of the truth—but you're alone amid the vastness of it all, aren't you? Just one little alga floating amid a green sea of them, convinced of your unimportance even as you threaten a hundred billion realities. I could pity you, if not for that threat."

"I..." Aislyn stares back at her. Alga? Is that another language? It sounds like the singular of *algae*. God, did this woman just call her a *microbe*?

"And now you have to live that truth," the Woman continues. She's not looming anymore—not as much, anyhow—but the air of patronizing concern that she radiates isn't much better. Aislyn stares at her, still trying to figure out whether she should be insulted. The Woman leans closer. "That's why you're afraid of the ferry. Half the people on this island absolutely dread crossing that water every day. They know that what awaits them on the other end isn't the power and glamour we can see from here, but bad jobs and worse pay, and prancing manbunned baristas who turn up their noses at making just a simple goddamned coffee, and prissy chink bitches who barely speak English but make seven figures gambling with *your* 401(k), and feminists and Jews and trannies and nnnnnNegroes and *liberals*, libtards everywhere, making the world safe for every kind of pervert. And the other half of the island *is* the baristas and chinks and feminists, ashamed they can't afford to live there and leave Staten Island for good. *You are them*, Aislyn! You carry the fear and resentment of half a million people, so is it any wonder that part of you wants to flee, screaming?"

By this point the Woman is doing more than looming. She is waving her arms, stage-whispering as loud as a shout, flaring her nostrils, wild-eyed. And Aislyn has reacted the way she always does when someone bigger and louder starts yelling; she's hunched in on herself, leaning away as the Woman leans in and holding her purse strap with both hands as if it is a shield.

She can think of only one thing to say as the Woman runs out of words and falls silent with a fleck of bubbled spittle on her lips. Aislyn blurts, "I... I don't have a 401(k)."

The Woman in White tilts her head. Looms less. "What?"

"Y-you said—" She swallows. She can't speak that word here at the ferry station. It's a home word. "You said, uh, Asian women take your 401(k). But I, I, I don't have one of those."

The Woman in White stares at her. It is the first time, maybe, that she has heard something crazier than herself. And after a moment, she bursts out laughing. It is an awful laugh. Delighted, but awful—high-pitched, too sharp, with an edge that reminds Aislyn of the mean girls back in high school, or maybe a cartoon witch's cackle. Passersby along the sidewalk flinch from that laugh, then stare at the Woman as if they've heard a warning from beyond.

And yet, after a moment, Aislyn finds herself grinning, too. Just a little. Then giggling, as the tension of the moment dissolves. The laughter is more than infectious. Aislyn is infected. Bonding by catharsis. All at once she and the Woman in White are laughing together, so hard that Aislyn's eyes water with the force of her own voice, and so richly that for a beautiful moment all of Aislyn's troubles feel as nothing. It's as if they've been friends for years.

When the laughter fades, the Woman in White dabs at one eye, with an air of regret. "Oh, my. That was lovely. I have to admit, I'll miss this universe when everything is said and done. It's hideous, but not without its small joys."

Aislyn is still grinning, high on her own endorphins. "Do you ever say anything, you know, normal?"

"Not if I can avoid it." With a little sigh, the Woman offers a hand to Aislyn. "But I want to help you. Please say you'll let me help you."

It's automatic to take a helping hand. Aislyn frowns, though. "What, uh, do I need help with?"

"This whole process. I've watched your kind go through it hundreds of times at this point, and it's always . . . fraught. I *like* you, Aislyn, little island, and it's terrible, what will happen to you if that primary avatar finally wakes up. He's a monster. I want to save you from him."

Through the lingering, head-clearing relief of her earlier laughing fit, it is obvious to Aislyn that the Woman is a crazyperson. Crazypeople are mostly in the city, she's always thought—homeless druggies and rapists who wear ratty dredlocs and (she supposes) have sores from all the lice and STDs. The Woman is well dressed and clean, but there is a high, manic gleam in her gaze, and her bright, cheerful voice sounds false. No one is ever that happy. She's clearly Not From Around Here. Maybe she's an immigrant, too—legal, of course. Maybe she's a Canadian who has been driven mad by the cold and socialized medicine.

Still, this is a crazyperson whom Aislyn finds herself liking. More importantly, the Woman has said that she wants to help Aislyn—and somehow she seems to know about the strange voices in Aislyn's head and the stranger compulsion that drove her to the ferry station. It makes Aislyn feel more sympathetic than she ordinarily would be.

So she sticks out her hand for the Woman to shake. "Okay,

then. I'm Ais—" And then she trails off, remembering that the Woman knows her name already. How ...?

"Staten Aislyn," the Woman fills in, and giggles as if that is not a joke that a thousand people have made to Aislyn over the course of her lifetime. Not for the last time does she regret her parents' choice to use an Americanization of *Aislyn*, rather than its softer Irish pronunciation. The Woman then takes Aislyn's hand and pumps it, too vigorously. "Yes. Pleasedtomeetyou is appropriate, yes? We're both composite entities for whom the boundaries of space, time, and flesh have meaning! Let's be besties."

"Uh. Okay."

The Woman gives Aislyn's hand another pump, and then practically flings her hand away. "Now. Since you seem to be of a sympathetic nature, let's get started on temporarily saving this local node of your consensus reality from existential annihilation, why don't we?"

"Well, I really need to get home—wait, what?" *Annihilation* is what took a moment to process.

"You know about the Bridge Incident?" Like *Woman in White*, this has already achieved capital-letter status in Aislyn's mind.

"Of course, but ..."

The Woman has turned back toward the Manhattan skyline, which arcs over the roof of the ferry station. The bridge in question is not visible from this vantage, but backwash from the incident has affected the whole Tri-state area all day. Even as they stand there, a trio of military planes *shoops* past overhead, angling to circle the East River. The Woman is bouncing a little on the balls of her feet.

"You know what made the bridge fall?" she says to Aislyn. "Me! I did that. It was an accident, mind you; I was aiming for that little shit, the primary." Her smile vanishes as quickly as it appeared. "Cities always fight when I come for them, but usually it's fair. Strength against strength, as it should be—but he actually threw *concepts* at me. I had no idea your kind had advanced to the point of using energized abstract macroconstructs in combat. Who expects microbes to go nuclear? That was when I knew the time for stealth had passed."

Aislyn is staring at the Woman, all her unease forgotten amid shock and horror. *Terrorist!* her mind cries . . . and rejects. Terrorists are bearded Arab men who mutter in guttural languages and want to rape virgins. This woman is just crazy. So she can't really be the person who broke the bridge—but she's possibly crazy enough to be dangerous. Aislyn decides to play along until she can get to someplace safe. "Oh. Um. O-okay."

The Woman in White's head swivels back to her. "I was asleep," she explains. "The bulk of me was, that is. Never needed more than a fraction of myself to function in this realm before now. But conditions are right, and I have gained a true foothold at last." She drapes an arm around Aislyn's shoulders again, before Aislyn can find a polite way to pull away. "There's five of you, you see, besides the primary. Five potential allies. Five weaknesses I can exploit."

The things coming out of the Woman's mouth keep *almost* making sense. Aislyn *almost* understands . . . but finally she shakes her head in frustration. "Primary what?"

"Primary avatar. Help me find him, and then you'll be free."

"Free? But I'm not—"

The Woman has begun to walk, pulling Aislyn along. They're headed toward the bus that Aislyn needs, astonishingly, so Aislyn still can't bring herself to shake off the Woman's arm. "Free?

You're not. Right now, you're part of him. Well, that's wrong; all of you are part of each other. I think? That's the best way I can explain it. This algal colony, this *microbial mat*, has nuclei... Hmm, no, wait, *all* of your kind have souls; that's a bad analogy." She sighs impatiently. "Well, six of you are more in charge than the rest. And those six are highly attuned to one another, naturally. Which means that finding one of you will help me find the rest of you." She grins, all teeth. "*That one* in particular."

They've reached the bus and stopped before its open doors. It won't pull away for another three minutes, according to the clock on Aislyn's phone. Aislyn has begun to worry, however, that the Woman in White will want to ride with her, or even accompany her home. She tries to think of excuses to give the Woman for why this cannot be.

"Now, head on back home," the Woman says, to Aislyn's great relief. "I've got other business to take care of. But until we meet again, here's a thing you need to consider." The Woman leans close for a conspiratorial whisper; Aislyn just manages not to twitch away. "Why did the others leave you unprotected?"

The question feels like a slap. In its wake Aislyn is stung, then numb. "Wh-what?"

"Well, I've managed to locate nearly all of you by now." The Woman extends her free hand and examines her nails. They're very long and curved. "The Bronx is a borough of angry, suspicious people who expect betrayal; she's canny and will take some planning to approach. Manhattan rolled up on top of a taxi and introduced himself to me, quite boldly; typical. Brooklyn, full of attitude and arrogance, came to his rescue when I tried to introduce myself back. And that damnable São Paulo is still here, somewhere, the rude fellow! He must be guarding the primary from me."

As Aislyn tries to process this (*there are five of you*), the Woman slides her needle further under the skin. "But no one has come to rescue or guard *you*. Manhattan and Brooklyn make powerful allies as they work together to track down the Bronx and Queens . . . but they haven't thought about you. Not. Even. Once."

Aislyn stares back, understanding at last. Five of them, plus some sixth who is *primary*. She is Staten Island and they are the other boroughs, plus New York itself. And are they like her, these other strangers? Do they feel the needs of thousands, hear the voices of millions in their heads? She wants to meet them. Ask them questions, like *How do you get your borough to shut up?* and *Is it really my friend or am I just that lonely?*

But she has not found them, because she chickened out of taking the ferry. Even if she had made it to Manhattan, how would she have located them? If Manhattan and Brooklyn found each other, there must be a way. Some kind of city-sonar or something, which would have activated if she'd tried to go to them. Without that effort on her part, however, the sonar has remained quiescent.

Well, why can't they come to her instead?

It's inconvenient, she reminds herself. *Coming to Staten Island is always inconvenient for people in the city.*

Yes, but this is important, isn't it? They know the city has five boroughs, damn it. And if they've chosen not to look for her . . .

Who's gonna believe you? her father's voice shouts, from memory. *Who's gonna help you? Nobody gives a shit. You don't fucking matter.*

Not words ever shouted at her, but Aislyn absorbed them

anyway, and now they are wrapped around her bones, a contamination as deep and toxic as lead. She can no more shake off the visceral belief that *she doesn't matter* than she can her fear of the city.

"I don't think they *meant* to forget you, mind," says the Woman. "They'll get around to remembering eventually, and then they'll come . . . but they hate taking the ferry. So slow and inconvenient. There's the Verrazano, but it's so expensive. What kind of borough makes itself so inaccessible? Didn't that Jew fellow, the one who sang jazz with all those Black people, call New York a 'visitor's place'? But not this part of it. He mentioned *Yonkers*, of all things, but left this entire borough out of the song. Staten Island, always the afterthought."

Aislyn sits there, hearing the words and hating them and knowing the truth in them. She doesn't fucking matter. Her island doesn't fucking matter. The others have forgotten her when she *needs* them, bridges are falling and everything is terrible, but she must find her own path to safety alone.

"Oh, now what's that face?" The Woman in White pulls away and grips Aislyn's shoulders in a sisterly way. "What's this sadness? Don't worry. They might have abandoned you, but I'm here! And just look." She turns Aislyn around again, cheerfully manhandling her, and then points over her shoulder at the doorway of the ferry station, which Aislyn ran through in a panic not twenty minutes before.

"What am I supposed to—" Then Aislyn sees it. On the metal sill of the door, curling out from a crack in the old painted metal, is the most peculiar thing. It looks like a fern frond, or a very long petal from an exotic flower. It's so white that it looks translucent, unearthly in its beauty. Aislyn inhales in admiration. "What is that?"

The Woman in White laughs. "Think of it as a camera," she says. "If you want. Or a microphone. If you ever need me, and you see something like that around, just speak to it. 'See something, say something,' right? I'll hear and come running."

It's more craziness. The Woman cannot possibly see and hear through a flower. Aislyn's got to get home to help her mother make dinner, so very gently, she pushes the woman's hands off her shoulders. "All right," she says. But she likes the Woman. It's nice to have a new friend, even if that friend is crazy, but she should at least know that friend's *name*. "But before I go, what should I call you?"

The Woman tilts her head, grimacing. "You won't like my name," she says. "It's foreign. Very hard to pronounce. I've told it to a few of your people and they've just mangled it."

Definitely from Canada, Aislyn decides. "Let me try anyway."

"All right, then. I'll need to whisper it in your ear, though. The time is coming when I'll be able to shout my name across the firmament and all will know its sound—but for now I'm only a whisper in this world. Are you ready?"

The bus driver is walking toward them, yawning and scratching himself. Aislyn needs to wrap this up. "Sure, go ahead."

The Woman leans close and whispers into Aislyn's ear a word that tolls throughout her skull like the most dire of great bells, shaking her bones enough that she stumbles and falls to her knees. The world blurs. Her skin prickles and itches and grows hot all over, as if burned by the wind of the word's passing.

Then someone else has crouched before her. "Ma'am?" It's the bus driver. Aislyn blinks and looks around. She's in front of the bus she needs to take home. How did she get here? Was there someone else here just now...?

The driver asks, "Ma'am, do you need me to call 911?"

"No..." Aislyn shakes her head, trying to convey that she's all right. But is she? The dizziness is fading but she feels wrong, all over. When she recovers enough to look down at her arms, which are bare given the light sundress she's wearing, she blinks to see them covered in faint, but rising, puffy welts. Hives. She's breaking out in hives.

The driver has seen them, too. He frowns, drawing back a little. "Ma'am, if you're sick, you shouldn't ride on public transportation."

"A-allergies," Aislyn murmurs, staring at her arms. She's allergic to pine nuts and basil, but she cannot imagine where she might have encountered any surprise pesto. "Just allergies. I, uh, I'll be okay."

The driver looks skeptical, but he helps her up, and when Aislyn is clearly able to walk on her own, he shrugs and gestures for her to board.

It's ten minutes into the ride, with Aislyn staring at the passing buildings and people and not-thinking other than to wonder whether she should start carrying an EpiPen, when she remembers the Woman in White. With a start, she looks around, but there are only the other bus passengers, a few of whom favor her with disinterested looks in return. The Woman has vanished, as easily as she appeared.

And yet. Aislyn's gaze alights on the STOP REQUESTED sign, and stops there... because just over the driver's head, dangling about a foot down from the sign, is another of those lovely white floral fronds that the Woman in White pointed out at the station.

Don't worry. I'm here.

What was the Woman's name again? Something that started

with an *R* is all Aislyn can remember. The rest was a blur of incomprehensible foreign sounds.

Rosie, Aislyn decides. She will call the Woman Rosie. It fits her, even; Aislyn smiles as she imagines the Woman baring a biceps on an old-fashioned poster. I WANT YOU, reads the caption. No, wait; Aislyn's getting her vintage posters mixed up. She can't remember Rosie the Riveter's slogan.

Well, it doesn't matter. Feeling immeasurably better, Aislyn resists the urge to scratch her hives, and settles in for the rest of the ride home.

INTERRUPTION

S omething is very wrong at Inwood Hill Park.

It's always difficult for Paulo to tell where he's going in another city. As a child—just himself, a quick and sharp-toothed favela rat, long before he'd become twelve million people—he had an uncanny sense of direction, enabling him to tell which way was east or south just by glancing at the sun. Even in strange places he'd been able to do that, but the ability vanished when he became a city. Now he is São Paulo, and his feet are configured for different streets. His skin craves different breezes, different angles of light. North and south are the same everywhere, of course, but in his land, it should be winter—never cold in São Paulo, but certainly cooler and drier than the muggy, searing summer heat of this ridiculous city. Every day that he spends here, he feels backward, upside down. Home isn't where the heart is; it's wherever the wind feels right.

Ah, he has no time for such maunderings.

The grid pattern of Manhattan and the pleasant Brazilian Portuguese voice of Google Maps both make up for his lost sense of direction, and presently he reaches the place that pings on his senses as intrusion, interference, inimical. Enemy. That sense has grown stronger in the hours since New York's birth, rather than weaker, as it should have—and it is changing, too, in a way he's never before experienced. Rising everywhere, tugging at his awareness like magnetic lines. Developing poles. The one at FDR Drive he expected, given the events that preceded New York's birth, though he means to go and inspect that site next in case it holds more clues. The one in Inwood is new.

He strolls through the park, enjoying the cooler air and fresher scents of greenery, though he remains wary. At first he sees nothing to explain the looming, prickling sense of wrongness that tugs him along, worse on one side of his body than the other as he orients himself. It's a workday and the park is nearly empty. The birds sing beautifully, however foreign their songs sound to his ear. Mosquitoes torment him; he waves at them constantly. That, at least, is no different from home.

Then he wends his way around a particularly thick stand of trees, and stops.

At the foot of the narrow walking path is a clearing, beyond which is a wide grassy meadow that overlooks what his map calls Spuyten Duyvil Creek. At the heart of the clearing is what he expected to see: a simple monument to the site where Europeans bargained to turn a beautiful forested island into a reeking parking lot and glorified shopping mall. (Paulo is aware that this opinion is uncharitable. He is disinclined to correct himself while he is stuck in New York.) It's a rock with a plaque on it. It also, he guesses given the history, represents a place of power for anyone who hears the city's voice.

The first thing he understands is that a battle has taken place here. The scent that tinges the air holds no longer purely green vegetation, but a saltier, briny whiff as well. He knows this scent. There's money all over the ground—and again, understanding something of the nature of Manhattan, Paulo knows at once that someone has used the money as a construct, to more precisely aim the power of the city. Aim at what? The Enemy. He does not know what form the Enemy took, but that's the only possible answer. And whoever fought the Enemy here won, or at least managed to walk away unbloodied.

But—this is the second thing Paulo understands, though it was the first thing he saw—the Enemy has left its mark, too.

The clearing is full of people. At least twenty of them mill about near the monument rock, chattering. He hears some of the chatter when the wind shifts. ("—cannot be*lieve* how low the rents are here, so much better than Brooklyn—" "—*authentic* Dominican food—" "—I just don't understand why they have to play their music so *loud*!") A couple of the people in the clearing carry food or drink: one woman has an expensive-looking waffle cone topped with at least three scoops; one's got a bottle of Soylent visible in his back pocket; one's actually sipping from a plastic wineglass of rosé. Most of them are white and well dressed, though there's a smattering of browner or grungier people.

None of them are talking to *each other*, Paulo notes. Instead they simply speak to the air, or into darkened cell phones held up to their mouths in speaker mode—or, in one man's case, to the small dog he carries in one arm, who keeps licking his face and whining and squirming. None of them face each other. The ice cream in the woman's hand has mostly melted, and three colors of dairy goo run down her arm and onto her clothes, apparently unnoticed. Pigeons have begun to gather where the melted ice cream puddles at her feet.

And all of them, Paulo has noticed, noticed *first*, are wearing white.

This is nothing that Paulo has ever seen before, but he's fairly certain that he has not happened upon a surprise white party in the middle of the park. Frowning, he lifts his cell phone and snaps a photo. It makes a faint shutter-sound because he hasn't bothered to turn off that option in the settings. At the sound, all of the people around the rock fall silent, and turn to look at him.

Paulo tenses. As casually as he can, however, he puts the phone in his pants pocket, and pulls a cigarette from his jacket pocket. He taps it twice before putting it between his lips. Old habit. Then, as twenty sets of eyes stare unblinking at him, Paulo pulls out his lighter and takes a good, deep drag. Folds his arms casually, the cigarette held between two fingers. Lets the smoke trickle from his nostrils slowly. It drifts up in clouds in front of his face.

Their eyes unfocus. Some of them frown and dart glances around, as if they've lost something and can't remember what. When Paulo backs away, around the trail-bend and out of their sight, they do not follow. After a moment, he hears their automatic, directionless chatter resume.

Paulo leaves quickly. The park is big and the walk is long, but Paulo does not slow his pace until he's at least a block outside of Inwood Hill's boundaries. Then, and only then, does he check the photo that he just took.

It's the scene he saw, eerie enough on its own—but every person's face is distorted as if the digital photo is an old Polaroid that's been heat-warped here and there. And although it's not clear in some cases, Paulo notes an additional distortion just behind each person's head, or near their shoulders. Indistinct, just a warping of the air, but consistent; he can see it on most of them. Something is there that he cannot see. Yet.

He goes into a tiny, poorly lit ancient restaurant whose staff are clearly all related. There he sits down and orders something at random. He's not hungry, but there is power in what he's doing, and he feels the need to bolster his defenses. This is not his city. He is more vulnerable here than he's used to.

Then, while he nibbles on some of the best pernil he's ever had, he texts the distorted photo to the international number. He adds, *It's boroughs. There will be five of them. And I'm going to need your help.*

CHAPTER FOUR

Boogie-Down Bronca and the
Bathroom Stall of Doom

B ronca shoves open the bathroom door. "Hey. Becky."

The tall Asian woman working on her eye makeup at the mirror sighs and does not turn. "You know I hate it when you call me that."

"I'mma call you whatever I want right now." Bronca goes over to stand beside her at the mirror, and does not miss the sudden tension in the other woman's shoulders. "Relax, I'm not here to kick your ass *that* way. We're gonna do this civilized. I'll use my words to tell you to fuck off, and you're going to find somewhere to fuck off to, at least for a few days. I don't want to look at your stupid face for a while."

The woman turns, scowling. "If we're going to be civilized, then you can use my actual name. *Yijing.*"

"I don't know, I thought we were being all familiar with each other. You know how like my name has a PhD after it but you always forget to call me 'Doctor'?" Bronca gets in the other woman's face and points a finger at her nose. "You submitted that grant application, most of which I *wrote*, without my name on it. How fucking dare—"

"I did," Yijing interrupts, even though they've got rules about that, interrupting women is sexist bullshit, but Yijing is bullshit, so Bronca isn't exactly surprised. Yijing folds her arms. "I thought hard about whether to include you, Bronca, but the fact remains that you're not doing any new work, and—"

Incredulous, Bronca turns and flings a hand toward the bathroom's back wall. Rioting over its surface is an abstract profusion of colors and shapes, photorealistic in places and airily watercolor-esque in others. The signature in the bottom corner: a heavily stylized graffitiesque curlicue reading *Da Bronca*.

Yijing grimaces. "I mean that you aren't *showing* anywhere, Bronca. The galleries—"

"I got a gallery, you dumb-ass, not even two miles from here!"

"Yeah, and that's the problem!" Exasperated, Yijing abandons her attempt to stay cool, raising her own voice. That's good. Bronca's seen Yijing get into it with other staffers and her various boyfriends on occasion; she's louder than Bronca, with the kind of voice that can crack glass. Bronca respects honest rage, however ugly it might get. "You're too local. The committee could give us a bigger grant, but to get it, we have to have broader reach. A *Manhattan* gallery."

Bronca curses, turning away to begin pacing. "Manhattan galleries don't want real art. They want inoffensive stuff from some upstate kid who went to NYU and majored in art just to rebel against her parents." With this, she grins fiercely at Yijing.

"You can try to make this about me, but that doesn't change the basic fucking point, Bronca." Yijing shakes her head, with just enough real pity in the gesture to infuriate Bronca. "Your work isn't relevant enough. You're not speaking to people outside this borough. And even though you like to brag about that PhD, you teach at a community college! I don't have a problem with that—this job doesn't leave enough time for academia, too—but you know that's not how grant committees think."

Bronca stares for a moment, too stricken to really register how hurt she's feeling. *Not relevant?* But it's old habit to lash back. "What, you sleep with the grant committee chair?"

"Oh, *fuck you*, Bronca—" And then Yijing slips into Mandarin, and her voice rises an octave and several decibels to well and truly curse her out.

Fine, though. Bronca squares up. She doesn't know enough Munsee to really go toe-to-non-English-toe with Yijing, but she's picked up a few of the worst bits over the years. "Matantoowi-ineeng uch kpaam! Kalumpiil! Kiss my 'irrelevant' Lenape ass!"

The bathroom door bangs open again, and both Bronca and Yijing jump. It's Jess, the director of the experimental theater program, glaring at them both. "You know we can hear you, right? People *down the block* can hear you."

Yijing shakes her head, throws Bronca a last reproachful look, and then circles around Jess to leave. Bronca leans against one of the sinks, folding her arms and setting her jaw. Jess watches Yijing go, then shakes her head and cocks an eyebrow skeptically at Bronca's posture. "Tell me you aren't sulking. You're like sixty."

"Sulking is petulant, pointless anger. Mine is righteous." And she's actually nearly seventy, but nobody needs to be reminded of that.

"Uh-huh." Jess shakes her head. "Never thought I'd hear you going in for slut-shaming, though."

Bronca flinches. Oh fuck, she did, didn't she? But she is angry—righteously, petulantly angry—and it's making her fall back on old bad habits. Like getting defensive when she knows she's in the wrong. "Bitch has bad taste. I could see it if she fucked men who were worth something."

Jess rolls her eyes. "And now with the 'bitch.' Also, you think all men are shit."

"My son's okay." But this is an old joke between them, and Bronca feels herself relaxing, which is probably Jess's goal. "I just...*Fuck*, Jess."

Jess shakes her head. "Nobody can deny what you've done for this place, Bronca. Not even Yijing. Cool the fuck down, though, okay? Then let's talk later about the grant. Right now I've got a problem brewing, and I'm gonna need you on your game."

It's exactly what Bronca needs to hear. She feels herself focusing, thoughts climbing out of their grim spiral (*If I'm irrelevant, is it because I'm old? Is this how my career ends, with a whimper instead of a bang? All I ever wanted was to give meaning to the world*) as she straightens and flicks imaginary lint off her denim jacket to compose herself. "Yeah, okay. What's going on?"

"New artists' group wants to do a show. They're connected to a big donor, so Raul's on it like a fly on shit. But the art is..." She grimaces.

"What? We've shown bad art before." Every publicly funded artist space has to, occasionally.

"This is worse." And there's something to the set of Jess's shoulders that finally does pull Bronca out of her own navel. She's never seen Jess truly angry, but it's there now underneath her professional veneer, along with affront and disgust. "So get it together and get out here." She closes the bathroom door and leaves.

Bronca sighs and glances at the mirror, more out of habit than any real concern for how she looks. Okay, she looks calm. Jess is going to want her to make up with Yijing soon, but that only makes sense; the Center's staff is small, and everybody has to be able to work together. Still, though...

"'Turning and turning in the widening gyre,'" says a woman's soft voice. As Bronca stiffens, belatedly realizing some poor sapette has been trapped in a stall this whole time by their argument, the voice laughs. This is bright, delighted laughter, almost infectious in its pleasantry. For a moment Bronca feels herself smile, too, but then she wonders what's so funny, and stops.

There's a row of six stalls in the women's room, and the three at the far end are shut. Bronca doesn't lean down to look for feet, mostly because she doesn't want to discover that there are *three* people who've gotten stuck listening to her and Yijing. "Sorry about the yelling," Bronca calls to the closed stalls. "Got carried away."

"It happens," replies the voice. Low, husky, despite the high-pitched laughter. It's a Lauren Bacall voice. Bronca loves Lauren Bacall's voice and has since she was a baby dyke. "Yijing is just young. Doesn't want to show respect like she should, to her elders. One *must* respect elders."

"Well, yeah." Abruptly Bronca realizes she doesn't recognize the voice. "Uh, sorry, have we met?"

"So often, 'the falcon *cannot hear* the falconer.'" Another of those little ripples of laughter. And no answer.

Bronca scowls. This must be another of Yijing's pretentious little NYU friends. "Yeah? I can quote Yeats, too. 'Things fall apart; the centre cannot hold; / Mere anarchy is loosed upon the world—'"

"'The blood-dimmed tide is loosed'!" The voice is positively gleeful now. "'And everywhere / The ceremony of innocence is drowned...' Ah, that's my favorite line. Gets right at the shallow performativity of so many things, don't you think? Innocence is nothing but a ceremony, after all. So strange that you people venerate it the way you do. What other world celebrates *not knowing anything* about how life really works?" A soft laugh-sigh. "How your species managed to get this far, I will never know."

Bronca is . . . not liking this conversation. For a minute she sort of thought the unknown woman was flirting with her. Now, though, she's pretty sure the woman in the stall is doing something other than flirting. Something closer to dropping veiled threats.

Don't get into it with patrons, she reminds herself, fussing with her hair in the mirror to displace anxiety. The hubs used to joke that she was hotter than Vasquez from *Aliens*, which was hilarious because while she was checking out Vasquez, he was eyeballing Hicks, and it was only a year or so later that each had fessed up to the other—

Another giggle from the closed stall, and with a sudden swift chill, Bronca realizes she has almost forgotten the person in there, just in the few seconds since the voice fell silent. Through the mirror, she fixes her gaze on the last three stalls. From this angle, she can't see *any* feet on the floor.

"Such innocence," muses the stall woman.

Okay, then. "Yeah, so, it's been nice exchanging poetry lines," Bronca says, flipping the spout and washing her hands just to seem like she's been doing something. "Hope everything, uh, works out in there." Since the woman's been on the pot for a good twenty minutes at least.

One of the three locked stall doors pops open. The loudness of the pop startles Bronca, and she whirls with dripping hands as the door slowly swings outward. No one inside.

"Things are working out just fine," says Stall Woman. "I've got a foothold, you see."

"On the toilet?" Even now, Bronca can't hold back the snark. She's going to die a smart-ass one day.

Giggle, giggle. They're all twelve years old up in this joint. "On so many things. On Staten Island. On this city. On this so-innocent world. Maybe even on you, sweet thing."

Bronca deliberately pulls a paper towel so the woman will know Bronca isn't standing around wigged out. Even if she is. "I'm about to become a grandma, honey. You sweet on old ladies?"

The second stall door pops open with a slower, grinding *ch-clack*. Bronca doesn't jump this time, but the little goose bumps on her skin do a thing as the door swings open, because it does so slooooooowly. Creaking the whole way, like something out of a horror movie. And all at once Bronca's hands fumble in the paper towel. She's hyperaware of everything—the hint of mold in the air, the stink of someone's former meal, the scratchiness of the cheap-ass brown paper towels she has to buy because that's all the budget can handle. The silence of the bathroom, its ventilation mechanisms on the fritz again. The closeness of the fetid air.

The last stall door, yet unopened.

"I'm sweet on everyone," says Stall Woman. Bronca can practically *hear* her grinning in there. "A whole city full of people so sweet that I could just gobble them up, and the streets and the sewers and the subways, too. Also, you're not old! Barely more than newborn. Old enough in spirit that the charm offensive isn't likely to work on you, though. That's the thing I never quite get about your kind. You're all the same kind of nothing, but your nothings don't function in the same ways. Have to use different approaches with everyone! So frustrating." Stall Woman utters a soft sigh of exasperation. "Have to watch that. When I'm frustrated, I speak too much truth."

It occurs to Bronca that she cannot see any hint of Stall Woman through the cracks around the door. Most bathroom stall doors aren't truly private, after all, just a kind of courtesy screen. Easy to see around. (Bronca's pretty sure men designed them.) For that last stall, there's nothing to see through the seam cracks. Just blank whiteness. It's as if someone has covered the cracks with sheets of copier paper—but who would do that? No feet visible under the door, either, she can now see.

"Truth's not a bad thing," Bronca says. Time to call this heifer out, so Bronca can stop feeling the little hairs tingle on her skin. "I've always thought it best to quit fucking around and just say what you mean."

"Exactly!" says the woman, almost proudly. "This doesn't have to be hard. If I could change your nature, make you less harmful, I would! I *like* your kind. But you're all so inflexible, and dangerous in your innocence. And none of you are likely to volunteer for genocide—which I suppose I can understand. Neither would I, in your shoes."

She pauses to sigh while Bronca thinks, *Wait, what did she just say?*

"But wouldn't you like to still be alive, when the end comes? You, and that sweet son of yours, and your grandchild-to-be. I'll even throw in your exes—the still-alive ones, I mean. Wouldn't you like this little, um, place of yours here to still be standing when all else has been flattened into nothingness?" Bronca bristles in mingled outrage and confusion, but the woman in the stall continues, oblivious or uncaring. "I can make that happen. Help you, help me."

Bronca has never, ever responded well to threats. Not even when everything about this situation, everything about this invisible woman, has her so unnerved that she's broken out in gooseflesh. But this ain't her first rodeo. She knows better than to show weakness.

"I think I'd like you to come out here and say that to my face," she snaps.

There is a startled pause. Then the woman in the stall laughs. It's not a giggle this time. This is a full-on, rich, rolling belly laugh, though with a scratchy edge that makes it less than pleasant to listen to. It goes on insultingly long, too, and finishes with "Oh, my! Oh, *honey*. No. It's been a long day, and this shape is such a pain. I've had to step into my parlor, so to speak, to rest. So trust me . . . you don't want me to open that door right now."

"Yeah, I really fucking do," Bronca snaps. "You gonna sit in a goddamn toilet and threaten me and mine?" It's bluster. She's *sick* with fear, even though fear usually pisses her off, makes her even more ready to fight. Now, though, every instinct is a-jangle with warning that somehow she isn't ready for this. She can't let this chick get away with threatening her . . . but she also doesn't want to see what's inside that bathroom stall.

"It isn't a threat," says Stall Woman. And suddenly, her voice is different. Less pleasant. Less husky, more . . . hollow. Like she's outside the stall somehow, speaking from much farther away. Like the stall is not a tiny cubicle but a vast, vaulted space; her voice echoes off surfaces that should not be in there with the toilet and the tampon box. And she's not smiling anymore, this unseen woman within a South Bronx bathroom stall; oh no. Bronca can practically hear the words being gritted through teeth.

"Consider it advice. Yes, *advice*, useful advice to counter your useless innocence. You willlll see things in these next few days, understand." Almost electronic, that extended word. Like the stutter of an audio file that's corrupted or otherwise incompatible with whatever system it's trying to run on. "Fresh things, *unique* thiiiings! When you d-d-do, remember this conversation, would you? Remember that I offerrred you a chance to live, and you ssssspurned it. I held out my hand and you *b-b-burned* it. And when your grandchild lies torn from its m-m-mother's belly, split and spilt upon the ground like so much garbage truck falloff—"

Bronca clenches her fists. "Oh, that's fucking *it*—"

And in that moment, something ripples through the room.

Bronca starts, looking around in momentary distraction from Stall Woman. That ripple felt like an earthquake, or the subway having a bad day, but nothing's rattling and the closest subway line runs three blocks away. Bronca hasn't moved, and yet she feels like she has. *Inside.*

Stall Woman is still jabbering, her voice growing louder and faster with every word. But somehow, Stall Woman becomes unimportant. There is a stretching…a snapping-into, like a puzzle piece finding its place. A *becoming.* And all at once Bronca is different. Bigger than herself.

Out of nowhere Bronca finds herself remembering a day from her childhood. She'd stolen—borrowed—her father's steel-toed construction worker boots so that she could walk through a brickyard on her way to do errands. The brickyard was full of rubble from a building demolished so long ago that it had sprouted flowers and ivy, but she'd decided to cut through it to avoid some of the neighborhood boys, whose catcalling and attempts to follow her had lately shifted from speculation into an active hunt. There had been one man (they were all grown men, and she all of eleven years old; her low opinion of men is so well earned) who moonlighted as a security guard, and who'd been especially persistent. Rumor had it that he'd washed out of being a cop somehow; something involving improper behavior with an underage witness. Rumor also had it that he liked Hispanic girls, and nobody around the Bronx could keep it straight that Bronca was something else.

So when she'd seen this man step out of the crumbling entryway of an old building shell, with a smirk on his lips and his hand prominently resting on the handle of his gun, she'd felt like she does now, fiftyish years later in an art center bathroom. She'd felt *bigger*. Beyond fear or anger. She'd gone to the doorway, of course. Then she grabbed its sides to brace herself, and kicked in his knee. He'd spent three months in traction, claiming he'd slipped on a brick, and never messed with her again. Six years later, having bought her own pair of steel-toed boots, Bronca had done the same thing to a police informant at Stonewall—another time she'd been part of something bigger.

Bigger. As big as the whole goddamn borough.

Stall Woman's voice abruptly cuts off its mad rant, midsentence. Then she blurts, with palpable petulance, "Oh, not you, *too*."

"Eat a bag of dicks," Bronca says. Veneza taught her that one. Then Bronca moves forward with a purpose, with her fists clenched and a grin on her lips because in spite of herself she's always loved a good rumble, even if it's the twenty-first century and nobody calls it a *rumble* anymore. Even if she's gotten old and "respectable." She is still Bronca from the brickyards, Bronca the scourge of Stonewall, Bronca who faced down armed police alongside her brothers and sisters in AIM. It's a kind of dance, see? Every battle is a dance. She was always a good dancer at the powwows, and these days? The steel-toed boots dwell permanently in her soul.

As she advances on the bathroom stall, its latch clacks and starts to swing open. There is only white around the edges of it— not light but *white*, and in the most fleeting of instants, Bronca glimpses a sliver of a room. It has a white floor, and in the distance is an indistinct geometric shape that seems to be . . . pulsing irregularly? What confuses Bronca more, however, is that the strange shape is at least twenty feet away. As if the stall is not a stall, but a tunnel, burrowed into the plumbing and lathing and somehow terminating *elsewhere*, because Bronca knows there's no space like that in or outside of the Bronx Art Center.

But before the door can swing open by more than a few inches, and before Bronca can catch more than a fleeting glimpse of something that her mind warns against even thinking about further, Bronca braces her hand on the nearby tile wall, lifts a foot, and kicks the fucking door in.

There is an instant of resistance. A strange, soft sound, as if she has kicked a pillow, followed by a thunderhead rumble of imminent lightning.

Then the stall door blurs away from her. It's as if it has flown off its hinges and down a rectangular tunnel sized to fit, or as if the door sees itself in a mirror of a mirror; now there are a dozen doors, a million, an impossible number wending away into infinity. There is a startled, furious wail from beyond it—Stall Woman, her voice skirling into a shriek so earsplitting that the glass in the windows spiderwebs and the industrial light fixtures sway and flicker—

Into silence. The stall door, hinged and ordinary again, slams inward from the force of Bronca's kick and whacks into the tampon box before bouncing back. The stall is empty. There's no tunnel, no other place, just an ordinary wall right behind the very ordinary toilet. The light fixtures stop swaying and the light steadies. There isn't even an echo of that shriek to linger in the air.

Then, in the aftermath of this, Bronca stands where she is, swaying a little as a hundred thousand years or so of knowledge falls into her mind.

This is a natural thing. She's the eldest of the group, after all, and the city has decided that she is the one best prepared to bear the burden of knowledge. So when the bestowing is done, Bronca stumbles back against the nearest sink and catches her breath. She's shaking a little, because now she understands what a close call she just had.

And yet. Even though she knows what must be done—they must find and protect each other and learn to fight together, it's crazy but it's true—she sets her jaw. She doesn't want this. She doesn't *need* it. She has responsibilities. A grandchild to nurture and spoil! She's been fighting all her life, goddamn it. Has to work five extra years just to be able to afford a semblance of retirement, and she's *tired*. Does she still have it in her to fight an interdimensional war?

No. She doesn't.

"The other boroughs will just have to look out for themselves," Bronca mutters, finally making herself straighten up and head for the bathroom door. The Bronx has always been on its own; let them learn what that felt like.

In Bronca's wake, the empty bathroom stall is silent and still.

Except for right behind the toilet. There, though it is barely more than a nub, its length having been burned away by Bronca's furious and unexpected retaliation . . . a stubby, not-quite-invisible white nodule twitches fitfully, then settles down to bide its time.

CHAPTER FIVE

Quest for Queens

They're waiting for the crosstown bus, and it's taking forever. This has given them time to strategize, however. Beyond knowing which boroughs have "awakened" or psychic-Bat-signaled or whatever they end up calling it, Manny and Brooklyn have no idea how to actually find their comrades once they reach those respective boroughs. Or rather, Manny has no idea. Once at the bus stop, Brooklyn declares that she needs to do some "research," which seems to consist only of a brief, terse phone call to someone that Manny tries not to listen to, out of politeness. After this, Brooklyn explains, "If my hunch is right, we'll know what's up with the Bronx in a few hours."

"*Is* it a hunch, though?" Manny looks up the street. They've been waiting for twenty minutes. Feels like forty. The afternoon has grown hot and close, the air thickening with humidity, and Manny's got three new mosquito bites. "It isn't coincidence that you could just…*feel* me, the way you did. And right now, with you, I feel…"

He is hyperaware of her presence. Sometimes, when she moves near him, the room seems to shift a little, its center of gravity adjusting in some way that he cannot see or feel—but he *tastes* it sometimes, which makes no sense. Gravity doesn't have a taste. But if it did, Manny thinks it would taste like sudden salt moving across the tongue, from slightly flavorless and sweet into a bitter, metallic weight that makes his eyes sting and his nose burn and his ears itch a little. In the other place, the Weird New York, he can see her shifting, an incomprehensibly huge firmament of cityscape matched only by his own jutting skyscraperness, both of them overlapping in ways that simply wouldn't make sense in the real world, but which fit the way they're standing next to each other. That's what's causing the gravitic shifts, he suspects; too much mass and breadth in one place at the same time. Perhaps because of this inherent contradiction with the laws of Normal New York physics, however, that vision never lasts. She always becomes Brooklyn the woman again.

And Brooklyn the woman looks as cool as if she just strolled out of industrial-strength air-conditioning. She's not sweating, doesn't look fazed by the long wait for the bus, and the mosquitoes have so far ignored her. "A hunch and a connection," she says with a shrug, when he trails off. "When I got off the train, I wasn't even sure what I was looking for—and then I just happened to pass a store selling TVs. All of them were playing a commercial for the local news. There was cell phone video of some dumb-ass riding on top of a cab down the FDR. You gon' be news at eleven, new boy."

"Delightful."

She chuckles at his annoyance, then sobers. He sees a very slight tilting of her shaped brows that lets him know she's as puzzled by all the mysterious happenings as he is. "As soon as I saw you, though, I knew who—*what*—you were. It was like . . . like seeing you, having a person to connect to the concept of *Manhattan*, helped me focus. Then I knew *where* you were, direction-wise. I figure we try public transportation again, and hope we get another hunch along the way."

So they just need an idea of who Queens is. A name, a face, a half-seen grainy photograph à la Bigfoot. Just a little help, to track down one person out of one and a half million. Easy.

Manny sighs, rubbing his eyes. "This is nuts. All of it. Before you showed up, I'd been thinking I should go to a hospital and see if I've suffered some kind of head trauma. But I didn't go because it also just feels..."

"Natural," Brooklyn fills in when he shakes his head in lieu of words. "Normal. Yeah, I get it. I was right there with you, on the brink of calling my therapist for an emergency session—especially when it popped into my head that Grandmaster Flash could save me from the invisible feather monsters. At that point it was just too goddamn weird to be something that came only out of my subconscious or alien airwaves or whatever." She loops a finger near her temple. "Still trying to figure out why your roommate could see it, though. Even in that video, I saw what you were fighting on the FDR, but no one else seemed to. Your roommate's the first person I've encountered—other than you—who has, uh, city-vision, or whatever."

"Actually, that happened on FDR, too," Manny says. "The woman who drove the cab for me saw the...big, uh...squiggly... thing. Other people did seem to know it was there, though, at least on some level. Enough to route around it if they had time. That's what caused the traffic jam."

"Need-to-know weirdness only. Okay." Brooklyn snorts at her own quip.

It feels right, though. Manny remembers how Bel kept squinting at the white things that had surrounded them—as if he could only just see them, and still wasn't sure they were real. Even then, however, Bel had seen more than most of the people on the FDR. So had Madison. They both needed to see the tendrils, or they would've been harmed by them...

But no. Manny frowns to himself as this rationale rings false to his instincts, and particularly to that calculating, brutally rational part of himself that seems to be a remnant of his old personality. That part of him offers an alternative explanation. *Bel was no good to you if he couldn't see the tendrils*, it says. *If he got taken over by the Woman in White, you would've had more trouble to deal with. As himself, he was at least... useful.*

Yes. Bel's cash had given him the idea to use the credit card—which he needs to cancel, yikes, since he just left the thing there—and concern for Bel had kept Manny focused. And Madison wouldn't have agreed to drive for him if she hadn't seen the giant fountain of tentacles erupting from FDR Drive. So need-to-know, as Brooklyn had said...but not Bel's or Madison's need to know. This is about *Manny's* need *for others* to know, so that he can use them as tools.

The city had done that to Bel and Madison just as it had coldly stripped Manny's identity from him, leaving nothing behind but a pleasant exterior and the ability to ruthlessly terrorize strangers into doing his bidding. And if that's true...Manny isn't sure it's safe to think of the city as an ally. Nor is it safe to assume himself to be one of the good guys.

Brooklyn's thoughts seem to be tracking with his. "Still want that crash course in New Yorker–ness?"

"Is it something I have a choice about?" He hears the bitterness in his own voice.

"Sure you do." When he looks up at Brooklyn in surprise, she shrugs. "Everybody's got a choice. Whatever weird-ass shit is happening, it's related to the city, so the obvious way to cut it all off is to leave."

That's...not quite what Manny was expecting to hear from her. But he feels the truth of it, as he frowns at her. Just leave. Go back to...He doesn't remember where, but it doesn't matter, does it? Go to Penn, hop the next train to Philly or Boston or anywhere else, break his lease and no-show for his grad program. He'll lose a lot of money and his pride, but maybe his memory will come back. And more importantly, he knows somehow that someone else will take his place as Manhattan. It will become someone else's job to fight the invisible deep-sea life and the possessed marketplace analysts—and he knows now that there will be more such battles. That's what the Woman in White promised, after all. All of this is just the precursor to something much bigger.

The city will go to war with the army it has, when that time comes. Does Manny want to be in that army? He's really not sure.

The bus has finally appeared, rolling with obscene slowness around a corner. He's got an MTA card; there was one in his wallet, bought by the man he used to be. He hopes that man wasn't too cheap to buy an unlimited card.

They get on the bus. (It's not an unlimited card, but proto-Manny has put fifty dollars on it. Go, proto-Manny.) As it pulls away from the curb—slow as molasses, God had better help Queens and the Bronx because by the time Manny and Brooklyn finally get there, New York will have crumbled into ruins—Manny decides to focus on what he can control, for now. "Tell me about New York, then," he says. "Tell it to me like I've never been here, or don't remember if I have. Because, uh, I don't."

"You don't...?"

Manny takes a deep breath. "I...don't remember who I was."

"What?"

It's hard to explain, Manny finds as he tries to do so. He tells her all about Penn Station, and how he can remember the lyrics to MC Free's songs but not his mother's face. When he falls silent, Brooklyn's staring at him. After a time, Manny is convinced that she won't comment on his amnesia—but then she says, "I hear music."

He frowns at this apparent non sequitur. She continues. "I hear it all the time. I was one of those kids who was always beat boxing, always thinking up lyrics, talking to myself on the subway platform, you know? But now it's, like, fucking *symphonies*. The click of a woman's heels on the sidewalk. An old car's bad timing belt, schoolgirls playing slaphands with a rhythm chant... all of it sets off something in my head. Like tinnitus, except beautiful." She rubs her face in her hands. "It's woken up a part of me that I thought was gone. But I let that part of myself go for a reason—so I could focus on shit that matters."

"Music doesn't matter?"

"Not as much as health insurance for my baby." She scowls. "I'd already been getting sick of the business before I quit, because it kept trying to push me to be someone I wasn't: sexier, harder, whatever. When my daughter came along, I decided I couldn't live that life anymore, and I'm *happy* as I am now. But this new music is, like, trying to drag me back to who I was. And it's wrong. I'm not Free anymore."

He hears: *I'm not free anymore* before he gets it, and then he understands why she's told him this. "You think becoming whatever we are is changing us," he says. "Remaking each of us, but in different ways."

"Yeah. I think that's, uh, the price of what we're getting. Your memory, my peace of mind, who knows with the others. But I guess that makes sense? Being the city..." She shakes her head. "Means we can't be just ordinary people anymore."

You definitely aren't human, Manny thinks, remembering what the Woman in White told him. It felt like a lie, but...

Abruptly Brooklyn groan-sighs and rubs her eyes. "Fuck it. Let's focus. Okay. New York for beginners." She turns on her phone, swipes past a couple of apps, and then turns it so he can see. It's the MTA subway map, familiar to him already.

"Manhattan," she says, pointing to the narrow island in the middle. He resists the urge to twitch. Then she starts at the top and moves in a clockwise half circle around the island, using a little stylus to point to each borough. "The Bronx, Queens, Brooklyn, Staten Island. That's the *official* city, even though Long Island's actually the same island that Brooklyn and Queens are on. Yonkers managed to keep from getting counted as part of the city; Staten Island tried to get away and lost. And then there's Jersey." She rolls her eyes.

"What about Jersey?"

"It's Jersey. So anyway, this map? It's bullshit."

Manny blinks at her. "But you just..."

"Yeah. And that's why I showed it to you. This is the first thing most people see when they come here. Even people who've been here for years think *this* is the city." She shakes the phone for emphasis. "They think Manhattan is the center of everything, when most of the city population is actually in the boroughs. They think Staten Island is some tiny thing, an afterthought, because they shrank it down to fit this map. But it's bigger than the Bronx, at least geographically. So, lesson one of New York: what people *think* about us isn't what we really are."

He eyes her, wondering if that was an intentional dig at him.

"Like how Council Member Brooklyn Thomason—Esquire—is secretly MC Free?"

"Ain't much of a secret, baby. Brooklyn puts it all out there." She taps the map again, in a different place. "Queens is what's left of old New York: retirees, the working class, and a whole lot of immigrants, all working their asses off for a house with a backyard. Goddamn techies keep trying to take over, and they'll probably win eventually, but for now all they got's a polluted-ass neighborhood called Long Island City. Which is *on* Long Island because Queens is on Long Island, but isn't *part of* Long Island. You follow?"

"No."

She laughs, and doesn't bother to explain further. She taps the Bronx. "This part of the city gets hit the hardest by everything. Gangs, real estate scams, whatever. Hard people, too, if they came through any of that . . . so in a lot of ways, this is the heart of New York. The part of itself that held on to all the attitude and creativity and toughness that everybody thinks is the whole city."

"So we're looking for a hardworking non-techie in Queens, and somebody creative but with an attitude in the Bronx? That narrows it down." Manny sighs. "What about—" He taps Staten Island on her phone.

Brooklyn's lips purse a little, more in disapproval than contemplation, he thinks. "That one will be a small-town thinker, even though they're part of the biggest American city. They don't *want* to be part of New York there, remember. They won't let you forget it." She shrugs. "An asshole with a chip on their shoulder, basically. And probably a Republican."

The bus eventually grinds its way to the subway station that they need, where they switch to the N train. "Should've grabbed a limo," Brooklyn mutters. Rush hour is in full swing; the subway is packed. They're standing, and Manny is trying not to elbow anyone by accident. It's his first time on the subway, but he's too distracted by the crowding to really enjoy it. "Well, street traffic might've been just as bad."

"A limousine seems excessive," he says.

"'Limo' just means a non-hailable cab, honey. Anything that's not a yellow or a green taxi, we pretty much call a limo, here—including the kind of fancy limos you're thinking of. Except it's also called a 'car service' in Brooklyn." She shrugs. "All of those are getting eaten up by Uber and Lyft anyway."

"Why is it different in Brooklyn?"

She gives him a look, which he supposes he deserves. It's different in Brooklyn because Brooklyn does its own thing. He's trying to learn.

They swap the N for the 7 at Queensboro Plaza. Manny's getting tired of standing when he starts to feel the tickle of imbalanced gravity again, and this time it's not coming from Brooklyn. He shifts his position to offset it, and sees Brooklyn do the same; they meet each other's eyes and nod. "Good," she says, pleased. "I was starting to worry we'd have to go all the way out to Flushing. Looks like our girl's in Jackson Heights instead."

They get off and head aboveground. As they stand on a corner across from a garblemouthed street preacher, Manny gets the bright idea to try a variation on the trick that Brooklyn used to track him down. He experiments with a few keyword combos on various local social media. On the "Queens" plus "weird" search, he finds many complaints about drag queens in poorly chosen ensembles. In addition to this, however, are several tweets from people located in Jackson Heights that mention children's screams and "a weird rumble." Then as they're watching that feed, someone posts, "Lol this old lady's pool tryna eat her kids, TMZ want pics?"

The photos are blurry—a backyard pool with a strangely dark floor, two flailing children, an equally blurry black-haired figure at the edge of the pool—but they're enough. Instantly, both Manny and Brooklyn feel the pull of the black-haired woman.

Then Brooklyn's cell phone bleats, and she plucks it from her purse to scan the message. "Well, well, well. I'll be damned. Looks like we just found the Bronx, too."

She turns her phone so that he can see. On the tiny screen is a photo of a mural. It's hard to discern, at first. There are lines amid the splashes of paint, but they tangle and cross in dizzying profusion over the rough brick on which they're painted. Then something orients in Manny's brain, and that other part of him inhales, and all at once he understands exactly what he's seeing.

It is the other place. The other *him*. The city he has become. New York City, as its whole and distinct self rather than the agglomeration of images and ideas that are its camouflage in this reality. He understands, suddenly, why he has seen that other place as empty; it isn't. The people are there, but in spirit—just as New York City itself has a phantom presence in the lives of every citizen and visitor. Here in this strange, abstract mural, Manny sees the truth that he now lives.

And he knows as well: the person who is the Bronx made this. He knows because the instant he understands the image, he feels that strange gravitic pull again, coming from somewhere to the north this time. Not as strong a pull as that of Queens, who is closer, but unmistakable.

"Somebody creative with an attitude, you said," Brooklyn murmurs, staring at the image, too. "That was just a guess on your part—but all my life, it's how I've thought of the Bronx. That's where hip-hop came from, and the best graffiti, and dances and fashion and…" She shakes her head. "I already had my people on the lookout for weirdness, but when you said that, I told them to look for a specific art piece. Couldn't remember where or when I'd seen it, but I remembered enough of the details that they found it. And that's her."

Brooklyn swipes her screen. Behind the photo is a text from Mark Vishnerio, Aide to NY City Council Member Thomason, from five minutes ago. *Currently on display at a gallery in the Bronx. Tag reads "Da Bronca"—the performance name of a Bronca Siwanoy, PhD, director of the Bronx Art Center. Painting title: "New York, the Really Real."*

Brooklyn glances up, gauging the sun. "It's already rush hour—starts at two or three o'clock here, by the way, when the early school buses start screwing up traffic. Unless Queens joins us quick or the Bronx works late, we're probably going to miss her if we go to the Bronx Art Center."

"Then we find her at home," Manny says. "She may not be safe alone."

Brooklyn sighs and shakes her head. "Only so much ground we can cover. We could split up?"

It would be the logical thing to do. But Manny grimaces. "That might just make us easier to pick off. Look, Queens needs us, right here and right now. Let's deal with one issue at a time."

"More boroughs, more problems," Brooklyn mutters, then nods in reluctant agreement.

Manny fiddles with the rideshare apps on his phone and picks a spot on the map that feels roughly close to where they can sense Queens. Then they're on their way, better late than never.

CHAPTER SIX

The Interdimensional Art Critic Dr. White

The pieces are bad.

Bronca walks along the display wall, slowly so as to give herself time to think. She can see Jess from the corner of one eye, standing by the reception desk. Close to the phone. Behind her, seated at the desk, is the Center's assistant, Veneza. Jess has got her poker face on, but Veneza is all big brown hostage eyes, which flick from Bronca to Jess to Yijing—yeah, Yijing, all hands on deck for this shit, and a united front, whatever else is going on between them—to their guests.

Their guests cluster at the center of the room, though their spokesman, a young white guy with a strawberry-blond man-bun and lumberjack beard, has positioned himself diplomatically between his group and Bronca. Says he's the manager for the group, which is some kind of artists' collective. The other members of the group are male and mostly white, too, though there's a little guy among them who looks white-with-a-generous-topping-of-Indigenous South American. He's got a scraggly version of the same dumb-ass beard, though. Trying so hard to fit in, he doesn't seem to notice it fits his face poorly. He'd have been handsome without it.

Gotta watch out for little dudes, Bronca remembers her ex saying once. By then they were still married, but had fully swapped teams; he was daddying half of Chelsea, and she'd cautiously joined Pink Crawfish, a lesbian dating service for women over fifty. Still friends, after weathering AIM lawsuits and AIDS die-ins and child-rearing together. Chris had always loved sharing all that earned wisdom with his friends. Such as: *Little dudes are like those tiny dogs that everybody thinks are so cute. But they never stop barking and they're crazy as fuck because their balls are too big for their brains.*

A true elder and warrior, Chris Siwanoy. She missed him. He might've had some idea what to do about *this fucking shit.*

She turns to Strawberry Manbun, who's watching her with an overly polite, fuck-you smile on his lips. He knows full well what she's thinking. He's waiting for her to say it out loud and violate the unspoken contract that covers white people who are doing everything short of tossing around the n-word in public. And hell, some even want that to be deniable.

"Yeah, okay," she says, half in reply to this thought. "Are you fucking with us?"

Yijing groans and covers her face. Jess, though, folds her arms, which is her version of taking her earrings off. This isn't going to be that kind of fight—Bronca hopes—but Bronca can see by the cold look on Jess's face that she's ready for anything. Little mean-ass Jewish chicks don't play this shit any more than old mean-ass Lenape chicks do.

Strawberry Manbun looks artfully stunned. He's a shitty actor, though his résumé says he's an understudy for a couple of

Broadway plays. Bronca figures that's a lie. These kinds of people always lie, and attack others, to cover their mediocrity.

That's what's extra offensive about the art, see. It's racist, misogynistic, anti-Semitic, homophobic, probably some other shit she isn't catching at first glance. But it's also *terrible*. Not that she really thinks it's possible to make good art when you hate so many people—art requires empathy—but the Center has a good reputation, and Bronca's used to having her professional time respected. Normally, people don't bring her crap.

This is crap. A collage of lynching photos, zoomed in on dead or agonized Black faces, the whole thing surrounded by stick figures drawn pointing and grinning in white greasepaint. A triptych of charcoal line art daubed with watercolor: in the first, a dark-skinned woman with comically exaggerated lips, nipples, and vulva lies tied in that Japanese rope-art thing that Bronca can't recall the name of. Her expression is somewhere between bored and soulless. In the second, a male figure is drawn on top of her, bare ass blurred to suggest thrusting movements. He's wearing a shtreimel and sidelocks; Bronca's amazed they haven't tattooed the Star of David on his ass just to make sure viewers get it. In the third, the man is now a long-haired jumble of Plains-nation stereotypes, including a damn war bonnet. (His shoddily rendered breechcloth and leggings are in the way, so there's a crude X-ray view through his body of the woman's oversized vulva pushed wide open. So that the viewer doesn't assume they're frotting, Bronca guesses? Who the fuck knows.) A line of men with cocks in hand—or knives, at random—wait their turn beside her. And in all three images, while the men take their turns, the emotionless woman spews quotes from well-known feminists of color.

There's more, most of it just tedious rather than rage inducing;

bad art makes everyone tired. The worst of these is a sculpture of a man bent at the waist to bare an enormous anal gape. It's clearly been shaped to fit a human fist. But the triptych is the one they seem proudest of.

Bronca points at the sculpture. "So, did 4chan put you up to this, or did you come up with it on your own?" She flicks a look at Veneza, who flashes her a quick nervous smile. Veneza's the one who taught Bronca about "chan culture." Bronca's proud of herself for remembering the name.

One of the people with Strawberry Manbun is a stoop-shouldered, pallid thing who looks like he's got consumption or some other Victorian-named disease. Doc Holliday, she decides. "I don't expect you to understand what I'm trying to do with this piece," he snaps. "It's *irony*, if you haven't figured it out. MoMA's got twenty-two abstract paintings of clitorises, so."

Bronca feels herself getting heated. Not good. She needs to keep her head. "And you think a kinky shock meme is the logical response to a clitoris? What's the gang rape supposed to be, in conversation with women's reproductive health?"

"It's a commentary on female genital mutilation," says this kid who looks fifteen. He can't keep the grin off his face. Can't even shovel his bullshit right. "See? She's Black. I mean, *African* Black."

Bronca takes a deep, steadying breath, and puts on her fakest smile. "Okay. I appreciate the time you gentlemen have put into today's meeting, so I'll keep this brief. The Bronx Art Center was incorporated in 1973, and it's funded by the city as well as private donors. Our mandate is simple: to showcase the cultural complexity of this magnificent borough, through art. We—"

"Are you giving us the spiel?" asks Strawberry Manbun,

sounding disgusted even as he laughs. "Is this some kind of, I don't know, commercial brush-off?"

Bronca's got a flow going now. "—embrace and celebrate the diversity of the Bronx through all of its races, ethnicities, genders, abilities, sexual orientations, national origins, and minority religions, as well as—"

"We live in the Bronx," says Fifteen, who's gone from giddily grinning to red-faced fury with a speed that speaks of a tantrummy childhood. "I grew up right here. I have a right to show my art here!"

Riverdale, Bronca guesses. Land of lawns and Tudor estates and NIMBY as a way of life. "That's not how it works," she tells the boy. "We exist to broaden the New York art scene beyond Manhattan, but we're still part of that scene, and we have to showcase *good* art if we want to make our bones. There's a million-five people in this borough, and a lot of them are artists. We can afford to be choosy."

"And even if we couldn't," Jess blurts, as she obviously thinks Bronca's getting off-track, *"we don't do bigotry.* No stereotypes. No rape-as-fetish. No homophobic gotchas..." She's turning blotchy herself; with one hand she flails at Bronca, obviously wanting her to take the thread back.

"So do you have any questions?" Bronca asks, in a tone that makes it clear she wants no questions.

"We haven't shown you the centerpiece yet, though," says Strawberry Manbun. When Bronca stares at him, affronted by his cheek, he favors her with a smile that sets off all her warning bells at once. There's a high glaze to his gaze, which might actually be high given the vape sticking out of his pocket, and which does nothing to conceal how pissed off Mr. Manbun is right now. He's up to something. "If you see our best work and still say no, we'll go. No hassle. Just take a look. That's all we ask." He spreads his hands, the picture of pissed-off innocence.

"Why would I want to see more of this?" Bronca gestures at the triptych. It looks like shit. She wants her rods and cones scrubbed.

"It's a more abstract piece," says Doc Holliday. He's turned to one of the other beard-wearers that Bronca hasn't bothered to name yet. That one trots out into the corridor. Bronca registered the plastic-tarp-covered piece when they came in, but forgot it during the assault on her senses afterward. The new piece is big, maybe ten feet on a side, and canvas to judge by how light it seems as they carry it in. The nameless one starts peeling tape off the plastic tarp. Holliday moves between this unpeeling operation and Bronca—Bronca assumes so she won't be spoiled by glimpses of whatever is beneath the tarp, rather than the full effect at once. Real artists don't do this. Only bullshit artists are this fucking dramatic. He's also super earnest. "I just want your opinion on it, please. I've gotten some good feedback from a gallery in Manhattan."

Yijing stirs. She's got a fixed look of disgust on her face, and for once Bronca loves that prissy way she pushes her chin forward. "Which gallery?"

The guy mentions one that Bronca's actually heard of. Bronca meets Yijing's eyes to see if Yijing's impressed enough by the name. Yijing purses her lips. "I see," she says, but Bronca suspects Yijing will soon call the dealer who owns that gallery to find out what the hell is wrong with them.

Strawberry Manbun looks a query at Doc Holliday, and together they move to position the piece against one of the open display walls. In a moment, they're ready. "I call this one *Dangerous*

Mental Machines," Doc says, and then they pull down the loosened tarp.

It's definitely not like the others, Bronca sees instantly. Those were caricatures of art—the kind of thing that people who hate fine art think constitutes the bleeding edge of the field. This is the real deal. In fact, as the colors resolve into intricate patterns-within-patterns, she begins to realize just how much skill must have been involved in making it. There is *technique* here. A lot of Neo-Expressionism, but some of the grace of graffiti. Everybody wants to channel Basquiat, but most people can't control it. Basquiat couldn't control it. Whoever made this, though—because Bronca knows full well Doc and Fifteen didn't—can.

But.

It's a street scene, or the suggestion of one. A dozen-odd figures wend, disproportionately, into the distance, along a busy road. Something about the density of the shops, and their clutter of signs, feels familiar. Chinatown. It's a night scene, and a rainy one; there's a sheen of colors like wet road pavement. The figures are barely more than ink-swirls, faceless and indistinct, but...Bronca frowns. There's something about them. They are *dirty*, these figures—clad in drab non-fashion, with sleeves rolled up to show blackened hands and shoes smeared with grime and aprons stained with blood and less identifiable bodily fluids. They loom, these dirty creatures, for whom the word *people* is a laughable misnomer. And as a haze in the air suggests the smell of wet garbage tangled with evening mist, Bronca can almost hear their chatter...

(It has grown dim and quiet in the gallery room. Strawberry Manbun stands at the edge of her vision as if spotlighted, smiling at her, watching her face greedily. No one else moves.)

But the chatter is not like what she's actually heard, walking through Chinatown. Real street chatter, there, is just talk—a pre-concert warm-up cacophony of tonal languages, English, and a smattering of European from the tourists, interspersed with the laughter of children and the shouts of angry drivers. What Bronca hears, here in front of the painting, is something higher pitched. A gabble.

(It's late afternoon. What she's hearing isn't what she should be hearing. The wheezy old HVAC should be rattling faintly as it strains against the summer heat. The Center faces a major thoroughfare, but where are the traffic sounds from outside? She should hear the buzz of a straight-line saw, now and again, as the woodshop turns out requests for Center artists. It's just never this quiet in the Bronx Art Center, not at this time of day. Bronca frowns... before the painting draws her back from this distraction.)

A gibber. The faces loom, seeming to shift as Bronca takes in the painting.

(Oh, wait. There's something. She can hear)

A *chitter*. Like the screechy, chitinous bree of an insect, broken up with distance and movement.

(Veneza's voice: "Old B. Yo, Old *B*. Buh-rr-o-nnn-ca." Bronca hates it when Veneza says her name like that, making a syllable of every phoneme. It makes her worry that she's having a stroke, which is why Veneza does it.)

Now a new sound. Something heavy and wet slapping the polished concrete of the Center's floor behind her. It makes her think of a docking line being pulled up onto a pier. She can even smell seawater faintly. She doesn't wonder why someone has unrolled a wet rope in the room, however, because the faces in the painting suddenly seem to loom closer, painted-wet and expressionless. *They're* what's chittering. Jittering.

The faces turn to follow her.

The faces turn and loom and *they are all around her—*

A hand grabs Bronca's shoulder and yanks her backward sharply.

There is a moment in which the universe pauses, stretching just a little. Bronca hovers, caught in the pliability of the moment for a long, pent breath—and then reality snaps back into place.

She blinks. Veneza stands beside her, frowning in concern. Her hand is still on Bronca's arm; she's the one who pulled Bronca back. The painting stands before them, just paint on a surface. Bronca has the sudden feeling that it never changed. The room around her, on the other hand . . .

Because Bronca is meant to be the guide, she understands precisely what has happened—although it's a complicated thing to try to think through, and she's glad she probably won't have to actually explain it to anyone. There's a lot to consider: particle-wave theory, meson decay processes, the ethics of quantum colonialism, and more. But when one really gets down to brass tacks, what's happened here is an attack. An attack that came dangerously close to not just killing her, but *destroying* her. And New York with it.

"Old B?" That's Veneza's charming nickname for her, which has caught on among the younger artists who use the Center. Veneza, whose middle name is Brigida, is Young B. "Feeling okay? You spaced. And . . ." She stops in midsentence, mouth still open for the next word despite her hesitation, and then she finally pushes on and says what she was going to say. "I don't know. Shit got weird for a second."

Understatement of the spacetime continuum. "I'm good." She pats Veneza's hand to reassure her, then turns to face Strawberry Manbun and his cronies. Manbun isn't smiling anymore, and Doc Holliday is frowning outright.

"Cover up that shit," Bronca snaps at them. "Took me a minute, but I get it now. 'Dangerous mental machines,' hah." She looks around and sees confusion on Jess's and Veneza's faces. Yijing, though. Yijing might be an ass, but she at least shares Bronca's love of expensive liberal arts university education. She's glaring at Doc Holliday, furious anew. So Bronca continues, "Yeah. That was H. P. Lovecraft's fun little label for folks in Chinatown— sorry, 'Asiatic filth.' He was willing to concede that they might be as intelligent as white people because they knew how to make a buck. But he didn't think they had souls."

"Oh, but he was an equal-opportunity hater," Yijing drawls, folding her arms and glaring at the men. "In the same letter, he went in on pretty much everybody. Let's see—if I recall, Black people were 'childlike half-gorillas,' Jews were a curse, the Portuguese were 'simian,' whatever. We had a lot of fun deconstructing that one in my thesis seminar."

"Shit, even the Portuguese?" Veneza looks impressed. She's half-Black and half-Portuguese, Bronca recalls, and doesn't get on well with her Portuguese relatives.

"Yep." Bronca puts one hand on her hip. They haven't yet covered the painting—which isn't a painting—but Bronca now knows better than to look into it for more than a moment. Jess and the others should be safe, because this attack was aimed solely at the city of New York, or a sufficiently significant portion thereof. "I could see it if you were trying to turn a mirror on Lovecraft. Show how twisted his fears and hatreds were. But this painting reinforces them. This shows you New York *as he saw it*, the chickenshit little fuck, walking down the street and imagining that every other human being he met *wasn't* human. So, gentlemen, again, what part of 'we don't do bigotry' do you not understand?"

Doc looks stunned that Bronca's still talking. Strawberry Manbun looks like he's holding in a whole heaping mass of mad—but he puts on a smile and nods for one of the others to rewrap the painting. "Okay," he says. "You gave it a chance and you still don't like it. Fair enough."

It isn't enough. Guys like this aren't really interested in fair. But Bronca steps out of the way to let the group wrap up and remove their work, ending up next to Yijing. For the next ten minutes or so, she and Yijing get to play United Flavors of Stink Eye at Manbun's whole operation.

But there's something weird about the whole group of them, Bronca muses while they work. Well, weirder than a bunch of rich-kid "artists" thinking that a taste for stereotypes and fetish porn make them avant-garde. First there's the painting. Doc and the rest seem immune to it, too, which means they're ordinary people, not like Bronca and the five others who are even now wandering around somewhere in the city, probably trying to figure out what they should do with themselves. But no one ordinary could have painted that thing. Second, there's the fact that they even tried this. Why waste time trying to get the Center to put their shitty art on display? Why not just use that as a pretext for the meeting, then come out of the gate with the big bad painting and catch Bronca with the element of surprise? Which means there must be more to this. Bronca narrows her eyes and looks them over for any sign of a wire.

She sees nothing—and, she grudgingly concedes, she wouldn't

know what to look for. She hasn't kept up on surveillance technology for a good twenty years or so. Her son gave her a smartphone, and she actually likes being able to watch movies on it, but it still feels like only yesterday that people were using rotary phones and dialing letter-number combos—

Something flickers. Bronca blinks, her attention caught. Wait, *is* that a wire after all? Down by Strawberry Manbun's ankle, as he carries the other end of a crate containing a piece of the bronze sculpture. No. Bronca might not know anything about covert listening devices in the twenty-first century, but she's pretty sure they don't look like . . . a loose shoelace? He's wearing thong sandals, so it can't be that. (She grimaces at his nasty toenails.)

But there, floating just above the long bones of his foot: something is sticking out of the skin. It looks like an especially long and wispy hair. White, not strawberry blond. At least six inches long . . . although as Bronca watches, it stretches upward as if trying to touch the crate he's carrying. Nine inches. A foot, just shy of the crate's wooden wall—and then it stops and contracts. Not long enough, apparently. It resumes its initial position, just resting along Manbun's foot, just a hair trying to play it cool. Maybe it'll try again once it's grown some more.

Bronca doesn't know what it is, exactly. It does not exist within the lexicon of knowledge that she has absorbed, and that in itself is deeply troubling. But she can add one and one.

So when the "artists' collective" is done, she follows Manbun to the door. It's close enough to the end of the day. She'll lock up early, give the staff a break after this. But first she says to Manbun, as he's walking out, "Who are you working for?"

She expects him to dissemble. He seems the type. Instead he only smirks and says, "Oh, don't worry. You're going to meet her soon. Face-to-face, she said. Without a bathroom door to protect you."

Bronca presses her lips together. It's like that, then. "Ask her how that turned out last time," she snaps, and shuts the door in his face. It's a glass door, which makes the gesture less of a fuck-you because she can't slam it without risking the glass, but it still feels good to see his smirk fade.

And then they're gone.

Bronca locks the door behind them and watches until they've gotten into their cars—one an enormous Hummer, the other a Tesla, both worth more than she makes in a year—and driven off into the trafficset. Then Bronca exhales and turns to face the others. They look shades of mad to worried. "Yeah, so that happened."

"I know some guys," Yijing says immediately. "I say I make some phone calls. Fuck those dudes up."

Bronca raises her eyebrows. "You. Know people about that life."

"Not unless that means a whole lot of lawyers." She folds her arms. "That was harassment with a side of intimidation. You can't tell me it wasn't. Bunch of fascist dudebros or whatever they are, coming into a place run by women of color, with *that* 'art'?" She puts her fingers up to make air quotes around the last word. "Fuck those motherfuckers."

Damn. Not that Bronca disagrees. Jess is quiet, though, so Bronca prompts her. "Jess?"

Jess blinks, then frowns. "I think we need to tell the people using the workshops upstairs that we're shutting down tonight, even for keyholders. Make sure the building is empty."

Bronca rocks back on her heels, floored, while Veneza goes, "Whaaaaaaaa?" Yijing immediately starts to complain, but Jess raises her voice enough to talk over all of them. "Just as a precaution," she says, but it's as sharp as a shout. "I'm just saying. Because I don't know if you ladies got a brownshirt vibe off those dudes like I did, but I've got two grandparents who would smack me sideways if I didn't say this. The others died in a concentration camp. Capisce?"

Bronca capisces, nodding slowly in grim agreement. Because, well. She grew up missing a few elders, too—and contemporaries, for that matter. It's not paranoia when people are actually setting fires and shooting up nightclubs.

But. "Not the keyholders," Bronca says. "I'll warn them, but some of them have nowhere else to go."

Several of the Center's artists in residence are literal manifestations of the term—kids kicked out by their families for being queer or neuroatypical or saying no, adult artists priced out of rooms of one's own, even one woman Bronca's age who recently left her husband. She makes the most amazing glass sculptures. He beat the shit out of her and destroyed one of her best sets before she started sleeping on a beanbag in her Center workshop.

The working spaces aren't really designed for habitation, so the Center doesn't run afoul of any housing regulations . . . technically. Bronca gets around it by periodically reminding the keyholders that the space is to be used only temporarily. She's been saying that to some of them for years.

Veneza, her expression grim, moves behind the desk and sits down at the reception computer, doing something Bronca can't discern. Jess sighs, but says, "Yeah, okay. Not the keyholders. But warn them, at least. And . . . you'd better call the board. Get them ready."

Bronca tilts her head, trying to follow where Jess is running. "For what, a protest or something?"

"Yeah," Veneza interjects. "Thought so. C'mere, I wanna show you guys something."

They all move behind the desk to see the monitor. Veneza has a browser window open to YouTube, and she's done some kind of search that's brought up a bunch of videos with lurid title cards and leering faces. Bronca's about to ask what she's supposed to be seeing when abruptly she recognizes one of those smirks. "Hey!" She points at the screen. It's Strawberry Manbun.

"Are you fucking kidding me," Jess mutters, before turning away with a groan. "Oh, of *course*."

"What?" Bronca frowns after her, then at Veneza. "What?"

"Yeah, so, I just did a reverse image search on that logo in their email." Veneza taps a mark at the corner of the video, which Bronca remembers seeing elsewhere now. On their emails and on their business cards. It was a warning of how terrible the art was going to be: a stylized *A* surrounded by vaguely Nordic runes and ugly curlicues. Completely unintelligible and hard to remember, which basically defeated the whole point of even having a logo. "It's the logo of the 'Alt Artistes.' This is their channel."

She clicks on one, enlarges it, and scrolls to somewhere in the middle of its timeline. The screen fills with Strawberry Manbun's face, looking ripely furious and with his manbun coming apart from the force of his gesticulations.

"—the nail in the coffin, the dunnit in the who!" he is saying. In the background is what looks like a hotel room. "This is what these *revisionists* insist upon, the disrespect for a superior culture that brought them Picasso, and Gauguin, and—"

"Mute it," Bronca says, already annoyed by the sound of his voice. Veneza does so, thank God. "We get the idea. So these guys are some kind of... performance artists? They make shitty art, try to get it into galleries, fail because it's shitty, but then they make a video telling everybody it's reverse racism?"

"I guess? It's not that logical. They say whatever gets their audience excited enough to click on the videos or send them donations. Also, Picasso stole from African artists and Gauguin was a pedo who gave a bunch of brown girls syphilis, but what the fuck do I know." Then she taps the bottom of the video, where Bronca has to squint to make out a number. It looks like . . .

"Tell me that 'k' doesn't mean *thousand*," she says, drawing back in stunned horror as she realizes it. "Tell me forty-two thousand people haven't watched this shit!"

"Yep." Veneza goes back to the search results and points out other horrifically large numbers. "That was one of their higher-count vids, but still. And, like, there's a whole industry of dudes like this. The more inflammatory they are, the more people watch them, and the more money they make."

"White dude whining as a growth industry," Jess says grimly. She's blond and cute and pale as paper, so Bronca guesses she gets a frequent dose of white dude whining from types who don't realize she's not quite on the same team before they start with the globalist conspiracy theories. "I was going to say we should warn the board about possible violence, but I forgot this is a thing, too."

"Yeah," says Veneza. "Fans of dudes like this are fucking cultists. Anything he says, they'll suck it up. They'll put your address on the internet, if they can find it. Send death threats to your boss, stalk your kids, send a SWAT team to your house, show up with a gun themselves . . . the works. You guys need to lock down."

"Lock down?" Bronca stares at her. "Lock down what?"

"Your identities. Your personal information. I can help you get started, but we're going to have to stay late."

They get into it, tossing around plans and fallbacks while Veneza hops on endless name-search sites and tries to tell them over a couple of hours how to hide the online paper trails of a lifetime. It's dizzying, terrifying stuff—scarier still when Bronca suddenly realizes something fundamental about what's changed since her real spitfire days. Back then she had to worry about the government tapping her phone. It still probably does, but all the other stuff's been *outsourced*. Now, instead of just a COINTELPRO operation, she's got to worry about that *and* some dude stalking her relatives from his mother's basement, *and* kids bombarding her with death threats because it makes them feel like part of the (terrorist) gang, *and* a troll farm in Russia using the Center as the next cause célèbre to whip up Nazis. All the people who really are a threat to the country; somehow they've been convinced to do its dirty work, more or less for free. She would admire it if it weren't so damn horrific.

By the time they've done as much as they can—because Veneza can only help them reduce the threat; there's no way to eliminate it entirely—it's late. Yijing and Jess head home, while Bronca and Veneza linger long enough to send out an email to the workshoppers about online safety.

Bronca goes outside to let down the night shutters. As she's finishing up, however, Veneza comes out of the Center's staff door, looking shaken. She's a sturdy kid in a lot of ways—and really, Bronca shouldn't call her a kid. Veneza's done with college—Cooper Union, because she's got a good head on her. But right now, the girl's brown skin is ashen.

"The bathroom," she murmurs. "I don't know, B. It's always creepy in there. But tonight that last stall just woogied me right the fuck out."

Bronca grimaces. She should've burned some sage and tobacco, or scrubbed that stall down with ammonia, or both. "Yyyeah. Let's just call that one haunted."

"Except it wasn't, yesterday. What the hell's changed between yesterday and today? It looks the same, but everything's weird all of a sudden."

Veneza turns to look over the street. The Center sits on a slope overlooking the Bronx River and the on-ramp of the Cross Bronx Expressway, which has finally stopped being a parking lot now that rush hour is over. But beyond this, in the distance, the nighttime cityscape spreads across the horizon. Northern Manhattan isn't as impressive as the part of the island that tourists like. Bronca likes this view better, though, because it makes clear that New York is a city of people, not just businesses and landmarks. From here, when the air isn't hazy, one can take in the endless apartment blocks of Inwood and the gigantic public schools of Spanish Harlem, and even a few of the stately row houses that remain on Sugar Hill. Homes and schools and churches and neighborhood bodegas, with only the occasional glass-and-steel condo high-rise to mar the view. This is a view of the city that only the Bronx sees on the regular—which is why, Bronca feels certain, Bronx people don't take any shit from arrogant Manhattanites. End of day, if people want to make a life in New York, they all gotta eat, educate their kids, sleep, and get by somehow. No sense in anybody putting on airs.

But Bronca also sees what Veneza's picking up on. The city *is* different, because yesterday it was just a city, and today it is alive.

There is precedent for this. There are always those more attuned to a city than others—though usually not when they're from completely different states. Veneza's a Jersey City girl.

Bronca probes carefully. "What do you mean when you say every-thing's weird?"

"The bathroom stall! Also? That painting those guys had. The last one." She shudders. "You were spacing out, so maybe you didn't notice. But *everything changed*. Like, the whole gallery. All of a sudden Yijing and those guys were gone, and the room was empty, and it got real quiet. The light was strange. And the paint-ing *wasn't* a painting—"

She stops abruptly, looking uneasy. And Bronca realizes all of a sudden that she's facing a choice about how to deal with Veneza. She can play it off. Tell the girl that what she's sensing is noth-ing. Daydreams, or a flashback from the mushrooms she once told Bronca that she tried. Veneza is so much of what Bronca could have been, if she'd come up in a better world—and so much of what Bronca is now, because the world is still a goddamn shit-show. Bronca wants so badly to protect her.

That's ultimately what settles the matter. Because if Veneza is seeing these things, then she needs to know that they aren't hal-lucinations. She needs to know to run.

So Bronca sighs. "The painting was a doorway."

Veneza's head whips around so fast that her Afro puffs jiggle. She stares at Bronca for a long moment. Then she swallows and says slowly, "And we weren't just looking at a painting of abstract people on an abstract street, were we? We were actually *going* there. To a place that actually looked like that." She takes a deep breath. "Old B, I really wanted you to tell me it was another mushroom flashback."

"People in hell want ice water. And technically that was an expressionistic street, but that's just me being pedantic to make myself feel better." Bronca smiles sadly. "Kinda glad I'm not the only one visiting Weirdshitistan, though."

"I mean, I got your back anywhere, B, but *dayum.*"

Damn indeed. Bronca sighs, rubbing her eyes, hating for the umpteenth time that this whole mess has dumped itself in her front yard. She's got other shit to deal with, damn it. She should be fixated right now on buying unnecessary cute stuff for her future grandson, granddaughter, or two-spirit child, but here she is up to her neck in otherworldly art attacks.

"Yeah, that's . . . okay, look," she says. "We gotta talk. Because you *can't* have my back on this, see? You don't . . . you're not." Is there a word for what she and the other five have become? The knowledge that has dumped itself into her mind is long on concepts but short on vocabulary. "You don't have the . . . boots."

Veneza looks down at the sandals she's wearing. "Yeah, it was like ninety degrees today, so."

Bronca shakes her head. "You drive?"

"No. Short on gas money 'til payday."

"Then come on. It's past the hour when the MTA and New Jersey Transit turn into pumpkins, so let me drive you home. There's, ah, something I need to show you, anyway, along the way."

"Oooh, a mystery. I'm all aflutter." Veneza hefts her bag, and they head for Bronca's old Jeep.

Bronca lays it all out on the drive toward Jersey City. It's easier to believe here, along one of the city's thicker arteries, watching the red blood cells of its people and commerce come and go. Above them, clouds backlit by the moon race toward the Palisades, and to the left, ever-present and ever a presence, is the light-speckled silhouette of the city. *Tell her everything*, that city whispers to Bronca, whenever she hesitates over some especially weird or frightening bit of intel. *The Enemy is different now, craftier, crueler. Help her survive. We like having allies, don't we? Real ones, anyway.*

True that.

Then while Veneza silently digests what Bronca has told her, Bronca turns off the expressway just before they would've crossed the bridge that leads to Washington Heights. They're on the edge of the Bronx. Traffic is light here, the streets relatively deserted given the time of night. Nothing but housing projects in the area, and the city's done everything it can to isolate the people who live in them—fences, highways that cut the neighborhood in half, a no-man's-land of industrial blocks hemming the residential area in. There's one sad-looking grocery store in the area that Bronca knows of, but they pass ten payday lenders and dollar stores while she drives, dotting every half-busy thoroughfare like fast-proliferating tumors.

When Bronca pulls into the gravel road that leads into Bridge Park, it's hard not to feel some apprehension. She remembers the days when the "park" was just a wasteland of rotted buildings, and nobody hung out here at night except bums, crackheads, and bored teenagers looking for somebody to fuck or fuck with—like a big brown-skinned Indian with a dyke cut who just needed someplace to hear herself think. It's not like that now, though. The park has been landscaped into a bland expanse of lawns and benches and dogwood trees that line the old bike trail. These days there's a whole other kind of danger, because Bronca's heard too many stories of the cops hassling neighborhood folks out of the park, so that the more affluent white people moving in will feel safer. And she's still a big brown-skinned Indian with a dyke cut, here late at night in the company of a young Black woman for no reason that a bigoted cop would be able or willing to understand.

She's not quite the same woman, though. As Bronca parks and gets out, she reaches for her city, and the city sighs a long purr of pleasure in response. *No one will interfere*, it promises without words. *This is our place, no matter what interlopers think. Come, and show her yourself.*

She shivers a little. Hearing voices—even if it's not so much a voice as a stream of impressions and feelings—really should freak her out. It doesn't, though.

"So, I'm a little freaked out," Veneza says. When Bronca turns, the younger woman is eying her skeptically. "Like, if you were a dude, I'd be pulling out the pepper spray that you don't know I have."

"Pepper spray is legal in the city. I know Jersey dumb-asses think we're all peace-loving hippies here, but read a website, damn."

"Oh. Well, just saying. You're being *unusually* weird."

Bronca laughs. "Yeah, that's not gonna get any better. But there's some things that I'm not sure I can explain with words. Come on."

The Harlem River spreads beyond the cobbled path and the railings. There's not much to see at this point, east of the more dramatic skylines of Washington Heights and well south of the true suburbs of Yonkers and Mount Vernon. Just a murky, poorly lit river running sluggishly in the warm night air. There's a low, graffiti-flecked wall on the Washington Heights side of the river, running along Harlem River Drive, but for the Bronx it's nothing but shoreline, which is twisty with fallen tree branches and moss-slimed rocks and a couple of old rusty shopping carts that have been there for as long as Bronca can remember. The water smells faintly of sulfur, because there's probably a sewage spill some-where. This part of the Bronx is on the come up, but it's been poor as shit for a long time, and this is a city where politicians don't care about infrastructure even for wealthier neighborhoods.

A different kind of infrastructure has made itself present, though, as of about 11:54 a.m. eastern time. Bronca walks down to the water, her footing sure and quick. Veneza follows, much more carefully. When Bronca stops, Veneza almost slips on a wet rock, though she catches herself. "Old B, if you've decided to go serial killer on me, just stab me on solid ground, okay? I don't want to die in this nasty shit, catching fucking chlamydia or something."

Bronca laughs, then holds out her arm for Veneza to grab onto. "You should be able to see it from here. Okay." She points down the riverbank. "Tell me what you see."

Veneza looks. Bronca can tell that all she's noticing are the darker shadows of tree roots and old pipes against the water. "Your tax dollars not at work. What am I *supposed* to be seeing?"

"Just shut up for a minute. Let me . . ." Hard to do two things at once, be in two places at once, think with two selves at once. But this is important. "I'm gonna flex."

If Veneza has a smart remark in reply to this, Bronca doesn't hear it, because she has subsumed herself into the sound of the water and the chirr of the insects and the endless drone of cars making their way over the expressways and the GW in the distance. But that isn't the only sound she can hear, is it? It is beneath the others, the pillar supporting them, the metronome giving them rhythm and meaning: breathing. *Purring.* A lot of stuff is fucked up and wrong in New York, but isn't that part of the city, too? Situation normal. So even though it is only half-awake, and its avatars are scattered and afraid, and its streets teem with parasites trying to burrow underneath and multiply and kill the host . . . here, in this place, the Bronx dreams peacefully.

Here, Bronca may be all that she truly is.

So she lifts a foot, and puts it down twice. Lifts it again, taps twice, turns. The city's hum rises to a song. Its heart beats—fast, *tap* tap *tap* tap *tap* tap. These are her rhythms. She turns with them, dancing from rock to rock, catching the weight of her movements with her core so that her steps fall lightly. This is the dance.

"This is the story," she says. Her eyes have shut. She doesn't need to see the rocks or watch for slippery spots; the rocks are grandfathers who have invited her feet, so she goes where they have bidden. The story is in her, flowing, guiding her steps. Dance is a prayer—and though she has not danced like this in years, not since she stopped going to the pow-wows and stopped enjoying the dyke clubs and stopped tromping through brickyards to embrace the strength of the land underneath, it comes back to her like she's never left. *Tap* tap *tap* tap *tap* tap.

This is the city.

Tap tap *tap* tap *tap* tap.

The city is her.

Tap tap *tap* tap *tap* tap.

"This is my finger," Bronca says aloud. She lifts one hand, palm down, fingers loose. Then she lifts her index finger.

In the near distance, maybe thirty feet off, one of the massive curving pipes that arcs into the river...moves. With a hollow metallic groan, it rises from the water. Uncurls, still rising, until it sticks straight out over the water at the same angle as Bronca's finger. Bronca keeps the arm up even as she turns and leaps onto another stone so that Veneza can see.

Bronca opens her eyes then and glances at Veneza—who is staring at the pipe, her mouth hanging open. Bronca smiles and brings the dance to a halt physically. In her mind, however, she's still dancing. She is the city *and* the land underneath, and because of that, she will always dance.

"This is what I've been trying to tell you," Bronca says, still holding her arm up. Now Veneza is staring at Bronca. "This is the change in the city that you've been sensing, and the truth you have to remember. Whatever you see . . . first and foremost, it's real. Second, it can be dangerous. Understood?"

Veneza shakes her head slowly, but Bronca suspects this is less denial than amazement. "Can you make, I don't know. Any part of the city, do anything?"

"Yeah, I can—some parts easier than others—but that's nothing." Bronca curls her finger again, and the pipe grumbles back into place. Then she lifts her other arm, grinning as she watches Veneza because even though *this is the dance* and she knows what will happen intellectually, it's still an altogether different thing to experience. And some things are best experienced through the eyes of the young.

So when *the river* rises into the air, the whole five-hundred-foot-wide expanse of it, and curls an elbow and a wrist and long, watery fingers like some kind of immense, spectral Rosie the Riveter parody, it is Veneza's delight that settles Bronca's heart. Bronca never wanted this. And even though she knows why she was chosen, how important it is, she has not known how to *feel* about any of it, except resignation and frustration and dread. Now, though, as Veneza goes, "Holy fucking shit," it feels good for the first time.

She allows herself a bit of smugness. "It *is* pretty damn rad, huh."

"Nobody says 'rad' anymore, Old B, damn."

"Yeah, well, they should. Always liked that one."

"You know, though..." Veneza frowns a little. "This is pretty small, if it's... symbolically part of you? I mean, if that's your arm, then the rest of you ends, like, just across the street from the park."

"It's not exactly proportional." Nor does the borough emulate her body in any predictable shape or way. This riverbank has a thousand potential fingers to her five, for example, and some of them have claws. The borough's heart is actually a different river—the Bronx River, of course. The borough's teeth, rotting but still sharp, are the isolated projects; its ears are a thousand recording studios, all born of the boogie-down sound. And its bones are the stones underneath it all, ancient as ancestors.

Veneza can't seem to take her eyes off the water-arm. "Can you make it flip me off?"

Bronca snorts and turns her hand to lift the middle finger. The river follows, twisting about, and when a fifty-foot column of water lifts from the middle of its fistlike mass, a spritz of droplets hits them both in the face. "Oh, *gross*," Veneza cries—but she is laughing even as she mops herself off. Then she blinks, staring. Because Bronca has lifted the river from its bed...and yet there is the river, flowing along quietly as it has for millennia.

"This isn't the same kind of real as what you're used to," Bronca says gently.

"What, it's a hallucination? Goddamn polluted river water in my face—"

"It's not a hallucination. It's just that...reality isn't binary." She sighs and uncurls her arm, relaxes her fingers. The great water-arm shifts back into the middle of the river and straightens out, becoming again the river that it has been all along.

"There are lots of New Yorks," she explains. "In some of them, you turned right coming out of the subway this morning. In others, you turned left. And you also rode a dinosaur to work, and somewhere else you ate some funky ant-ball snacks at lunch, and somewhere else you've got a side gig as an opera singer. All of those things are possible. All of them have *happened*. Got it?"

"Like science fiction?" Veneza tilts her head, eyes narrowing in thought. "The many-worlds interpretation? Quantum physics? Is that what we're talking about?"

"Eh, if it wasn't on *Star Trek*, I don't know." Though Bronca does have a vague memory of a weird episode about a mirrored universe where everyone was evil, somehow signified by men wearing goatees? And in this universe they wear manbuns. Whatever.

"I'm going to tell you a creation story," Bronca says. "It's not like the ones my people tell. Not even like the ones your people tell. The one I'm about to tell you is ..." She considers, then laughs as she thinks of a term. "More like a *unified field theory* of creation. So try to follow along.

"A long time ago, when existence was young, there was just one world that was full of life. No one can say if it was bad or good. It was life." She shrugs.

The river beside them runs through other planes where other Broncas speak—a thousand other tellers telling a thousand other tales, beneath ten thousand different skies. If Bronca concentrates, she can see them, skies where a second sun has risen or the night air is purple and gold and burns with what would be toxic to her. She tries not to see them, however. Veneza deserves her full attention for now ... and it's dangerous even to look at some things. The city has warned her about this.

"That first world, that first life, was a miraculous thing. But each decision those living beings made fissioned off a new world— one where some of them turned left, and another where some turned right. Then each of those worlds fissioned off more worlds of their own, and so on, and so on. How do you top a miracle? You don't; you just make another universe, which will start making its own miracles. And so life proliferated—across a thousand million universes, each one stranger than the last."

Bronca repositions her hands, one flattened in the air a few inches above the other. Then she ladders them, one above the other, to suggest many layers. A mille-feuille of worlds, she means to suggest, each building on the other, forming coral columns that rise and split and twist apart and split again. An endlessly growing tree, sprung from a single tiny seed, whose branches are each so wildly different that life on one would be unrecognizable to life on another. With one important exception.

"Cities traverse the layers." In this world Bronca points at the skyline that rises above the trees of Bridge Park, on their side of the river. "People still tell stories of how terrible the Bronx is. At the same time, somewhere, some realtor is talking up how amazing it is, so that people with money will come and buy up everything. At the same time there are the folks who live here, for whom it's neither terrible nor amazing; it just is. All of these things are true, and that's just within our own reality. It's not just *decisions*, is what I'm trying to say. It's . . . Every legend of this city, every lie, those become new worlds, too. All of them add to the mass that is New York, until finally all of it collapses under its own weight . . . and becomes something new. Something alive."

Fuck yeah, says the voice in her head.

Shut up, sweetie, I'm busy, she sings back.

Veneza is turning, looking at the trees and the water and the night-lights as if it's all new. It is. She says, in a tone of wonder,

"Always used to look at the city from the rooftop at home. It always looked like it was breathing."

"It was. Just a little, then." Fetuses breathe their own amniotic fluids, consuming themselves as practice for the day when they will metabolize something wholly different. "But today, everything changed. After today, the city's going to be alive in a way that it wasn't before."

"Why today?"

Bronca shrugs. "The stars aligned? The Creator got bored? I don't know. The timing doesn't matter; the event does."

"Yeah, I guess I'm not paying attention to the right things." Veneza sobers. "That painting today. Tell me about that."

Yeah. Bronca needs to stop showing off. She sighs and turns away from the rocks, beckoning for Veneza to follow her back toward the Jeep. "Right, the painting. Basically, one of the realities out there is not super jazzed that our reality exists. Fuck if I know why—but whatever the reason, something from that reality tries to kill cities whenever they become alive the way New York has just done. They tried this morning, and did some damage, but failed in the big push."

Veneza's eyes widen. "Oh, shit. The Williamsburg!"

"The Williamsburg." Bronca nods grimly. "Which could've been a lot worse; it was going for the whole city, like I said. Something stopped it. Someone like me, another person who is now the city."

"What, like . . ." Veneza pauses, frowning. "There's more people who can make the river move?"

"There are six of us. One for each borough, and another who's the whole city. That's the one who stopped the attack this morning. That entity from the other universe"—*the Enemy*, her mind whispers—"is still here, though. And something's changed about the way it presents itself. It's *supposed to be* a horrible big thing that attacks cities at the moment of their birth. That's how it's always happened before—always, across thousands of years. Now, though, its tactics have changed."

And that's got Bronca very worried. There is nothing in the lexicon about the Enemy co-opting human minions to deliver monstrous paintings. Are the others having this kind of trouble, too? Maybe she should…

No. *No.* Beyond preparing Veneza as best Bronca can, she's staying out of this fight.

"The painting." Veneza, whose thoughts have obviously followed the same path, shivers visibly. "Stuff in it was…moving." She trails off, her voice haunted.

"Remember what I said about life from those other places not being something that even looks alive, to us."

"What, there are actually people who look like two-dimensional paint smears somewhere out there?" Veneza shakes her head. "Fuuuuuck."

That was what had made the paint-figures so creepy, really. To know that the things she was seeing weren't just mindless, swirl-faced monsters, but things with minds and feelings? Minds as incomprehensibly alien as Lovecraft once imagined his fellow human beings to be.

They get in the car, and Bronca turns them back toward the expressway, heading for New Jersey. Veneza's quiet beside her, digesting what she's said. But there's one more important bit that Bronca has to get across.

"So." She takes her eyes off the road just long enough to fix them on Veneza. This part is important. "Remember that thing I did with the river? I did the same thing at the Center today. If I'm careful, if I do things right, I can push those people, the Enemy, back into their world, or at least out of my immediate vicinity. You, though, you can't do that. So next time you see some fucked-up shit—"

"Come get you. Got it."

"Uh, well. Yeah, that works, too. But if I'm not around? Book it. Run *away*, not toward it like you did today. Okay?"

At this, however, Veneza scowls. "If I hadn't run toward the crazy, and pulled you back when they started reaching for you with all their little..." She waggles her fingers and makes a face. Bronca frowns in surprise. Those things had been reaching for her? "Then you would have been, I don't know, paint food."

She's so damn stubborn. "Well, if I'm not in imminent danger that you can save me from, get the fuck out. Because I don't want to think about what will happen if those things grab *you*." When Veneza's jaw sets, Bronca pulls out the big guns. "Please. Do it for me."

Veneza winces, but some of the stubbornness goes out of her. "Damn it. Fine. Okay, then." She frowns a little, though, troubled. "But why could I see it, when Yeej and Jess couldn't? They didn't move, actually, while it was happening. It was like they were in a freeze-frame, with the lights down low. Same with those guys who brought the painting. You, though, were normal-looking. And me, I wasn't frozen at all. Why?"

"There are always people around who are closer to the city than others. Some of them become like me, and others just serve the city's will, as needed."

Veneza gasps. "Oh, shit, you mean I *could've* been like you?"

"Maybe, yeah, if you weren't from Jersey."

"Oh, fuck." It's a testament to the fact that Veneza isn't a kid, though she acts like one sometimes, that she doesn't seem thrilled by the prospect of developing extradimensional superpowers. She grips the Jeep's door handle instead, as if she needs it to feel more secure. "Jesus, B. So, I mean, it's awesome that, uh, you're a city? Congratulations! I want to be accepting of this new stage in your identity formation. But if people are showing up at work to try and swallow you with paint-monsters, what are you going to do if you get doxxed? Those things *in your house*."

Bronca's been trying not to think about that. "Hell if I know."

Veneza remains silent for the rest of the ride to Jersey City, which is only another ten minutes or so. When Bronca pulls up to Veneza's apartment building—a small, nondescript low-rise across the street from a half-vacant lot—she stops at the curb. Veneza doesn't get out, though.

"You need to crash with me?" she asks Bronca, in perfect seriousness.

Bronca blinks in surprise. "You live in a studio."

"Right. No roommates. Luxury living."

"You don't have a *couch*."

"There's a whole two-by-six trash-free space on my carpet, I'll have you know. Or hell, share the bed. I changed the sheets, like, five days ago. Seven! Eight. Okay, I'll change the sheets."

Bronca shakes her head, bemused. "No homo. Not with *you*, anyway."

"I swear I won't ravish you in your sleep, B." Veneza glares at her despite the banter. "Even though you did just tell me that an entire universe's worth of city-eating monsters is out there trying to fuck you up, so maybe you could stop worrying about your virtue for a minute and think about your *life* instead?"

She really is a sweetheart. Bronca sighs, then reaches over to ruffle her puffs. Veneza pretends to dodge, but then she permits it because she doesn't really mind, and because Bronca makes sure they still look cute afterward. "I can keep those things out of my building," Bronca says. "I think. But to do even that much, I need to be *in New York*. The city I'm part of? Which is not the city we're in right now?"

"Oh." Veneza sighs. "Right. Forgot this whole thing has *rules*."

She gets out of the car, taking more time to get her purse out of the back seat than is strictly necessary. By this, Bronca knows she's still trying to think of a way to help. "Hey." When Veneza looks up, Bronca nods at her. "I'm gonna be fine. I was at—"

"'Stonewall, I stomped on a cop,' yeah, I *know*. Informants aren't paint-monsters from the fucking id."

It's called the Ur, Bronca thinks, but she's scared Veneza enough. "Either way, I got this. Good *night*."

Grumbling, Veneza shuts the door.

Bronca watches 'til she's inside, then heads home. And as the city welcomes her back within its borders, she prays to any god that will listen, across any dimension, that her friend will be safe.

CHAPTER SEVEN

The Thing in Mrs. Yu's Pool

The Queen is in Queens, contemplating the stochastic processes of a trinomial tree model, on the strange warm day when everything changes. The Queen—whose real name is Padmini Prakash—doesn't want to be working on her Computational Analysis project, which is why she happens to be daydreaming about some Lovecraft meta that she read on Tumblr, and looking outside, in the moment of the city's rebirth. The meta wasn't so much interesting as funny, science-side Tumblr arguing with fantasy-side over the comical notion that non-Euclidean geometry could somehow be sinister, and concluding that Lovecraft was probably just scared of math. The view through her window isn't especially interesting, either. Just a westerly view of Queens' myriad of neighborhoods and churches and billboards, with the very Euclidean spires of Manhattan looming beyond. It's a bright, sunny June day, all of 11:53 a.m., and the day's a-wasting as Americans say, so with a heavy sigh, Padmini turns her attention back to her work.

She hates financial engineering, which of course is why she's getting a master's degree in it. She would prefer pure mathematics, where one might elegantly apply theories toward the cleaner (or at least decontextualized) goal of understanding processes, thought, and the universe itself. But it's a lot harder to get a job in math than finance these days, especially with the H-1B lottery getting tighter and the ICE gestapo waiting to swoop in on any pretext, so here she is.

Then something—instinct, maybe—prompts Padmini to look up again. Thus she is staring directly at the Manhattan horizon in the precise moment when a titanic tentacle curls up from the East River and smashes the Williamsburg Bridge.

She actually doesn't know which bridge it is, at first. She can't remember one from another. Still, the tentacle must be pretty big for her to be able to discern that it's a tentacle at all. *That's not real,* she thinks, with the instant scorn of any true New Yorker. Just two days before, big white film-production trailers took over her entire block. That happens all the bloody time these days, because movie people invariably seem to want multicultural working-class New York as backdrop for their all-white upper-class dramedies— which means Queens, since East New York is still too Black for their tastes and the Bronx has a "reputation." Given that the tentacle is enormous but translucent, rising above the waterfront condos of Long Island City and flickering like a poorly connected monitor—or cheap special effects—naturally Padmini concludes that it's some kind of hoax: *2012 called; it wants the Tupac hologram back.* And then she giggles, inordinately pleased by her own cleverness. Math Queen's got jokes.

But the tentacle is awfully heavy-looking as it strikes the bridge. Padmini must concede that they got that detail right in the special effects; heavy masses displace more air than smaller things, and the lag caused by that much friction would make for visibly sluggish momentum. This tentacle is going just a little too fast to be in free fall, but Padmini figures they can tweak it in postproduction. Or maybe they'll play it off by saying the tentacle is just phenomenally strong? That wouldn't ruin the audience's suspension of disbelief.

As the tentacle hits the bridge, the bridge twists up in holographic silence—but an instant later, the wind shifts and carries with it the sound of metal tearing and concrete cracking and horns blowing. Padmini's apartment building shudders. And... now there are screams, Dopplered by distance but unmistakable. All the way in Jackson Heights, miles from Williamsburg even as the crow flies, Padmini can hear *screams*.

Then riding somewhere behind that sound wave comes a wave of... emotion? Anticipation? Dread and excitement. Something is wrong—but also right. All around her there is a sudden and *intense* rightness, shivering through the trees of her building's backyard and thrumming up through the old frame house's foundation. Dust puffs through cracks in the walls. She inhales the faint scent of mildew and rat droppings, and it's disgusting, but it's *right*.

At her desk she pushes herself up, driven to her feet by restlessness. In the same instant, not far off, a subway goes by along one of the elevated tracks. For an instant she is rushing along with the train, *is* the train: fast, powerful, aching for a coating of graffiti along her sleek-but-boring silver skin—and then she is just herself. Just a tired young graduate student, past her prime at the ripe old age of twenty-five according to fashion magazines, leaning close to the window of a borrowed bedroom and trying to understand how the world has suddenly changed.

All at once, her mouth goes dry with the instinctive awareness that something else is wrong, and this time it's a lot closer than the East River.

Near. Here. Her head whips about almost of its own volition, almost as if something has taken hold of her ponytail and yanked on it to direct her attention where it is needed. *There*: the backyard. Not the one attached to her own building, which is paved over and contains only weeds and the rusted-out barrel of their downstairs neighbor's former barbecue pit. The one next door. Mrs. Yu lives in that garden apartment, and she's decided that a backyard needs a pool, probably because she used to live in Texas where that was a thing people did. It's just a little above-ground thing, dingy and cracked after only two New York winters. At barely more than eight feet wide, it takes up nearly the entirety of the yard. Still, it's a hot June day, so two of Mrs. Yu's grandsons are hard at play in the water, giggling and squealing loudly enough to almost—almost—drown out the screams from Williamsburg.

And do they not notice the way the water suddenly changes color, as the bright blue plastic bottom of the pool transforms into something else? Something grayish white. Something altogether stranger than plastic. Something . . . *moving*, with a slow organic undulation that Padmini can see even through the rippling water.

No. They don't notice because they are unironically playing Marco Polo, yelling at each other in a mix of Mandarin and English and splashing wildly to get away from each other. One's got his eyes closed, the other is fixated on the first, and neither has put his feet down on the pool bottom. They're small boys, but the pool is tiny, too. They're going to touch the bottom eventually.

Padmini is up from the desk and tearing through the apartment to reach the door before she can think. If she did think, she would decide that she's being foolish. If her conscious mind were fully engaged, she would tell herself that even if her sudden intense belief about touching the grayness at the bottom of the pool is rooted in any sort of truth, she cannot possibly make it to the ground level, and to Mrs. Yu's front door, in time. She cannot make it through Mrs. Yu's house quickly enough, if the old woman even lets her in without first wanting a half hour's worth of small talk because Mrs. Yu is lonely, and into the backyard, before the boys touch the bottom of the pool. If she were thinking, she would convince herself that her sudden intense belief is irrational. (*Really?* she would ask herself in scorn. *And what's next, stepping on a crack really does break your mother's back?*)

But she *knows* it's real. It has been given unto her to understand the mechanics of the whole business, so she instinctively knows that water is the helpmeet of the Enemy: not a doorway in and of itself, but a lubricant of sorts, facilitating easier traverse. The thing in the pool will do worse than kill the boys; it will *take them away*. To where and for what? Who knows, but it can't happen.

So in her panic, Padmini pelts through the door of the apartment and halfway down the fourth-floor flight of stairs without so much as stopping to grab her keys. (The door swings wide open behind her. Aishwarya Aunty calls after her in startlement; her baby cousin starts crying. Padmini doesn't even close it.) She puts her hand on the bannister and thinks, *Now, must get there now*—

—and because she is what she is, she envisions herself *accelerating* to get there, not magically but mathematically, through the walls and the backyard fences and air and space. The transit from point A to B would take

$$T = \pi \sqrt{\frac{a^2 - r_0^2}{ag}}$$

time, where

$$g = \frac{GM}{a^2} = \frac{4}{3}\pi\rho \, Ga$$

is the surface gravity of the arc of a hypocycloid—

And the instant she thinks this, a voice inside her head answers, *Oh, that's what you want to do. Okay, no problem.*

Then the walls of her old building bend around her, warping, until she is not running down stairs but *flying*, more than flying, rushing through a tunnel as if she is a bullet and the whole world has become the gun—

And then she is running across grass, she is in Mrs. Yu's backyard, she is at the edge of the pool grabbing one boy and hauling him out by the shoulders. He screams, kicking, and punches her in the face, knocking her glasses onto the grass. The other boy screams, too, for their grandmother. Padmini has the first boy on the grass, he's safe there, the grass is solid ground and feels *right*, but the boy is still screaming and he kicks at her, grabs her hair, tries his damnedest to impede her as she tries to get up for the other boy. The first boy weighs all of fifty pounds, but he goes for her knee and then punches her in the belly. "I'm—" Padmini cries, but before she can get the next word out there is an entirely different kind of scream from the pool that stops both of them cold.

Mrs. Yu comes out onto the back porch, a bamboo strainer brandished in one hand. She stops and stares at the pool. They all stare, in fact.

In the pool, the other boy has stood up on the grayish-white bottom—which, close up, is not just grayish white but *mottled*, and some of it is *scarred*, because it is *skin* and not plastic or earth.

And now tendrils of that grayness have whipped up from the bottom of the pool to wrap themselves around the boy's legs.

After a moment's horrified staring down at himself, the boy starts screaming again, this time splashing wildly to get out—but he can't use his legs. As Padmini watches, the tendrils move up and over his trunks, up his waist. He swats frantically at them and they whip up to catch one arm, lickety-split, pinning it down. And his feet are gone, all of a sudden. They have vanished into the now-amorphous gray substance, which is bubbling and rising around him, swallowing him from the ankles up and dragging him under—

Mrs. Yu shouts and runs down to the pool. Padmini belatedly shakes off shock and runs over as well. Between the two women, they grab the boy's flailing hand. The gray stuff is fearsomely strong as it pulls on him. Padmini pulls back with everything she's got, but she is an overweight, overworked graduate student, not the Rock. The boy is terrified, his face staring up at them even as fingers of the gray stuff start worming up around his face. She can't stand the sight of it. She doesn't want to touch it, and indeed every particle of her screams against doing so because it is somehow inimical to her—and yet she cannot let this child be taken without using everything she's got to fight back.

And, suddenly, she thinks of fluid mechanics.

Fluid mechanics are beautiful. The equations jump and ripple, push and ebb. It is nothing to Padmini to run the equations for flow velocity through her mind. Nothing to change the variables to increase that velocity, down close to the boy's skin. Water is a lubricant, but if she can just imagine something that is a better lubricant . . . *between* his skin and the gray substance, faster and more fluid than water should ever be . . .

The pool is a tumbling rapids of churning water. Padmini cannot see the tendrils anymore amid the froth, but she is hyper-aware of them as she pulls, and Mrs. Yu pulls, and even the first boy grabs onto Mrs. Yu's waist from behind and pulls. "No!" Padmini shouts in defiance at the gray thing in between desperate gasps for air, but meanwhile she is thinking,

$$\rho\left(\frac{\partial \mathbf{u}}{\partial t} + \mathbf{u} \cdot \nabla \mathbf{u}\right) = -\nabla p + \nabla \cdot \mathbf{T}_\mathrm{D} + \mathbf{f}$$

where f equals *infinity* if that's how much force it takes to get this disgusting thing off the child—

It works. The thing's tendrils slip free, and the boy comes skeeting out of the pool as if buttered and fired from a buttered-child cannon. Padmini takes the brunt of the blow, which is good because Mrs. Yu has osteoporosis. The boy bowls Padmini back, and though she lies winded on the ground with a small, sobbing child curled up against her, she is elated. Ecstatic! Who knows if the thing in the pool will stay there, or if she'll be able to save anyone if it crawls out of the water and tries to eat them again. It doesn't matter. For the first time in years, it seems, she's done something not just because she's expected to do it, but because she's *chosen* to do it, and done the hell out of it besides.

"And don't fucking bring your squamous eldritch bullshit here," she gasps, grinning, without really hearing herself.

It is as if these words set off a bomb. She feels something, a wave of outgoing force, seem to tingle away from her feet and the crown of her head and her butt where it crushes the grass as she sits up. She can even see the wave as its energy crawls across the grass and over Mrs. Yu's apartment building—and the old pool. There is a hiss from somewhere below the pool as this force moves across it. The water in the pool roils; the boy in her arms cringes and makes a sound of fear. But Padmini knows that this is a good thing, this change. She staggers to her feet (the boy is heavy), but by the time she's up, she already knows what she'll see. Mrs. Yu's pool bottom has turned back to pale blue plastic. The portal to another place, where pool bottoms are made of devouring skin, is gone.

So Padmini wraps her arms around the weeping child, shuts her eyes, and privately vows to make an immediate offering at her tiny, neglected puja table. Well, the bag of fruit she bought last week has already manifested flies and might have gone moldy. Okay, she'll offer incense instead, the really good stuff.

And a little while after all this, two very weird strangers show up.

"Good thing we came here first," Manny says. He's standing by the backyard pool that almost swallowed Queens. It's just an ordinary pool now, but in the other world that Manny can see, the entire empty, twilit backyard (it never seems to grow fully dark in Weird New York, or fully light) is layered over with the massive, glowing parallel marks of *something* that has clawed at this place, and very nearly rent it open. The marks are healed now, just. Manny can feel their rawness. Worse, the air smells of strange, oceanic aldehydes, and somewhere else—not in Weird New York, but troublingly close by—he can hear the very faint, lingering roar of frustration from something immense and inhuman that almost broke through.

Back in this world, he can hear Mrs. Yu through the apartment window, still saying soothing things to her grandsons while she feeds them to calm them down further. The younger boy has taken no lasting harm from his encounter with the pool-bottom monster, though Manny's pretty sure he'll never be coaxed into a swimming pool again, and even bath time might be a problem from here forth. Not that he blames the boy. Manny's creeped out just standing five feet from where it happened.

"Is it really a good thing?" Brooklyn asks. Mrs. Yu's place sits on a gradual hill. They gaze out over endless backyards and houses, sloping away from where they stand. "We got here too late. If that young lady hadn't figured out how to push this thing back into wherever it came from, we'd have gotten here to find all these people dead. Or . . . gone."

Manny shudders at the thought. Some things, he understands instinctively, are worse than death. "I guess you're right. She got lucky. We all have been, so far." Though he does not add, *But it only takes one mistake.* Brooklyn knows it anyway.

"It sounds like the thing that was in this pool is a more, uh, violent version of the patches of tendrils—or feathers—we've seen," Manny says. And then he has a horrifying thought. "It might even be the *same* thing. I keep thinking about how, at the park, she kept switching between 'we' and 'I' like the pronouns were interchangeable. Like she couldn't keep the words straight, and they didn't really matter anyway."

"Maybe this isn't her first language."

That's partly it. But Manny suspects the problem is less linguistic than contextual. She doesn't get English because English draws a distinction between the individual self and the collective plural, and wherever she comes from, whatever she is, that difference doesn't mean the same thing. If there's a difference at all.

"Those things in the park did what she wanted," Brooklyn says. "It's also clear that she's responsible for what happened at the bridge, somehow, and apparently FDR Drive. And here. You saw how much time it's taken us to travel from one point in the city to another; she couldn't possibly be in all these places personally. Some of this stuff happened at the same time, across the city from each other. So maybe she's...I don't know. Like a fungus. Everywhere, all over the city, but we only see the bits that poke up here and there."

"Ew," says the woman they've come to meet, who excuses herself and then turns away from where she's been carrying on an intent conversation with an older woman nearby. She's still sitting on Mrs. Yu's backyard steps. The older woman, standing beside her, settles into an aggressively defensive posture with her arms folded and chin jutted forth, but she says nothing as Padmini speaks. "Did you have to go to fungus?"

The living embodiment of the borough of Queens is a tiny thing, busty and dark brown, with a wealth of long black hair that's stiff from having been soaked in chlorinated pool water and not rinsed before it dried. She's introduced herself to them as Padmini—"Like the actress?"—and has apparently resigned herself to having a name they do not recognize. Manny has to work very hard to remind himself to call her Padmini, however, because of course her name in his head is Queens. But that is a name she must choose. He has no right to force it upon her.

Brooklyn smiles at the girl wearily. "I call things like I see them—but you're right, fungus isn't where I wanted to go, either. Speaking of other things I don't want to hear but that do have to be said...This thing came directly at Manny and me, but attacked a neighbor in your case. Any idea why?"

"Why are you asking me?" Padmini looks aggrieved. She starts to wring out her hair again. It's actually dry, but the gesture has the look of a nervous tic. "Before, what, three or four hours ago? I didn't know about any of this."

They have by this point explained everything to her that they can. It's gone more smoothly than Manny expected, probably because Padmini just saw a pool try to eat two children. It's been awkward, too, however, because Padmini's relative—the older woman, whom Padmini has introduced as Aishwarya Aunty—has come down to see why Padmini apparently ran out of their apartment at full tilt and then teleported to the neighbor's backyard. Aunty hasn't said much, but she's hovering and radiating protectiveness in a way that Manny would admire if so many of her hostile glares weren't directed at him and Brooklyn.

But he knows the answer to Brooklyn's question, so he decides to interject.

"Going after collaterals is good strategy," he says, sighing as he slides his hands into his pockets. "Family, neighbors, coworkers—anyone who isn't capable of defending themselves. Start some kind of high-profile chaos involving people the target cares about, which might both lure her out of a safe position and distract her with worry or grief. Then attack while she's off guard."

He's abruptly aware that Brooklyn has narrowed her eyes at him. He knows why. There's just nothing he can do about it. Her voice is neutral, though, when she speaks. "How was she in a safe position beforehand?"

"Yes, how?" That's from Aishwarya Aunty, who looks like a taller, fortysomething version of the avatar of Queens, and is pretty regal herself in a gloriously sunset-orange-themed cotton sari. "If you aren't just crazy." Padmini tries to hush her.

Manny turns to point at Padmini's apartment building. It's an ordinary-looking wooden frame house, four stories high. She's told them she lives on the top floor with Aishwarya and Aishwarya's husband, and their new baby. "That building," Manny says. "It's glowing, isn't it? We all see that?"

Brooklyn turns to look, and Padmini gasps. *Glowing* isn't exactly the word for what they're seeing, Manny suspects, but it's close enough. The sun has slanted toward sunset, backlighting the building in a way that would be eerie if this were Amityville instead of Jackson Heights. That's not what Manny wants them to notice. What he hopes they see, and what all of them except Aishwarya clearly do, is that Padmini's building is different from Mrs. Yu's, and from every building around it. Brighter, somehow. More defined? Almost as if the building has been Photoshopped for greater sharpness while the rest of the block retains a fuzzier contrast. Somehow, that building is *right* in a way that the Checker cab had been, now that Manny thinks about it—and his own apartment building, once he'd stepped off the elevator. He noticed the change at the time, but hadn't understood it.

"I don't think the Enemy can get into that building," Manny says. "Something has made it *more* Queens, so to speak, than the rest of Queens."

"You're saying I did that?" Padmini shakes her head. "I didn't do anything. Until you two showed up, I had no idea why any of this was happening. Why would I be able to—" She gestures at her building in frustration.

"I don't know. But I wish you could tell us how you did it. This thing is targeting us one by one, and I don't think it's going to stop. There doesn't seem to be an instruction manual or a wise old mentor anywhere to help us figure out the rules, but if we keep playing catch-up, it's going to win, eventually."

Manny sighs and rubs a hand over his face, suddenly very tired.

It's been a long day. Between them is a little plate of baozhi that Mrs. Yu put out for them, and he bends to take one, suddenly ravenous. It's delicious. He takes another.

Brooklyn sighs as well. "Look, I'm worn out, and I missed lunch riding up to Inwood to save this one from the feather monster." She jabs a thumb at Manny. "I think we need to rethink trying to do this all at once. Not going to do anybody any good if we drop where we stand."

"Shouldn't we go to the Bronx?" Manny frowns. "Since we know who she is. And, uh, what's the fifth borough, again? I forgot, sorry."

"Staten Island," Brooklyn says. "I have no idea how to find her, though."

"'Her'?" asks Padmini.

Brooklyn blinks. "Huh. I don't know where that came from. It feels right, though. Doesn't it?" She looks at each of them. Padmini frowns and nods slowly. Manny does, too.

"Well, okay, then." Brooklyn shakes her head, plainly uneasy about the strange knowledge dropping into her head. "My point was that the, uh, that woman, has probably already gone after the Bronx and Staten Island, same as she did all of us. And the fact that those boroughs haven't exploded or something means that the people who represent them have figured out enough to survive so far. They're probably confused as hell, but they may not need our help any more than she did." Brooklyn nods toward Padmini.

"*I* am certainly confused," Aishwarya Aunty mutters. Padmini pulls her to sit down on the step beside her, and they start having a hastily muttered conversation in some other language. Tamil, Manny knows. He knows so many things that he should not.

"There's another of us," he blurts. When they all look at him,

Aishwarya with narrowed eyes, he explains. "Not five, but six. The Woman in White, she kept going on about another. Someone who'd fought her—beaten her—but not completely. That's why she's still able to attack us."

"Six?" Brooklyn frowns. She's been staring at the baozhi, and now finally gives in to temptation, taking the last one. Almost immediately the door behind them cracks open, and Mrs. Yu puts out another plate of three. Manny nods to her awkwardly, but she doesn't bother looking at them before closing the door again. Meanwhile, Brooklyn continues, "Ain't but five boroughs, Manny."

"Five shapes that fit together make one whole," Padmini says, shrugging. Manny blinks in confusion, but Brooklyn inhales.

"You mean *the city* as a whole," she says, her eyes widening. "Not a borough at all, but... New York? The city of New York, all in one person." She whistles, shaking her head, but it's clear that she believes it. Manny does, too, now that the concept exists in his mind. "He must be all kinds of crazy."

"But strong," Manny murmurs. A shiver passes through him; the hairs on the back of his neck prickle. Why? He doesn't know. But he does not want to question his assessment, or Brooklyn's assumption that the embodiment of New York is male. "If he fought whatever it was that took out the bridge, by himself, we need him."

Padmini slowly holds up a hand. "Uh, then if we're voting, I vote with Ms. Brooklyn. You both look exhausted. I *feel* exhausted. It will be dark soon, and I would like very much to have some time to think about all this. Maybe we could, ah, adjourn for the night, and reconvene in the morning?"

"That's foolish," snaps Aishwarya Aunty. They all stare at her, and her scowl deepens. "You just said something was *hunting* you. You want to split up now, and make it easier to pick you off? Together you can at least watch one another's backs."

"Aunty? You believe us?" Padmini asks. She looks wide-eyed, hopeful, and very young.

Aishwarya shrugs. "It doesn't matter if I do or not. Craziness is happening, so let's figure out a way to get done with the craziness quickly so you can get back to your life, yes?"

Padmini laughs a little, but Manny sees the gratitude in her eyes.

Brooklyn sighs. "I have to get back, anyway," she says. "I told my daughter I'd be late, but I don't want to be out all damn night trying to hunt down borough-people. And city-people. Especially when we have no idea where to start, with two of those."

Manny feels the same, but some of that is the general jangling restlessness that he's been feeling since Padmini mentioned an overall embodiment of the city. They need each other, he feels certain, but they especially need this sixth one. And he feels especially, instinctively certain that they need to hurry up on that last bit.

"This must be happening in other cities," Padmini says, interrupting Manny's reverie. She's scowling, as if annoyed that the world makes less sense today than it did the day before. "We can't be the only weird ones, can we? Have there been disasters like the bridge anywhere else today?"

"No," says Aishwarya. She sighs. "The usual bad news everywhere, but nothing like the bridge."

Then Manny remembers. "The Woman said something about São Paulo being here." With the person who is New York.

"The city of São Paulo?" Brooklyn asks. "It has a . . . person? Shouldn't that person be *in* São Paulo?"

"I don't know. But if it's true, then what's happening to us is something that must have already happened in that city. And that settles something I've been thinking about since you brought it up." He nods to Brooklyn. "When you said that we can leave, and the city will pick someone else. I think you're right about that; it feels right, and that's pretty much all we've had to go on so far. But I also feel like...past a certain point, we're no longer going to have that choice. The whole city is probably supposed to be like Padmini's building, safe from the Woman in White. It isn't, not just because we don't know what we're doing, but because something's *wrong* right now. We're incomplete. Without each other, and the one who is New York, we can't secure the whole city. But if we ever manage to do that..."

Brooklyn groans. "I get it. Then *we'll* be like São Paulo. Wherever we go, even if it isn't New York, we'll be...New York."

Padmini sits up, looking alarmed. "What, forever? But—no!"

They all look at her in surprise. Even Aishwarya. Padmini grimaces. "It's just...look, this is a lot to deal with! It's nice that both of you have come to help, but—" She shakes her head, a coronal rather than lateral movement, conveying her struggle to articulate the problem. "I don't know. I just...I can't become Queens. I'm not even a US citizen! What if my internship company doesn't hire me, and I can't find another job that will give me a visa? Then I'll be puttering around Chennai, being Queens! That can't be right."

They all stare at each other in uncomfortable silence.

Mrs. Yu opens the door again, just enough that they can see half of her face. Manny's getting used to ignoring her; she's obviously eavesdropping, but that's also just part of life in a city. She doesn't put another plate out this time, however, just peering out at them through the slit between door and frame. Her gaze roams them all and lands on Manny. "You hùnxuè'ér?" she asks. "Hapa? That's what the young people call it now."

Manny blinks out of trying to understand why he understands Toishanese. "Uh, no." Not that he knows of.

"Hnh." She examines them all again, then presses her lips together in annoyance. "In China, many cities have gods of the walls. Fortune aids them. It's normal. Relax."

"Okay, what the fuck," Brooklyn says.

"Yes, exactly," says Aishwarya. Padmini frowns at her. "There are many in my country who believe that, too. Lots of stories. Lots of gods, lots of avatars—probably hundreds. Some are patrons of cities; you could call them city gods. It's wild to think *you're* one." She glares at Padmini, whose expression takes on a sort of aggrieved blankness. An old habit of tactful silence, Manny guesses. "But if you are, then you are."

"Yes." Mrs. Yu opens the door more. Behind her, on one of the apartment's couches, her younger grandson is asleep. His brother sits nearby reading a school textbook as if they did not just fight for their lives that afternoon. "Real gods aren't what most of you Christians think of as gods. Gods are *people*. Sometimes dead people, sometimes still alive. Sometimes never lived." She shrugs. "They do jobs—bring fortune, look after people, make sure the world works as it should. They fall in love. Have babies. Fight. Die." She shrugs. "It's duty. It's normal. Get over it."

And there's really not much they can say to this.

Brooklyn's expression softens. "Sorry, ma'am. We've been here for a while. We should get out of your hair, shouldn't we?"

"You saved my grandsons' lives. But yes."

So they get up and file out, which necessitates going through Mrs. Yu's house. Manny takes care to thank her for the dumplings.

Aishwarya stops on the sidewalk outside, glaring at them as if they have personally conspired to trouble her. "You both will have to stay with us," she tells Brooklyn and Manny. "If our building is a safe place, and if having you around makes Padmini safer. I don't have any clothes to fit you, and there's only the floor..."

"My apartment building will work, too," Manny says. Then he grimaces. "Uh, but it might be the final straw for my roommate."

Brooklyn, however, is shaking her head. "I've got a place that should do, actually, if this whole business works the way I think it does. More than enough room for all of us. Hang on." And she takes out her phone again, turning away from them to begin dialing.

Manny wonders if she's asking her aides to create some kind of safe house for half-apotheosized cities to hide out in. Padmini is staring at him oddly, though, and he raises his eyebrows. "What?"

"I thought you were a little Punjabi, maybe, until I heard what Mrs. Yu said. What are you, then?"

"Black." It comes out instinctively, and feels true.

"You look...half-white?"

"Nope. Black."

"Black Latino or maybe Black Jewish or, what is it, Creole...?"

"Plain old ordinary Black." It feels like a familiar conversation. He *has* gotten this a lot, throughout his life. "I mean, probably other stuff besides Black somewhere back down the line, but I don't remember if I ever knew what. Or cared." He shrugs. "America."

She chuckles at this. Aishwarya is watching Brooklyn; Padmini seems to relax a little amid this reprieve from her aunty's disapproval. "Queens—the borough, I mean—looks like you, too. So many shades of 'what-are-you' brown. But…" She inhales with a little *ah*. "Manhattan has Harlem. And Central Park used to be a Black and Irish neighborhood; I read about that online somewhere. They took the land from those families to make the park. And there's that memorial downtown, at Wall Street, where they found a bunch of Africans buried in unmarked graves. Slaves. I guess some were free? But there were thousands of them, all buried under…" She grimaces. "Uh, where I work. So, what Manhattan is now, white people run so much of it, but it's literally built on the bones of Black people. And Native Americans and Chinese and Latinos and whole waves of European immigrants and… everybody. That must be why you look so… everything."

"Okay." Manny focuses on what's more interesting. "You work on Wall Street?"

At this, she slumps a little, looking disgruntled. "It isn't my fault. I'm not a citizen. To get a worker visa after graduation, my best chance is an internship with a company that can afford to pay the fees, and right now only finance and tech—"

"Whoa, it's okay, I'm sorry." Manny holds up his hands quickly. "I don't judge."

"I do." Padmini's expression settles into anger. "My employer does terrible things. I can't think about it or I won't sleep at night." She sighs. "I hate this city. That's the irony of this whole affair. Me, part of New York? That is bullshit. Such bullshit. But I've lived here for like a third of my life, and my family's hopes are all tied up in me being successful here, so… I can't leave it, either."

And that, Manny understands, is why she has become Queens.

Brooklyn turns, tucking her phone into her purse. "I just let my father know we're on the way. Everything is set up. Ready?"

Aishwarya purses her lips, reluctantly impressed by such efficiency. She eyes Padmini. "I assume you've decided to go with them?"

Padmini sighs. "Yes, that seems best. And I'm not going to get up to wild orgies or anything, I promise."

Aishwarya snorts in amusement. "Just make sure your orgy partners are US citizens, free of bad diseases, and not too old or ugly. You had better get some clothes to take with you, kunju."

"Oh, right." Padmini smiles gamely at Manny and Brooklyn, then starts toward her building. She stops, however, frowning as Manny and Brooklyn move to follow. "I'll only be five minutes."

"The Woman in White could kill you in five minutes," Manny says. "Or us, for that matter."

Padmini stares, and then probably thinks about Mrs. Yu's pool. "Fine, then," she says, and they all follow her inside.

It takes longer than five minutes. That's because, as soon as Padmini opens the front yard's gate, the garden apartment's window slides up, and a tiny old white woman peers out at them. "Paddy-me, was that you screaming?" she demands of Padmini, and Padmini goes over to crouch by the window and explain that, yes she screamed, but it was because there was a horribly big cockroach in Mrs. Yu's pool, and she just happened to be over visiting, and she *really* hates cockroaches. That seems to mollify the old woman, who mentions that she's baking some pies and will bring one up to Padmini's apartment when she's done.

"Sorry," Padmini says, looking sheepish as they move on from this.

"Ms. Kennewick does make extremely good pie," Aishwarya says to Brooklyn and Manny, in an aside. "My husband eats them like a pig."

After they climb the steps and go inside the building, it happens again. Each of the floors has been split into two small apartments. The 1A tenant is a young man whose dog they can hear barking through the door before he cracks it open, with the chain still in place. He eyes Brooklyn and Manny for a moment, then asks in a low voice if Padmini is having any "trouble." Padmini beams and assures him that she's fine and the new people are friends and everything's well. So the young man mutters an order and the dog—a very large pit bull—goes silent. Both of them continue glaring, however, until Manny and Brooklyn are out of sight.

"That was just Tony," Padmini says as they climb steps. "He's very nice. He makes me black cake in December, with *rum*, and I get so tipsy! He must be a freelancer, because he's home all day, which is why I suppose he's such a good cook. I don't know what he does for a living."

"I do," Brooklyn says with a grin at Manny.

It's like that all the way up. They don't meet 1B or 2A, both of whom are at work according to Padmini, but 2B is rented by a stoop-shouldered older Black man in a kufi, who thanks Padmini for looking after his cat the week before. When she shyly asks for a few sticks of incense, he beams and hands her some from a shelf near the door. "I've always liked this scent for when I pray," he says, clearly approving of her newly remembered spirituality.

"Her, pray?" mutters Aishwarya, but the man in the kufi doesn't hear.

"I do, too, pray," snaps Padmini, but she blushes a little and hurries on up.

The whole third floor is one family—relatives of the owner, Padmini says. The door doesn't open, but Manny can hear small children inside playing. One of them gets close to the door and yells, "It's Padmini! I hear her! I want to say hi to Padmini!" before someone else inside the house shushes him and moves him away from the door.

And somewhere between the third floor and the fourth, where Padmini lives in Aishwarya's place, Manny gets it. This is just one building amid thousands in Jackson Heights—but here, in this four-story walk-up, is a microcosm of Queens itself. People, cultures, moving in and forming communities and moving on, endlessly. In such a place, nurtured by the presence and care of its avatar, the borough's power has permeated every board and cinder block of the building, making it stronger and safer even as the city as a whole totters, weakened, against its enemy's onslaught.

It makes Manny ache, suddenly, to feel the same wholeness all over the city. Shouldn't everyone here have this? He's been here only a day, and already he's met so many vividly interesting people, seen so much beautiful strangeness. He wants to protect a city that produces such experiences. He wants to help it grow stronger. He wants to stand at its side, and be true.

There is a kind of ringing that sounds, suddenly, through his soul. He stops in the middle of climbing the steps, startled—and Brooklyn turns as well, inhaling a little. Padmini, facing the opposite direction on the next landing to lead them up, stops and shuts her eyes for a moment. He feels the reverberation between them, and it shakes him into the other space—where, for the first time, he realizes that he has never been there *as a man*. He's a city. When he stares at the strange empty streets, the damage (mostly healed now, because they are growing stronger), the wavering beautiful light, it suddenly strikes him that this is the equivalent of looking at his own navel. And in the instant that he makes this connection, his perception reels and rises and pulls back until suddenly he sees the whole of himself: he is Manhattan. And in the near distance, barely dwarfed by his own skyscrapers—another! She is Brooklyn. And beside her, close enough to join hands, sprawls a new marvel. Padmini is *enormous*, endless miles of low-story sprawl. When she turns, he hears the melodies of a thousand different instruments, sees the faceted sparkle of stained glass and industrial fiberglass and occasional specks of diamond, tastes salt and bitter earth and sharp fiery spices that bring tears to his eyes. Right there! His other selves. The city they need to be. He lifts his hands in the other world, the world of tiny people, and through the pounding of his own pulse he becomes aware of them doing the same. Yes, like this, *together*, they can be so very strong if they just—

All at once Manny's perception snaps back into his flesh-and-blood body. He stumbles on the steps and falls, clumsily enough to face-plant on a riser; blood floods his mouth. A solid ten seconds pass before Brooklyn and Padmini react; Aishwarya beats them both to it, gasping and trotting down the steps to help him sit up before the other two do the same. It's taken that long for Manny to figure out why he's on his face.

What did you expect? laughs something, not quite a voice, in his head. It's a good-natured laugh, not the malicious kind. Laughing with, not at. *You're not New York, you're Manhattan. Nice try, but pulling everyone together is his job, not yours.*

Abruptly, he is somewhere else.

Somewhere in Normal New York. Down—underground? It's dark. He glimpses white tile walls shaded with shadow, a gray concrete floor. A subway station. Smell of dust and a whiff of ozone, oddly clean of the ambiance of stale urine that Manny remembers from his one experience of the subway. Somewhere nearby, but not too nearby, a train rumbles past; in the shadows cast by a shaft of sunlight coming from somewhere above, pedestrians hurry past one another. And before him—

Before him, on a bed of ancient newspapers, curls a sleeping young man.

Manny stares down at him, transfixed. The young man is a slight figure, painfully thin, dressed in dirty jeans and worn old sneakers, his gangly-looking limbs sprawled a bit in repose. Manny cannot see his face clearly, though he is bathed in the mottled light from above. Something about the shadows, the angle ... He wills himself closer, suddenly aching to see more, but nothing happens. It isn't enough, this mere glimpse. He needs ... He needs ...

I'm his, he thinks suddenly, wildly. *I want to be ... oh, God, I want to be his. I live for him and will die for him if he requires it, and oh yes, I'll kill for him, too, he needs that, and so for him and him alone I will be again the monster that I am—*

Blink; the vision is gone. Manny finds himself sitting on the stairs again, the others around him, his mouth still full of blood, his mind blank. Padmini and Brooklyn have sat down, too, both dazed. Brooklyn glances up at him and her expression tightens minutely, in a way that Manny cannot read. A politician's poker face.

"You saw him," she says. Not a question. "So there really is a sixth. New York."

Yes. Manny swallows and nods, tonguing his bottom lip where his teeth have cut it. His nose is bleeding, too. He hears the shakiness of his own voice; it's a good match for how he's feeling all over. "So. Visions. That's new."

"*Group* visions. Yeah." Brooklyn takes a slow breath. She sounds a little shaky, too. "I'd say it was all in your head, but apparently it's in mine, too." Manny nods unhappily.

"And mine," says Padmini. Aishwarya is sitting near her now, but Padmini's still managing to look wobbly on her step. "Do either of you know where that was?"

"I've only been here one day," Manny says. He pushes himself up a bit more and pinches his nose shut, tilting his head back.

Brooklyn shakes her head, too, however. "Not a clue. Bet it's not Brooklyn, though."

"Wh—" Because the vision came to Manny most powerfully. "Oh."

"Describe it," Aishwarya says, frowning at him.

He shakes his head, too out of it to marshal his thoughts. Padmini speaks for him, and as she does so, he marvels at the clarity with which she has seen into his mind. "We were somewhere underground. A subway station, but a strange one. Dark. Except there was sunlight. And there was a boy lying on some newspapers."

Young, but not a child. Early twenties, Manny would guess. Black, dark-skinned. Lean. Probably quick when he moves.

"Newspapers?" Aishwarya looks from Padmini to the rest of them, her eyes wide. "Like a puppy or something?"

"No. Like a bed." Brooklyn rubs her eyes, then gets to her feet. "Stacks of papers, some still with the straps on. He was lying on a bed of newspapers, somewhere in a disused portion of some subway station. Which narrows it down to, oh, like twenty possible places. Hell, every now and again, we find tunnels we *forgot* over the years, so he might be in one of those. I don't even know what the hell this is about." She's watching Manny closely. "I get the sense you do, though."

"Do you want to go to a hospital? I can call a rideshare." Padmini has found a tissue somewhere on her person and is ineffectually trying to dab at Manny's nose. He takes it from her and swabs the blood off his face.

"No," he says. "Thanks. This'll stop in a minute."

"You hit that step hard. What if it's broken?"

"Not my first broken nose, if so." Manny shifts his attention over to Brooklyn. "I don't know anything more than you do. I think I saw him, *we* saw him, because there are three of us here. If we want to see more, more of us need to be together." The Bronx, or Staten Island. Or maybe all of them will need to be together before the knowledge of where the sixth one, the true New York, lights up in their minds like a HERE THERE BE DRAGONS pointer.

Brooklyn says nothing for a moment. Then she murmurs to Padmini, "Go on up and get your stuff, baby. We'll catch a Lyft or something, but still, best to travel light."

"Oh. Right." Padmini gets to her feet with Aishwarya's help, and they hurry on up the stairs. When the door to their apartment has closed, Brooklyn shifts to sit on the stair above Manny.

"You remember more about who you used to be?" she asks. It's casual.

He checks his nose. Seems unbroken. The bleeding has slowed, too. "Some." It's casual.

She purses her lips. "I, uh, got a little more from that vision than just that boy. New York, I mean. I think I picked up on some of you."

Yes, he rather suspected that she had. Padmini doesn't seem to have, but maybe she's dealing with so much strangeness that this is just more of the same. He waits for Brooklyn to make her point.

"When did you start remembering?"

"I don't. Not really." Some of that, however, is because he does not *want* to remember. His real name is on his ID, for example, but he has kept himself from looking closely at it. There are contacts in his phone that he isn't interested in calling, texts he does not mean to answer. These are choices, he understands, as meaningful as his choice to remain in the city rather than fleeing on the next train to God knows where. He can be who he was if he wants to be, but only up to a point. Something about the old him is incompatible with the new identity that the city wants him to have. So he has chosen to be Manhattan, whatever that might cost.

"Hmm," Brooklyn says. Noncommittal. Leaving him space.

Manny's tired. It's been a long day.

"I used to hurt people," he says, sitting back against the stairwell wall and gazing into the middle distance between them. "That's what you want to know, isn't it? I don't remember everything. I don't remember *why*, but I remember that much. Sometimes I did it physically. More often, I just scared them into doing what I needed them to do. But for a threat to have any teeth, sometimes . . . I followed through. I was good at it. *Efficient*." Then he sighs, closing his eyes for a moment. "But I'd made the choice not to be that person anymore. I remember that, in particular. That's why most people leave their old lives and come to the big city, right? New start. New self. It's just turning out to be a little more literal for me than for most people."

"Mmm," she says, taking a deep breath. "Serial killer?"

"No." He doesn't remember feeling pleasure in the things he did. But he does remember that causing pain and fear was as easy for him as terrorizing Martha Blemins had been, in the park. Meaningless. He's not sure that's any better than being a serial killer. "It was...a job, I think. I did it for power, and maybe money."

But somewhere along the way, he'd chosen to stop. He clings to this proof of his humanity as if it is the only thing that matters. Because it is.

"Well, that's pretty damn fitting, for Manhattan." He can feel the weight of her gaze. "You've got some weird feelings about that young man."

Manny sighs a little. He'd been hoping she hadn't gotten that, too. Some things should remain private, for God's sake.

"Sorry," she says. "I wasn't exactly expecting to get yanked into, I don't know, a Vulcan mind-meld or whatever, so I didn't think to, uh, not look. Hope you didn't get any of me."

"I don't think so."

"Good." She folds her arms and leans on her knees. Her legs are primly aligned, her skirt not at all rucked up; she is the picture of elegance in this ugly, wood-paneled old stairway. But that's worry on her elegant face. "So, between us, I'm getting a bad feeling about what happens if and when all six of us finally get together. If that was a taste of it...I don't think I want five other people in my head."

Manny shrugs. He doesn't, either, but it's becoming increasingly clear that they must find one another, or die. "Maybe it won't be so bad when we find the—the New York. Maybe he'll... regulate it. Or something."

"You're very optimistic for a possible serial killer. I like that about you."

It makes him laugh, which he apparently needed, because he feels much better. "How are you doing with all this, apart from existential dread?"

She shrugs, but he's good at reading people. It must have been a professional skill for him once. She's terrified, in her quietly elegant way. "I'd think about leaving—not that I want to, of course. New York is my home. Fought for this city all my life. But just to keep my father and my daughter out of the line of fire, you know? I'm doing this instead, for now, because seeing this through offers a possibility for both: help the city *and* keep my family safe. But if things get too tight . . ." She shrugs eloquently. "Not sure I love New York enough to die for it. Definitely don't love it enough to sacrifice my family for it."

"You said your daughter was fourteen."

"Yep. Can't nobody tell her nothing." Brooklyn relaxes visibly with the change of subject, and smiles with fond exasperation. "Dad says she's payback for all my lip when I was her age. But she's got a good head on her shoulders, too. Just like her mama."

Manny chuckles. He can't remember whether he was mouthy growing up, but it's nice to imagine that he might have been. "Anything I can do to help your family, I will."

Her expression softens. Maybe she likes him a little more. "And I hope you get to become the person you actually *want* to be," she says, which makes him blink. "This city will eat you alive, you know, if you let it. Don't."

Then she gets up, because Padmini is coming out of her apartment, still trying to stuff things into a backpack while Aishwarya hands her things she's forgotten and bags of food. Brooklyn moves to help. While the women murmur and work together on getting the pack zipped, Manny chews on Brooklyn's words. They feel like a warning of many things.

Then the women come down, and he gets up to take any baggage that Padmini will let him carry, which isn't much, though

Aishwarya readily plonks two filled reusable grocery bags on his arms and a tiffin stack into his hands. "Ready," Padmini says, looking at them anxiously. "And, ah, I have dinner for us, if you want. Also, I called my supervisor and let him know I won't be able to come in to my internship for the next few days. I now have the flu." She coughs a little, experimentally. "You get a cough with the flu, don't you?"

"Sometimes," says Manny, fighting a smile.

"Oh. Well, I did mention a fever of 110 and that I had my period, too. He'll think I'm delirious from one or the other."

"Get well soon," Brooklyn says drily. "Let's go, then."

They catch a Lyft that carries them along the Brooklyn-Queens Expressway. The nighttime cityscape of Manhattan is perfectly positioned for Manny to stare at for most of the drive, and he does so greedily, fascinated despite the knowledge that he is staring at himself. He's a little overwhelmed by all of it: the bright, startling order of the highway, even as half of its drivers seem determined to run their own private speed races. The high-rises that loom over or alongside the highway, and the fleeting vignette glimpses he gets into other people's lives: a couple arguing in front of an ugly painting of a boat; a roomful of people, which must be a dinner party; an old man pointing a remote at a TV with both hands and yelling. At one point their highway runs between two other highways, underneath a third, and alongside a service road that's actually bigger. It's madness. It's amazing.

It's nothing more than what any large city has...and yet it *is* more. Manny feels the pump and life of it. When he rolls down the window, he sticks his face out as much as the seat belt allows, and inhales the rushing air. (The driver gives him a skeptical look, but shrugs and says nothing.) He lets this breath out, and the wind gusts hard enough to shake the car a little, making the driver curse and Brooklyn clap a hand over her hair to keep it from being too messed up by the open window. She throws him a warning look, knowing full well what he's been up to, and he smiles back apologetically.

He can't help it, though. He is falling in love with a city, and men in love are not always considerate or wise.

When they arrive at the address Brooklyn has given the driver, it's deep in a neighborhood that the map calls Bedford Stuyvesant. They emerge from the car to face a pair of brownstones, stately narrow things, which seem to have been similarly renovated and decorated. One is still in the traditional style, with an ironwork gate opening onto a stoop of steps; there's even a historical landmark plaque beside its first-floor door. The other, however, has been modified: no steps, no gate, and the garden apartment door opens directly onto a pretty brick-lined and plant-strewn courtyard. The arched double-door entryway is much wider than that of the other brownstone, and its doors are more modern. Manny spots an automatic door-opener button to one side.

Padmini whistles. "This is very rich," she says, admiring the building. Then, to Brooklyn: "*You're* very rich."

Brooklyn snorts, although she also stops on the sidewalk to let them gawk, plainly enjoying their admiration. And, Manny notes, she doesn't deny the "rich" part. "We'll be staying there," she says, nodding to the traditional brownstone. "Unless either of you have issues with steps? My family lives in the accessible one; Dad uses a wheelchair. You'll get a little fourteen-year-old attitude from my daughter, but if you don't mind that, we can all crash there, too."

"I'd love to meet your family, but steps are fine," Manny says.

Padmini agrees, so Brooklyn leads them up the steps of the traditional brownstone.

Inside, Padmini's *very rich* gets compounded with *and stylish*. Someone's renovated the place; original details like a fireplace (with a marble mantel!) and a carpeted, mahogany-bannistered stairwell have been joined by a modernist chandelier that looks like a frozen explosion, and trendy furniture that's too visually striking to be entirely comfortable. Manny likes it anyway.

And best of all: the instant they walk inside the building, Manny feels a skin-shivering return of the sensation they felt in Padmini's and his own apartment buildings. The architectural lines look sharper, the walls' texture finer. The light brightens just a touch; the room smells fresher.

"Yeah, thought so," Brooklyn says, grinning. "Ain't nothing more Brooklyn than a brownstone, baby."

"Are you in real estate?" Padmini asks, still a bit wide-eyed.

"Not really. Only own these two buildings. I grew up here, see." Brooklyn sighs as she slips her shoes off. Manny and Padmini quickly follow suit. "Dad bought both buildings in the Seventies. Just sixty grand for this whole entire building. The city was struggling in those days. White people ran off to the suburbs because they didn't want their kids going to school alongside little José and Jaquita, so the same bad economy that hit everywhere else did double damage here. But Dad held on to the buildings, even when the property taxes nearly ate us alive. When I was fourteen, I was snaking toilets and moving furniture. Jojo don't know how good she's got it."

"Your daughter?" asks Padmini.

"Right. Short for Josephine, named after Baker." Brooklyn shakes her head, then grins. "Anyway, now both buildings are worth millions." She grins and beckons for them to follow as she starts giving them a tour. "Just managed to finish the accessibility mods to the other building before the whole block went historic-landmark, thank God, or I'd still be in a paperwork fight with the city. And I still had to promise to never modify this one, to soothe all the ruffled feathers."

"People had a problem with you making a brownstone that a wheelchair user could live in?"

She snorts. "Welcome to New York." She gestures to the airy, crown-molding-accented kitchen. "Anyway, we rent this one out to tourists for the extra income." She shakes her head in amusement. "'Historic townhome! City views! Vintage accents!' Five thousand per unit per month, bam, and more during special events or holiday seasons. Dad calls it the 'Clyde Thomason Pension Backup Fund,' since the city keeps threatening to take 'em away."

Brooklyn shows them each to a neat little guest room, and orders Chinese for dinner. Queens has the meal that Aishwarya packed for her, but she nibbles from the fried rice, and freely shares the fragrant lamb curry and idlis from her tiffin. It's a humble, quiet supper as they sit around the kitchen island, but it's such a relief to just be able to relax for a while that Manny savors it.

He does feel guilt because, somewhere in the city, the avatars of the Bronx and Staten Island are alone, possibly afraid, and definitely in danger. And somewhere beneath them all—in the subways, in the dark—the avatar of New York slumbers alone on a bed of trash, with no one to keep him warm. No one to protect him.

Not for long, Manny vows privately. *I'll find you soon.*

And then . . . well. Manny came to New York because he no

longer wanted to be what he was. The city has taken his name and his past, but only because he was willing to give those up in the first place. Perhaps he should not be ashamed that the city has laid claim to the rest as well, including the parts he thought undesirable or unsavory. Of course New York would find a use for those. No city can exist without someone like him—this city in particular cannot—and maybe it's time he accepted that.

And is it so terrible to be terrible, if he puts all the awfulness of himself into the service of the city?

It is unexpectedly comforting, this possibility. When he settles down to rest, he drops off to sleep almost immediately, and dreams eight million beautifully ruthless dreams.

INTERRUPTION

The instant Paulo climbs out of the cab, he knows what he's seeing. The apartment building is unobtrusive in nearly every way, except that it is *more Queens* than any other part of the sprawling borough that Paulo has seen. It has become the locus for a city avatar's power.

He can also sense the prickle of the Enemy's work nearby—but somehow, unlike Inwood, this breach has done less harm. After the cab leaves (with a substantial bill, since Paulo told the man to drive around a bit so that he could pinpoint the area of disturbed dimensional integrity), he slips down the narrow dark gap between the framework houses, and hops over the chain-link fence so that he can get a better look at the site. An aging plastic aboveground pool. It has the same pale, acrid scent as whatever infected the monument rock at Inwood. More power has been applied here, decisively and precisely, excising the infection with a surgical efficiency that Paulo cannot help but reluctantly admire. Between this and its proximity to the apartment building locus, and possibly other factors that Paulo cannot fathom, it seems unlikely that this site will attract... hangers-on.

He hears a voice calling in Chinese to someone else within the house, and quickly he exits the backyard. At the apartment building, he presses the buzzer for the topmost apartment, meaning to work his way down. When an indistinct feminine voice, fuzzy with feedback, murmurs through the intercom speaker, he says, "I'm looking for someone who knows about what happened to the pool in the backyard next door."

There is a pause. Then the voice says, again indistinctly, "[Something something] ICE? We're here legally, and whichever [something] reported us can go to hell!"

"I'm most definitely not with ICE, the police, or any organization you've ever heard of." Paulo steps back, onto the building's walkway, so that anyone looking out the window can get a good look at him in the walkway lighting. He sees someone at the window, but they're there and gone too quickly for him to discern. Going back to the intercom, he debates whether to ring the apartment doorbell again or move on to the next floor. Then there is another indistinct murmur through the speaker, and the building's front door buzzes to let him in.

On the fourth floor, a plump fortysomething woman in a sari cracks open the door to peer at him, without bothering to take the chain lock off. Paulo can see a middle-aged man in the background, on his feet and scowling belligerently, with a baby's feeding bottle in one fist. The woman is defensive, too, but Paulo understands this. Everyone is wary of strangers, in a city.

Her gaze rakes him as he reaches the top landing of the stairs. "You don't have permission to enter," she says at once.

"I only want to speak," he says. "I can stand right here and do that."

This makes her relax fractionally. "What now?" she asks, in accented, annoyed English. "Are you a reporter? I heard that someone mentioned it on Twitter, but it's still hard to believe you've come about a pool. It's the middle of the night."

"My name is São Paulo," he says, expecting it to mean nothing to her. Most of the Americans he meets have never even heard of him. Or else they think he's part of California. "I'm looking for—"

Her gasp catches him by surprise. "They *said*—oh. You're real?"

He lifts an eyebrow. "Quite real, yes." There's only one reason she would ask such a question. "You've seen things that aren't real lately?"

She shrugs. "Craziness. Everywhere in this city. But most recently, next door, yesterday. Other people came, who talked about the craziness. They were ... like you." She narrows her eyes at Paulo then, as if trying to discern something she cannot articulate. "I don't know."

"Other people?"

"One was, mmm, Manny? I think that was the name. The other was Brooklyn Thomason, one of those city council people. Tall and Black, both of them, fair man and dark woman. They said our Padmini was Queens."

They've begun to find each other, even without his help. Paulo can't help smiling. "And they've left? Can you tell me where ...?"

She tilts her head, thoughtful, and her gaze is suddenly shrewd. The man in the background has come forward and now stands just behind her, and their stances are alike: subtly protective. The man follows the woman's lead, however, and the woman says, "Who are you to ask, then? They said something was hunting them. Some*one*. A woman."

Paulo's skin prickles all over, as it did at the Inwood rock, and by the suspicious swimming pool. Could the Enemy have reactualized harbingers already? It is as if the birthing-battle did nothing. "That should not be," he says, slowly and softly. "But...hunting. Yes. I believe that's true." New cities usually had very healthy survival instincts, because they had to. If the avatars of New York believed that a hostile foreign presence was hunting them down, they were probably right. "A woman, you said?"

Her mouth pulls to one side. "I suppose you're not a woman. Still, why should I tell you anything?"

"Because I'm here to help them."

"Lot of good you've done so far."

Paulo inclines his head in acknowledgment of this. It's not an apology. "Truthfully there isn't much I can do," he says. "My task is to advise. In the end, the battle is theirs to fight, and survive. But I can't even advise them if I can't find them—and any knowledge, at this stage, will help. They need every bit of help they can get."

The woman considers this. Paulo thinks his honesty has helped; she doesn't have a high opinion of him, but at least it's marginally positive. Her husband murmurs in her ear in some other language, and even without translating the words, Paulo can recognize a *Don't tell him anything, we don't know who this man is*.

The woman nods a little, but there is a sad look on her face as she regards Paulo again. "I can't help her, either," she says at last. "She's my cousin's daughter. Smart girl, good, pretty when she bothers to try, but they sent her here alone, can you believe it? It was all they could afford. And only us to look after her."

"She has more people to help her now," Paulo says, as gently as he can. Her concern is genuine. He can't reassure her, sadly. If this woman's cousin is indeed the avatar of Queens, then she is in terrible danger and might not survive. But Paulo can be truthful about this much. "A city is never alone, not really—and this city seems less solitary than most. More like a family: many parts, frequently squabbling . . . but in the end, against enemies, they come together and protect one another. They *must*, or die." The woman is watching him now, sorrow giving way to fascination. "There are five other people out there who will be this for her. Six, if you let me help."

After a long moment, she sighs. "They were tired," she says. "Hungry. They went to Brooklyn—with Brooklyn—to rest for the night."

They should not be either tired or hungry. Nothing about this city's birth is going as it should. Paulo restrains a sigh and says, "That could be good. If they know how to create protective loci . . ." He glances around at the walls of the apartment building's corridor, seeing more than the ugly wood paneling. In a place protected in this manner, they would be proof against attack. Safer, together, than they could ever be with Paulo. He nods to himself. "Then the three of them can take care of one another, for now. But that leaves two alone." The Bronx. Staten Island.

"They said they would go to the Bronx in the morning. It sounded like they had an idea of where to look."

It leaves the avatar of the Bronx to fend for themselves until then, but if the others have some inkling of the avatar's location, then they're doing better at tracking each other down than Paulo is. "What of Staten Island?"

"What about it?" The woman looks skeptical now. "They said they didn't know how to find that one."

Staten Island is the smallest borough, according to Wikipedia. Geographically vast, but only a few hundred thousand people in population. There's a chance that Paulo might find the avatar simply by going there and driving around, if he rents a car. Cities—even small ones—make a weight upon the world. With enough proximity, one can feel the pull they exert.

"Then I'll begin there," Paulo says. He reaches into a lapel pocket, past the half-empty pack of cigarettes, and pulls out a business card. Paulistanos are infamous workaholics; other Brazilians joke about their obsession with meetings and office politics and all the trappings of business. There is a touch of power in the card when he hands it to her, but he does not attempt to expend that power. She's not one of his, after all, and Queens is likely to take it poorly if Paulo gets pushy with her relatives. He merely says, "Please give your cousin that number when you speak to her again. The country code for the call, assuming she has an American phone, will be fifty-five."

She takes the card and frowns at it. There's nothing on it except, in elegant block capitals, the words MR. SÃO PAULO, and a phone number. Underneath the name, though above the number, is a smaller subhead: CITY REPRESENTATIVE. "Why should she have to make an expensive international call to talk to you? Get an American phone."

"Forcing others to acknowledge my point of origin provides a latent strengthening effect." She draws back a little, utterly confused. Paulo nods to her, and to her husband, then turns to go.

"Is that all, then? Just call you?"

"Yes." Then Paulo stops at the top of the steps. "No. Tell her to text me the location of the Bronx, and I'll meet them there after I've found Staten Island."

"They said they didn't know exactly where the Bronx—"

"They will." That they've managed to find each other thus far is proof that the city is helping them, however weakly—pricking their intuition, calling their attention to seemingly innocuous details or facts, guarding their places of rest. That won't be enough to keep them safe for long, but it helps. They need every bit of help they can get.

The woman shakes her head, sighing. "She has studies. A job, a life. When will all of this be *over?*"

"When they find the primary avatar," Paulo says. But this feels like a lie. Something strange is happening in this city—something he's never seen before, and that the others have never mentioned. No way to be certain that it will end when the city is whole, because nothing here has gone the way it should. So he amends, "I hope."

Then he heads off, to track down the smallest borough.

CHAPTER EIGHT

No Sleep in (or Near) Brooklyn

Brooklyn tells herself that she's just crashing in the vacation unit to be polite. Padmini's stressed out, poor child, considering she only just learned about all this city business a few hours ago. And Manhattan—despite being a scary motherfucker behind that nice face of his—is still a new kid in the big city. Brooklyn tells herself that she's sticking around in case they need anything.

It's a lie, though. The bed she's lying on is new, with a fancy European-style mattress and one-thousand-thread-count sheets, but it's still her old bedroom. And as Brooklyn settles in to rest, having cracked open the window so she can listen to the night sounds of the city—crickets and passing cars and the soft laughter and music of a house party somewhere on the next block—she finds herself needing comfort, too, and finding it in the familiarity of the old walls, the old ceiling, the old scent of the place that's still there, ever so faintly, underneath the new paint and hardwood floors. Back in the day, her room would've been sweltering; they couldn't afford air-conditioning units or the resulting electric bills, just fans. And Brooklyn would've been looking at the night sky through burglar bars, which everyone needed at the height of the crack epidemic. Still. Back then she had been a teenage girl so full of dreams, whose only real worries were passing the Regents and not getting knocked up by her boyfriend of the time. (What was his name? Jermaine? Jerman? Something with a J. Lord, she couldn't even remember.) She hadn't yet become MC Free, vanguard of a movement; she was just a kid trying out freestyle lyrics in the dark, forgetting half the best ones because she kept falling asleep in the middle of composition.

And back then, she sure hadn't been expecting to transform into a goddamn living embodiment of this wild, incredible, stupid-ass city.

But there is a kind of poetry to the whole situation that Brooklyn accepts—because this wild, incredible, stupid-ass city has given her so much. That's why she ran for city council, after all: because she believes that only people who actually love New York, versus those merely occupying and exploiting it, should dictate what it is and becomes. Becoming a borough is just the literalization of something she's always done, so she's okay with it. More than she ever expected to be.

She knows who it is as soon as the phone rings. "Are you coming home?" asks Jojo, in a carefully bored tone so as to let Brooklyn know she doesn't actually care. It's cool. She's fourteen, which she thinks is almost grown, so she absolutely resolutely does not miss her mama.

"I'm right next door."

"Which is why I asked if you were coming *home*."

Brooklyn sighs, although it's fond. "I told you. This place still feels like home to me, baby. Just let me have this for a little while, okay?"

Jojo's sigh is almost a match for her own, but Brooklyn hears the amusement in it. "You're so weird, Mama." Then, in the background of the phone, Brooklyn hears her getting up and doing something involving a grunt and a wooden rattle—oh. Opening her window, too. "I guess you used to look out at this view and think up lyrics?"

"Mostly I just looked at the sky. Did you finish that paper you were supposed to do for English?"

"Yes, Mama. Five paragraphs, just the way the SAT likes it." Singsong boredom. "I miss Ms. Fountain, who used to let us write *interesting* stuff."

Brooklyn agrees. Jojo has gotten into one of the coveted specialized high schools of the city, Brooklyn Latin. It's a more old-fashioned school than Brooklyn likes—actual classes in Latin and uniforms and other stuff that would've made Brooklyn herself vomit at that age, but Jojo chose it, and she's mostly thriving there. The beloved Ms. Fountain, like a lot of teachers in the city who don't want to squeeze in with roommates for the rest of their lives, decided to accept triple the pay from a tony private school up in Westchester—and Brooklyn can't blame her one bit for that. She feels sorry for Jojo, though, and the other public school kids who've lost a good thing.

"Well, that's why I proposed that program I told you about," she says to Jojo. "To help public school teachers get affordable housing."

"Mmm-hmm." It's not really disinterest. Jojo is usually more invested in Brooklyn's current life as a politician than she is in Brooklyn's past life as a rapper, which makes Brooklyn very happy. The girl is distracted now, though. Over the phone, there's another sound: the cell phone bumping up against a window screen. "I can't see anything."

"You gotta open the screen, baby."

"Ew, Mama, mosquitoes will get in! I'll get West Nile malaria."

"Then you better kill them. The sky over the city has too much light, baby. You can see the stars a little, but you gotta work for them." Brooklyn grins. "Can't let anything stand between you and what you want."

"Is this another lecture about goals? You said you were gonna stop lecturing me about goals."

"It's a lecture about the stars." And also goals.

There is a moment's pause while she hears Jojo rattling the screen and finally getting it up. "Oooh. I do see ... three stars in a row. That's Orion's belt, isn't it?"

"Probably." Now it's Brooklyn's turn to go wrestle with her bedroom window. Fortunately she had the shitty, paint-crusted old single-panes replaced during a gut renovation a few years back; the new double-paned windows are much easier to open. Once she's raised the screen and poked her head outside, she looks up. "Oh, yeah. Definitely Orion."

Then she looks over. The two buildings have flush back ends. In the dark, her daughter's silhouette waves at her, and she waves back.

Then Brooklyn pauses as she notices something else in the dark, down in the paved backyard of the other building, where her father sometimes likes to barbecue for the family. At other times of year it's mostly just occupied by an old ironwork table and some uncomfortable chairs, and a lot of dead plants in pots. (Her father gets after her for those, but she's busy. Green thumbs take time she doesn't have.) She keeps meaning to get a landscaping company in, have them do something interesting with the space.

Right now, however, there is a strange glowing thing stretched over one corner of the yard.

She leans farther out the window, frowning as she tries to figure out what that is. Did somebody string up a tangle of neon tape? Do they even make such a thing? But this does not have the slightly yellow glow of things made with luminescent dye. It's untinted white and ghostly, and seems to waver a little as she looks at it, as if it isn't quite there.

Then it moves.

Brooklyn jerks violently, and there is a terrifying instant in which she tips a little, where she's balanced herself against the bottom windowsill in order to lean out. It would only be a one-story fall, but people have died from less. She catches herself, fortunately, and gets a grip on the window frame, though her hand has gone sweaty and numb with chill.

Because now that she's gotten a good look at it, there is something like a three-foot-wide spider moving around the backyard that her daughter leans out over. It has only four legs—if those even qualify as legs. They don't taper. They don't bend as they come away from the tiny central body; the whole creature must just be lying on the ground, spread out along the concrete flagstones in a flat cross. That's all it is. But when it moves, it is vaguely spiderlike, contracting into a single flat line and then scissoring out into four lines again, all joined at a small rounded hub. An eldritch daddy longlegs, brought to you by the letter X.

And then another scrabbles over the chain-link fence, between tendrils of her neighbors' gone-wild grapevine. The creature pauses for a moment, one leg sticking straight up as if to test the air.

The phone is still in her hand. Her mouth dry, Brooklyn pulls it back to her face. "Jojo. Go inside."

"What?" She can see her daughter, still looking up, start a little.

"Whoa!" For an instant she loses her balance, too, and Brooklyn suffers a horrified second of fearing that she will watch her only child tumble into the backyard with those things. But Jojo catches herself as her mother has already done, then looks around. "You see something, Mama?"

"Yes. Go inside! Shut your window and move away from it." Better still—"Go to Dad's room. Get him up and in his chair."

"Oh, shit," Jojo says, and immediately darts inside. She's a smart child when she isn't being a smart-ass—and she is herself a true child of New York, enough to know that Brooklyn doesn't warn of danger without good reason. Under the circumstances, Brooklyn's going to overlook the profanity.

The moment Jojo slides the window closed—with a loud thump—the white X-spiders in the backyard react, shivering and then x-ing forward a few steps. There are three now, Brooklyn sees; another has just folded its front two legs over the lip of a wooden planter that it was apparently hidden behind. She's guessed what they are now, though. They have a different shape from the white feathers that menaced her at the 2 train station and surrounded Manhattan in Inwood Hill Park, but they feel of the same prickling, jangling *antithesis of presence* that everything else associated with the Enemy seems to radiate. As if they erase some tiny part of New York with every iota of its space they occupy.

And now there are six of them in her family's backyard.

Brooklyn runs to the bedroom door and down the hall. She hears a startled snort from one of the guest rooms as her feet drum down the corridor; Manhattan, waking from sleep. Can't wait for him to help, for whatever good he'd be. She's only wearing satin pajamas, no shoes, and carrying no gun, not that she ever would, given how many friends she's lost to things like that. All she's got is an illegal-in-the-city-of-New-York collapsible baton—which she snatches from the umbrella stand as she runs past—and fear for her daughter and father, which have so charged her with adrenaline that she feels as if she could tear apart ten men bare-handed. But what's menacing her little girl isn't men.

Oh, but, baby. You know how to handle up on these things, too, laughs the city in her mind as she wrenches open the apartment door and the outside door and runs down the brownstone's stoop steps. Her bare feet slap on the sidewalk as she jumps the gate—too damn old to do stuff like that without suffering tomorrow, but she manages the vault credibly, thank God for her personal trainer—and then she stops. She's panting, shaking, and utterly horrified as she turns to face both buildings and finally understands the depth of her mistake.

Because when Brooklyn came home, to this block that is hers and to these buildings that are hers in this borough that is so much hers that deep down she would've been surprised if someone else had gotten the job of becoming it, *she did not go inside* the brownstone that her father and daughter now occupy, along with a few tenants on the upper floors. She didn't need to, because she always keeps a few clothes and toiletries in the vacation unit. And so, when the peculiar power of the city filled the brownstone that she did enter, suffusing it with *Brooklyn-ness* and making it impregnable against the incursions of the Enemy, she had simply assumed that the power would encompass both brownstones. But the power does not recognize property ownership—and worse, the modified brownstone has been shorn of the stoop that once connected it to the neighborhood. This amputation is a still-healing wound that makes the building even more susceptible to attack by foreign organisms. She should've been even more careful to protect this one.

And because of Brooklyn's folly, now *dozens* of white X-spiders twitch-crawl over the entire building's facade. As Brooklyn watches, one of them drops onto the brick pathway and then x-wriggles under the front door, passing through the crack as easily as a sheet of paper.

Brooklyn knows not to panic. That's how people get killed when the bullets start flying—and this is a trap, she knows, just as much as Mrs. Yu's pool was for Padmini. This is how the Enemy has lured her out of the safe building. Instead of giving in to the urge to hyperventilate or scream or run blindly into danger, she closes her eyes. Tries to think something other than *Sweet Jesus one of those things is in there with my baby*. She listens to her own panting breath, which hitches because she's not *that* in shape, and she prays for her city to help her somehow because God hasn't come through yet. And that is how she finally notices

pant (gasp) pant pant (gasp)

A perfect b-girl backbeat, which some part of her mind has noticed even amid her terror.

That's all she needs. Because she has been trained in the use of *this* weapon. She is a veteran of these sorts of battles. And if she must find a way to transform her old weapons into a new form? Then it's done.

Swagger first. She squares herself, pushes back her shoulders, bounces a little on the balls of her feet. Okay. Here she goes.

"'Battle Brooklyn? Well, let's go.'" She whispers this aloud, to focus her mind. They are the lyrics that first made her famous—but already she is spinning new lines, remixing what she needs from aether and the memory of an entire catalog of musical history. Even as she thinks the next words, she feels the power come on, shaped more by her mind than anything else. The words are just a conduit—a construct, to which she's already given a shape. A myth. A legend. The heroic power to tear apart ten men, or fifty fucked-up extradimensional spider monsters, with extreme prejudice.

You thinking I should go high? Nah! I go low.

She's running at the building. Shouldering the door, low, at the lock to break it open. (It shouldn't work. The door is heavy old wood in a metal frame. But the city has entered her bones and strengthened her muscles; she *will not* be denied.) Just beyond the door, the invading X-spider has already woven its web: lines of white, ugly light crisscrossing and tangling from the floor to the ceiling, forming a net meant to ensnare her for doing just this thing. Up close, Brooklyn can see that the lines aren't just light. They are living things themselves, strands that whisper and shiver, covered in weird little holes like the thorns of roses turned inward—But she is *Brooklyn*, goddamn it, and when she makes claws of her hands and slashes at the spider-strands like a cat, a sheath of power surrounds and protects her fingers as the webs tear and burn away to ash. She hears the spider—because web and creature are one and the same—shriek once, and then go silent.

I'm the core of this city, either live or compost.

Your appealing lines really? Like rinds your rhymes tossed.

There is another shriek, from further into the apartment. Jojo. In her father's bedroom.

There ain't no way, no level you could defeat this.

I'm a queen, a boss, with no weakness. / I'm Superman, but the kryptonite don't work. I'm too advanced, you tyke.

Brooklyn runs in to find Jojo and her father all right—but not for long, because a big X-spider is sliding into the room between the frames of the window. The damn things are infinitely two-dimensional when they want to be. But as two of its legs finish the slide through and spread out to brace against the wall, its body puffs up and the legs become thicker, cylindrical things again. And now Brooklyn sees that the little holes all over its legs are *moving*. They are tiny, tooth-ringed mouths gawping open and shut—

...*Go do your homework*, Brooklyn thinks savagely, before she charges forward and slams her palm against the thing's fat middle body. It looks translucent, as visually insubstantial as the feather things—but there is something solid under Brooklyn's power-sheathed palm for just an instant, cold and buzzing and jittery and feeling less like something alive than like a sack of infinitesimal Legos tumbling apart and trying to re-form under her hand. Around her hand. *Incorporating* her hand.

What Brooklyn is, though, defies the thing's attempts. She's one woman—but in this instant she is *also* two and a half million people, fifty trillion moving parts, the biggest and baddest borough of the greatest city in the world. And the stuff that binds her—the will and allegiance and collective strength that screams, *We are Brooklyn*—is far, far more powerful than the force that holds the X-spider together.

So when her hand crushes the X-spider, it catches fire in a brief blue-white flare that Brooklyn barely feels. An instant later, it shrivels away like the web did. It is more than dead. Brooklyn has annihilated it.

Then, with a shout, Brooklyn drops and slaps both hands against the floor. This is *her* floor. Her house, her family, her city, and oh how *dare* these fucking things invade it—

Now take it end to end and run it back again. And every time that I see you, you catch a smack again. Send you home running and crying, another ass whoopin'.

—and the wave of city-energy that ripples from her hands and throughout the building is so intense, so pure, that the entirety of New York shivers and rings with one soundless tone. For an instant she is tempted to merge herself into that harmony, lay claim to the whole city as Manhattan tried and failed to do...but no. She is content to be just Brooklyn. It's always been enough for her to be able to take care of what's hers.

So she *feels* the X-spiders crawling all over the building, and she feels it, too, when they stop and shriek as they are destroyed by wavelets of Brooklyn-ness cascading forth from the old brownstones. And the block, and the neighborhood. Bed Stuy, do or die. Crown Heights, stand up. Flatbush, represent. She lays claim to all of it, from Greenpoint to Coney Island, Brooklyn Heights to East New York. She wills the contamination that has spread over so much of her city to die. It ain't gotta go home, but it *gots* to get the fuck out of Brooklyn.

It works—but that's all she can do. When the wave of energy reaches the borders of the borough, Brooklyn can push it no farther. Even doing this much—alone, without the support of the others—leaves her utterly drained. She collapses to the floor in a heap, barely aware of Jojo's hands as the girl runs over to her, hearing her father call her name but lacking the strength to reply.

She grins to herself, however, even as her vision darkens and she hears Manhattan come thumping in. "Still got it," she murmurs.

Jojo's panicking. "Got what? Mama? Granddaddy, I can't get her to sit up—"

"Let her rest," says Manhattan. Brooklyn feels his hand touch hers, and something from him flows into her. She twitches a little in reaction, because so much of him disturbs her on a fundamental level—but his voice is kind, and it is good to know that she doesn't fight alone. The infusion of strength is enough to pull her from the brink of something like a coma back to merely exhausted sleep. She understands with the clarity of epiphany that this is a lesser version of what they'll all need to do for the one who embodies the whole of New York City, whenever they find him. Their touch will strengthen him the same way, and he will in turn strengthen them all. Then they can protect the whole city. Soon. Good.

And as she drifts off to sleep, she smiles as, this time, she makes sure to finish her victorious rhyme.

. . . So think again before you ever try to pass Brooklyn.

It's late afternoon the next day before Brooklyn finally drags herself out of bed. So much for getting an early start on finding the Bronx.

But then she comes into the family kitchen to find Jojo, her father, Padmini, Manhattan, and even the family cat, Sweater, sitting around the living room table in silence. They're staring at some kind of business letter, which sits open on the coffee table; her father must have pulled it from the day's mail.

"What's going on?" Brooklyn asks, shuffling forward. She's moving but still tired, and half the muscles in her body ache from overuse. Too goddamn old to fight transdimensional rap battles in the middle of the night. But she comes alert a moment later as her mind processes what she's seeing. The Certified Mail postcard on the back of the torn-open envelope. The furious look on her father's face. "Dad? What—"

"This is an official notice of eviction," Clyde Thomason says.

"*Eviction?* That's bullshit, Dad. We're not renters. These buildings have been paid off for years."

Jojo seems so shaken that Brooklyn goes over and puts a hand on her shoulder. The girl says, "Yeah, but some kind of city agency says we didn't pay arrears on taxes, or something—"

Brooklyn can't help it; she chuckles. Her family has always made fun of her control-freakish eagerness to pay all of her bills as soon as she can. She doesn't like having the weight of unpaid debts hanging over her head. "This is a joke. Somebody's fucking with us, Dad. Check the ID, the spelling of the name, it's probably a mistake."

"I called the city." He picks up the letter and shakes it. "Took an hour, but I actually talked to a person. *They got the deeds.* This building and the other, both have been *sold*, right out from under us. Something about a third-party transfer of title, or something..." His voice breaks. He's holding it together, but Brooklyn knows her father; he's on the brink. "And we have until next week to move out, or they'll come with marshals to *throw* us out."

Too stunned to think of a response, Brooklyn takes the letter to read. It's true, she realizes as she reads it. Her home is not her home. It has been stolen, the goods sold before the crime's victims even noticed the theft.

And the most brazen part of it? The thief's name is right there on the letter, big as day: the Better New York Foundation.

CHAPTER NINE

A Better New York Is in Sight

No one burns down the Center overnight, and the keyholders report no suspicious or hostile activity when Bronca comes in late that morning. She's only half-awake, after having spent a fitful and uneasy night at home; nothing attacked, but she worried, and now she's got under-eye baggage as souvenirs. There's a message on her office voice mail from the board's development chair, Raul: "Bronca, I respect your opinion about the Alt Artistes' collective. We can't promote bigotry of any kind. But like I told Jess, the collective is connected to a prospective donor, who—"

"Blah blah blah blah," Bronca says, hanging up with the message unfinished. It's always blah with Raul. Bronca's still appalled at Yijing for sleeping with him. Granted, Bronca is only lukewarm on dick at the best of times, but not even four-alarm dick is worth that much aggravation.

There were two other messages in the voice mail box, but Bronca decides to listen to those after she's had time to calm down and wake up. She grabs her morning coffee from the machine in the break room, then starts her usual post-opening walk-through of the Center.

It's easy for a nonprofit administrator to lose touch with her purpose. Life can become nothing but grant applications and payroll problems, supply orders and fund-raising schmoozes, if one isn't careful. Bronca's an artist, so she takes pains to keep art foremost in her routine, if not her mind, every day.

Today she heads for their newest and most interesting exhibit. This one is a kind of summons, she's always thought—and before yesterday at around noon, she didn't quite know *what* she was trying to summon. The room contains photographs of graffiti found around the borough—graffiti by a very particular artist, whose work is distinctive, yet curiously eclectic in its composition. Bronca's made out spray paint and house paint amid his materials, along with a little road tar and the occasional handful of natural pigments. (She hadn't realized there was any indigo growing in the Bronx, but the university analysis she paid for is probably correct.) Whatever the artist could find, in other words, or buy or steal or make on a tight budget. His themes are strange: a giant howling mouth with two teeth. An enormous brown eye, giving a sly side-eye to the generic glass-and-steel condo being constructed next door. A strangely plain mural of sunset over a meadow, painted onto the side of an old twelve-story derelict factory, which somebody really needs to knock down before it starts killing people with falling bricks. There's an arrow painted into the middle of the idyllic meadow scene, wide and bright red, pointing down at a ledge underneath the meadow. Bronca was confused by that one until she finally had an epiphany. The meadow is a red herring; what matters is that the ledge is a *handhold*. A convenient place for something enormous to grab on and steady itself. What? Who knows. But it fits a pattern.

The same artist, Bronca suspected before yesterday—and

knows with certainty now. The same unseen ear, which hears the city's song so clearly. Yes. This is the work of another of her people. Another of *her*, part of New York. She's collected these pieces because the work is amazing, and because bringing them together is a kind of call-out to him. (Somehow she knows he's a him.) Photos of the works, life-sized where the photographer got the right shot and poster-sized otherwise, now dominate Murrow Hall, which is the Center's largest and best display space. BRONX UNKNOWN is the show's title, hanging from the ceiling on a placard suspended by fishing line, and it's almost ready to go. Maybe, when they get some media coverage at the July opening in a couple of weeks, her artist will come to find her and become less unknown. Since she's not planning to go find him.

Bronca stops short, however, at the sight of someone in Murrow Hall. She only just unlocked the Center's doors, but already there is a woman in a white pantsuit and matching CEO heels examining one of the photographs. It's certainly possible that someone could've entered the Center while Bronca was getting coffee, but usually Bronca hears anyone who comes in. The Center is old, and its hardwood floors creak. The woman is carrying a clipboard, her back to the hall's door. Is she some kind of inspector?

"Powerful, aren't they?" asks the woman as Bronca stands there staring. She's looking at Bronca's favorite piece, although it's also the one that feels as if it has a slightly different eye. In the image, seen from above, a body curls sleeping atop what looks like a bed of old newspapers—not just *Village Voices* and *Daily Newses*, but really old stuff that Bronca barely remembers from her childhood, like the *New York Herald Tribune*, and obscure stuff like the *Staten Island Register*. The papers are in bundles, still wrapped with twine or plastic. The figure atop them is centered and almost photorealistic amid a pool of light: a slender young dark-skinned Black man in worn jeans and a stained T-shirt, asleep on his side. His sneakers are nondescript, canvas, dirty, and there's a hole in one of them. He can't be much more than twenty years old, though it's hard to tell because his face is turned into the papers, hidden except for one baby-smooth cheek. There's a little meat on him—wishful-thinking biceps peeking from the sleeves of his shirt, a suggestion of deltoids underneath—but overall he's skin and bones, to the point that Bronca's tired maternal instincts make her want to just feed the poor child 'til he fills out.

The framing of the painting is the really interesting thing— as Bronca has tried to capture by having the photograph cut into a circle. The whole thing is circular, positioned above the painting's subject, as if the painter is gazing down at him from the top of an open well. Bronca thinks there is adoration in this framing; it emulates the gaze of a lover, looking down upon a sleeping partner—or a parent, watching over a small child. She has seen the same tenderness of positioning, the same lighting, in classical painters' depictions of the Madonna. But then, she knows why this painting is different. It is a self-portrait, but the boy didn't paint it.

"This one especially," says the woman in the white pantsuit. On a whim, Bronca walks into Murrow Hall to stand beside her, looking more at the woman than at the photograph. She's almost as pale as her outfit, Bronca sees, though this is exacerbated somewhat by her tawny, near-white hair. She doesn't look at Bronca, keeping her avid gaze on the image of the boy. "I feel like it's trying to send me a message."

It is, but not to some random stranger. Bronca folds her arms and decides to play along, though. "We're all big fans of Bronx Unknown here," she says. "What message do you think he's trying to send?"

"I think it's saying, 'Come here,'" the woman says. "'Find me.'"

Bronca stiffens and turns to stare at the woman, who grins. In profile, this makes Bronca notice the woman's canines before anything else. They're badly proportioned, out of alignment with the rest of her upper teeth and slightly too big. The white suit looks expensive. Anyone making that much money ought to be able to afford custom orthodontics.

And that is completely beside the point, Bronca realizes, as a ripple of unease prickles over her skin. Unease and . . . recognition? If something so atavistic can be called that. When a mouse that has never before seen a cat spots one for the first time, it knows to run because of instinct. Something in the bone knows its enemy.

Not that she's a mouse, though, so Bronca only regards the white-haired woman evenly and says, "Maybe so. But I'm getting a lot of warning vibes off it, too."

The woman frowns a little. "What do you mean?"

"Well, it's subtle. All of this is conjecture given that we don't know anything about the artist, but I'm thinking Unknown is homeless, or in such precarious circumstances that he might as well be." Ignoring the woman for the moment, Bronca steps forward and points at the unfashionably torn jeans, the dirt on his plain white T-shirt, the worn-out, generic shoes. "These are the kinds of clothes you get out of a Goodwill pile when you've only got a few dollars to your name. And he's not wearing anything that would make him stand out. No hoodie. No colors or accessories. White folks will call the cops on a Black kid for wearing just about anything, but he's dressed as down as you can get without going naked."

"Ah, the better to go unnoticed. You think he's hiding from something?"

Bronca frowns at the photo, startled to realize it's a good question. But he's supposed to be fine at this point, isn't he? The city is alive. Then again, Bronca's supposed to be fine, too, and she's been seeing too many signs in the past day that something is very wrong with the city.

For the third time that morning, she wonders again if she should try to find the others—

No. "Yes," she says, to the woman's question. "I think he is hiding, now that you mention it. Huh."

"What could it be?" The woman asks this with such wide-eyed innocence that her tone alone sounds like a lie. "What frightens such a bright, vibrant young man into concealing himself?"

"Your guess is as good as mine." Then Bronca remembers that she's trying to make a point. She taps the boy's hand, which has been rendered in marvelous detail. They are the hands of an artist or a basketball player or both: long-boned and long-fingered, with a broad palm. Across the knuckles there are faint, old, keloidal scars. "He's a fighter, though. That's the warning. He hides, runs when he has to, but corner him, and that's your ass."

"Hmph," the woman says. Her tone is inflectionless, but Bronca hears the scorn in it. "Yes, that explains a great deal. Wouldn't have thought him so vicious, to look at him. Such a scrawny thing. Barely more than a child."

Yes. The young avatar of a very young city—relatively and globally speaking—that seems more bluster than bite. But anyone who actually thinks that has never noticed the large canines amid New York City's own charming smile.

"The thing a lot of people don't get about fighting is that it's not really the big guys you gotta worry about." Bronca turns, which puts her between the woman and the painting—not blocking the woman's line of sight, but planting herself at the side of the portrait. This is a place of art, and symbolic gestures matter. "Big guys, sure, some of them have been tested, but a lot of times, they don't have to fight much *because* they're big and intimidating. The ones who'll tear you a new one are the kids like this: the scrawny pretty-faced ones, poor and dark and wearing cheap clothes. Kids like that have to fight all the time. Sometimes the abuse breaks them, but sometimes—often—it makes them dangerous. Experienced enough to know exactly how many hits they can take, and ruthless enough to apply scorched-earth tactics."

"Hmmph." The woman sounds disgruntled. She has folded her arms as well, in a way that Bronca reads as sullen. "Some might say it also makes them monsters."

Bronca lifts an eyebrow. "*Some*, I guess. But I always figure those people must be the ones starting all the fights." Bronca shrugs. "Abusers know kids like this are the ones who sometimes grow up—if the abusers don't kill them first—to fix the world wherever it's broken. *Enough* kids like this equals the end of abusers."

"*That* is pie in a sky," the woman says. Bronca frowns a little at the odd phrasing. "Cruelty is human nature."

Bronca restrains the urge to laugh. She's never liked that little bit of bullshit "wisdom." "Nah. Nothing human beings do is set in stone—and even stone changes, anyway. We can change, too, anything about ourselves that we want to. We just have to want to." She shrugs. "People who say change is impossible are usually pretty happy with things just as they are."

It's a dig at the woman, with her expensive suit and power-professional haircut and the whole more-Aryan-than-thou aesthetic she seems to be working. All Bronca's life, women like this have been the ones to watch out for—"feminists" who cried when their racism got called out, philanthropists who wouldn't pay taxes but then wanted to experiment on kids from broke public schools, doctors who came to "help" by sterilizing women on the rez. Beckies. That's why Bronca's not going to call Yijing that name anymore. It should be reserved for those who earn it.

The woman starts to open her mouth, then picks up on Bronca's insinuation. Instead of ignoring it or getting snitty, though, she grins. It's a huge grin, showing nearly all her teeth. How has her mouth opened that wide? Jesus.

"I'm White," she says, holding out a hand to Bronca. Bronca suffers a moment's confusion before the woman adds, "Of the BNY Foundation? *Dr.* White, that is."

Bronca shakes. "*Dr.* Siwanoy," she says, with the same emphasis and a smile. She shifts to her white voice, too, since this feels like that kind of party. "But please feel free to call me Bronca."

"Director Bronca." The woman is still smiling with all those teeth. It looks like it hurts her face. "I understand you spoke to some friends of mine yesterday. A lovely group of young artists."

Well, fuck. Bronca keeps her smile in place, but it takes doing. "The 'Alt Artistes,' yes," she says, deliberately using the name the group didn't give. "I'm afraid their work was in violation of our center's longstanding policy against promoting bigotry."

"Oh, but bigotry is such a moving target, with art." The woman wrinkles her nose a little, still grinning. "Is it parody, or serious? Maybe they meant to *fight* bigotry."

"Maybe so." Bronca's still smiling, too. Smile versus weaponized smile, in the arena of professional fuck-yous. "But our policy is based not on *intentions*, but outcomes." Bronca shrugs. "There are ways to subvert stereotypes that don't simultaneously reinforce them. Good art should be more layered than just thoughtless regurgitation of the status quo."

"Layers," says Dr. White, her smile fading at last. For a moment, she looks weary. "Yes. So many layers to existence. Hard to keep track of them all. So let's make this simple." She turns the clipboard around so that Bronca can see the business check attached to it. Frowning, Bronca leans over for a better look—and freezes as she sees the amount.

"Twenty-three million dollars," says White. "I believe that would cover a substantial portion of your operating and capital budgets for the next few years? There is a catch, though. Of course."

Bronca stares at the check. She's never seen that many zeros written out by hand. And White has put little doodles on some of them—pupil-spots in the zeros to make them googly eyes, and little eyebrows over them, in pairs. She's gone a little nuts with the zeros for cents, however, which each have multiple eye-spots all over the place. This last bit makes Bronca frown up at her. "Is this a joke?"

"No. Would you prefer a wire transfer?" White tilts her head. "You should have gotten a call from a board member about me, verifying my identity—and that the funds being offered by my foundation definitely exist."

Shit. Bronca remembers hanging up on Raul's message before finishing it. Still. This is bullshit. It has to be. People do this sometimes with nonprofits—dangle money and expect them to hire incompetent relatives, name buildings after dead pedophiles, and so on. And there's actually some wiggle room for all that. Cost of doing begging-for-money business. But not as much as people seem to think.

"Let me make sure I understand you," Bronca says. She's still smiling, although it's taken a hit. "You want to make a donation to the Bronx Art Center? Of twenty-three million? We're delighted, of course, but . . . you mentioned a catch."

"Mmm-hmm." White's smile has crept back, though not as broadly, becoming instead something sly and smug. "We just want you to make room in your gallery for some of the Alt Artistes' pieces. Not the ones you object to!" She holds up a hand quickly as soon as Bronca opens her mouth. "You did explain your policy, and I'm in complete agreement. But they have a lot of pieces, beyond what they showed you yesterday. I'm sure they've got *something* almost completely bigotry-free. Let's say you put up three of their works. Just three."

It sounds reasonable. Slippery slopes always do. Bronca narrows her eyes. "I've seen their videos. Their whole shtick is trying to prove they're being discriminated against because they're a bunch of rich white boys—"

"So put up some of their art to prove them wrong." Dr. White looks at Bronca as if this is the obvious solution.

"Dr. White, I'm afraid your friends' work isn't very good. *That's* why I rejected it." And it isn't very good because they're a bunch of rich white boys making art as a prank—and apparently expecting a wealthy benefactor to open doors for them.

White sighs as she lowers the clipboard. "Look, we both know that sometimes you have to make compromises. This one is simple: put three of their works up, get twenty-three million. Unrestricted funds."

Unrestricted? That, Bronca really doesn't believe. Philanthropists don't think nonprofits know how to spend money—or that they won't just embezzle it all. Because that's what they would do if the chance presented itself, she suspects, and they figure everyone has the same wonky moral compass. It's time to call bullshit.

"What's your gain from this?" Bronca demands. It comes out belligerent. She's lost her smile, too, because she doesn't like being fucked with. "Are these boys your relatives? Are you with, I don't know, some kind of religious group or something?"

Dr. White's smile has turned pitying. "No, no, nothing like that. I just believe in ... balance."

"How is—" Okay, this is pointless. Trying to reason with bigots is always a losing game. And Bronca can already tell there's going to be an epic explosion from the board if she refuses the donation. With a frustrated sigh, Bronca rubs her eyes. It *is* a small concession to make, isn't it? A few terrible paintings on the walls for a few weeks, in exchange for enough money to keep the Center running at peak for years, even if the city reduces its funding. With that kind of money, Bronca could make a real difference in the lives of the keyholders. She could hire more staff, finally make Veneza full-time, offer more programs. She could—

"Also," says White, sliding that into the silence as if she can smell Bronca's imminent capitulation, "there's just one more thing. I'd like these taken down."

And she nods at the photographs of Unknown's graffiti.

Bronca inhales in shock before she can think not to. "What? Why?"

"I just don't like them, that's all." White shrugs, then extends her hand to Bronca again. "Those are my terms. Do let the board know of your decision by the end of today, will you? They'll take it from there if you decide to accept."

Bronca stares at her, though she takes the proffered hand. Habit. When she does, there is a quick, sharp stabbing sensation in many points all over her palm, which makes Bronca jerk back in surprise and stare at her hand. "Ow, shit!"

White sighs in palpable irritation and says, "Something wrong?"

"I don't...Felt like something...I don't know." Allergies? Eczema? Maybe she's getting shingles. She's heard that hurts. "Sorry."

White smiles again, and it feels put-on this time. "Well, you've got a lot to think about. I'll leave you, for now." More odd phrasing. Bronca follows as White turns and heads out of the Center. Privately she marvels at how quietly White moves. She's wearing pumps, but the floor creaks only faintly beneath her feet. Light-footed as a dancer.

And then, just as Dr. White lets the glass door swing shut behind her, Bronca notices something else strange. White stops on the threshold for a moment as if to let her eyes adjust to the bright sunlight outside. Then she...*wavers*, sort of. There is a heat-haze flicker, a channel-change interstitial instant. It passes before Bronca can really register it, and then White visibly sighs and turns to walk out of sight—but a few startling observations lodge in Bronca's mind at once. First, that White sort of shakes herself a little with that sigh, which is just an odd movement for her to make. Like she's shaking off the unpleasantness of Bronca's presence, or something. Second, wasn't White's hair white or platinum blond, a moment ago? Now it's honey blond. And her heels aren't white, but a pleasantly summery yellow.

And lastly, in that half an instant, Bronca noticed White's shadow. Moving, before she started moving. Contracting, for one fleeting glimpse—as if it were much, much bigger a moment before.

Then White is gone.

Bronca lifts her hand to examine it, in the wake of that strange jabbing prickle. It's fine. Didn't even hurt much, really. But there are tiny indentations all over the palm, like if she grabbed a hairbrush bristles-first.

Bronca casts about in the lexicon of knowledge that she possesses, but finds nothing that can explain the encounter. The Enemy has been a thing of immensity and animalistic savagery for tens of thousands of years. It has never been a small rich passive-aggressive white woman. Which means that Bronca's just seeing danger under every extremely large check.

Still.

Yijing wanders in, texting something on her phone with one hand and waving absently to Bronca with the other, either not seeing or ignoring Bronca's tension. Bronca heads to the reception desk. Veneza is part-time and doesn't come in 'til later, so Bronca's the front line 'til then. She sits there for a minute, processing that whole interaction—and coming to the rapidly growing conclusion that lexicon or no, something was very, very wrong about Dr. White.

Then the phone rings. It's Raul. "I know what you're thinking," is his lead.

Bronca's thinking of closing her office door and trying to squeeze in a nap once Veneza comes in. "Well, hello to you, too, Mr. Development Chair. Is that an official 'I know what you're thinking,' or an off-the-record one?"

"It's a warning," Raul says, which yanks Bronca wholly back to business. "The board members have been discussing White's donation all night, by phone and email and even text. When money's involved, some of these people don't fucking sleep."

Yeah, that about fits Bronca's observations of the Bronx Art Center board of directors. A few are prominent artists, but those aren't the important ones. The ones who really control everything are CEOs, scions of old-money families, consultants for think tanks, and retired versions of Bronca who were clearly better at their jobs than she is, because they ran nonprofits and somehow came away millionaires. "Okay, and the consensus was—wait, let me guess. Take the money."

"Unrestricted funds, Bronca."

"Not unrestricted. She wants *our principles* in exchange!"

He lets out a slow, careful sigh. Bronca respects Raul, his loose regard for power dynamics in workplace sexual relationships aside. He's one of the artists on the board, and unusual in that he's got equal talent at sculpture and at wrangling prickly business-types who have no idea how art works. Where he falls down is wrangling prickly artist types like Bronca.

"That's very melodramatic," he says. "And not at all true. The Better New York Foundation—"

"Jesus, *really?*"

"Yes. Very well resourced, very private, and very dedicated to raising the city from its gritty image to the heights of prosperity and progress."

Bronca actually pulls the receiver from her ear to glare at it for a moment. "I have never smelled a bigger pile of horseshit. That's—" She shakes her head. "It's gentrifier logic. *Settler* logic. They want the city without the 'gritty' people who made it what it is! Raul, what she wants—"

"Isn't too much to ask. That's what the board concluded."

There is a finality to his voice. Bronca's heart clenches as she understands. This is all going so fast. "Are you saying this is do-or-die, then? Take the money, or...?"

"What do you *think*, Bronca?"

Her first instinct is to start yelling. She knows that's the wrong response, the response that isn't going to help, but she wants to do it anyway. Her grandfather always did complain that she was too prone to bluster and bludgeoning. Her people have survived by hiding in plain sight for generations, passing as Black or Hispanic or whatever worked, but all that time pretending has left its mark. She tries to always remember that the way of the Lenape is cooperation, but it's a struggle sometimes.

"Listen to me. If we remove Unknown's works and replace them with stuff from, from . . . *a bunch of profiteering neo-Nazis*, you think people aren't going to notice? Think about what kind of message—"

"Have you looked at the profiteering neo-Nazis' latest video? Have you checked your fucking email, Bronca?" When Bronca falters and falls silent, startled, Raul sighs into the gap. "Go look. And consider the fact that the board started getting emails on this overnight, too. Then call me with your choice."

She flounders to speak. "'Do it or get fired' isn't a choice, Raul."

"It is. You can refuse the money, get fired, and doom the Center's staff and artists to years of financial uncertainty and fuck-knows-whatever kind of leadership they'll hire after you. The new director will almost surely be someone who's more likely to obey the board, which means they won't be half the advocate for your people that you are. That's what matters here, Bronca. You can't do them any good if you're—"

"You're making a choice, too! Between racist hacks and somebody who's spent her life fighting that shit! You're choosing them!" Yeah, so much for not yelling.

"That isn't how the board sees it. And yeah, I know that's how it *is*." He rides over her retort. "Jesus Christ, Bronca, you think I don't get it? I'm Chicano as fuck. My parents were illegal—I *get* it. But these people are always gonna tell themselves that a little fascism is okay as long as they can still get unlimited drinks with brunch!"

Bronca has fallen silent, though she's shaking. She's out of arguments. From the corner of her eye, she can see Yijing lingering nearby, clearly eavesdropping; Jess has come to the door of her office as well, after Bronca's shout. Veneza is walking up to the Center's door, since it's almost time for her shift to begin. Without really thinking about it, Bronca moves her hand to press the speakerphone button. Raul's long sigh is heard by an audience this time.

"Look," he says. "I'm just the messenger. You know I fought this, but . . . Take some time to think about it, Bronca. I know you, and I know you're right, but I don't want to lose you. And watch your back. This got ugly fast." Then he hangs up.

Bronca does, too, and lifts her eyes. Jess has a hand to her mouth, horrified. Yijing sighs and turns her phone around to display some social media thing or another. Bronca can't see the tiny text. "The Alt Artistes' video has gone up," Yijing says. "My mentions have been flooded with 'kill urself' crap all morning, and I couldn't figure out why at first. Different accounts, but all variations on the same thing: Why does @BronxArts hate white men, how can we say we don't discriminate when we clearly do, isn't it Affirmative Action if we only showcase artists who aren't white, blah blah blah. With a lot of 'chink bitch' and rape threats on the side."

"What the hell?" Bronca asks, stunned.

"Me, too," says Jess. She looks tired already. "They called my *home phone* last night. Five times—'til my husband took the phone off the hook, but I bet our voice mail is full of specialness and love. Guessing they got my name off the Center's website and figured out my personal info from it, like Veneza tried to warn." She sighs, rubbing her eyes. "I'm scared to check my email, to be honest."

"Yeah, don't," Veneza says as she comes into the room. She's got her laptop bag in one hand, and her eyes are bleary. "One of my exes texted me last night. The Artistes' video is extra fucked up. He was trying to tell me to leave my apartment, but *my* name isn't on the staff page." She rolls her eyes. "First time I've ever been glad you guys are too cheap to pay me benefits."

Jess goes still. "You think we're going to get doxxed?"

"You already have been." The words send a chill through Bronca; Veneza sighs and opens up her laptop, clicking on something. Then she turns it around to show them. There's a page on some kind of forum. At the top is the forum subject: OPERATION FUCK THESE LEZBICHES WITH BIGG FAT DILDS. Then dozens of posts. Bronca tries to parse it and can't; the text is too small, and there are too many people "talking." She's tried to stay on top of the internet, she really has, but at times like this, she feels like a damned Luddite.

"So, it turns out that there's a whole campaign about this," Veneza translates.

Yijing, who's clearly better at reading this stuff, squints at the screen and then curses. "The fucking *dates*. Oh my God. They planned this in advance."

"Pretty much," says Veneza. Her expression is pained. "All that stuff I told you guys yesterday about how to hide your business online? It was already too late, sorry." She taps the screen over one of the forum comments, and abruptly Bronca recognizes the words there. It's her home address and phone number. Beneath it, someone has posted "got her yaaaah" without punctuation.

"Oh, these sons of bitches," Bronca growls. But inside, she's shaking. What happens if some of these people show up to burn down her house in the middle of the night? Or if they break in while she's sleeping? She has a gun—illegally, can't get a permit because of her arrest record for AIM protests and "vandalism," which is what they call it when artists put murals on derelict building walls. But is that what it's come to?

Jess groans. Yijing shakes her head, her eyes moving rapidly back and forth as she scans the screen. "They're even trying to find your Social and your bank info, but they haven't gotten it so far. You have to call your bank, the cops, everybody you can."

Bronca puts a hand over her face for a moment. She can't think. And what can she do? The city's power can't help her with this.

Then Veneza nudges her, and when Bronca lowers her hand, Veneza is watching her, eyes dark with compassion. "Hey," she says. "Remember. *Six square feet* of floor space. I gotchu."

It's so ridiculous. And Bronca loves her so much.

So she takes a deep breath and tries to rally. "Right," she says. "Okay. Calling the bank."

"We need to get online," Yijing says, scowling. "Do some counter-campaigning. You handle your business, Bronca—but while you do, we've got to start fighting back."

It becomes a whole big thing, Bronca realizes, through the endless day that follows. She's still dazed by the looming threat of employment termination, but that's only one gun in what turns out to be a fucking broadside. The Artistes' video—which Bronca watches, despite Veneza warning her that it would only "heat up your brain"—is almost a masterwork of insinuation. At no point do they come right out and say that Bronca rejected them because they're white men; that's unprovable, and actionable. They say everything else, though. That Bronca is an out lesbian and Indigenous-rights activist with an Ivy League PhD ("I thought Indians were supposed to be poor," sneers Fifteen, who's included in the video as a guest expert on something). That Yijing's own work has appeared in the gallery ("They're just promoting themselves and their friends!" someone has typed into the video's comments). That Jess is Jewish, which seems horrifying to them all in

itself ("And now we know who's *really* behind this," Strawberry
Manbun says, leaning forward to glare into his video cam).

The messaging is all there, carefully divorced from specific con-
clusions or calls to action. And judging by the comments, their audience is eating the whole thing up like IHOP. The Artistes are clearly
the victims of a conspiracy by uppity women "of color" and ques-
tionable sexuality to promote their own indisputably inferior art
over the work of skilled, deserving artists who just happen to be cis-
het white men. In conclusion, the Artistes instruct viewers to "let the
Bronx Art Center know what you think"—after which they display
the names of the board from the Center's own newsletter masthead.

They knew exactly whom to target, and their goal was precisely what's happened: Bronca's job is in danger.

Yijing and the others are on it. Jess calls and texts a number of the Center's artists while Bronca's on the phone with the
bank. Bronca's mystified by how Jess is picking her calls, until Jess
explains: not the biggest names, but the ones with the widest reach
on social media. She gets them to start posting about the situation,
which Veneza has already bullied most of her art-school buddies
into discussing online. The goal, Jess explains, is something that
will look like a spontaneous show of support from the public.

There *is* a spontaneous show already occurring, as Veneza
shows them. It's just unfocused. There are quite a few posts floating around asking why people seem mad at the Center, which
has done so much good for the community, and trying to figure out how an anti-racist mission statement is getting called
racist. But within an hour, Yijing is on a conference call with
three arts-media reporters and a news feature editor, where she
explains that the Center's director has been asked to remove the
work of a talented artist in order to make room for "hate art."

BuzzFeed posts something about the situation; so does Drudge but everything was already cockeyed on that side of the looking glass anyway. Veneza's started something she's calling a counter-hash—#BronxNotBigots, although at one point she gets annoyed because some helpful wit has also started using #ArtNotAlt. "That's a dilution of our message!" she proclaims—but as far as Bronca can tell, both messages are working just fine. When Yijing shows her how to look at all this fiddly social media stuff, there are *thousands* of people tweeting and blogging in support of the Center. It's the most beautiful thing she's ever seen.

And then, toward evening—a good hour or two after the Center should have closed, but of course they're all still here again—Bronca's direct line rings. Raul's number.

Bronca takes the call in her office. It's brief. When she emerges to find the other women sitting there staring at her, she has to laugh. It's a weary but much-needed cathartic release after this ridiculous day.

"Yeah, so... the board has reviewed the situation, and pub-licly put its full support behind the freedom of expression that any champion of the arts should... blah blah blah blah." Bronca shrugs. "Translation: They've rejected the Better New York dona-tion. Also, they're not firing me."

Veneza jumps up and yells in triumph. Jess looks like she's going to faint. Yijing is furious. "Translation: the entire goddamn internet jumped on them, and they didn't want to look bad. But are they going to apologize? For even *considering* this Dr. White's offer?"

"It's the board. You know that's not how they roll." Yijing opens her mouth, and Bronca holds up a hand. "Look, this is bullshit, but it's bullshit we survived. Go home. Have dinner before nine o'clock for a change. Forget about this place for a while. And . . . thank you, all of you, for saving my job."

That silences them for a moment. Yijing looks at Veneza; Veneza makes some kind of face at her, trying to convey something that Bronca cannot interpret. Finally, Yijing looks exasperated—but she turns to Bronca and draws herself up a little. "I have a guest room," she says. A little stiffly, but still, given how much they hate each other, it's a gesture that makes Bronca regret half the things she's said about Yijing over the years. (The other half she'll stand by 'til she dies.)

"We'd kill each other by midnight," she says back, but it's gentle, and she smiles. "Thank you, though."

Yijing shrugs, putting her shoulders back. "Putting up with you seems like a small price to pay to stick it to these fuckers. But what are you going to do, then? It probably isn't safe for you to go home for a few days."

Bronca rubs her eyes. A hotel is out of the question for the moment. Her bank has dealt with the problem of possible identity theft by canceling her debit and credit cards—which means that Bronca's got nothing to her name but the cash in her wallet, until she can get to a bank branch and replace her cards. She's already called her neighbors to warn them. Her house is half of a semi-attached two-family over in Hunts Point. The neighborhood can be a little rough for outsiders, which is why Bronca could afford to buy there—and really, the kinds of people who might want to try this stalking shit are probably too scared to spend much time there doing so. Still, Bronca knows she should do what's safe.

"I'll stay here," she says finally. "I can't afford a hotel and don't feel like trying to see if I'm being tailed while I drive to one. And here, there are the keyholders to watch my back. I'll crash upstairs with them." She's done it before, and even has an air mattress in her office, along with some spare clothes and a go-bag that she's kept since the blackout of '03.

"Uh, weren't we just warning the keyholders about possible violence yesterday?" asks Jess.

"Yeah. But if there's going to be violence, I'm better off with half a dozen people for backup than on my own." Bronca shrugs. "It'll be what it'll be. Go *home*, ladies. I'm good—really."

So they start gathering their things. Bronca goes to sit in her office for a little while, mostly trying to recoup her energy. And when Veneza stands in the doorway for a little while, watching her, then comes over to give her a hug, Bronca needs it more than usual.

"I'm gonna stay here with you tonight," Veneza declares. "Us and the keyholders can gather round the glassblowing furnace and sing campfire songs. I think I stuck some marshmallows in the file cabinet at the front desk."

"A glassblowing furnace would blast marshmallows to powder in about half a second. Do I want to know why you have marsh-mallows in the file cabinet?"

"For my hot chocolate." Veneza gives her a *duh* look. "They're the fancy Whole Paycheck kind, too, square, with Madagascar vanilla. Or Indonesian vanilla. I can't remember, but they're fair trade."

Bronca laughs again, shaking her head. And for a little while, in the wake of all this, it feels like everything's going to be okay.

Bronca's asleep, dreaming of being other people and in other places, when suddenly her city nudges her. *Hey. Trouble.*

She grunts awake and sits up, with an effort. Her left ass cheek is numb because she's too fat to sleep on an air mattress without her hips actually resting on the industrial concrete floor. She's gone stiff, too, just because she's old. Still, she wrestles out from under the weird foil emergency blanket—which was surprisingly warm—that was in her go-bag, and struggles to her feet. Because. Trouble.

They're on the third floor of the Center, where the workshops are located. Access to this level from the Center is locked during the evenings, but keyholders can get in using the freight elevator, which isn't moving at the moment. All around Bronca are the sleeping forms of six people—several of the keyholders, draped over beanbags or curled up on couches. One woman is sleeping in the palm of her own sculpture, which is a giant chiseled-marble hand. Veneza is scrunched up on her side in a bright green plush chair, muttering in her sleep.

Moving quietly so as not to wake them, Bronca prowls through the level, angling around half-finished found-art constructions and shelves of unfired pottery. Nothing up here. *Downstairs?* she asks the city.

It answers her with sound, echoing faintly in her ears as if from far away: the slow, furtive scrape of something dry on concrete. A soft male giggle, followed by another voice's whispered shush. Some kind of liquid *glug*, splattering on a hard surface. And a sound that any painter would know: the rattle of canvas against wood.

Bronca doesn't even think before she hurries to the stairs. On the inside, the stairwell is bright with colorful murals that the various kids' and teens' classes have drawn all over the walls: dancing subways, racing street signs, cheerful pizza guys holding out a slice and a soda, smiling laundry ladies. Bronca immediately knows something's wrong because the murals are *damaged*; somehow, someone's gotten into the stairs and partially damaged the artwork in broad strokes. It's as if they dragged an eraser over the spirals and swirls. Erased *paint*, leaving raw gray cinder blocks underneath. How . . . ?

As she stands there, fists clenched, she becomes abruptly aware of a new sound. Sobbing. Babbling. From downstairs? She tilts her head, but can't tell. She can just make out the words.

"I'm *trying*," babbles the sobber. "Don't you think I . . . that? Yes. Yes, I *know* that." A woman's voice, familiar although Bronca can't place it. It's one half of a conversation, distorted oddly, wavering in and out of audibility. Someone on the phone? But the voice echoes as if they're shouting. "Stop it! Haven't I . . ." Waver out. Waver in again. ". . . everything you asked of me? Aah!"

That's a cry of pain. Bronca starts down the steps again, compelled by that voice. It's not from downstairs. It's all around her, and yet . . . not. Distant in a way that makes it sound like it's not in the building. Not anywhere nearby.

"I know it I know it I know . . . made me for this, but am I not a good creation?" Gasp. Sob. Now the voice hitches. "I . . . I know. I see h-h-how hideous I am. But it isn't my fault. The particles of this universe are perverse—" There's a long pause this time. Bronca has almost reached the ground level when the voice chokes out, now thick with bitterness, "I am only what you made me."

Then silence. Bronca pauses for a moment with her hand on the ground-floor door's latch, listening, but there's nothing more. She sets her jaw and turns the latch.

On the ground level, where it's dark except for low-power lighting, she can hear them clearly: several people moving around inside. How did they get in? Doesn't matter. What does matter, she sees when she passes Murrow Hall, is that they've pulled all of the photographs of Unknown's work off the walls. The frames have been haphazardly piled in the middle of the hall—and someone's sprinkled *lighter fluid* on them, she realizes as she gets close. Her nose wrinkles, half at the smell and half in fury. She catches the edge of her favorite, which is facedown on top, and turns it over... to find that someone has scratched all over the young man's sleeping face with what looks like a black marker. "Oh, you *motherfuckers*," she snarls.

"There are remarkably few of your kind who actually do that," says a voice that makes Bronca stiffen with recognition. *Stall Woman*. That was her in the stairwell, too, Bronca realizes now, though her voice was less clear there.

"I expected much more mother-fucking, when I first came to this city," Stall Woman continues. She isn't distraught anymore; now she sounds detached, bored even. "Given how often New Yorkers use the term, I honestly thought there would be mothers getting fucked in every alley. A veritable plague of mother-fucking, unless of course mothers like being fucked, which I presume they do. Then I suppose I should call it a *bounty* of mother-fucking. But there really isn't that much at all. Strange."

Bronca looks up. Murrow Hall has a thirty-foot ceiling, which is why the taller installations usually end up in it. Right now, however, Bronca spies something moving in that corner of the room. Under the white paint, somehow, as if the paint is still wet; she inhales a little at the sight. The shape under the paint is spider-like, although flat to the wall, and lacking several legs. Not large, maybe palm-sized? Whatever it is, it doubles in circumference as Bronca watches, and then doubles again. Abruptly there is a tearing sound, and the crack—because that's what it is—suddenly splits apart. The wedges of the opening begin to peel back, not like something organic, but like something *computerized*. Pixels overlapping each other, piling up and then spilling away to reveal a space beyond.

What should be there is the ceiling of the next gallery over, or maybe some insulation and ductwork. What Bronca actually sees, however, is a white ceiling that is much farther away than it should be—farther than is possible, given the dimensions of the Center. The second floor, maybe? It's throwing off Bronca's sense of perspective. But the color of the ceiling that she sees is different from the warm white paint used throughout the Center. This is gray-toned, cool. The texture is off, too: grainy, rougher than drywall, flecked with tiny crystals here and there. Pretty. But there's also something off in the proportions, in a dizzying way that makes no sense to the eye.

Bottom line: it is very much not any space within the Center that Bronca has seen. And Bronca's got the sudden sense that once again, she's catching a glimpse of what was really happening in Stall Woman's stall that day.

She shouldn't look. The lexicon warns . . . but she cannot tear her eyes away from that tiny, flat, featureless spot of otherness.

And as Bronca keeps staring, something small slips through this opening. It's whip-fast—so fast that her eyes cannot follow it. It's on the floor in front of Bronca in an instant, and it's already bigger, elephantine. There is another waver, and for an instant Bronca yelps as suddenly there is a *wall* of pebbled, grainy whiteness in front of her, immense . . . then it's human-sized. Just a lump of white clay, uncurling and taking shape. A *person*, straightening and turning to Bronca—and Bronca catches her breath and stumbles back as she realizes the person *has no face*.

There is another pixel-flicker, and the person resolves suddenly, becoming a smiling woman in white.

She is not the same woman Bronca met that morning. Bronca has looked up the sponsors of the Better New York Foundation by this point, and spotted "Dr. White" in a photograph; her family name is actually Akhelios, not White. From a big wealthy Greek shipping clan known for its right-wing political contributions. This is not Dr. Akhelios, who was brown-haired and ordinary in the photo. The person who has materialized before Bronca is definitely not ordinary. She is tall as she draws herself up and adopts an oddly elegant pose: something like ballet third position, with her hands held before her upturned, gracefully and unnaturally poised. Her hair is the same tawny white as that of the woman Bronca met before, but there the resemblance ends. The Woman in White has the kind of angular, high-boned face that Bronca has only ever seen before on high-fashion models, and other women deemed beautiful for their ability to act as living props. This one is even more modelly than most, however—in a way that pushes her past beautiful and into uncanny valley territory. Her cheekbones are just a little too defined, her lips too perfectly Cupid's bow, her eyes just a touch too far apart. The smile that she wears seems fixed, painted on...but that, at least, is familiar. Somehow, even though this is a completely different woman, Bronca knows she's finally met the *real* Dr. White.

There is a call from the Murrow Hall entrance, and Bronca turns to see that her old friends the Alt Artistes have clustered there, blocking her exit. It's not all of them—just Manbun, Holliday, and Fifteen, the lattermost wearing some kind of hilariously silly ninja getup that looks more like oversized black satin pajamas—but that's still three more people than Bronca can easily fight, if it comes to that. In the dim night-lighting they are grinning; she sees the gleam of their teeth. They think she's in trouble.

The fact that they're right makes her maybe more belligerent than she strictly needs to be as she turns back to White. "Trouble at home?" she asks, remembering the groveling, resentful tone that she heard in the stairwell.

White does something shruglike. It's too sinuous a movement to just be a shrug—too much head, not enough shoulder. "We all have a board, of sorts, to answer to."

Bronca laughs a little, surprised to feel sympathy. "I think I'll take my board instead. Do you even have a PhD? What's it in, Weird Shit?"

White laughs. Her mouth opens very wide as she does so, showing nearly all her teeth. "By the standards of my people, I'm barely more than an infant, hopelessly unteachable. By yours, I am ancient and unfathomable. I have knowledge of mysteries you haven't even begun to wonder about. It's very nice to meet you in person, though, The Bronx."

"*Bronca*." She knows why White is calling her that, but goddamn it, her name is her name.

White considers, then shrugs. "Such meaningless things, names. You cling to them in this world, where all is chaos and separation and differentiation—*and I understand*." Her hands move, extend, implore; her expression turns tragic. "I have lived in this world for countless human lifetimes! I've seen how your kind—especially *your kind of* your kind, must fight simply to be seen as the same kind, and not be consumed into the mass. Which is why I regret more than ever what must be done."

As Bronca puzzles over this, White splays the fingers on her upraised hands. All at once, the white walls of Murrow Hall,

stripped of Unknown's vibrant paintings and pathetic in their bar-
renness, blossom with colors and slashes of paint. New murals
suddenly unspool over the walls as if with a colossal paint roller,
though the hand of their painter remains unseen. But Bronca's
stomach clenches as she recognizes the style of this work—and
sees faceless, paint-strewn figures resolve out of the spreading
swirl of colors. They stand around the walls, a watching crowd,
a few seated or kneeling while others climb, elbows and knees
a-jut, over the walls themselves. One of these last, a creature that
is more radial than symmetrical with five leglike limbs, tilts its
head sharply toward her—

Bronca jerks her gaze away. The mural is on every wall,
though, and spreading over the ceiling in her peripheral vision.
Her heart's pounding. The mural scares her far more than Manbun and his buddies ever will.

"I don't understand," says the Woman in White. Her head tilts
suddenly, sharply, in a parody of puzzlement. There's no kindness
in her voice anymore. "Wasn't it you who tried to barge into my
toilet stall? Didn't you want to come in and see me? And I left the
door open for you, too, oh yes I did, but then you *kicked* me, and
the door shut. *Rude.*" Her smile vanishes abruptly, replaced by
annoyance. Then she sighs. "But I haven't given up on you, The
Bronx. My offer—from the toilet?—still stands. If you work with
me, I'll help you. There's no need for you and your favorite indi-
viduals to die in the conflagration to come, or at least not for some
time as you reckon it. I can see to it that you, The Bronx, are the
last to be enfolded. All I need you to do is find him for me."

And she gestures down at the pile of Unknown's photo-
graphed art. On top is Bronca's favorite, still beautiful despite its
desecration.

Looking at this, at the clean lines that are still visible despite the marker and the distancing secondhandness of photography, steadies Bronca through her fear. She remembers the day she found the real image. It was a mural that someone had painted onto the wall of a crumbling low-rise in the South Bronx, near one of the 4 train stations. Another brickyard. Bronca can't seem to stay out of them. But then, amid decay and despair, she'd seen this. The self-portrait of a young man who'd drawn it without hands, without paint, from miles away. *The city painted it for him*; that was why the eye for that painting felt different. And now the avatar of New York is somewhere underneath the city, she knows instinctively; somewhere in the subway tunnels. He's sleeping in the image, and at last Bronca understands what this means. Something *has* gone wrong. The avatar's sleep is unnatural, enchanted, a desperate last-ditch measure to conserve strength while the city labors through an unexpected crisis. The reason the city is so dangerous, so infested with the Woman in White and her ilk, is because all of its defenses are at their lowest ebb, and faltering.

Why? Why is the city's avatar sleeping?

It comes to her almost painfully fast, as if the city has just been waiting for Bronca to ask this question. Because New York is too much for one person to embody. Because its avatar embodied it anyway when the city needed him—and he fought, and won, because otherwise the city wouldn't be here—but doing this, using that much power, nearly destroyed him. Now he waits for Bronca and the others, the ones who are meant to help him. They must heal him. He can't wake up without their help.

Bronca could tell the Woman in White this. She doesn't know which subway station the painting depicts, but she could share what she does know. Right now, Murrow Hall's walls are an open doorway into another universe—one that is so fundamentally inimical to everything that Bronca is (human, woman, individual, flesh, matter, three-dimensional, breathing). One step in any direction might take her there. A shove. A tug—and even one moment spent there, clashing with its alien atoms and trying to breathe its alien air, will rend her to her core. (*Is* there air? Is that a thing that would exist in such a place?) She knows this as surely as she knows her own names, as surely as she knows her own kin and skin. The Enemy is not just at the gates but at her throat, and if she means to live, she has no choice but to surrender.

But there is something else she knows as well as skin: that she is a warrior.

Not born, maybe. Chris once told her that she had a gentle soul wrapped in razor wire, but the sharp edges are not her fault. The world trained her to violence, to ferocity, because it hates so much of what she is. This isn't the first time Bronca has been surrounded on all sides by those who would invade her, shrink her borders, infect her most quintessential self and leave only sanitized, deadened debris in their wake. It's not even the first time she's had the power to fight back.

This is just the first time it's happened since she became the goddamn Bronx.

"No," Bronca says to the Woman in White. "I don't fucking think so."

The Woman sighs. "I'm sorry, then." She makes a little twitching movement with one hand. Something behind Bronca makes a sound. It's nothing she can easily describe. *Da-dump*, at its baseline: a low, gulping, almost musical double reverberation, like something electronic. Except this is *organic*, she knows. It is the hunting cry of a beast that has no voice, an organism that has never known laws of physics congruent with her own—and it is close. The Artistes, sycophants that they are, snicker or start jeering. They can see whatever's coming for her, she guesses—though Fifteen abruptly blanches as he gets a good look at it. He steps back quickly, shaken, and looks away. By the angle of his gaze before he retreated, Bronca knows the thing is right behind her.

And Bronca . . . laughs.

She can't help it. Some of this is nerves. The rest is fury. These *people*. They have come into her borough, her territory, and ripped down good art. They've tried to *force* her to accept their disgusting mediocre bullshit instead. And here is this white woman, who is not a white woman at all but who has tried to manipulate mechanisms of power against Bronca just like the worst of them, demanding that Bronca capitulate. Like *fuck* she will.

The Woman in White frowns at Bronca's laughter.

"I don't know who the hell you think you are," Bronca says, and she is spreading her arms. "And I don't know *what* you are. But you don't know who I am if you're coming at me with this weak-ass game."

The Woman's eyes narrow. "You're The Bronx."

"Yeah," Bronca says. "And I'm also the one who got all the knowledge of how this works." She is setting her feet. "The others probably don't know how to do this yet, but I do."

A wind has begun to blow within the hall, stirring papers hanging along the Center's corridors. Bronca does not notice. The world has divided into two: Murrow Hall, where the Woman in White curses as jittering figures amid the wall-mural draw back in what Bronca suspects is alarm; and the other New York. There's a Murrow Hall in the other New York, too, but what has changed is its perspective and focus. Now Bronca stands expansive, mountainous. She has legs bolted to a million foundations, and arms of a hundred million joints of rebar. The flesh that fills the gaps is the soil where a thousand generations of Bronca's mothers grew and thrived, which has been invaded and poisoned and built over again and again—but it survives still. Survives *strong*.

And before her, small and insignificant, cavorts a white blankness of a thing. It's dangerous; that much she knows. It can hurt her very badly—both of her. All of her. It can drag her true self into a place where the completeness of her can be killed for all time, never to recover or be reborn. That will destroy the Bronx. Without the Bronx, all of New York will die.

So Bronca touches a steel-clad toe to the ground, lightly as any dancer. It lands with the pounding force of ten thousand block parties, boom cars, and drum circles—and sends forth a wave of energy that obliterates everything in its path. Everything that's not of New York, that is.

Around the Woman in White and Bronca, the mural is suddenly empty of people. The Alt Artistes have fallen to the ground, unconscious or groaning, because Bronca's manifestation has killed every tendril of White in the Center. It was in them. It was in the bathroom, Bronca notes with belated chagrin, infesting the third stall; damn it, she should have double-checked. It has grown into the electrical system and begun crawling up inside of the stairwell walls, damaging the children's murals along the way—but now that contamination is gone.

Now it's just the two of them, living city and eldritch abomination, face-to-face and ready for the showdown to come. Today? Maybe. Bronca waits to see.

And after a long, pent moment, the Woman in White exhales. She is unharmed by Bronca's attack, which is peculiar. However, she says, "I'd hoped to recruit you to my cause." Her voice is soft. Humility, maybe—but Bronca knows better than to try to interpret anything she does by normal, human standards. "We have so much in common, you and I. We both want to survive! We've both had to stand on our own, ally-less and undervalued, lost in the shadow of our supposed betters. We've both chosen to do what's right, regardless of what it will cost us in the end."

Bronca shakes her head, unwilling to feel sympathy anymore. "I'm not a settler from another damn dimension."

"No, you just threaten the existence of an *infinity* of dimensions, and more lives than your species has numbers to count," White snaps. Bronca frowns, but then the Woman sighs. "I suppose I cannot blame you, however. We all do what we must. Very well; I can't destroy you—yet. We'll meet again, perhaps, when circumstances have changed."

With this, the Woman in White jerks her head a little. The murals on the walls—figureless swirls of muted color now—vanish, rolling up into nothingness as readily as they appeared. There is one last soft *da-dump* behind Bronca before it, too, fades into silence. She would swallow to relieve her dry throat in the thing's wake, but it's important to show no weakness right now. She is the Bronx. The Bronx don't back down.

The Woman in White inclines her head. There is respect in this. "My minions won't bother you again," she says, "until the day that all masks are set aside, of course."

"Of course," Bronca says, wry. Minions. It's almost comedy. Bronca lip-points toward the Artistes, not bothering to look at them. "And them?"

The Woman glances at them. Bronca gets the sense that she is genuinely puzzled by Bronca's question. "I have no more need of those parts. Consume or repurpose them as you please. They're very malleable."

Then she turns, without another word, and steps forward. It is as if she's stepped into a hole in the air that Bronca cannot see. First the front half of her is gone, and then she picks up her trailing foot, and the latter half vanishes.

Bronca edges forward cautiously. But when she steps forward and swipes at the air with her hand, her hand passes through empty air. Any opening that was there has sealed itself. Exhaling, Bronca straightens and turns to the Artistes—only to find Veneza just beyond the pile of men, staring at her with wide, shocked eyes.

Bronca considers her protégé, putting her hands on her hips. "You okay?" she asks. The look on her face means that Veneza must have witnessed at least some of that whole confrontation. She's going to have questions.

"Well, I mean, just the sight of something awful and incomprehensible isn't going to send me off frothing at the mouth," Veneza says. It's nonchalant, but there is a shaken note to her voice nonetheless. "I'm from Jersey."

Bronca coughs a laugh. "Thought I told you to run if you saw weird shit."

"I *saw* these asshats." Veneza lip-points at the Alt Artistes; that's a Lenape thing she's picked up from Bronca. One of the Artistes sprawls facedown, and Bronca can't see him breathing, so she really hopes he isn't dead. The other two are almost spooning; Fifteen, who's still conscious (but fetal, and groaning with his hands pressed over his face), is the little spoon. It would be cute if they weren't racist sexist homophobic dipshits. "So I came to make sure you were okay. And then I see—" She falters a little. Her gaze flicks to the wall behind Bronca. Where the *da-dump* lurked.

"Yeah, that would've been the time to leave."

"Couldn't think." Veneza shakes her head and presses the heels of her hands to her eyes for a moment. Bronca tenses, but Veneza makes no move to tear her eyes out. The lexicon warns that that can happen. "Fuck, I'm gonna have nightmares for days. So that's what's after you? For real, I mean? Just, like, working through esses resíduos de pele? That White bitch?"

Bronca tries, she really tries, to be a role model sometimes. Occasionally. Okay, not often. "We shouldn't use 'bitch' to refer to women in the pejorative—"

"I'm using it to refer to a nonhuman nonwoman. So is this whole scheme like, an extradimensional shakedown or some kind of fuckshit like that, is that what I'm seeing?" Veneza's voice has gone more than shaky; it is seismic. She's trembling, too, and now her hands are rubbing tears from her closed eyes. Bronca sighs and goes over to her. "Skippy the tentacle monster sends her little bigot fuckbois to harass you on the internet? Like, is that how Lovecraftian horror *works* now, because . . . I can't . . ."

Bronca just holds her. It's what they both need, for a while.

Then they hear feet on the stairwell, and one of the keyholders pushes open the door. It's Yelimma, the glass sculptor with the abusive ex-husband. She's carrying an aluminum baseball bat. Two other keyholders, both homeless twentysomethings, hunch behind her, peering out at Bronca. Yelimma takes in the sprawled Artistes and Veneza's visible distress. Her nostrils flare. Bronca shakes her head quickly, though she's not quite sure what Yelimma is signaling that she intends to do, or what she's telling Yelimma not to do. She hopes it's Do Not Use Bat, or at least Not For Now.

"Call the police," she tells Yelimma. "I'm gonna go pull the videos from our security cameras for them."

"Make a *copy*," Veneza snaps. She's better now, though her eyes are red and she's still a bit twitchy. "What's wrong with you? Make a copy and a backup copy and a hidden backup copy. NYPD gets the originals and you'll never see them again."

"I don't have time for all that," Bronca begins, and of course as soon as she says this, Veneza makes a disgusted noise and heads toward the reception desk.

"*You* call the police, then," she tells Bronca. "*I'll* make sure they don't fuck up the video evidence. Yelimma, hit the Artistes if they give you lip." Then she's off.

Yelimma comes over, a wry look on her face. "You okay?"

Bronca, who has closed her eyes for a moment to disengage with the waiting, ready, martial spirit of her borough, lets out a long slow breath, and then nods. "Yeah." Surprisingly, under the circumstances. But she is.

It takes the police a fucking hour to show up. It's still the South Bronx. By then one of the Artistes—Doc—has come to, although he seems more confused and high than anything else. He sits shivering against the wall while Yelimma watches him with a taut attention born of experience. He keeps saying that he's cold, and asking how he got there. Bronca supposes that whatever the Woman in White did to him could have affected his memory, but she also knows that the Woman in White could not have used Doc and company unless there was something sympathetic, *synchronistic*, within all of them. So even though Manbun might actually be comatose or catatonic instead of just unconscious, Bronca can't muster much in the way of pity for him. She just hopes he doesn't die in her gallery.

When the cops do finally show up, they try to talk Bronca into not pressing charges. The Artistes are nice white boys from well-connected families, it turns out, caught breaking and entering by a bunch of hippie brown women; of course the cops don't want the smoke they're going to get from these families' lawyers or the press. Veneza gives them a thumb drive featuring footage of all three men crowbarring the Center's shuttered exhibit door—the only door in the place that isn't on the alarm system because a sensor got damaged a while back, which they knew somehow. The footage shows them sneaking in, one carrying a visible can of lighter fluid. Veneza's also added time-stamped photos that she took of Murrow Hall, and the piled-up, marker-vandalized paintings. Bronca makes sure the cops note the smell of lighter fluid, still very detectable on the absorbent photo paper. One of the cops makes noises about how it could interfere with the investigation if Bronca shows the video footage anywhere, "like online or to the news." Bronca smiles and says, "You and the DA handle things the way they need to be handled and we won't have to."

So finally they take the Artistes away in zip-cuffs, or in Manbun's case, on an ambulance stretcher.

By this point, it's dawn. The keyholders are all up, doing what they can to help put the Center back together. At Bronca's request, they put up the Unknown self-portrait again, despite the damage. Takes more than a marker to destroy something that amazing. Veneza runs out for donuts and coffee, and as word spreads on social media about the break-in, other artists and patrons from around the borough start showing up. They bring brooms and tools. One guy whose uncle runs an ironworks shop shows up with the business's truck, carrying several beautifully worked iron gates. He measures and mumbles but is eventually able to fit one that can replace the busted exhibit door shutter. It will be better than anything the Center's budget could afford. He's installing it for free.

When Bronca finally takes a moment to sit down in her cluttered office with the door closed, she puts her hands over her face and cries for a minute.

Then someone knocks, and she knows it's either an emergency or one of the many strangers in the place right now, because the Center staff knows better than to bother Bronca while the office door is shut. Scrubbing the back of a fist over her eyes, she grabs a tissue for her nose and calls, muffled, "What."

The door opens, and three people stand there. Even if Bronca hadn't been raw inside, she would know them by the sudden, almost painful ring of recognition that sounds throughout her soul. They are kin, battle companions, the missing fragments of her self. They are Manhattan, Brooklyn, and Queens, and they're grinning, ostensibly elated at having found Bronca.

"What the shit do *you* want?" Bronca demands.

CHAPTER TEN

Make Staten Island Grate
Again(st São Paulo)

Aislyn is up on the roof again, gazing at the distant city in the night, when her mother scares the life out of her by touching her from behind. She yelps loudly enough for her voice to echo from the nearby houses, and turns to glare at her mother. "Mom! Are you trying to give me a heart attack?"

"Sorry, sorry," her mom says. "But are you sure you should be up here? That allergy attack you had..."

Aislyn has spent the past twenty-four hours on Benadryl to try to reduce the hives she picked up at the ferry station. They're mostly gone now, and not as itchy, though the Benadryl has made her dreamy-headed and slow. Sitting on the roof is one of her favorite pastimes ordinarily, but between the drug and the soft, constant song of the city, the experience has become sublime. "I'm good, Mom. It feels nice out here. The wind's so cool, and you can smell the harbor even from here..." It feels so good, in fact, that on impulse she adds, "Sit down. Look at the city with me."

The roof of the Houlihan home isn't much more than an

access door and some satellite dishes, though her father jokingly calls it their "rooftop bar." Aislyn's put two folding lawn chairs out here, and she knows that her father often takes advantage of them, because she has to pick up his beer bottles and put away his binoculars whenever she comes up. This is the first time her mother has ever climbed up, however, so she watches with some interest as Kendra (she's thought of her mother as this since her teens, because it's what her father calls her) settles gingerly into one of the lawn chairs. It creaks and slides back a little beneath her weight, which makes her yelp, then laugh nervously.

"Sorry," Kendra says again. "I don't like heights." But then she falls silent, gazing at the cityscape. Aislyn is pleased to see her mother's face, too, relax into wonder. Manhattan is scary to contemplate up close—and, apparently, full of bees—but from this safe distance, it is a jewel to behold.

They sit for a few moments in companionable silence, and then her mother says, "So, did you make it to the city yesterday?"

Aislyn starts, her heart constricting, though she doesn't know why.

Aislyn does not understand her mother. Kendra is basically an older version of herself, black-haired and slender and so pale that sometimes there's a green cast to her skin. Aislyn often finds herself hoping that she'll grow up to be as beautiful as her mother, since Kendra has only fine threads of gray hair and a few minute wrinkles, even in her fifties. Black Irish holds the years well. However, Aislyn does not want her mother's eyes. All of Kendra's age lives here, not in lines but in constant, darting flickers and a slow, sad weariness. Back when Aislyn was a teenager, she often thought of her mother as dull. Since then Aislyn has come to understand that women sometimes have to pretend to be dull so that the men around them can feel sharper. Adult Aislyn has had to do the same thing, with increasing frequency as she's grown older. So she and her mother are finally beginning to become friends...but it's fragile, like any friendship formed amid stress. And her mom has never intruded so far into territory that Aislyn regards as inviolably hers before.

She shifts a little, trying not to show her discomfort, although the rickety lawn chair betrays her by creaking loudly. "How did you know?"

Kendra shrugs a little. "You usually take your car to go shopping. The bus is so slow. But NYPD photographs license plates at the ferry station."

And her father almost found out anyhow, because of her panic attack. Aislyn sighs in careful frustration. "I just..." And then she can't think of anything else to say. Her mother has also lived nearly her whole life on Staten Island. How can Aislyn say, *I just wanted to leave you and Dad and everything I've ever known to go to the city you've spent years warning me against?* And for what? *To meet total strangers who are part of me, part of New York, and I am part of New York, I don't think I want to be but I am*—

And then Kendra destroys Aislyn's entire image of her, and perception of herself, with a single sentence. "Really hoped you would make it," she says quietly.

Aislyn flinches hard enough to make the chair shift back. She stares at her mother. Kendra offers another of those tired smiles, though she doesn't look at Aislyn while she does it. Just keeps her gaze on the city.

"Wanted to be a concert pianist when I was young," she says, further flooring Aislyn. "I was really good. Got a scholarship to Juilliard and everything. Wouldn't have had to pay a dime except

MTA fare every day." She sighs softly. "I mean . . . I was *really* good. Fucking amazing."

Aislyn can count on one hand the number of times that her mother has dropped an f-bomb over the entirety of her life. But that isn't the thing that's jolted her the most. "Um . . . I've never seen you touch a piano. You don't even listen to music on the radio, except when Dad does."

Kendra smiles a little, with just one corner of her mouth, while the rest of her face remains its mournful, immobile self. She doesn't say anything.

Aislyn can't believe this. "Because . . . your parents said no?" Her maternal grandparents are dead now—heart attack for Grandpa, undiagnosed liver cancer for Grammy—but Aislyn remembers them as being very traditional. Stolid, no-meat-on-Fridays Catholics. Aislyn's strongest memory of them is Grammy telling her how she should dress and carry herself if she wanted a good husband. Aislyn had been seven when she died.

"I was pregnant, love. Married your father not a month after I got the acceptance letter."

Aislyn knows about this: Conall, the brother she should have had, but did not due to a miscarriage. Aislyn was born a few years later. No one really knows if Conall was going to be a boy, of course. He was a blob with flippers by the time he left the building. But when her father drinks, he talks about what he could have had: a brother-in-arms to help the family face this terrible world, instead of a daughter who is only another useless thing to protect.

Aislyn knows that the idea of working motherhood is anathema to both her parents. But since Conall . . . wasn't, and it would've only meant working wifehood, Aislyn frowns. "You still could have gone. Couldn't you? If..." She has tiptoed around Conall for years. Her father still grieves. Her mother keeps her own counsel on the matter because that's what women have to do sometimes, she has always told Aislyn.

"I meant to go. Your father wasn't much help with, oh, anything, but I was determined to find a way to make it work." Her mother smiles again. That little half-a-mouth smile, less than a quarter of her face. Her gaze is distant, somewhere well beyond the city. "That's why I had the abortion."

Aislyn's mouth drops open.

"But afterward, he was so heartbroken that I..." Kendra sighs, the smile fading. "I decided it was right that I should give something up, too."

God. Aislyn has to swallow, hard, to muster words. "You never told Dad?"

"Why would I?" So many answers wrapped up in that one. Why would she tell a conservative, son-hungry man that she'd aborted his baby? Why tell a husband that it was his fault for forcing her to choose between one dream and another? And then there is the matter of how he would have reacted.

Aislyn shifts again, realizing she's drawn back from her mother a little. She didn't mean to. It's just...a lot.

But her mother isn't done. "So I hoped you would make it out. I thought at least one of us should, I don't know, see the world? Try new things. It's why I sent for those brochures from colleges in the city." She grimaces a little as Aislyn stares at her again in shock. Aislyn had gotten in so much trouble for those brochures. Her father had assumed she'd requested them. He'd ranted for most of the night about how terrible the city was, and how much he'd sacrificed to keep her safe, and how it was her choice of course but he expected her to make good choices. A week later, she'd enrolled in the College of Staten Island.

"Jesus Christ," Aislyn mutters—and then she winces, realizing she's forgotten herself. Her mother has always grumbled about blasphemy when her father says the same thing.

"Yeah, that was a real shitshow, wasn't it?" her mother says. Okay, Aislyn's going to stroke out any minute now. "Sorry."

Finally, though, her mom gets to her feet and turns to Aislyn. All at once Aislyn finds herself imagining a different version of her mother: still the same woman, still limned by the distant light of the city—but wearing a stylish little black dress and with her hair elegantly coiffed instead of just a fraying bun at the back of her neck. The way she's seen concert pianists dress on TV. There would be fewer lines in her face, Aislyn decides, considering this stranger who has been her mother for thirty years. Lighter circles under her eyes, if any. And her eyes would be just beautiful, instead of beautiful and tired and sad.

Then the moment passes, and Kendra is just Kendra again.

"Don't stay here," she says to Aislyn. "Just don't . . . if the city calls you, Lyn, listen to it. And go."

Then she pats Aislyn on the shoulder and heads for the roof access door. Aislyn sits there for a long hour more, staring not at the city, but at the door that her mother passed through.

As Aislyn comes downstairs, she realizes someone else is in the dining room with her father. That's unusual enough; Aislyn's father doesn't like intruders on his territory. But when she leans around the door to see who it is, she is surprised to find her father sitting at the dining table with a man of about Aislyn's age whose entire appearance screams antifa. Or commie, or weed head, or any number of other things that Matthew Houlihan has called young men who look like this. The young man is wearing perfectly rectangular black-rimmed glasses and a conspicuously old-fashioned mustachio, curled and waxed at the tips. His arms—mostly bare; he seems to be wearing only a short-sleeved button-down with suspenders, the kind of outfit her father has called "gay" on other men—display unimpressive biceps and such a profusion of tattoos that Aislyn cannot make any one of them out. He sits close to Aislyn's father, kitty-corner at the table edge, showing him something on a tablet computer; they're both snickering at whatever it is, like small boys at CCD lessons on Sundays. Her father, a broad man even up to his balding pate, is literally twice the younger man's size. It's like watching a bulldog snicker at a dachshund's jokes.

Then they both look up, and Aislyn is caught staring. Her father immediately beams and beckons her into the room. "Hey, yeah, Apple, come on in. I want you to meet a friend."

Aislyn comes in, trying not to frown so that she can be polite, but...her father does not have friends. He has "guys from work," who are cops as well—and to judge by his comments about them, her father regards most of those as rivals for the rank of detective, which he has been striving to achieve for most of Aislyn's life. He goes drinking and occasionally to ball games with them, however, and this apparently serves as enough of a substitute for friends that he's never sought anything else. And yet here is her father, grinning as he says, "This is Conall McGuiness—" And then he laughs, as Aislyn cannot help widening her eyes at the name. "Good Irish name, right? Always liked that one."

Conall laughs, too. "Blame my father." Matthew chuckles and slaps him on the back, while Conall regards Aislyn. "Very nice to meet you, Aislyn. I've heard a lot about you."

"Um, hopefully all good," Aislyn banters by rote, trying not to squirm. She's gotten better at this since she was a child, when she would simply stand before strangers without speaking, having frozen up—but she's still not *good* at it. Usually, her father knows this and gives her plenty of warning before he brings a stranger home, for her sake. "Nicetomeetyoutoo, thanks." And to her father, just because the curiosity is killing her, she adds, "Is this, ah, somebody else from work?"

"Work? Eh, no." Her father's still smiling, but all at once Aislyn knows that he's lying. But what is the lie? Conall doesn't look like a cop. He doesn't *feel* like a cop, although Aislyn's cop-dar is understandably limited in its scope. But maybe Conall is a friend of cops, in general. "We're just working on a thing together, kiddo."

"A hobby," Conall adds, and then he and Aislyn's father dissolve into boyish snickering again. Aislyn has no idea what's so funny.

When they recover, Conall is the picture of pleasantry. "Apple, huh? That's cute. I figured you'd have a nickname based on Aislyn. Dreams, dreamer, dreamy, you know."

That's the meaning of Aislyn's Gaelic name, which Aislyn looked up in a book once when she was a child. "You really are a true son of Ireland, huh."

Conall grins. Aislyn's father nods approvingly and adds, "Apple 'cause she's my little apple, here in the Big Apple. I started calling her that when she was little and she loved it."

Aislyn has always loathed this nickname. "Do you, uh, need anything to eat or drink, Conall? Dad?"

"We're good, kid. Hey, but, Conall, Aislyn's a great cook. Even better than her mother. Kendra!" It's a sudden bellow that makes Aislyn jump, but for once, her father isn't angry. Kendra appears immediately, and Matthew gestures vaguely toward the back of the house. "Make up the guest room, babe, Conall's going to stay with us for a couple of days."

Kendra nods, nodding again to Conall in lieu of a greeting. Then she hesitates. "Lyn and I already ate, though." And the leftovers are already put up for the night, if Conall's hungry. It's also a commentary on the fact that Matthew came home later than usual tonight.

Matthew's smile vanishes almost instantly, and Aislyn's belly clenches almost as fast. "Did I ask when you ate?"

She is relieved when Conall straightens a little, drawing both her parents' attention back to himself. "Thank you for looking after me," he says to Kendra, and flashes a charming smile. "Wow, Matt didn't lie, Mrs. Houlihan, you really are beautiful."

Kendra blinks in surprise. And Aislyn's father—who normally *hates* being called Matt—laughs and companionably whacks Conall again. "Trying to sweet-talk my wife, huh? What the hell, you." Just like that, everything's laughs again.

Aislyn looks at Kendra, without quite intending to. She's learned over the years that she and her mother cannot *appear* to be allied, even if they are. But Kendra seems just as puzzled by the whole situation. She goes off to make up the guest bed, and Aislyn decides to beat a retreat as well.

Just before Aislyn completes her turn away, however, a flicker of movement snags her attention. She jumps and looks back sharply, frowning. Conall and her father have returned their attention to whatever's on the tablet, and they've dropped their voices to continue talking. Just like best friends. All very abnormally normal. What was that movement, though?

There. On the back of Conall's neck. Something long and thin and white sticks up from somewhere around the sixth or seventh cervical vertebra, and just above his crisp shirt collar. One of those weird little tendrils that the Woman in White kept putting on people and objects.

Conall glances up again, and raises his eyebrows at her stare. "Something wrong?"

"Nothing," Aislyn blurts, and then she nods something farewell-like before hurrying upstairs to her room.

By 3:00 a.m. it's clear to Aislyn that she's not going to get any sleep. As she's done with previous bouts of insomnia, she gets up and heads into the backyard. There's nothing here but the family pool, which her father installed ten years ago, and which Aislyn's swum in maybe twice. (It isn't that she doesn't like swimming. It's that she can't stand the fear that someone might be ogling her in her swimsuit—even though there's a twelve-foot wooden privacy fence around the entire backyard. It's not rational, but neither is her fear of the Staten Island Ferry.)

But even though the pool is useless for swimming, it's not bad for meditating—if moping beside a pool while clad in jammies and her favorite Danny the Dolphin plush slippers qualifies as meditation. This time, however, she's been out there for about five minutes, mournfully contemplating the distant, increasingly desperate call of the city, when something shifts beside her. She jumps and whirls to find her father's houseguest Conall sitting in a poolside lounger not five feet away.

He's been there the whole time, Aislyn realizes with some chagrin; she was just so caught up in her thoughts that she didn't notice. He's muzzy-faced as he yawns now and blinks at her, and there are lines from the lounger's straps on one cheek; he must have been asleep. There's dried drool on one side of his mouth.

276 • N. K. Jemisin

Aislyn doesn't laugh at this because she's also a little appalled to see that he's wearing nothing but a pair of her father's old pajama pants. He's double-tied them, but they're still tentlike on him. As he's without a shirt, she sees now that he also sports a farmer's tan and a series of additional tattoos across his chest and belly that are a lot less ambiguous than the ones on his arms. One's an older, nicely done Irish trinity knot over which the number 14, and a separate 88, have been etched in jagged, more amateurish lines. She remembers reading something about those numbers, and though she can't recall what they're supposed to mean exactly, she doesn't think it's anything good. A couple of the tats are semi-comprehensible outlines of what look like Norse gods? They're very muscular. Part of Aislyn is mildly offended by the conflation of Nordic stuff with Celtic, because the Vikings were invaders—but it is the tattoo on his left pectoral that makes her tense up. There, right over his heart, is a thickly etched swastika. So maybe this isn't really the time to quibble over mixed mythological metaphors.

Conall chuckles. "Well, you haven't run screaming. Your dad did say you were a true daughter of the isle."

"What's Ireland got to do with..." Aislyn gestures at the swastika.

"Just that there aren't enough girls like you out there making the right choices." He reaches down, and belatedly Aislyn sees the bottles next to the lounger. Her father's favorite beer brand. In addition to this, there's a metal flask surrounded by several airplane-sized bottles of harder liquor. All appear empty. Aislyn cannot see the white tendril on his neck from here. Can the Woman in White watch her through it? Is she part of him, somehow? Aislyn is groping for a way to ask, *Did she tell you her name, too?* when Conall sets the bottle down and says, "Ever fucked a Black guy?"

"Wh—" Her thoughts freeze. The question doesn't make sense on any level—that he would ask such a thing of a stranger, that he would ask it of *her* of all people, that he would ask it of a supposed friend's daughter, that he would put that string of words together in that order. "*What?*"

"You know. Ever took a swing on the old jungle gym? Or made the beast with a wet back?" Then he laughs at her face. As if it's the funniest thing in the world.

"I'm just saying," he continues, "if your father's trying so hard to set you up with me—which he is—I should know what kind of goods I'm buying, right? I mean, you're a pretty girl, but you're from Staten Island." He grins as if this is supposed to mean something in particular. "I'm just asking who's, uh, stretched you out. Broken you in."

His eyes rove her body while he talks. Aislyn suddenly feels that her worn, oversized T-shirt and faded dolphin pajama pants are the height of indecency. She should have put on a robe. That's why he's talking to her like this, because she's dressed like a whore. She should have—

He laughs again, and this time it's lazy and friendly. "Calm down, calm down, I'm just fucking with you. I tried to tell your dad that you weren't really my type, buuuuut..." He picks up the flask, which is open, and swigs from it, then grimaces as if its contents have burned his throat going down.

She needs to leave. He's gross, and drunk. But the words are actually starting to anger her, now that her shock has given way to comprehension. She is here in her own home, he is a guest, and he speaks to her like this? "I'm definitely not your type," she says.

Then she turns her back on him—but does not leave, because she refuses to look like she's fleeing from him, even if she wants to.

He snickers. It's infuriating. "Aww, hey, hey, Aise, I'm sorry. Friends, okay? Let's be friends. Hey, I wanna show you something." When she deliberately does not turn, he shifts a little, making the lounger scrape the concrete. At this, she jumps and whirls because some part of her is abruptly afraid that he's going to get up and... What? Now she's being irrational. Her father is a cop, and a shout away; Conall wouldn't dare. But Conall is still in the lounger. He's sprawled out more, in fact, spreading his legs and planting his feet on the pool deck, and... and that isn't a bottle tenting his pants. Aislyn flinches and starts walking away, hotfaced and disgusted.

Conall catches her hand as she goes past, to her astonishment. "Sure you wanna go?"

"Let go of me," she snarls.

"Look, Aise," he says. He's dropped his voice into something low and persuasive. "We both know you'll die in this house if some guy doesn't marry you away."

That. Aislyn freezes. That's.

He reads the horrified acknowledgment of reality in her shock, and grins. "And we both know you've never done *anything* with *any* guy, let alone any big fat jungledicks. I've seen your type. Good Catholic girls, too scared to do shit. Wanna know a secret? Nobody likes virgins, Aise. It doesn't make you pure or special, just a shitty lay whenever somebody finally gets around to you." His hand, already tight enough that she's going to have to struggle to break his grip, pulls her down a little. "Daddy's Girl, still living at home. Never had a boyfriend. But you *want* to leave, don't you? You dream about having a real life. You want to get away from this shitty island. Be somebody. Right?"

"Let go of me," Aislyn says again, but this time it's weak because some of what he's said has struck entirely too close to home. She's shaking, too, and she hates it, because he can feel that. But she is surprised to realize, in a sudden epiphany, that she isn't shaking out of fear. He's said a lot of things that are accurate, but—

this shitty island?

Her hand twitches in his, and he tightens his grip in response. He thinks she's trying to get away. She isn't.

Shitty?

"So here's your ticket," he says, bumping his hips up so that his erection bounces in obscene suggestion. "Your dad just loooooves me. But you don't want to be his anymore, do you? Be your own woman; suck my dick. Or we can even get started on grandkids for him, if you want. I got a fat creampie all ready up in here." He grins and then fumbles at the drawstring of his pants, trying to tug them down. "Or if you're really committed to the virginity thing, anal's good, too. Doesn't hurt at all." He laughs.

He's revolting. Aislyn cannot understand why her father has befriended this creature, brought him home, put him up in their house. Or, rather, a part of her is especially shaken because she does understand why: because on some level, her father *is* this man. She cannot imagine Matthew Houlihan being this crass with her mother, or else her maternal grandparents would never have let Kendra marry him—but beneath her father's veneer of traditional respectability, he is also a beer-swilling, controlling boor. Aislyn loves her father; of course she does, but Conall is right on one level: her whole life, Aislyn has had to scrape and struggle to maintain her own emotional real estate. If she doesn't leave this house soon, her father will snatch it all up and double the rent on anything he doesn't want her to feel.

Conall is very, very wrong, however, about something important. He thinks that the meek, shy girl that her father has described, and whom he is currently terrorizing, is all there is to Aislyn. It isn't.

The rest of her? Is as big as a city.

"I *told* you," she says to Conall, finally jerking her hand free, "to let. *Go.*"

On the last word, a sphere of pure force balloons outward from Aislyn's skin. It presses Conall into the lounger and then— as he inhales in shock—bodily lifts both him and the lounger, then flings them all the way across the pool deck. Man and furniture smash through the wooden fence amid a clatter of splinters and the snap of boards and one strangled, belated, "What the *fuuuuuck?*"

Aislyn straightens at once, her eyes going to the cameras edging the pool area. "'Everything that happens everywhere else happens here, too,'" she murmurs quickly. It is her father's favorite saying. "'But at least here people try to be decent. *Try to be decent.*'"

Something ripples around her. An edit of perception. The recording-lights on the cameras flicker a bit. And as Conall struggles to his feet, covered in leaves from the neighbors' euonymus hedge and bits of shattered wood from the fence, staring at Aislyn in something like terror, she glares at him. "I wasn't here," she snaps. Then she steps over his mess and walks out of the yard.

She doesn't know where she's going. It doesn't matter where she's going. She's got no money and no ID, and can't go far anyway because she's walking in puffy slippers shaped like dolphins. But as she walks, her limbs moving with tight, brisk efficiency, her jaw full of tension, she feels the island, her island, editing perception around her. No one notices or pays attention to a lone young woman walking down the middle of the street (because her street has no sidewalks). It's not that they don't see her, the drivers of the cars that pass, or the neighbors who chance to look outside after hearing a loud noise from the Houlihan house. It's just that, as they notice her, something else catches their attention. A movement in the trees, a car rolling past with speakers blaring, a bus in the distance stopping on screechy brakes. The front door of the house opening as Matthew Houlihan comes out with a sawed-off shotgun in one hand, heading around to the side of the house where the fence has been shattered. He doesn't see Aislyn, either, even though she's only maybe twenty feet away in that moment. He sees what she wants him to see. Everything that happens everywhere else happens on Staten Island, too, but here people try not to see the indecencies, the domestic violence, the drug use. And then, having denied what's right in front of their eyes, they tell themselves that at least they're living in a good place full of good people. At least it's not the city.

And at least Aislyn is not at this very moment being raped by a man in whom her father sees himself. This, and the fact that she's heard her father make fun of rape victims, is why she doesn't bother to tell her father what Conall did. This is why, if her father checks the video feed from the cameras, he'll see an indistinct figure—not Aislyn—standing by the pool, who then gets into a struggle with Conall, and runs away after bodily throwing Conall through the fence. Evil comes from elsewhere, Matthew Houlihan believes. Evil is other people. She will leave him this illusion, mostly because she envies his ability to keep finding comfort in simple, black-and-white views of the world. Aislyn's ability to do the same is rapidly eroding.

This is why she stops on the corner with her head down and her fists clenched and her shoulders tight. She's sucking in breaths to try to get a hold of herself, and trying not to cry. It's late enough that the street that winds past her neighborhood is quiet. A car passed a moment ago, and the next one coming is at least a mile behind it. Here, in this liminal silence, Aislyn can be afraid and angry and bitter about all the forces that have conspired to make her what she is. She can wish for better. She can—

The car that's been coming along the road for the past minute or so reaches her. It's going slowly, and as it gets closer, it slows more. Finally it stops right before her, the driver leaning over to roll down the passenger-side window. Aislyn tenses, bracing herself for the catcall or solicitation.

The man inside is ferociously lean, dark-haired, and something other than white. He's got a lit cigarette held tightly between his lips as he stares at her for a moment. Then he says, "Staten Island?"

She jerks upright—and for an instant the world changes. Highrises wheel past, buses squealing between them, docks and piers bristling into a defensive configuration. Before her looms a foreign, neon-bright skyline so immense and building-studded that it casts her into shadow. And then it is only the thin brown man again, who is staring at her with narrowed, cynical, knowing eyes.

"Get in," says this total stranger. Aislyn starts toward his car without a second thought.

Before she can reach for the door handle, however, there is a stir at her feet and a playing-card-quick shuffle of realities around her—and then suddenly curling, lashing white flower fronds whip up from the earth between her and the car.

Aislyn stops, her eyes widening, and the man curses, throwing the car into reverse and trying to back away from them. Still growing, the fronds swiftly become taller than Aislyn herself. Then they lunge away from Aislyn . . . toward the car, which they rapidly rise to surround and entangle. She can hear them slapping and hissing as they hit and sear at its chassis.

And as Aislyn stumbles back from the frond mass, the Woman in White catches her from behind with tight hands on her shoulders, leaning forward to peer into her face. "Whew! He almost got you. Are you all right?"

"What? No! Let go!" Aislyn shakes her off reflexively. Where the hell did she come from?

In the same instant, from within the lashing tangle of white flower fronds, there is a strange not-sound—a vibration, but with no tone that her ears can detect. It sluices through part of the thicket of fronds, dissolving them, and then the car lurches forward with a screech of tires. Out of control, it skids a little onto the grassy slope off the main road, then stops, brake lights glaring.

Aislyn barely notices, almost tripping over her puffy slippers in her haste to scramble away from both the remaining fronds and the Woman in White. The Woman looks wholly different from the last time Aislyn saw her, two days ago at the ferry station. This time she's wearing a tracksuit, which makes it easy to see that she's much plumper and shorter, with her white hair—streaked here and there with a few strands of faded bottle auburn—now in a shoulder-length soccer-mom bob. Her face is . . . *Not the same woman,* Aislyn realizes with a frisson of shock. This is someone wholly different. And yet . . . she is also the Woman in White. Every instinct that Aislyn possesses identifies her as the same woman from before. Same manic energy. Same bright, too-earnest eyes, as she holds up hands as if to soothe a skittish beast.

(Aislyn's mind thinks of a name, but flinches away before

she can recall all three syllables. Or is it two? Three but slurred, maybe. Starts with an R. Rosie. She'll stick to Rosie.)

Doesn't matter. "Stay away from me," Aislyn snaps. She's shaking. In her mind's eye, she is seeing that delicate white frond growing from the back of Conall's neck. Once, she thought those fronds were beautiful, but the Woman said she could see what was happening through them. That means she saw—and did not stop—what Conall just tried to do. It infuriates Aislyn. "I thought you were my friend! You said you would help me!"

The Woman frowns, looking genuinely hurt and confused. "That's what I'm trying to do! That fellow, he's another city and I hate him, did he hurt y—"

"*Your* fellow!" Aislyn feels so stupid. Was the Woman watching while Conall held on to Aislyn and invited her to suck his Nazi cock? Did she do nothing to help because it did not involve cities or boroughs or any of the other bizarre business that has taken over Aislyn's life? "In my house! In my own home!" Somehow, this is an extra bit of insult.

In the meantime, the brown man has gotten out of the car and is walking toward them. He's taller than she realized at first, dressed in an open-jacketed dark suit with no tie, the cigarette a red warning at his mouth and a business card held like a switch-blade in his fingers. He radiates stylish menace, and . . . with a deep chill, Aislyn realizes he isn't her. Isn't part of New York. Whatever spell he wove before, which made her want to go with him, is gone. Now she can only think that he is bigger and stronger and a man and *foreign*.

Aislyn backs away from him, too. The man reaches the asphalt and stops, on the other side of the patch of wavering fronds. The fronds twitch toward him at once, and he sucks smoke from the cigarette and blows it at them without looking. It's just cigarette smoke, as far as Aislyn can tell—but the white fronds react as if they've been attacked with chemical weapons. They lash away from him, squealing and shriveling, and within seconds the remaining fronds have flattened, dead and fading rapidly from translucence into absence.

Amid the new silence, the three of them face each other in a triangle of tension.

The Woman is staring with wide, angry eyes at the brown man. Her head has tilted to one side, and Aislyn is amazed to note that her posture is defensive, almost frightened. "I'm getting very tired of you, São Paulo."

"We have had an understanding for thousands of years," says the man, who isn't a man. She's never heard of a city called São Paulo. Maybe it's African, or in India? It sounds exotic like that. The pronunciation of *São* that the Woman used is weird, too. Something like "song," all round and back-of-throat. The same nasal musicality is in the man's accent when he speaks. "Once a city has been born, your attacks *end*. Always before, this has been so."

The Woman laughs a little. "Please. There was never any understanding. There can be no understanding because your kind *don't understand anything.*"

São frowns at this, then tilts his head. "Try me," he suggests. "You never have before; you just tried to kill us. Of course we fought back! But if you can speak, and if you are a . . . a person, then you can explain what you want. Maybe we don't have to fight."

The Woman in White's face has become a study in incredulity. "What I *want*?" Her eyes narrow even as she laughs. "Oh, sometimes I hate you people. One by one, you're fine. Better than fine—some of you are wonderful; so funny and peculiar. But there's a thing you always do, and I despise you for it. Did you really need to hear me speak to know that I was a person, São Paulo? Do people have to *protest* their own assault before you'll stop?"

The man stiffens, and Aislyn does, too, at the word *assault*. But yes, it's there in his face amid the confusion and anger: guilt. He did something, this brown foreign man. Something he felt entitled to do—maybe to the Woman, maybe to some other woman. And all of a sudden, whether or not the Woman has been complicit in what Conall did, Aislyn finds herself hating this São Paulo. It isn't personal. In this moment, Aislyn just hates all men who feel entitled to help themselves to things they shouldn't.

So she glares at him. "What do you want?"

São Paulo blinks away from the Woman in White to focus on Aislyn, plainly surprised by her tone. Or maybe he did not expect someone like her to have voice enough to speak. Maybe he's Muslim, or some other kind of woman-hating heathen barbarian. "I came to find you," he says. His tone stays even, but she can tell he's puzzled by the question. "You and the others. This city requires your help to complete its maturation."

"Well, I don't need *your* help," Aislyn snaps. "So you can leave now."

He stares at her—and then he looks at the Woman in White, his eyes narrowing in suspicion. As if he's trying to figure out whether the Woman somehow *made* Aislyn say what she just did. As if he cannot believe that Aislyn is capable of speaking for herself.

At which point Aislyn. Is just. *Done*.

"You don't belong here," she snarls. Her hands have become

tight fists. "Not in this city, not on my island. I don't need you. I don't want you here!"

And because Aislyn is still deep in communion with her borough after tossing Conall through the fence, still thrumming with energy and anger and thirty years of suppressed fury finally finding its outlet at last, she rejects São Paulo as fiercely as she did Conall.

It shouldn't work. She's seen his other self, which is absolutely massive—bigger than the whole of New York. More importantly, he is whole and powerful in ways that New York is not. And yet. She is Staten Island. She stands upon her home ground, where he is an interloper, and he is far from the pollution-shrouded towers of his home city. So the wave of force that Aislyn used on Conall ripples forth again. It catches the Woman in White, who cries out and flings up her arms and suddenly vanishes, as quickly as she appeared. What stands in her wake is a pudgy middle-aged woman with a spray tan and deep Clairol-red hair, who blinks and looks dazed before turning away from them and starting to walk back toward the next neighborhood over, ignoring the whole tableau.

But that was only collateral damage, because the Woman in White was not Aislyn's intended target. The wave of *You don't belong here* hits São Paulo full force, and the effect is far worse than what she did to Conall—because Conall was, after all, just a man. São Paulo is blasted by this power as if by an invisible flame-thrower, and she sees him take the blow in two ways at once. On one plane he raises his arms as if to ward off Aislyn's rage, and she sees the bones of his forearms snap just before he is lifted and flung off into the darkness beyond his parked car.

In the other reality, she sees from up high as an earthquake shivers its way across the greater metropolitan area of São Paulo. Older buildings fall, especially in some of the city's favelas. A quadruple-lane highway along the great city's flank splinters like bone—although thankfully it does not break apart entirely, which would spill hundreds of vehicles into the nearby river in a Williamsburgian echo of horror. Beyond that, it's bad, though. A city's commuter conduits are its lifeblood. For days, the fifteen million citizens of São Paulo will struggle to work, to reach the hospital, to stay connected in all the myriad of ways that a city requires for health and life.

In that other place she sees girders blur and realizes that something flails toward her—though she gets the sense this is more reflex on São Paulo's part than malice. People who grow up fighting learn to hit back even as they're going down. Reflex or not, the strike lands, and in the other place Aislyn feels the rake of urban rail lines across her core, which slice through her like claws. They *hurt*, a deep and terrifying burn that seems to tear something inside her—not organs or tendons, exactly, but something just as vital, though more existential. Her soul, maybe. She gasps and doubles over, clutching at her middle and blinking against pain-tears. Instinctively she knows that Staten Island has taken damage somewhere. Her island hurts with her.

But. Aislyn is still standing, and São Paulo isn't.

Aislyn has subsisted for so long on mere survival that the endorphins and elation of victory, of feeling strong even for a minute, go right to her head. She starts laughing despite the pain in her middle, and for a dizzying instant she cannot stop. But then, slowly, she takes a breath, and then another, and forces herself to calm down. She sounds as crazy as the Woman in White. She *feels* crazy. But she can also feel São Paulo still out there, wounded somewhere in the dark, so she forces herself upright, sucking air through her teeth to get past the pain, and calls after him. "Stay away from me. Or... or else."

It's not the most badass threat she could make, but he does not reply. Maybe he's unconscious, or sulking. Doesn't matter. She won.

Then Aislyn staggers back toward the house, with her ribs aching and her skin flushed and her thoughts bouncing around like Daffy Duck on a woo-hoo binge. The house is lit up when she gets there, but her father is in the backyard taking a statement from Conall. Two more cop cars pull up just as Aislyn climbs the front walkway, but the men inside don't seem to notice her as they stroll toward the backyard. Inside the house, Aislyn's mother is at the back door watching them. No one's thought to check on Aislyn, who's supposed to be upstairs safe asleep—so she simply slips up the stairs and goes to her room.

With her window cracked for fresh air, she can distantly hear her father speaking with Conall in a raised voice. It sounds like he thinks Conall was drinking and threw the lounger through the fence himself. Conall is protesting this with equal loudness. ("I'm telling you, I got jumped! It was a big Black dude!") Aislyn is a little curious to know how the argument will resolve itself, even though she knows her father will soon go check the security videos and see Conall's "big Black dude," which is actually a 120-pound white woman overwritten by the illusion she fed the cameras. Some part of her still hopes for justice to prevail, and for her father to realize what a monster Conall is... but the rest of her knows better. Her father has always been right: the only true justice is having the strength to protect oneself against invasion or conquest.

"If the city calls you, listen to it," she murmurs to herself; her mother's words. And São Paulo echoed this, telling her that the city needed her. But Aislyn decides in this moment to ignore the call. Her borough is what protected her—not Manhattan or Queens or Brooklyn or the Bronx. *Staten Island.* Everything she needs in life is right here. The city can go hang.

With this thought in mind, she falls into bed, and exhausted sleep.

A few miles away, in a trash-strewn train yard, MTA engineers and police gather and murmur, mystified by a series of four massive, parallel trenches that have appeared, breaching the tracks of Staten Island's lone, nameless subway line. The trenches were actually glowing hot and smoking when they were first discovered by a sleepy conductor going off shift—as if they weren't dug but *sliced* into the gravelly earth with a giant hot knife, or maybe an industrial-strength laser. Since then, they've cooled off enough that investigators can put ladders down to try to figure out what kind of incendiary device could have caused such damage. Each trench is fifteen or sixteen feet at its deepest point, shearing through soil, metal, concrete, bedrock, and even the electrified third rail. As if someone rent the earth itself with great, girder-sized claws.

Repairs will be simple enough—fill the holes with rebar and cement, replace the broken tracks—though they will take several days. In that time, many of the island's poorest people will struggle to get to and from work, or to visit their sick parents, or to pick up their kids from school. A city's commuter conduits are its lifeblood.

And sometimes even shallow wounds fester.

Aislyn sleeps.

CHAPTER ELEVEN

Yeah, So, About That Whole Teamwork Thing

Bronca hates them instantly, these avatars of the other boroughs who now sit or stand in her office. Brooklyn's the one who pisses her off the most. Oh, she recognizes the woman at once—MC Free, one of the first female MCs from back in the old days, who'd felt plenty free to start beefs with every other woman in the field and drop all the same kinds of homophobic bullshit that the men had done, while having the nerve to call herself feminist. Figures she'd turn politician. Also figures she's the one who turns up her nose at the messiness of Bronca's office, refusing to sit on an available chair because it's got dried oil paint on it.

But Manhattan is no better, with his friendly smile that shows too many teeth. She thinks at first that he might be kin; something about the set of his features feels familiar, even though he's obviously so multiracial that he could be anything. Then she finds herself leaning toward him, listening to him a little more than the others as he speaks, and belatedly she gets it. Maybe the Dutch smiled like that when they gave trinkets to people of the Canarsee—a band of the Lenape—and laid sole claim to what all others had shared for millennia. Probably every ethnic group he meets thinks he's one of theirs, at least partially. It's a subtle, manipulative bit of magic, and Bronca resents the fuck out of it as soon as she figures it out.

Queens is the one Bronca probably shouldn't hate, because she's just a girl too overwhelmed by everything to be one of the movers and shakers in this, but Bronca finds herself distrusting the girl's apparent innocence anyway. She's *Queens.* Queens can't possibly be that gormless. But of course, Bronca herself is the Bronx, and the Bronx don't trust nobody but the Bronx, so maybe her distaste for everyone else is just as inexorable as Manhattan's charm. If so, she leans into it, because it's been a rough few days and she doesn't feel like trying to be better.

"I don't need you," Bronca says. It's the third time she's said it, and they're not listening. She's about to throw them out. "I pushed that culo in white out after she attacked my place. Did it *by myself.* I needed you then and none of you were here, so I handled it, and I don't need you now."

They all look at each other. Brooklyn sighs and turns away, either giving up or just not caring, so Manhattan's the one who tries again. He's smooth, she'll give him that. Could talk rings around Raul. Yijing's probably gonna throw him her panties when he leaves Bronca's office.

"I don't think I understand your objection," he says. "Manny" he calls himself. It's bullshit. He's bullshit. That's her objection. But he actually has the nerve to look hurt. "We all know what we are. I know you feel it, too. Why choose to protect only one borough when by working with us, you can secure the whole city?"

"Because I fight my battles alone," she snaps. "Always have.

And because when I *do* 'work with' others, I prefer to do it along-side people who would walk through fire for me. Will you?"

Of course he frowns. "Maybe. I have to get to know you first."

At least he's honest. "Well, then. I don't want to know you, so."

"The fire we've got to walk through is *here, now*, sis," says Brooklyn. But she says it with her back to Bronca, while looking through the office's inner window at the exhibit hall beyond. It's disrespectful as fuck, and Bronca suspects Brooklyn's not even trying to be disrespectful. She's just naturally an asshole. "Door's hot, alarms going off, stop, drop, and roll."

"I'm not your sis. And don't act like you'd piss on me to put the fire out."

Poor Queens—she gave another name, but Bronca doesn't remember it, and anyway, she's Queens—just looks confused. "Do you all know each other?" she asks the room. "I feel like there's bad blood here."

"Always bad blood between the Bronx and the rest of the city," Brooklyn says. Bronca's nastiness has finally earned her full atten-tion, however; she's turned to face Bronca now, with her arms folded and an *Oh, so it's like that* expression. Time for the earrings to come off, then. Bronca braces herself. "Plenty of good stuff here in this borough. Lots of good people. But they can never get their stuff together enough to exploit it properly—so when everybody else does, the Bronx throws a shitfit and claims it's disrespect. It ain't even that, though, *sis*, see?" Brooklyn plasters a thin smile on her face. "Disrespect would mean we care."

Bronca plants her hands on her desk and pushes to her feet. "You can see yourself right the fuck out of my office."

Brooklyn snorts and is halfway to the door before Bronca can draw another breath. Manny glares after Brooklyn, but then spreads his hands to plead with Bronca. "None of us is going to survive this alone—"

She shouts, "Get. *Out!*"

They leave. They stare at her like she's crazy while they do it, but they go.

In their wake, Bronca sits down again. She's shaking. She doesn't know what she feels. She's eaten half a donut. She's running on a couple of hours' sleep amid one of the worst three-day periods of her life, and she has faced death at least twice in that period. (Maybe three times. She has an idea that if she'd been any less powerful in the moment that she kicked the bathroom stall door...well. At least twice.) Maybe she's being irrational. In fact, she's pretty sure she's being irrational. But for fuck's sake, they were getting on her nerves.

She's sitting there, seething and staring at the uneaten half of the donut, when the door opens. She inhales at once to start shouting again—but it's Veneza. Veneza is always okay. So Bronca subsides into quiet seething while Veneza comes over and sits down in the chair that Manhattan, whatever he calls himself, once occupied. She just looks at Bronca, expressionless.

That's enough. Bronca crumples beneath this gentle, silent admonishment, falling onto the desk and putting her forehead down on her hands. "I can't take this," she says. It's more of a sob than a declaration. "I'm too fucking old for this. I'm scared and I can't go home and *I'm not me* anymore. I can't. I just can't."

Veneza takes a deep breath and blows it out through pursed lips. "Yyyyeah, I figured they were hitting you with a lot all at once." She's silent for a moment. Veneza has always known when to let Bronca have silence. "Want me to tell 'em to come back later?"

"Tell them to never come back." But she knows that's not going to fly, so she sucks in a breath to let Veneza know she's not completely crazy. "Tell them to give me an hour."

"Gotcha." But Veneza's got more to say, Bronca's pretty sure, since she doesn't move. After a long moment in which Bronca finally starts to calm down, Veneza says, "You know...I hated New York before I met you. You're the one who showed me how to love it."

"Kiss my ass." Bronca says it to the desk. She's sulking and she knows it and she wallows in it. "I hate this city."

Veneza laughs. "Yeah, well, you New Yorkers—everybody except the new ones—always say that. It's dirty and there's too many cars and nothing's maintained the way it should be and it's too hot in the summer and too cold in the winter and it stinks like unwashed ass most of the time. But ever notice how none of you ever fucking *leave*? Yeah, now and then somebody's elderly mom gets sick down in New Mexico or something and you go live with her, or you have kids and you want them to have a real yard so you bump off to Buffalo. But most of you just stay here, hating this city, hating everything, and taking it out on everybody."

"Your cheering-up technique needs work."

Veneza chuckles. "But then you meet somebody fine at the neighborhood block party, or you go out for Vietnamese pierogies or some other bizarre shit that you can't get anywhere but in this dumb-ass city, or you go see an off-off-off-Broadway fringe festival play nobody else has seen, or you have a random encounter on the subway that becomes something so special and beautiful that you'll tell your grandkids about it someday. And then you love it again. It *glows* off of you. Like a damn aura." She shakes her head, smiling to herself a little wistfully. "I get on the train to go home every day, and sometimes I look around and see all these people *glowing*. Filled with the beauty of this city."

Bronca, frowning, lifts her head to stare at Veneza. Veneza is looking through the glass block window that dominates one side of Bronca's office. You can't really see anything through it—just the blurry shapes of people as they pass along the sidewalk, and the occasional bus. Still. It's a little bit of the city, moving and vivid and alive. The colors and light of the glass play over Veneza's face in a way that makes her momentarily ethereal. For not the first time, Bronca wishes that she'd had a daughter. Veneza is amazing, everything she could have wished for in a child. But Bronca is content to have an amazing friend instead.

With a slow, tired smile, Bronca sighs. "Yeah. Okay. An hour. *Uninterrupted.*" Then she will apologize to the other parts of herself, swallow a bit of pride, and join them as she knows she should. She still doesn't fucking like them, and might never. But. She needs them to save the city that Veneza loves. That's enough of a reason to put up with all this shit.

Veneza grins as if she hears this thought, and heads out to tell the others.

Bronca's surprised by how much the others don't know. She is the one who was given to know the history of the whole business, but she thought they would've gotten *something*. It lessens her anger a little; if they literally had to figure out everything from scratch, including how to find each other, then maybe she can cut them some slack. It also turns out that they intended to find her the previous day, but then they lost it to Brooklyn nearly burning herself out by sealing off the entirety of her borough. Bronca resists the urge to yell at them about this, because they're not supposed to *do* that. They need each other, working together, to amplify the power and reduce resistance and do other stuff for which there are no words. They need the primary avatar to focus all of it. But she can't yell at them, not even Brooklyn, because they didn't *know*. And, really, that's her fault.

So it's time she explains a few things.

While Yijing and Jess handle the business of the Center, Bronca has a sit-down with her fellow boroughs in the staff break room. Veneza's there, too—mostly to keep Bronca in line, she jokes, but it's not really a joke and Bronca is grateful for her presence. (The others give Veneza the hairy confused eye for a moment, then Veneza starts offering around the bag of microwave popcorn she's brought. Queens goes, "Ooh, kettle corn," and that's it, Veneza's in.) It's actually been several hours rather than just one, because Bronca had to divert some time to interviews by two news crews who showed up unannounced to cover the vandalism and arrests. Naturally, spotting a city council member on the premises, they roped Brooklyn Thomason into commenting, too. Brooklyn gave a pretty good impromptu speech, too, answering the question of what a council member from a different borough is doing helping a Bronx institution with, "An attack on the Bronx is an attack on all of New York," which even has the virtue of being true.

So now they're all sitting around eating delivery pho. With real food in her, Bronca's inclined to be a little less of an asshole, so they're all getting along better. Brooklyn even apologized for being an asshole back, and it turns out they actually tried to call her when it became clear they wouldn't make it to the Center before this morning. (Uselessly. Voice mail's full of hate messages and nobody listened to it.) They're all buddies now. Which is good, because Bronca's got some stuff to tell them.

"Okay, so," she begins. "We've got to find Staten Island. With four of us together, that should actually be pretty easy; we're already calling to her, but together we can narrow down her location and go to her—if she doesn't find us first. But what we really need to focus on, even while we're looking for SI, is tracking down the primary avatar."

They stare at her like she's just spoken in Munsee. (She checks with Veneza, because sometimes when she's tired she does slip into that; she spent a few years trying to learn the language when she was younger, and it comes out at odd times now. Veneza shakes her head. Nope, just incomprehensible English, then.)

"So there really *is* a sixth one," Brooklyn finally says. She throws a look that Bronca can't read at Manhattan.

Good Lord. "Uh, yeah there's a sixth one. You didn't know that?"

Now both Queens and Brooklyn are looking at Manhattan. Manhattan grimaces a little, then takes a deep breath. "We... suspected. But our source for information was that woman." He doesn't need to describe her; Bronca nods. They all know who the Woman is. "And, uh, a vision."

Okay, that's not something Bronca was expecting to hear. She raises her eyebrows. "A vision."

He's light-skinned enough to blush visibly, which is almost cute. Then Queens clears her throat and adds, "I saw it, too. We all did. That's how we knew it wasn't just, oh, car exhaust fumes."

"But we didn't know what to make of it," Manhattan continues. He still looks distinctly embarrassed. Bronca's starting to wonder what exactly happened in this vision of his. "None of us really understands how this works, or why it's happened to us, so naturally we've, uh, had a lot of denial to work through first."

"Can't see why you would," Veneza mutters under her breath, though more than loudly enough for all of them to hear. "Squiggly shit coming out the damn walls..."

Manhattan shakes his head and focuses on Bronca. "You seem to understand more about this than the rest of us. How?"

Bronca's briefly tempted to spin them some bullshit about it being a Lenape legend. She doesn't because she's too tired for bullshit. So she says, "All cities know it. It's like...I don't know. Ancestral memory, or something; it comes from the other cities that have made it this far. When we become avatars, the knowledge pops into our head. Or in our case, since there are six of us— one is the usual for most cities—the knowledge popped into *my* head. Have to admit, though, I figured you guys would've gotten at least some backwash."

"There are a lot of things in my head," Manhattan says, without apparent irony. "Nothing about why cities turn into, uh, us." He gestures around the table.

"Yeah, well," Bronca says. "There's stuff we can all do, but then each of us gets unique skills on top of that, because each borough contributes different strengths to what makes New York what it is. Bronx has the most history." Endless generations of Lenape stretching down the lines of the past—changed, though not destroyed, by colonialism. The survivors moved to south Jersey and thrived, but the Bronx is their ancestral land. "So I got the memory of what came before."

"I don't think I got any weird skills," Queens says. She sounds sad about it.

Brooklyn considers. She looks tired, Bronca realizes at last— and when she recalls why Brooklyn is so tired, the realization pivots her perception of Brooklyn, just a little. Securing her borough had wiped her out for the whole day, and she's lucky it didn't put her down for longer. Maybe her manner is not so much distance and hauteur as exhaustion and some kind of simmering anger—the latter not aimed at Bronca, though as Bronca has seen, Brooklyn's more than willing to let rip at all comers. But there's something going on with her, something besides turning into a living city. Bronca files it away for later.

"I'm not sure if I got any weird abilities, either," Brooklyn says. "I hear the city's music, but maybe that's just because, you know, former musician."

Manhattan's got that distant look on his face again. Bronca pokes at it deliberately. "Well?"

He takes a deep breath. "That painting downstairs. The one the vandals defaced, which you call a self-portrait of Unknown. I, ah... That was the vision I had. That *exact* thing—same angle, same lighting. I couldn't see his face, either."

Interesting. "So you know where he is?" asks Bronca.

"No. If I knew, I would be there." Manhattan shifts, a momentary irritation flickering over his expression before he controls it. "He's alone, and that woman is after him. Someone has to protect him. *I* am supposed to protect him." He blinks once, and pauses, and there is something about his manner that hints at sudden surprise. "I am *supposed to* protect him."

"Sounds like we've found your thing, then," Brooklyn drawls.

Queens, the kind soul, leans forward and puts a hand on his shoulder. "We'll find him," she says.

"Yes." And then Manhattan's gaze shifts, sun to moon, warm to ice. The speed of the change is breathtaking, and Bronca doesn't unnerve easy. He's not even looking at her, just the floor, speaking his desire into existence. "We will."

And God help anyone who gets in his way. Bronca shakes her head, though, just to warn him that she's got nothing good to offer on that count.

"I don't know where the primary is, either. And we might not be able to find him without Staten Island. But to track him down, we have to, uh, become what we are in the other place? Here?" Suddenly it's hard to explain, not because of English but because words are inadequate. They all nod as if they get it, though; okay, so far so good. Warming up to her subject, Bronca leans forward. "When we do, we'll see the full complexity of our existence. There will be a deep point that draws us in; that will be him. Then we switch back to this world, and . . . voilà. We'll know him in this world, too. If it works."

Queens is looking around at all of them. "Wait, so, all these, well I guess, visions I keep having, of us as both people and as huge cities, are me seeing into an actual *place*? I thought the whole thing was just . . ." She grimaces. "I don't actually know how to say it. Representations of the world? Like a mandala."

Bronca says, "I don't know anything about mandalas. It *is* a representation of this world, if that's what you mean. But it's also a world in itself—a real one, where things like position and distance and size don't mean the same thing as here. It sounds a lot like different things I've read about over the years. The Australian dreamtime. Jung's collective unconscious. Vision quests and sweats, like what some of my people do."

Queens inhales. "Oh, I thought you were Latina. You're the *other* kind of Indian."

"Original flava, baby," says Veneza, hunting in her popcorn bag for any remaining kernels. "This side of the planet, anyway."

Bronca rubs at her short hair. She really needs some sleep. And it feels weird to be telling this story now, in the summertime. Stories are for winter, when the animals have gone to sleep; that was what her mother always said. But maybe this doesn't count as a story so much as a lesson.

"So, here's the thing," she tells them. "*All* of that stuff is true. All the other worlds that human beings believe in, via group myths or spiritual visitations or even imaginations if they're vivid enough, they exist. Imagining a world *creates* it, if it isn't already there. That's the great secret of existence: it's supersensitive to thought. Decisions, wishes, lies—that's all you need to create a new universe. Every human being on this planet spins off thousands between birth and death, although there's something about the way our minds work that keeps us from noticing. In every moment, we're constantly moving in multiple dimensions—we think we're sitting still, but we're actually falling from one universe to the next to the next, so fast that it all blends together, like…like animation. Except there's a lot more than just images flipping past."

She stops to see if they're following. They're more than following; all of them are staring at her, completely rapt. It's a little unnerving, but Bronca knows why: because on some level, they can perceive it. Because of what they've all become, their minds work differently now. It's a lot easier to explain something that people already innately understand.

So she takes it to the next level, and makes the gesture that she did for Veneza: one flat hand topping the other, then she ladders them. Layer over layer over layer.

"What we are transcends the layers between worlds. Actually, when a city is born—when *we* are reborn as cities—the birth process kind of smashes through them." She keeps holding one hand flat, then arrows the other down into it, making the flat hand crumple and curl up. "What we are, what we're made of, is many worlds coming together. Reality and legends. This world where we're just people, and that world, where we can be miles-wide cities that just happen to be sitting a couple of feet across from each other because the laws of space, physics, don't work the same way."

Manhattan blinks, realizing something. "When I first arrived, there was damage there. Busted lights, cracks in the ground. Like an earthquake had happened. And as soon as I became part of the city, I forgot my name."

"You forgot—" Okay, maybe Bronca's going to have to cut them a *lot* of slack. "What, like amnesia?"

He nods, jaw set and brows furrowed, then glances at the others. "All of us have a similar story. Sometime in the morning, the day before yesterday, we all had a...moment. That's when the city changed. I think I arrived here right after that moment. Something *happened* in that moment; some kind of fight. That was the damage I saw, and I think the loss of my memory is how it affected me in this world. Then not long after, that thing on FDR Drive..." He puts a hand to his side and grimaces, as if his ribs hurt. But it's memory, and he lowers his hand after a moment. "If I hadn't stopped it, it would've killed me. That's the takeaway, here. Something hurts the city, it hurts us. Something *kills* us, and... what, the city dies?"

"More like explodes," Bronca says.

Silence. They're all staring at her. Yeah, she kind of figured that would get their attention.

"Sssso," she says, sitting forward. "This process? It happens all the time. All over the world, wherever there's a city. Enough human beings occupy one space, tell enough stories about it, develop a unique enough culture, and all those layers of reality start to compact and metamorphose. Eventually, when it's close to that, uh, *moment*"—she nods to Manhattan for the word—"the city picks someone to be its ... midwife. Champion. A person who represents the city and protects it, as we do—but that person gets the job even before the city becomes something new. That person *helps* it happen."

"Poor sucker," mutters Veneza. Manhattan frowns at her.

"If all goes well," Bronca continues, "the city becomes whole. The Enemy can't touch a whole city, not directly, or at least not without a lot of effort. But the birthing process can go wrong. If the Enemy catches the primary avatar, for example, and rips him to shreds before the city can do its thing, then the city isn't born; it dies. It dies *hard*. We don't know the names of some of the cities that have died this way, but the ones we do know will tell you what we're up against: Pompeii. Tenochtitlán. Atlantis."

"Atlantis isn't a real thing," says Brooklyn. Then before Bronca can say it, she inhales. "Or ... it isn't a real thing *anymore*. What you're saying is that it *was* a real thing once, but its avatar failed."

Bronca nods. "In Plato's stories, Atlantis was swallowed up by earthquake and floods. But the real disaster is that Atlantis *became just a story*. It failed so catastrophically that the entire human race shifted into a branch of realities in which Atlantis never existed at all."

They all stare at her, and each other. "Holy shit," Veneza murmurs, which seems to cover everyone's expressions. "Jesus, B."

Bronca lets out a slow, careful breath. "Yeah. But we're good on that count; our primary succeeded. New York obviously survived."

Now they all start talking at once. Manhattan blurts, "Then why is he sleeping—" and Brooklyn pronounces, "Well, *something* seems to have gone wrong," and Queens shakes her head and says in an irritated tone, "Then why does he need us?" And Veneza gives Bronca a skeptical look and says, "Uh, are you sure about that? Because, squiggly shit."

As noisy and rude as children. Bronca pushes through their talking. "It survived," she says, and pauses 'til they shut up, which at least doesn't take long. "But the battle was hard. And the primary, who did not understand that we were necessary to him, fought alone." Brave, strong young man, her Unknown. "He won, but it took all his strength. He fell into . . . well, I guess we could call it a coma. He can't wake up, can't strengthen the city as he should, until we find him. And we *need* to find him. We're not supposed to do this alone."

With deliberate emphasis on this last line, she looks at Brooklyn, who still radiates visible weariness even after they allowed her a day to recover. Brooklyn, already frowning, catches this look and understands instantly, inhaling a little. But then, surprisingly, she turns to gaze at Manhattan. "Guess I owe you more than I thought. Bad time for a coma."

Manhattan nods, looking amused. "If I'd realized what was happening sooner, I would've helped more. Next time, don't go charging off in your pajamas alone."

Meanwhile, Queens has shaken off her irritation; now she looks excited. "The equations always suggested simultaneous events, not purely conditional. The cat is alive *and* dead in the box! A universe for each outcome, and probably one in which it's both!" She beams at all of them, clearly expecting them to share her excitement.

"Uh, right," Manhattan says.

Queens sighs with the air of someone who is used to not being understood. She takes out her phone and starts texting someone, her bottom lip poked out a little.

Brooklyn's expression turns grim. To Bronca, she says, "You said becoming a city punches through other universes."

So she's not stupid. Bronca inclines her head to the woman, in respect if not in approval. "Yes."

"Okay, so." Brooklyn visibly braces herself. "So what happens to those universes that our city *punches through*?"

Manhattan's got a terrible look on his face. Queens goes on an entire face journey—shock to calculation to dawning horror to anguish. She puts her hands to her mouth.

"They die," Bronca says. She's decided to be compassionate about it, but relentless. None of them can afford sentimentality. "The punching-through? It's a mortal wound, and that universe folds out of existence. Every time a city is born—no, really, before that. The process of our creation, what makes us alive, is the deaths of hundreds or thousands of other closely related universes, and every living thing in them."

Brooklyn shuts her eyes for a moment. "Oh my God," Queens breathes. "Oh my God. We're all mass murderers."

"What's done is done, though," Manhattan says. His voice is soft, his gaze distant and unreadable. "From the moment we came to be."

Queens flinches and stares at him, openmouthed. "How can you say that? What's wrong with you? That's . . . what, trillions of people? I can't even begin to calculate it! All dead? And we killed them?" She looks on the verge of tears. Her hands have begun to shake. "For fuck's sake!"

Bronca's expecting Manhattan to go cold again. He does that so easily, she's noticed, even in just the few hours that they've known each other. Instead, however, he looks away for a moment, then takes a deep breath and moves to kneel in front of Queens. He takes her shaking hands in his own, and looks her in the eye, and says, "Would you prefer to offer up all of your family and friends to die instead? Maybe there's a way we can."

Everyone goes still. It sounds like a threat, even though it's just a suggestion. Bronca's not sure how Manhattan makes such a quiet statement sound so awful—but maybe it's the fact that there is compassion in his gaze, instead of coldness, when he says it. Coldness would be reprehensible, horrifying. Compassion is worse, because it cannot be dismissed as evil.

And Padmini stares at him for a long, pent moment. Then, slowly, her shakes still. She shuts her eyes and lets out a long breath. Manhattan doesn't move, doesn't press. It's not the approach that Bronca would have taken . . . but then, Bronca's approach would probably have been wrong. Something about Queens makes Bronca feel toward her as she does toward Veneza—as if Queens is younger than she actually is, a surrogate daughter to be protected. She isn't, though. Padmini is Queens, land of refugees who've fled horrors, blue-collar people working themselves to death, and spare daughters mortgaged for an entire family's future. She knows all about brutal choices and unavoidable sacrifice—and Manhattan's question, cruel as it seems, is one that respects this knowledge.

Finally, like the shading of the evening sky toward night, Bronca sees the change come over Queens as she accepts the inevitable. She doesn't slump, but there is nevertheless an air of sorrow about her as she presses her lips together. "Of course not," she says to Manhattan. It just pisses me off, that's all." She takes her hands out of his...but then nods to him, in graceful concession. "The world might be awful, but we don't have to *like* it that way."

Manhattan, to Bronca's surprise, smiles at this, with his own air of sorrow. "Exactly," he says. Then he gets up and goes over to the little window that looks out on the main gallery, his back to them.

Bronca lets out a long, uneasy sigh. This was hard knowledge for her, too, when it came. And yet. "It's also nature," she says. "Many things die so that something else can live. Since we're the ones who get to live, we should offer thanks to those worlds for contributing themselves to our survival—and we owe it to them, as well as our own world's people, to struggle as hard as we can."

Queens and Veneza stare at her. This is a general problem of city-people, Bronca knows—because she, too, was born and raised in a city, and had to learn the lesson late in life. Chris took her hunting once, over her vehement objections. And though Bronca would not fire the gun that took down the deer, Chris and the other Indigenous woman they'd been hunting with had made Bronca help with the butchery. It was important, they'd told her, to know where her food came from, and to understand that not just one, but *many* deaths had enabled her survival. Therefore it was crucial that she use every part of the animal, as much as she could, and take no more than she needed. To kill under those circumstances, or to survive, was respectful. To kill for any other reason was monstrous.

Manhattan gets this, Bronca notes. So does Brooklyn, who's probably seen some shit in her day. And, Bronca suspects, so does the avatar of New York City, in his peaceful enchanted sleep. It seems like a New York sort of thing to understand.

After a moment, Manhattan takes a deep breath and turns back to them. "So what's our next step?" he asks. "Since you seem to understand best how this works."

"Now, we find Staten Island."

"Problem," Brooklyn says. She holds up her phone for some reason. "I've had my people on this—the ones who aren't trying to figure out who stole my damn house—and there hasn't been a single bit of weirdness on social media that we can zero in on."

It's Bronca's turn to be confused. "Weirdness to zero in on…?"

They explain their process to her, and Bronca finally gives up being angry with them for not finding her until now. The whole thing is entirely too loosey-goosey for her tastes. But the gist of it is that their method's not working with respect to Staten Island— which is about what Bronca expected. Staten Island gonna Staten Island.

They go around for a while before Brooklyn finally sighs and rubs her eyes. "Look, there's enough of us now to just go there, rent some Zipcars, and drive around until our city-dar or whatever it is kicks in. It's the only thing I can think of to do—"

"I don't know how to drive," says Queens. "Sorry."

Veneza leans over to her. "I couldn't drive 'til last year. Solidarity, babe."

"—aaand maybe we should concentrate on trying to find the primary avatar anyhow," Brooklyn concludes. "It sounds like he's the more important target anyway. At least we're all, uh, awake, and able to defend ourselves if those white things, or the Woman in White, finds us. Staten Island must be able to do it, too, since the island's not a crater right now."

"It's harder, fighting alone," Queens says, looking troubled. "Scarier, because you don't really know what's going on."

"We'll find her as soon as we can," Manhattan says. "But if there's a way to find the primary..." He looks at Bronca, leaving this sentence a question.

"Maybe," Bronca says. "Like I said, it might not work without all five of us. But we can try it now, if you want."

"I want," Manhattan says. The other two aren't as decisive about it, but they at least look interested.

"Uh, should I go?" Veneza asks, frowning at Bronca. "Shit gets weirder when you guys are doing, uh, weird stuff."

"It should be safe, but up to you," Bronca says. To the others, she adds, "Now, do whatever you normally do to step into that other place. Meditate, pray, sing, whatever."

"Math," says Queens. She looks sheepish. "I, uh, never got anything less than 100 percent in math, back in high school. Stupid kids made fun of me for it. Called me 'Math Queen,' like I would think that's an insult. I'm a bloody math *goddess*—" She flushes, apparently realizing that she has digressed. "Anyway, when I, um, engage with that other part of me, I do math in my head."

"Whatever floats your boat, kiddo," Bronca says.

Brooklyn nods, thoughtful, then falls silent. After a moment, she starts murmuring softly to herself, or maybe subvocalizing, and bobbing her head to some inner rhythm as she concentrates.

Only Manhattan looks troubled. "I've never controlled it," he says. "It just comes to me, whenever I'm, uh, feeling New Yorkish."

"And when you think about *him*," Brooklyn says, pausing in her freestyling or whatever she's doing.

He blinks, then sobers. "Uh. Yeah."

Bronca shakes her head slowly. "Well, you did say you're, I guess, his bodyguard. If *he's* your thing, then that's what you've got to go with."

"Yeah, okay." He sighs and rubs at the back of his head. More quietly: "I don't know what this means."

Bronca shrugs, then offers her usual solution for awkward interpersonal interactions. "It means you ask him out for coffee, once he's awake. And then you hope for the best, same as regular people."

He blinks, then chuckles a little, relaxing as if Bronca calling a spade a spade has finally made him feel better about the whole thing. Probably gets laid a lot with that face, but no idea how to do an actual relationship. Also figures that the personification of Manhattan is two-spirit, too. She snorts a little at the thought. Maybe Stonewall was worth something after all. Anyway.

"Let's get to it," she says.

She isn't in quite the right headspace for a spiritual journey, not here in this cold place lit too brightly by fluorescents and smelling a little too much of chemicals and cleaning solvents. Still, they're standing in the Bronx right now, with her people's songs still reverberating through the ground. No need for a journey at all, really. Her city is right here.

Bronca feels the change before she opens her eyes, because all of a sudden she has become vast. She stretches, upward because her sprawl is checked on all sides, and downward into the tunnels and caverns that are her root. When she opens her eyes, the world is strange and the sky is twilit and she beholds herself: bright and dark, a spirit-form of blurred lines and stained concrete and built-over brickyards. She is the Bronx.

And around her, suddenly, joined and overlapping in a way that somehow does not create paradox or cause pain, are her kin. Bright Manhattan, tall and shining, but with the deepest of shadows between his daggerlike skyscrapers. Jittery, jagged Queens, pan-amorous in her welcome to all, genius in her creative hustle and determination to put down roots. Brooklyn is old, family-solid, a deep-rooted thing of brown stone and marble halls and crumbling tenements, last stop for the true-born of New York before they are forced into the wilderness of, horror of horrors, Long Island.

And together, they turn and behold their lost sister at last: Staten Island. She is dim compared to their light, suburban where they are dense, thinly populated in comparison to their teeming millions. There are actually *farms* somewhere amid her substance. And yet. She bristles with tiny throwing daggers in the shape of ferries, and defensive fortifications built in semi-attached two-family blocks. They can feel the strength and attitude of her, blazing more brightly than any sodium lamp. She is so different, so reluctant... but whether she wants to be or not, and whether the rest of them are willing to admit it or not, she is clearly, truly, New York.

It's strange, though. Even though Staten Island is right there—and there is no space in this place—she's somehow also distant from them. And dimmer than she should be, her high-rises shadowed and streets oddly clouded, as if something's laid down fog in thick obscuring lines. Bronca reaches, but cannot touch her. Manhattan tries, too, and comes closest, his bustling businesses almost brushing her commuter hubs... but at the last moment, she shies away. *Very* strange.

Not the only one they've come for, however. The others stir restlessly, so Bronca takes hold of the wheel of them and spins it. She is the guide. And in order to see where the singularity of New York is, she must back out of the other world. She must shift her perception up a level, and then up again, until it becomes possible to see the entire universe. (She feels Queens' awe, because she alone understands the scale of what they are seeing, but Bronca shies away from the girl's eager grasp of the numbers. They are immense. They contain multitudes. That'll do for Bronca.) And then they shift up again.

Before them floats the immensity of space and time as Bronca now understands it: not just here but everywhere, not one universe but an infinity of them. It is an endlessly growing broccoliesque mass, here in the no-place of perception. Each branch consists of thousands of universes stacked atop each other like plates of mica, forming columns that snake around and branch off, dominoes set up by someone with no sense of order. There *is* an order to it (and she hears another part of herself, Queens, thinking loudly, *A fractal tree!*), but in its immensity and dynamism, in the ferociously energetic churn of creation, it's almost an overwhelming thing to grasp. Not limitless, as Bronca first thinks, but vast beyond her ability to easily imagine. A thousand branches (that Bronca can see) grow and then crank out two thousand fissioned-off children that then generate four thousand grandchildren, and . . .

But abruptly there is a hollow *thoom*, and a ripple, and one of the bigger thickets of branches collapses before them. It happens so fast. There is a fleeting blue-shifted glow, and then that whole twisting cluster burns away, all the way back to the stem it branched off from. Bronca feels the others shudder in anguish and horror, and she shares it. As beautiful as that brightly burning chain is—like the most amazing fireworks ever—they all know what it means. Countless universes have just died, or become as never-were, like the branchings that must once have spawned Atlantis.

But Bronca draws their attention to what floats in this branch's place, tiny but bright, not connected to the other universes but blazing and stable all on its own. A singular point of light.

Bronca spins them, and again they behold themselves: *they are such a light.* They have witnessed the birth of another city like themselves, somewhere in the multiverse. Many such lights dot the tree, interspersed among its splits and folds—thousands of cities, glowing like jewels against the formless dark. There are places in the distance that seem to lack those lights; the tree's trunk, maybe? But amid the nearby crown? Cities. Everywhere.

And now Bronca uses the strength of the other four to direct them *back* and *down* and *in*, to the centerpoint of them all—

Before them, in a pool of mottled light, lies the primary avatar of New York. He curls atop a bed of ancient newspapers, asleep. There's a layer of pale dust on his Black skin; he's been here for days. He looks so alone there, self-contained but unguarded, so young, so fragile. The thought comes: *I will do anything for him,* which is not Bronca's thought—Manhattan, whose conviction is part knight-errant discovering the quest to which he needs to devote his life, and part raw lust. Still, Bronca feels it with all the conviction of her own heart. *Ours,* is what she does think, which surprises her because she's never been the possessive type. Someone else in their gathering reacts to this, but there is pleasure in the reaction. *Yes,* flows the thought, echoed this time by all of them. It doesn't really matter anymore who it comes from. *Ours. He is*

ours, and we are his, of course, but

wait, this isn't good, how are you in my head

Focus, Bronca pushes through their growing anxiety. Too many strong egos all tangled up together. This isn't going to last long. *Where?*

The pool of light spins, and for the first time they get a good look at the walls of the place where the primary lies, albeit fleetingly. There are white tiles in patterns, arches decorated with a mosaic of colored bricks—(Bronca gasps suddenly. *She knows those tiles.*) There is no real sense of placeness or direction. Bronca tries to stop the spinning, reaching out—down—toward the primary again, but she cannot control it—

And far below them, as they pull away, the primary avatar's one visible eye suddenly opens.

Getting warmer, he says without words.

Then he opens his mouth, and they twist and fall again, into the yawning blackness between his teeth—

Someone shakes Bronca roughly. She resents the hell out of whoever's done this. "Leave me alone," she snaps. "I'm old. I need my fucking rest."

"Old B, if you don't get up right now, I'mma pour cold coffee on you, and if that doesn't kill you with a heart attack, you're gonna die from cussing me out. *Get up.*"

So Bronca pulls herself awake. She's lying on the rattier of the two couches in the staff meeting room, which means she's going to be sore and achy whenever she manages to sit upright. Some of the keyholders are busy upstairs; she can hear one of them distantly doing something with the circular saw, and it's a testament to how tired she is that she actually slept through that racket. There's still daylight coming in through the exhibit hall glass, so she couldn't have slept that long. It's maybe 8:00 p.m.? In June, the sun doesn't really set 'til around nine.

The others are still there, flopped across the chairs or couches. Veneza's the only one on her feet. Manhattan's actually sitting on the floor near a couch, which Bronca feels compelled to warn him against; he's not going to have any feeling left in his ass if he spends too much time on industrial concrete flooring. Too late, though, because he's blinking blearily as if he, too, just woke up. Brooklyn's awake, barely. Queens is rubbing her face, but then she rummages in her backpack and pulls out a packet of chocolate-covered espresso beans, popping a handful into her mouth. She offers some to Brooklyn and then Manhattan.

And then someone else walks into their circle: a tall Asian man in a business suit, maybe in his fifties, with a face like carved marble and a mouth set in a permanent downturn. He's not Bronca's main concern, however. The man is carrying someone else over his shoulder. A limp body in a more stylish suit, although grass-stained and filthy.

"Oh my God," Brooklyn says, reaching for her phone and immediately thumbing the "emergency call" button. Manhattan scrambles to his feet, shaking his head to clear it.

"Put that away," snaps the stranger to Brooklyn. He's got an accent, but it's unusual. Chinese-inflected British English, Bronca decides. "He's a city. Paramedics can't fix this."

They all stare, but Brooklyn puts her phone away. The Asian man flaps his hand rudely at Queens until she gets off the couch, and then he lays the unconscious man across it. This man is younger, leaner, Latino-ishly brown although in a more ambiguous way than usual. He reeks of cigarette smoke. There's no blood that Bronca can see, but he's *gray* in a way that has nothing to do with skin color. It's the strangest thing to see—as if the whole of the world is in HD color, but this man has somehow regressed to the days when televisions were just three channels and grainy black-and-white pixels. And there's something...around him?

Bronca blinks, squints—and then, when she shifts her awareness partly into cityspace, she understands. There is a kind of translucent envelope surrounding the unconscious man and suffusing his flesh. It has an attached line, like an umbilicus, which trails away to someplace in...South America. Brazil, she guesses, though she's only 50 percent sure she could pick that country out on a map, and she can't remember the names of any cities there except Rio.

She blinks back to find the older man examining her. "Not useless, then," he says, which makes Bronca stiffen in fury. Then he glances around at all of them, assessing in the same way, unimpressed by all. "But none of you even noticed his injury, even though he was within your own borders."

"He's a city? What's happened to him?" Queens reaches out and touches the unconscious man gingerly, though she draws back her fingers at once when the envelope around him dimples preemptively, averse to her touch.

"And who the hell are you?" Brooklyn's still sitting, but she's shifted her weight forward a little, aggressively. Manhattan stands at her back, his whole posture very still. That they are both braced for some kind of attack is obvious. But Bronca shakes her head, pushing herself to her feet so that she can wave them calm. Because she can see this stranger in the other place, too, and he's definitely not another variant on the Woman in White.

"Call me Hong," he says, glaring down at the unconscious man. With a sigh, he bends and rummages in the man's jacket—the envelope does not resist him for some reason—and takes out a packet of cigarettes and a lighter. "He said the situation here was a mess, but he's dramatic. I didn't think it could be so bad. Yet here we are."

Manhattan looks around at the rest of them and mouths, *Hong...Kong?* Bronca nods. She's never been to that city, but she's seen its skyline in photographs—that one dick-shaped tower is distinctive—in her memory and in the other realm, where she sees the totality of him. The city of Hong Kong is standing before them, scowling and lighting up a cigarette.

"Hey," Bronca says. When he glances at her, she points at the sign on a nearby wall: NO SMOKING.

"Fuck off," he says. It's said with so little heat, not even the same emotion that one would use to say *no*, that Bronca's mouth falls open. She's not really offended, just surprised. Then, however, Hong coughs and turns a sour look on the cigarette. "I hate smoking."

"Then why the hell—" Veneza begins. Before she can finish, however, Hong takes a deep drag from the cigarette, then leans down and blows the smoke out in a long stream over the unconscious man.

It is as if his whole body absorbs the smoke. He shivers all over, and some of the grayness and blurriness fades. Now he is sepia toned, almost as clear as a Nineties-era third-tier computer monitor. Bronca gasps in spite of herself. Manhattan comes forward quickly. "Maybe you should do that again," he says to Hong.

"No," says Hong, stubbing out the cigarette. "Once is all I could have done, and even that barely works because it's me that's doing it, not him. What he really needs is the polluted air of his own city, but it isn't safe to travel through macrospace right now. And unless one of you is willing to get on a ten-hour flight to bring him there—as I just got off of a fifteen-hour one, and don't want to see a plane again for a week—then I'm not sure what else to do to accelerate his recovery." He slumps into a nearby chair, rubbing his face.

"Okay, wait," Veneza says. "You're Hong Kong? Who's he?" She points at the unconscious man.

Hong lifts his face long enough to glower at her. "São Paulo, of course. Who else could he be?"

"Rio? Some whole other city?" Queens stares at him. "How are we supposed to know?"

"Rio has not yet been born," Hong snaps in an acid tone. "Only two cities in this hemisphere are currently alive: his, and yours. That is why he's here. As the last city born, it's his duty to help you through your time. Now do you understand? Are you caught up yet?"

Queens stares at him for an instant, stunned at his rudeness—and then she flares. "You don't have to be such a fucking asshole!"

"Don't I?" Hong stabs a finger at São Paulo. "I see him barely capable of manifesting in this world, half-dead, but none of you seems remotely concerned. And none of you has asked the obvious questions of a supposed ally: Who did this to him, and how might he be avenged?"

"São Paulo, São Paulo." Veneza, murmuring to herself, slides off her chair and trots over to the meeting room fridge, starting to rummage through its freezer. The others stare, but Bronca, long used to the girl's peculiarities, ignores this.

Manhattan moves over to Hong and the unconscious man; Bronca wonders if it is intentional that he has positioned himself between the strangers and his fellow boroughs. Queens leans around him. "We don't know this guy," she says to Hong. "You seem to expect that, but if he was supposed to help us, he didn't. Is he going to die?"

"São Paulo still stands, doesn't it?" After delivering this cryptic remark, Hong leans back in his chair and regards them all with a hard, dispassionate glare.

Brooklyn says, with strained patience, "Look, we don't know this guy from Adam. I'm sorry your friend is hurt, but there's pretty much only one person who could've done this to him, if I understand all this correctly. We've been calling her the Woman in White, but—"

Hong is smiling. It's a far more unnerving smile than even Manhattan's, because it's so obviously false. Bronca's never seen active hate in Manhattan's eyes, and there's definitely a glimmer of it here. "*She* didn't do this," Hong says.

Brooklyn is so thrown as to actually exchange a look with Bronca. Who shakes her head, because she doesn't get what Hong Kong is on about, either. "And you know this how?" Bronca asks.

"This kind of injury happens only when we step within the boundaries of another city and that city takes exception to our presence." Hong's gaze rakes over each one of them. "In this place, at this time, only New York could have hurt São Paulo so badly."

"Whoa, wait, that's crap," Manhattan says, scowling. Belatedly, Bronca registers that she's never heard Manhattan curse. What a strange trait for the island of Fuck You. "None of *us* did this. We were all here, anyway, except—"

Silence. Slowly, inexorably, the realization hits. Brooklyn groans softly. Queens shakes her head in disbelief. Manhattan's expression hardens. Bronca doesn't want to believe it herself... but the conclusion is undeniable.

Hong watches each of them—evaluating them, Bronca realizes. Checking to see if any of them is faking surprise or dismay. "Well," he concludes finally, his tone softening just a bit, "I'm told that New York has five boroughs, and I see only four of you. And that one." He nods after Veneza, who has by now worked most of her upper body into the freezer. She seems to be digging for something behind the ancient tub of Neapolitan ice cream left over from the staff birthday party for Jess.

Staten Island. Attacked São Paulo. And because it happened here in New York, where São Paulo did not have his city nearby to protect him, the attack has injured him badly.

"No." Manhattan gets up and starts pacing. "It has to have been some kind of misunderstanding. She's *part* of us."

"Maybe . . ." Bronca rubs a hand over her hair. She's tired. Not enough sleep in the past few days, plus gallivanting all over the multiverse takes it out of you. "Maybe Staten Island thought he was the Woman in White. Maybe this was an accident."

"Or maybe," says Brooklyn, who has moved to lean against the wall, her arms folded, "it's just like what always happens with Staten Island. We should have expected this."

Manhattan rounds on her. "*What?*"

She laughs humorlessly. "Right, you wouldn't know, new guy. Staten Island is the sore thumb of this city. The rest of New York votes blue, the island goes red. The rest of us want better subways; the island just wants more cars. You know why the Verrazano Bridge toll is so high? *They* wanted that. To keep the 'riffraff' from Brooklyn out!" She makes a disgusted noise. "So if anybody's gonna stab an ally in the back, it would be that borough."

"We can't awaken the primary without all of us." Manhattan still hasn't raised his voice, but his words have grown clipped, his tone dangerous. "We *need* her."

"Then one of us is going to have to go talk to her," Bronca says. "Convince her to work with us."

Silence.

Hong sighs and takes a silk handkerchief out of his pocket, mopping his face and neck with it unnecessarily. "He was right; this *is* worse than London. Though I suppose that's why this 'Staten Island' turned on the rest of you, if she figured out the danger."

"What danger?" Bronca frowns at him in confusion. "What's London got to do with—"

Then Veneza exclaims in muffled delight and emerges from the freezer. In one hand she's got a plastic grocery bag, which has been partially wrapped around some kind of square tray inside. Immediately she crouches, and yanks the bag open. "These are frozen, but you can still kind of suck on them," she mutters. "I was worried my mala half brother would eat them when he comes over to my place, because he would, so I stored them here at work, then forgot about them . . . Ha!"

And she triumphantly lifts a small round chocolate-looking thing out of the plastic container.

"What the fuck," Brooklyn says.

Veneza rolls her eyes. "Brigadeiro. Some kind of Brazilian candy thing, like, oh, truffles. My dad's Portuguese, not Brazilian, but we eat them, too, because yay colonialism. And it's not specific to São Paulo, but . . ." Hurrying over to the couch, Veneza crouches and holds the brigadeiro to the man's lips. If Bronca hadn't already been staring, she might not believe what she now sees: São Paulo shivers all over and gains more clarity, just at the touch of the sweet. Now he's full color, if still a bit undersaturated. Veneza murmurs something in Portuguese, coaxing, which seems to help in itself; he shivers brighter, closer to human color. São Paulo opens his mouth. She pops the little thing in—and to everyone's relief, after a moment he starts to chew. "Ah, beleza.

Fucking beautiful. I was just faking the São Paulo accent, though; I hope he doesn't think I was making fun—"

São Paulo opens his eyes. "Valeu," he replies, and then sits up.

Queens claps in delight. Then she slides over to crouch beside Veneza, stage-whispering to ask if she can have one of the brigadeiros.

Hong regards São Paulo with disfavor. "Good, you're not dead."

São Paulo glares at him blearily. "It took you three days to get here?"

"I had to take a plane. Planes take time."

"It still shouldn't have taken—" Then São Paulo's eyes narrow. "The Summit. You notified them, and they balked. *That's* what took you an extra day."

Hong snorts a little in amusement, and then he takes out his smartphone and starts scrolling through it. "I've told you that it's nothing personal, Paulo. The old ones hate the younger cities on principle. And maybe they think you're arrogant."

"Of course I'm arrogant, I'm São Paulo. I'm also *right*, and they don't want to admit it." Paulo extends his arms for some reason, examining them as if he expects to see something other than his own limbs. He flexes his hands, and whatever he feels satisfies him, so he relaxes. "So they'll deny the facts on the ground and make this to be incompetence on my part. You keep asking me why I hate them? *This* is why."

"I set the bones when I found you. Healed them with some Café do Ponto coffee that I had in the car. Thank fancy New York airport coffee shops for that, and thank me for my foresight. Brazilian cigarettes taste like shit, by the way." Then Hong finds whatever he's looking for on his phone. "Here's a thing that should concern all of us." He turns his phone around.

Bronca comes over to see, as do the others. Paulo glances at the image from where he is, and sighs. The others gasp, but all Bronca can make out is a blur. With an irritated sigh, she pushes through them and takes the phone from Hong, lifting it close enough to see.

It's an aerial photograph of New York City, taken at sunset. She's seen photos like this before, artsy shots taken from drones or helicopters and using specialized equipment. This one is typical in centering Manhattan—but unusual in not excluding the other boroughs from the shot. The helicopter seems to have been hovering somewhere around the midpoint of the island, maybe over Central Park, pointing south. In the foreground spreads lower Manhattan, with its cluster of skyscrapers huddling uneasily on the tongue of landfill that makes up that part of the island. To the left—the image is slightly curved, a deliberate distortion probably meant to suggest that New York encompasses most of Earth— is probably Long Island City, Queens, and maybe Bay Ridge in Brooklyn, curving away toward the Verrazano Bridge. To the far right is Jersey City, or maybe Hoboken; Bronca can't tell. All of it sparkles in energy-efficient LED-lit squares. The photographer has added a slight orange filter, to warm the coldness of the lights and give the whole image more life. It's New York at its brightest and most beautiful.

Except for the farthest point of the image, across a dark stretch of water from the lowermost tip of Manhattan. Staten Island.

Its lights are much dimmer—so dim, in fact, that Bronca wonders why she hasn't heard anything about a brownout. But as she squints at the image, she realizes the problem isn't dimness. It's that Staten Island seems much farther away than it should be. She blinks, shakes her head. No. The borough is where it should be, but its perspective is off. An optical illusion, maybe, caused by the distortion of the photograph? Whatever it is, it looks as if Staten Island is miles farther from Manhattan than it actually is.

Her thumb bumps a button on Hong's phone by accident, and the image shifts to let her see that the photo is part of some kind of social media thread. Most of it's in Chinese, but there are a few English-language posts. "MORE TERRISM?!" shouts one spelling-challenged alarmist.

Hong takes his phone back. "This has never happened before," he says. It's mostly to Paulo, though he glances at all of them. His jaw is tight. "Cityspace is cityspace. Peoplespace is peoplespace. They are different universes, normally bridged only through us. Yet this photo reflects the fact that one borough of this city, *in cityspace*, is actively attempting to withdraw from the rest. And the denizens of peoplespace have *noticed*."

Paulo has pushed himself to his feet, though he needed Veneza's help to get all the way up. (She blushes, Bronca notes, when he nods to her and murmurs something that's probably *good thinking on the brigadeiro* in Portuguese, and which she's clearly hearing as *come with me to the Casbah*.) "This is what I've been trying to tell all of you old shits," Paulo snaps, his accent lengthening the last word into *sheets*, though otherwise his English is only lightly inflected with another tongue. "Something here is impeding the normal postpartum process—something more than just the fact that this city hasn't finished its maturation. The dimensional overlap is unstable. The Enemy is *too* active, active in ways it never has been—"

"Yes, yes." Hong dismisses him and focuses on Manhattan, who he seems to have arbitrarily decided is the leader of the group, probably because he's the only other man present. "I saw you and your cohort attempting to synchronize with your primary. Did you find him?"

Manhattan shakes his head. "No. We saw him, but..."

That's when Bronca inhales, remembering what she'd suddenly noticed during their whatever-it-was. "Those tile patterns," she says. "I *know* those fucking tile patterns." And then she turns and heads for the meeting room door. Behind her, the others are still for an instant, then she hears them scramble or stumble to follow.

Beyond the meeting room, the Center has closed for the evening. Yijing's left a sticky note on the monitor of Bronca's office desktop, even though she knows that Bronca only turns the damn thing on when she has to: "600K in new donations!!" Bronca stares at it for a moment, unable to process the number, then she puts the note aside to focus on something that makes sense. Like tracking down the living embodiment of New York City from clues she picked up in a dream.

By the time the machine has finished its endless boot-up sequence, she's gone to one of her bookcases and yanked out a big photo book titled *Beaux Arts Century*. And by the time the others have crowded into her office to try to figure out what she's figured out, she's found it. "This. This!" She slaps one of the photos in the book, then turns it around for them. It's a full-color, high-quality picture of a room with a beautifully vaulted ceiling, tiled with what looks like decorative gold bricks.

Manhattan leans down to peer at it, and a muscle in his jaw flexes. "That's the style. Not the place."

"Yeah, I don't think the primary is sleeping in the Grand Central Oyster Bar," drawls Brooklyn. She's frowning, though. "But I do feel like I've seen tiles like this in other places."

"You have," says Bronca, grinning, "because back before people with no taste started replacing every beautiful thing in this city with cheap bullshit, it was one of the most distinctive architectural forms in the world—an art movement that was centered in New York. They're called Guastavino tiles. Obsolete now, but back in the day they were designed to be fireproof and self-stabilizing. Perfect for a city that's half-underground and full of flammable trash." She taps the ceiling in the photo. "There's only a few examples of this left in the city. So . . ."

"Ohhhhh, yeah, I got you," says Veneza, sliding into Bronca's desk chair and pulling the keyboard toward herself. Bronca sees her typing in "Guastavino tiles" and "Manhattan."

Manhattan, meanwhile, has been thumbing through the book. "This says a lot of the Guastavino vaults were in old tenements," he says, looking troubled. "Buildings that are derelict—" He stops. Bronca sees how his eyes widen. Then he turns the book around so fast that the motion knocks over a cup of pens on Bronca's desk. "Here," he says, his voice tight as he points. "*Here.*"

Brooklyn looks, and chuckles. "Oh, my God. Of *course.*"

Veneza looks, then grins, and turns the desktop monitor so they can see the web page she's pulled up. DECOMMISSIONED SUBWAY STATION IS ARCHITECTURAL JEWEL IN THE CITY'S CROWN, the header reads. It's the same place that Manhattan has found in Bronca's book. "Old City Hall Station."

"Then that's where he is," Manhattan murmurs. He leans on the desk, letting out a sigh of relief. "We can go and find him, finally."

"It's not easy to get to," Brooklyn warns. "That station is defunct, closed to the public most of the time. Only way in—if you don't want to sneak onto the tracks and risk electrocution, getting run over by a train, or getting arrested—is via the Transit Museum, but they only do tours once in a blue moon. I think I've got a favor I can call in, though." She reaches for her phone.

"Can't you get there on the 6 train, when it turns around?" Veneza asks Brooklyn. "Tourists do it all the time. I did it once."

"Yeah, but they don't let you *out* of the train. It doesn't even stop."

Hong has come to peer at the book while they're talking. Then he shakes his head impatiently and glowers around at them. "Fine. You'll need to get there as soon as you can. We'll have to hope that the strength your primary gains from consuming you four will finally allow him to awaken and properly protect the city, even without the fifth borough."

Silence falls for a moment.

Then Brooklyn says, "I'm sorry, *what*?"

CHAPTER TWELVE

They Don't Have Cities There

In the morning, after Aislyn has made breakfast and eaten with her parents—and Conall, who did not look at her the entire time—she heads off to work. On the doorstep of the house she stops short, however, surprised by the sight of an enormous twenty-foot-wide white pillar taking up most of the front yard.

It's nothing identifiable. Just a big, smooth-sided and feature-less cylindrical white thing jutting up from the ground and out of sight into the sky above. Aislyn stares at it, trying to understand how someone has built something this big in their front yard without her noticing, and without anyone in her house remarking on it. And so fast, given that it wasn't there last night! Then she realizes she can see a flock of passing Canada geese through its translucence...and she understands, sort of.

The pillar is like the flower fronds, and like the woman who always wears white; neither is From Around Here. And like the flower fronds, no one other than Aislyn can see the pillar—which is why, when her father passes her on the way to his own car, he waves without remarking on the titanic tower that now shadows his house. Her mother won't be able to see it, either, Aislyn is pretty sure. Only Aislyn knows it's there.

When she steps into the driveway and gets a good look at the horizon—their house is on a slight hill—she spots another, similar pillar in the distance. Somewhere over near Freshkills Park, she's guessing.

Aislyn has a car—a used Ford hybrid that she bought a few years back. Her father hates it because he thinks only liberals should care about the environment, but he put up with her choice, and even gave her half the purchase price so that she could buy it outright without a car note, because at least it's American made. She pays for gas and insurance with the money she earns from working at the local library, where she has an off-the-books job. (It's nothing illicit, but it has to be off the books because she doesn't have anything but a two-year associate's, and the city requires a four-year degree. Her father agreed to "lose" some outstanding parking tickets for the head librarian.) But she can't drive the car much because her father monitors the mileage, and because she suspects he's put a GPS tracker in it somewhere. He does things like that. When Aislyn wants privacy, she takes the bus.

Right now, though, sitting in the car and staring at the tower in her yard, and thinking of the strange man—the city of São Paulo, apparently—who approached her, and thinking of Conall and her fear of leaving the island and . . . everything, Aislyn abruptly feels like she just can't take much more of this.

So she looks up at the rearview mirror, where a thin, barely visible white tendril wafts about. "Hey," she says. "Can you come here? I need to talk."

For a moment nothing happens. Then, abruptly, the rearview mirror changes. One second, it features a stunning view of the

Houlihan driveway. In the next, it opens onto a vast space. She can't see it well—only a hard gray-white floor, which is so stark with shadows that it feels like there's a spotlight somewhere, just out of view. She can't see what's making the shadows, but then one of them shifts, and a moment later the Woman in White sits up from somewhere below the rearview mirror. She's different again, Aislyn notes. Still white, but this time there is a hint of epicanthic fold about her eyes, and exotic angles to her cheekbones and the spacing of her nose. Russian, maybe? Her brows are white. Her hair— Aislyn blinks.

"Lyn, my person-shaped friend! I figured out why you were angry with me last night. What a bad boy that minion was. And how foolish, to get grabby with a city! You could have smushed him."

Aislyn nods absently. "Are you bald?"

"Am I—" The Woman pauses. Abruptly, lush tawny-white hair tumbles around her face, nearly crowding her features out of the mirror. One lock falls artfully over an eye. "No, I am not bald."

"Ohhhhh-kaaaaay." Then Aislyn frowns, remembering that she *is* supposed to be mad at the Woman, after all. Despite Conall's subdued manner, Aislyn's father had been delighted with him that morning, slapping the younger man on the back and calling him "son." Apparently the current story is that somebody came into the backyard, and Conall fended the intruder off despite having drunk too much to remember the intruder's face. A real hero, in Matthew Houlihan's eyes. "So you know what Conall did."

"Yes, that one." The Woman smiles brightly. "You should know that the guide-lines—the things you keep calling flowers?—don't *control* people, not precisely. They just . . . guide. Encourage preexisting inclinations, and channel the energies from same into more compatible wavelengths."

What Aislyn gleans from this gobbledygook is that Conall got grabby because Conall is a grabby bastard to begin with, who might have attacked Aislyn whether he had a flower growing from his neck or not. But that, and the explanation, does not console her. "Why are you putting *anything* in people?" she asks. "I didn't think it meant much at the ferry station. Now, though..."

It is indisputable that the flower fronds, or guide-lines or whatever they're called, have a purpose. That this purpose is something other than control makes it no less unnerving. What does happen, then, when the guide-lines get inside a person? Aislyn has a sudden memory of watching a nature show on a slow day, about parasites. One episode had been all about a fungus that grew inside ants as a kind of webwork throughout their bodies, eating them as it grew, and controlling their behavior. Then once all the juicy bits of the ant were gone, the fungus popped out of their heads in order to release its spores.

From the back of the head, Aislyn remembers, incidentally. What would be the nape of the neck on a person.

In the mirror, the Woman in White leans closer, narrowing her eyes. "Hmm, you're getting the wrong idea, I can tell," she says. "It's not, uh, whatever you're thinking. Let me explain. But this is awkward. Hold on a moment, I'll come to you."

Something shoots from the mirror, past Aislyn's face and into the back seat. Aislyn catches her breath and jerks away in pure reflex, but she doesn't quite have time to register what she's seeing as something frightening. As far as she can tell, it's just a long, thick tongue of featureless white substance, which skeets through the mirror frame as if it isn't glass, but the opening of some kind of tube or delivery chute. What she sees when she turns is not a puddle of goo, as she is half expecting, but feet. White, featureless boots, attached to nothing, although the bottoms of the boots are beginning to develop texture and color. Then something pixels up from these to form legs, primly crossed at the ankle. Then hips, a waist, all of it achieving realistic definition only belatedly—and finally the Woman in White sits there, beaming, with a little clutch purse in her lap.

There is an instant in which Aislyn's mind tries to signal an alarm, doom, existential threat, all the usual fight-or-flight signals that are the job of the lizard brain. And if the gush of substance had been different somehow—something hideous, maybe—she would have started screaming.

Three things stop her. The first and most atavistic is that everything in her life has programmed her to associate evil with specific, easily definable things. Dark skin. Ugly people with scars or eye patches or wheelchairs. Men. The Woman in White is the visual opposite of everything Aislyn has been taught to fear, and so . . . even though intellectually Aislyn now has proof that what she's been seeing is just a guise, and the Woman in White's true form could be anyone or any*thing* . . .

. . . Aislyn also thinks, *Well, she looks all right*.

The second thing that stops her is the latent, not-quite-acknowledged realization that the Woman is dangerous. What will happen if she screams? Her father will come running to defend what's his, and Aislyn is fairly certain that the Woman cannot be harmed by any ordinary human being. And then will the Woman put one of those parasite-flowers into him? He is already a man inclined toward violence and control. Will he become worse? She will do nearly anything to avoid this possibility.

The third, and possibly most powerful of the things that stop her, is that she is agonizingly lonely, and the Woman has begun to feel something very like a friend.

So Aislyn does not scream.

"Now, you just drive to work," the Woman in White says, reaching forward to pat Aislyn's shoulder. Again there is a fleeting ghost of a sensation, like a sting that is short-circuited on its way to causing pain. Aislyn flinches now, realizing what that sting means—but there is no white tendril on her shoulder when the Woman takes her hand away. The Woman sighs a little. Aislyn lets out a shaky breath.

(She does not parse the Woman's sigh as disappointment. She does not parse her own sigh as relief. The alternative is to challenge her own belief that the Woman in White isn't so bad. This would force her to question her own judgment and biases and find them wanting. And given how hard she has fought lately to feel *some* kind of belief in herself, she is not ready to doubt again. So it's fine. Everything is fine.)

Focusing on what matters, Aislyn jabs a finger at the huge white towerlike thing in her front yard. "What is that?"

"Mmm, think of it as an adapter cable," says the Woman in White. "You know what those are, don't you?"

"Yes. But that's not a cable."

"Of course it is. It's just a very *big* adapter cable."

Aislyn shakes her head. She's going to lose it in a minute. "Okay. Fine. What's it adapting, then?"

"Weeeeelllll, an adapter usually connects one way of doing a thing to a different way of doing a thing, right?" The Woman shrugs. "You want to listen to music. You have speakers designed to work with one kind of music-maker, but all of your music is on a different kind of music-maker. Yes? Irritating and inefficient. There's a simple fix for the problem, however." She gestures at the white tower.

It shouldn't make sense, but it does. Aislyn shakes her head slowly. "But what, I don't know, *way of doing a thing*, could you possibly be adapting with *that*?"

"My universe to yours."

"I—" Aislyn stares. Then closes her mouth. She really can't think of anything else to say to that.

The Woman sighs impatiently and then waves a hand at the steering wheel. "Drive, drive! I don't want you attracting any more attention by veering from your usual routine. I can't watch you all the time. That's why that nasty little São Paulo almost got to you last night." Then she grins in delight, clapping her hands in just a little too much glee—but it is infectious, her giddy delight. "But you showed him, didn't you?"

It *had* felt good to send that awful man tumbling. Just like Conall. São Paulo's car is gone today, she notes, and there have been no police or emergency vehicles around that morning, so she assumes he got up and drove himself away. With two broken arms? No matter. Aislyn smiles to herself, then turns to the steering wheel and starts up the car. "Yeah. Okay. But if you're going to ride to work with me, you have to tell me what's going on."

"That's the plan, lovely." Aislyn pulls out of the driveway as she hears the Woman settling into her back seat. There is an odd moment when the car bumps across the gutter into the street. The whole vehicle seems to dip lower than usual. The struts groan, and she hears something in the car's undercarriage scrape loudly against asphalt. The Woman in White mutters something like "Damned *gravity*, always forget the exact ratio," and then the car rises back to its usual height and pulls away with no more difficulty.

"The adapters are *possibility*," the Woman says as Aislyn drives. Aislyn tries to look at her in the rearview because it's polite to meet another person's eyes during a conversation, but the Woman isn't sitting in that area of the back seat. "A just-in-case. And I have no choice but to put them in the few rare places where this universe's muons have become somewhat friendlier—which unfortunately means your front yard. Also, on top of the ferry station, over at that park that used to be a landfill, and at that college you used to attend. Where do you work?"

"The public library branch at—" Then Aislyn understands. She went to the park after work once, and was ogled the whole time by a park service employee who was picking up the trash. That was last month or so. "You're putting those things wherever I go?"

"Not wherever you go. Just places where you've rejected this reality to some degree or another. Even before you were a city, such acts had power. Superpositioned objects change state depending on observation, after all."

"Okay." She doesn't like it. She doesn't even understand it. But it can't be a big deal because the Woman in White is a nice woman who looks okay, and so Aislyn has no real reason to be afraid, or to feel used. And anyway, she's telling Aislyn about it, so isn't that better than lying? "Oh...ah...okay, then."

"That's why I like you, Lyn." It is her mother's nickname for her. Her father has never called her Lyn. She's never allowed anyone else to do so, either. "You're so accommodating. Who would have thought *this* city, of all of them, would have such an accommodating component? Such a tolerant girl-shape."

Yes. Aislyn has always tried to be tolerant. She takes a deep breath. "So, the . . . adapters?"

"Oh, right. Well, if I can just put down a few more like the one in your yard, I'll be able to align the . . . hmm. Errrf." Aislyn hears the Woman in White shift in irritation, maybe fidgeting. "This place is so primitive. I'm not even sure I can come up with enough analogies to explain it, since you barely understand how this universe works, let alone others."

"Oh, wow, I didn't know there was more than one."

"See? How could you not know something so basic? But oh, there are ex-approaches-infinity-llions. *Hakretimajillions.* More every minute!" But for once, the Woman in White does not sound delighted by this. "That's the problem, of course. Once, there was only one universe. One realm where possibility became probability, and life was born. So much life! On nearly every plane and surface, floating along every layer of air, stuffed into every crack. Not like this stingy universe, where life huddles on only a few wet balls surrounding a handful of gassy balls. Ah, Lyn, if only you could see how beautiful it is."

And in the rearview mirror, something changes, as if in response to the Woman's wistfulness. Aislyn tries not to stare because she's driving, and even though it's only a two-lane road in an area where there are fields and stands of woods in between neighborhoods, she still isn't interested in learning what a head-on collision feels like. And yet . . . In quick glances at the rearview, she no longer sees the car that's tailgating her or the road beyond it, or the school bus that should be turning onto that road from an intersection she just passed. Instead she sees that empty, shadowed room again, from when the Woman first spoke to her. Then she notices a swirl of vapor in the air . . . or is it liquid? Or is it, more simply, just color? Just a sinuous swath of color that darts and flows across the mirror like something liquid, but also like something alive, and pinky pale against the stark shadows of the background. Something else moves across it—and here Aislyn feels a bit of alarm because it is a black something, and black things are usually bad. It's only a little bit of alarm, though, because then she sees that the black thing is a rounded, cylindrical blackness, and nothing bad ever came in that shape. This thing makes her think of hockey pucks. She likes hockey, even though the Rangers aren't very good. (She prefers the Islanders, even if they're not of *her* island, exactly.) Or maybe this thing is something like those chocolate cakes that used to come wrapped in foil when she was a kid, and which she hasn't eaten since she was thirteen because her father once said she was gaining too much weight. What were those called? Ring Dongs? Ding Hos? Regardless, once upon a time she loved them, so when she sees this thing scuttle across the mist-stream of pink and sort of erase it, she just thinks, *Huh, weird but kind of cute*, and keeps driving.

(*Is* that movement scuttling, though? The pink mist flinches away. She hears a faint, high-pitched gibber that makes her think of pleading, of pain and struggle and then hopeless despair—and then the mirror is empty again, and the road demands her attention.)

"There are no cities in that first universe," the Woman continues as they pass woodlands and strip malls. "There are wonders you can't imagine. Convolutions of physicality and intellect beyond anything this world might ever achieve, but nothing so monstrous as cities. It seems strange to you, I know, to think of something so central to your existence—you *are* one!—as monstrous. But to the people of that realm, there is nothing more terrifying and terrible." She utters a little sad laugh. "Than cities."

Aislyn contemplates this, and finds it not at all difficult to understand. She has stood on the docks of the ferry and gazed across the water at distant, looming Manhattan, and she has trembled in its shadow. "Cities *are* monstrous," she says. "Filthy. Too many people, too many cars. Criminals and perverts everywhere. And they're bad for the environment, too."

"Yes, yes." The Woman flicks a hand; Aislyn sees the edge of fingers in the rearview, momentarily occluding the stark-shadowed place. When the Woman's fingers have passed, Aislyn sees that the black cylindrical thing is back, lingering now at the edge of the mirror. It's not still; it's bouncing up and down, arrhythmically. Weird, but cute.

The Woman continues, "All of that is true, but that's not what really makes cities so awful. You must understand some of it now, yes? You've seen beyond this realm into the edge of other realities. It is the nature of all thinking entities to know ourselves, at least to some degree."

"I—" Aislyn starts to protest. She dislikes being told that she is this thing she loathes. She also doesn't understand whatever the Woman is trying to say. "I guess?"

"Yes. Well." Another hand flutter. The hockey dong—Aislyn snickers at this, it feels dirty, better go with Ding Ho instead—abruptly stops bouncing or pulsing or whatever it's doing, as if it has noticed the Woman's movement. As if the two images have anything to do with each other. But the place of stark shadows isn't real, is it? It seems farther away, somewhere well beyond the rear window of the car. She has been sure, until this moment, that it was an optical illusion—a reflection off one of the back seat windows, combined with passing shifts of sunlight. Or a weird daydream. She did have corned beef hash for breakfast; maybe the mirror stuff is undigested beef or underdone potato.

(Much, much, much later, when the whole business is nearly over, she will look back on this incident and think, *Confirmation bias is a bitch.*)

"The problem," the Woman continues, now working up to a real rant if Aislyn reads her voice correctly, "is that cities are rapacious. There is infinite room in existence for all the universes that spin forth from life—even universes as bizarre as this one! Room for everyone. But some life forms cannot be content with just their ecological niche; they are born invasive. They *punch through*—and when they do, they turn ten thousand realities into nothing, like that." She snaps her fingers. "And they can do much, much worse, if they put their backs into it. Or even if they don't."

Something odd is happening in the world of stark shadows. The Ding Ho—is it bigger? No, just closer to the mirror, although the perspective seems off. Abruptly there's a faint waft of cold air on the back of Aislyn's neck, which feels like bliss. It's June, and the car's air conditioner isn't working well; it only sporadically spits out gusts of actual cold. Probably needs fluid. Maybe the Woman in White has opened one of the vents in the back seat.

"That, uh, sounds awful," Aislyn says, trying to keep an eye on her speed. She'll never hear the end of it from her father if she gets a ticket.

"It is a catastrophe that makes the end of your entire species a mere triviality." Aislyn actually hears her shrug. "What's one more extinction, after all, when numberless intelligent species are wiped out every day by the horror of *cities*?"

The Woman has just lost Aislyn. "Wait, what?"

"You work in a library. Have you read any Lovecraft?"

Aislyn rubs the back of her neck. The cold is starting to give her a muscle spasm or something. She wants to say something to the Woman in White about shutting the back seat vent, but around them, the occasional woods have given way to auto shops and gas stations, and billboards for shopping malls in New Jersey. This means they're almost at the library where Aislyn works. She's got some muscle relaxants in her purse if it gets too bad.

"I've read him a little," she replies. Science fiction and fantasy have never really been her taste, except in romance; she enjoys giggling over stories about alien men with big blue penises. One of the senior librarians is a big Lovecraft fan, though, and he kept insisting that she read some until she finally gave in. "I mean, *The Shadow over Innsmouth* was really rambly, but I get why people make movies about the monsters. I tried some of his short stories, too." Those had been even more rambly. Still, the one she'd read that was about New York—set in Red Hook, where Ikea is—had sounded pretty accurate to how her father describes Brooklyn: full of criminals and scary foreigners, and gangs of foreigners being criminal. She'd liked that one, at least, because its protagonist was Irish, and afraid of tall buildings.

The Woman's voice has grown grim. "Lovecraft was right, Aislyn. There's something *different* about cities, and about the people in cities. Individually, your kind are nothing. Microbes. Algae. But never forget that algae once wiped out nearly all life on this planet."

"Wait, what?" That doesn't sound right. Algae? "Really?"

"Really. Cities are an endemic problem of life amid these branches of existence: put enough human beings in one place, vary the strains enough, make the growth medium fertile enough, and your kind develops...hybrid vigor." Aislyn can actually hear the Woman in White shudder elaborately, the cloth of her outfit shifting. "You eat each other's cuisines and learn new techniques, new spice combinations, trade for new ingredients; you grow stronger. You wear each other's fashions and learn new patterns to apply to your lives, and because of it you *grow stronger*. Even just one new language infects you with a radically different way of thinking! Why, in just a few thousand years you've gone from being unable to count to understanding the quantum universe—and you'd have made it there faster if you didn't keep destroying each other's cultures and having to start over from scratch. It's just too much."

Aislyn frowns. "What's wrong with learning a new language?" She taught herself some Gaelic as a child. It's hard to pronounce, and with no other Gaelic speakers around that she could practice on, she's forgotten nearly all of what she learned, outside of a few colorful phrases and some songs. But she cannot comprehend how learning it was a bad thing.

"Nothing. I'm just describing your nature. I don't judge. But it's a problem because as *you* grow, *your cities* grow. You change one another, city and people, people and city. Then your cities start bringing multiple universes together—and once a few such breaches have occurred, why, the whole structure of existence is weakened."

Now the Woman in White leans forward. Aislyn can see her hand on the headrest of the passenger seat. "Countless people, dying on countless worlds, and you don't even notice. Galaxies crushed beneath the dread, cold foundations of your reality. Some of your victims are aware enough to cry out to you, you know, but you do not hear. Some try to fight you, flee to nearby realms in hope of sanctuary, even worship you in hope of mercy—but not one of those poor souls has a chance. Does that sound fair to you, Aislyn? Do you understand why I have to stop you?"

In a horrible way, Aislyn does. And if it's true . . . God, it's awful. But . . . she frowns, and feels a little guilty for thinking this, but . . . is it *evil*? To some degree, what the Woman is talking about sounds like what Ms. Pappalardo, one of the librarians, who's also a vegan, always tells Aislyn: *Countless living beings have been enslaved so you could have honey in your tea.* Aislyn's read that this is wrong anyway; the bees make more honey than they can use, and the relationship between bees and humans is more symbiotic than slavery. But the real reason Aislyn doesn't stop putting honey in her tea is because . . . for God's sake, it's just honey.

"Maybe there's another way," Aislyn finds herself saying. She recalls a bumper sticker on Ms. Pappalardo's car. "For all of us to . . . coexist?"

"No. It's been tried." Then the Woman sighs, a little sadly. "The thing is, I know you're not evil. I was created to help the people back home understand you, after all—and I do, more than any of them ever could! But understanding doesn't always help."

Da-dump.

Aislyn, in the middle of making a turn, twitches the steering wheel a little late, distracted by both the conversation and that weird sound behind her. The car's turning radius is off; she hits the curb and curses out loud, jerking the wheel sharply to correct. She overcorrects at first, and then has to slew the wheel in the other direction to keep from hitting an oncoming car. The whole car lurches from side to side, and once again it feels weirdly sluggish and heavy as she does so—

"What— Damn it, I *told* you to stay in the staging area," the Woman snaps as Aislyn finally regains control of the car. "Now look what you did."

Stung, Aislyn blurts, "Sorry! I just— There was a weird sound—"

"I didn't mean you, Lyn dear, sorry." Abruptly there is the sound of a door being firmly closed, and then the cold draft stops. The car lifts immediately, struts up-creaking in what Aislyn imagines is relief. She's going to have to get those checked.

Pulling into the library's parking lot, Aislyn picks a parking spot, shuts off the car, and lets out a little breath of relief at the close call. She's going to have to have her front rims checked for dings, too, and her dad's going to kill her if she's damaged the car badly enough to need major repairs, but she's glad it wasn't worse.

When she glances at the rearview, it's normal again: the parking lot, the street beyond where cars pass, a guy walking by while picking his nose. She turns around and finds the Woman in White turned around as well, glaring out the back window as if she is personally, deeply offended by nose-picking. It's weird, but no weirder than usual, so Aislyn says, "So, do you need me to call you a Lyft or something?" She really doesn't want the Woman in White following her into work.

"What? Oh. No, dear." And the Woman smiles as she turns back. It is a kind, fond smile. "Always so thoughtful. I'm going to miss you."

"Are you going somewhere?"

"No. Listen." She reaches out to touch Aislyn's hand where it is braced on the passenger seat. "You understand that I don't hate you, yes? Belief matters in the multiverse, and I'm just enough like you to crave trust and connection and all that other nonsense. So...do you believe me? When I say that I care about you, and wish circumstances could be different?"

"Of course I do!" Aislyn has never had it in her to hold good intentions against people. And the Woman in White seems so sincere in her regret; Aislyn's heart goes out to her. She cannot imagine a world where people who mean well can do any real harm. She cannot reconcile all these big, elaborate topics—multiverses and inevitable doom and life as a living city—with the simple reality of the Woman, who is a genuinely nice person. The world needs more nice people.

So she pats the Woman's hand awkwardly, given their positions. "It will be all right. You'll see."

The Woman smiles. "You're a good dimension-crushing abomination," she says. "I'll do everything I can to take care of you, for as long as I can."

And then—if Aislyn hadn't been looking right at her, she wouldn't believe it—the Woman in White vanishes. There's no puff of smoke or popping sound or magical door opening and closing. She's just gone.

Aislyn sits there for a moment, stunned and confused and wondering why she smells a whiff of ocean brine. But she's about to be late, so after a moment she just shakes her head, accepts the things she cannot understand, and hurries into work.

CHAPTER THIRTEEN

Beaux Arts, Bitches

It's what happened with London," explains the living embodiment of the city of Hong Kong, with barely concealed impatience. "There were well over a dozen avatars in that case. Then something happened and there was only one—but the city was safe from then on."

Silence falls. After a moment of this, in which Manny and the others stare at Hong, speechless, he seems to grow even more irritated. He glares at Paulo. "You haven't told them?"

Paulo, still leaning on Veneza, sighs loudly. "I haven't *met* them, until now. And I would have explained it once they were ready, in a way they could understand, because I am not a *blundering insensitive ass*."

"Consume us," Manny says, speaking slowly to be sure he understands. "As in 'eat.'"

"As in 'cannibalism,'" Queens blurts, her eyes wide. "As in, 'death'!"

"As in Sodom and Gomorrah," Hong says, putting his hands on his hips. "Although I'm told the Enemy killed the former before the merger was complete—while they were in a transitional state akin to what you are, now. 'Fire and brimstone' consumed them then, the legends say; it was a volcanic eruption. The actual event destroyed *four* cities in the region, including two that weren't even alive yet."

Manny's shocked to realize Sodom and Gomorrah were real places. *No volcanoes here, at least*, he thinks, in a kind of giddy, terrifying denial. New York is islands on the edge of a sea—and climate change looms. A flood is more likely.

"Something like that is what could happen here," Hong continues, as if he has heard Manny's speculation. He's relentless. "If New York doesn't hurry up and eat all of you, it *will* happen. Except, given the interconnectedness of this metropolitan region, we believe the resulting cataclysm will take out parts of New Jersey, Long Island, Pennsylvania, and Connecticut in the process. Possibly western Massachusetts, too. There is a significant fault line in this region."

Okay. Maybe not flooding. Or maybe an earthquake and then flooding, followed by chunks of the East Coast falling into the sea. So many choices, really.

Everyone looks floored. Manny's feeling it, too, but maybe the person he used to be has a lot of practice at reacting quickly to shocking, horrific news. "You're lying," he snaps. Hong's jaw tightens, though he seems more disgusted than angry. "You're trying to manipulate us. Scare us, into doing…"

Into doing what the city requires. Into sacrificing themselves, if that's what it takes to keep the Woman in White from turning the Tri-state area into a crater.

"I'm telling you what has to be done," Hong says. He says it slowly, in icy-crisp English, as if they are all bad students whom he's been forced to teach. "I'm telling you what *has happened*, in every other case where a composite city—a city made of cities, like yours—has been born. There's a primary avatar and one or more sub-avatars of the boroughs or exurbs or shantytowns or whatever they're called. The birth is incomplete, and the city isn't safe, until the primary devours the others."

"If this is a story you've heard, 'devour' doesn't have to be literal," Bronca says. She's speaking slowly, too, though Manny suspects this is a processing thing for her. Chewing the idea over, out loud. "It could be . . . I don't know. Spiritual. Sexual, who knows."

"Sexual is not better!" says Padmini. She sounds horrified as she glares around at them.

"I don't know how the 'devour' part works," Hong admits. "But I told you: with London there were many, and then there was one. She was traumatized. For many years she would not speak at all. Now, she is . . . different, even for one of us. When she'll talk about the issue at all, she claims that she doesn't remember what happened." He sighs and folds his arms. "It clearly isn't anything *good*."

Manny wants to attack someone. Anyone. The urge to do violence runs under his skin like a current—but violence toward whom? He will not hurt the primary avatar. Lashing out at anyone else is pointless, because everyone in the room is either the messenger or another passenger on this ride to surreality. When he takes a deep breath to try to calm himself, it actually works, and has the feel of old habit. Yes. He is not some monster, lashing out wildly. Violence is a tool to be controlled and directed, and used only for worthy purpose. That is the man he has chosen to be.

He focuses on Paulo, not to attack, but to understand. "There is no way," he says, "that you could have soft-pedaled this to us."

Paulo still doesn't look good, Manny thinks, assessing him clinically. Here in Bronca's office, he's standing on his own near the microfridge, but his posture is decidedly off from true vertical. There are dark circles under his eyes. Still, he draws himself up with careful dignity. "I would have begun by explaining the stakes," he says. "You're all selfish. Anyone would be—but one *cannot* be, and be what we are. Thousands or millions of lives depend on a city's avatar. The Enemy is within the gates; there's no more time. If you have located the primary, then you must go to him." He takes a deep breath. "And then do whatever is necessary."

Padmini is the one who explodes. Manny wasn't expecting that. She seems like a nice girl. But she pushes away from the wall and lunges at Paulo, shoving him into the microfridge. "You want to let that—thing—kill us? *Eat* us? You haven't even been here when we needed you, and you just show up and tell us to die? How dare you! How *dare* you!"

Manny reacts without thinking, catching her by the shoulders before she can do more. He does this for two reasons: first because Paulo grimaced when she shoved him, as though he has injuries greater than what they've realized—or as if her shove hurt much more than it should have. *Only New York can injure São Paulo so badly, here within the city.* Unreliable ally or not, Manny suspects they still need Paulo.

The other reason that Manny reacts is more visceral. It's because Padmini called the primary *that thing.* "Stop it," he snaps at her. He knows he shouldn't. She's upset for good reason. But he cannot bear her rejection of the primary—of New York. They are all New York. He feels it, too, in the parts of himself that did not exist before three days ago: the same thing that any of them can do to a foreign city, they can do to each other. But New York cannot war with itself without dire consequences, any more than a man can stab himself in the guts and still be fine.

Padmini wrenches away from him, her hands immediately turning to fists. Manny braces himself for a fight, both as a man and as an island of fragile, built-by-the-lowest-bidder skyscrapers. Fortunately, she only shouts. "Be quiet! I don't want to hear anything more from you! You're crazy. You probably *want* to be eaten by him. Why would I want to be part of you? Oh—" And she turns away, hands in the air, making a sound like a growl.

"I don't want to die, either," he replies, then pushes on before he has time to think about Padmini's accusation, that he wants to be devoured. "And we don't know that we will! Paulo said it himself: *something different* has been happening here, beyond the usual process." He lifts his gaze to glare at the foreign cities. Paulo is trying not to be conspicuous about leaning on the microfridge to keep from falling over. Hong merely regards Manny impassively. "I know tap dancing when I hear it. Everything from the way we've awakened to the way the Enemy is acting—time after time, you've both been *surprised* by what's happened in this city. You're nearly as in the dark here as we are!"

"Maybe so," Hong agrees readily. He looks bored. No wonder Paulo hates him. "It's true that every city birth is different. Would you rather I not have mentioned that in every precedent we know of, the sub-avatars have vanished?"

"No. We needed to know that," Brooklyn says. Alone of all of them, she hasn't gotten to her feet. She still sits in the largest of Bronca's mismatched chairs, her legs primly crossed and hands folded in her lap. Maybe only Manny sees how pale her knuckles have gone.

Hong regards her for a moment, then inclines his head to her in a "just so" nod.

Padmini turns away to begin pacing in the narrow space on that side of Bronca's office, muttering to herself. She's meandering between Tamil and a few creative English imprecations. Manny tries to ignore her muttering, to leave her that much privacy—but then she says, "Kan ketta piragu surya namashkaaram," which translates to something like *Why look at the sun after you've already been blinded* or *Why bother doing morning yoga if you got up late*, and he cannot stop himself from reacting.

"None of us are enemies to each other," Manny says. Padmini stops and stares at him. "We've got one enemy—the one who's already attacked each and every one of us, sometimes more than once. The primary hasn't done anything to harm us. He's on our side. He has no reason to want to kill us—"

"You don't know that," Bronca says, with a sigh.

"It doesn't matter if he *wants* to kill us or not, new guy," Brooklyn says. Her voice has hardened. She folds her hands, regarding Manny over them. She's still showing the toll of both her battle against the creatures that attacked her family, and the shock of learning that she's lost her home. "Lots of bad things that happen ain't personal. This primary could love us all like brothers and sisters, but in the end he's going to do what he's got to do. So would we in his position. Millions of lives in exchange for four?" She shrugs. It looks nonchalant but isn't. "That ain't even a debate."

Manny nods at her, grateful for the support. She regards him back, her gaze frank and cool. By this he knows that she did not say it for him.

Hong then nods, too. "Well. Now you know. Let's go, then."

They all turn to stare at him. Even Manny shakes his head in pure incredulity at the man's complete lack of tact. "Too soon, man," says Veneza. God knows what she thinks of all of this, but it's clear that she gets the dynamics. "*Way* too fucking soon."

"I don't care if it is or not," Hong says, without heat. "All of you deserve to know what will happen, but Paulo is correct in that there's no more room for sentimentality or individualism or cowardice. Just on the ride from JFK, I saw blankets of white tentacles covering entire blocks. They are forming *structures*; did you notice that?"

"Structures?" Bronca frowns. "Like what?"

"Like nothing I have seen that can be compared. On Staten Island, I saw . . ." For the first time, he hesitates and seems disconcerted. Then he shakes his head, and it's gone. "A tower, of sorts. I have no idea what it's for. But if our enemy has built it, there can be no good reason for that."

Veneza abruptly gets up and exits Bronca's office, leaving the door open. It's getting late, though sunset-tinted light still comes in through the main gallery window because they haven't put down the shutters yet. They all stare as she stops at the big window, bathed in slanting red rays, and leans forward, peering at something in the distance. Then she points out the window, and turns to call to them, "A tower, right? Uh, like that?"

They all hurry into the main gallery and cluster at the window beside her.

It's difficult to see from here. Small with distance, though it arcs above the trees and buildings and the zooming cars of some kind of highway. Manny has to squint to see it—but it looks like a cross between a giant toadstool and the Gateway Arch in St. Louis: an arch that is irregular, misshapen in its twists and curves, and flattened at the top. There are slowly undulating streamers coming off the flat top's edges, attenuating into a thinness too difficult to see clearly from this distance and angle. It's easy to guess where most of those streaming, moving tendrils are going, though. Down. Thinning into filaments and spreading onto the streets below.

"I saw that when I went out for lunch today," Veneza says softly as they all stare. "I thought it was, you know, a guerilla art installation, bad marketing gimmick, whatever. I was going to go check it out after work today. But when I texted a friend about it—she lives there, it's Hunts Point—she said she didn't see anything."

Bronca groans softly. "I live in Hunts Point. Fuck, that thing is probably right over my house."

Hong regards Veneza for a moment. "It wouldn't be a good idea to go near it."

"Yeah, you think?"

"What is it?" Paulo asks.

"No idea." Hong sighs. "I suppose you were right about this city being an unusual case."

"Yes, I was." Paulo glares at him. "Thank you ever so much for throwing me under the bus, by the way."

"You're welcome," Hong says evenly.

"Look," says Bronca, in a soft tone of horror. She's pointing at the street right in front of the Center. On a sidewalk across that street, a group of Latino teenagers walks by, perhaps heading home from an after-school activity. They're laughing and joking with each other, punching each other as boys do, making a lot of noise in their young joy.

There are six of them. Three have tendrils curling up from the backs of their necks or shoulders. One of the infected ones has

fronds all over his arms, too, and a small one growing from his face just below one eye.

Everyone falls silent for a while.

Bronca breaks the silence with a noisy deep breath. "I need... shit. Let's go for a walk." When the stares turn to her, she tightens her jaw. "Just around the block. I've been in here without a break for going on forty-eight hours. I need more than just talking with you people to get a feel for what's really happening out there."

They look at each other. Hong starts to open his mouth, and Paulo elbows him. Bronca makes a sound of annoyance, then turns to go on her own.

Manny immediately moves to join her, though she stops and glares at him. "You can't go alone," he says. She narrows her eyes at him, and it's definitely an intimidating look, even though she's shorter than him. He doesn't care. (He's faced worse, he knows, though he doesn't remember what.) "None of us can go anywhere alone until this is done."

"This is bullshit," Padmini mutters. Veneza claps her on the shoulder awkwardly, but then moves to join Bronca and Manny.

"Do you have a construct ready, to defend yourself should the Enemy attack?" Hong asks.

Bronca curls her lip at him; it's not a smile. "I always have my boots." She's not wearing boots at the moment, Manny notices, but Hong seems satisfied with that. Hong eyes Manny, who grimaces as he realizes he doesn't. It's not difficult to guess what Hong means—but what quintessential Manhattanism can he think of to weaponize in a crisis? He's been here three days and spent less than one of them in his own borough.

Well— He reaches back and finds his wallet. There's the debit card. As long as he's not broke.

Hong gives him a skeptical look, then nods at Bronca. "Well, it's her borough, anyway. Try not to get in her way."

Manny winces, but follows Bronca and Veneza outside.

The instant they step outside, however, Bronca stops, frowning. Manny notices her wince and put a hand to one hip, as if it pains her. "Shit, I should've come out of there before. *Everything* feels wrong."

"Yeah, but it's a dry heat," Veneza says. Bronca only shakes her head and starts walking, with a noticeable limp.

The Center sits on the gradual slant of a hill, so they start up its slope toward some smaller avenue that Manny can see up ahead. Everything looks fine to his eye, apart from the occasional people or cars that pass by with tendrils on them. There are no big, FDR Drive–esque plumes of tendrils that Manny can see, but if this many denizens of the borough are being infected, then there's something, somewhere. Those structures, maybe. Maybe the thing on FDR Drive was developing into something like them—a tower—when he stopped it.

Bronca strides forcefully despite her age, glancing at every example of the infected and muttering something in a language Manny can't parse, for once. Something that apparently isn't spoken much in Manhattan. She's rubbing at her side, too, in addition to the hip. Both gestures feel familiar. When she does it again, grimacing as if she's got heartburn, Manny says, "When I fought that thing on FDR, it felt like it was digging into *me*, not just the asphalt."

Bronca sighs. "Oh, good. I was worried it was rheumatism."

At the corner, however, Bronca comes to an abrupt halt in front of them, her face a study in shock. Manny tenses, sliding a hand into his pocket for his debit card, but what she's staring at is simply an empty rubble field on the opposite corner. It looks like a building there has been recently torn down. There's nothing left but tumbled bricks, and a newly painted plywood fence announcing whatever's coming soon to replace it. He can't see anything to be upset about, but Veneza, too, inhales as she sees it. "Oh noooo," she says. "Oh, my God. Murdaburga."

"What?" asks Manny.

"Murdaburga's gone!" Her whole posture radiates tragedy. "Those were like the fattest, juiciest burgers you ever had. And that place had been there longer than I've been alive. It's a Bronx *institution*. When the fuck did they knock it down? And why? There were always people inside buying burgers. I thought it was doing okay!"

Bronca sets her lips in a grim line and stomps across the street, her shoulders tight. Manny hurries to keep up. When she stops again, he realizes she's staring at the poster that's been put up on the fence. LUXURY LIVING, it reads at the top, above a lovely architect's drawing of a modernist mid-rise stack building.

"Condos," she snarls, in the same tone that others might say *cobras*. "Murdaburga was the storefront on a building that dozens of families lived in for years. I'd heard there was trouble a couple of months ago, something about jacked-up rents—but my God. They just threw all those people out. For overpriced, ugly-ass *condos*."

"Yo, Old B," Veneza says, with sudden urgency. She has peered through one of the murky plastic windows set into the plywood fence; now she steps back and points at it, wordless and wide-eyed. When Manny and Bronca share the view, it's hard to see at first— but then Manny catches his breath.

All over the brickyard, like the newest of sprouted seedlings, short white tendrils have wriggled up from between or within the bricks. It's a whole field of them. As they watch, an older woman totters past the far edge of the brickyard, pushing a granny cart laden with laundry and groceries. She stumbles suddenly, frowning as she catches herself on the cart, and bending for a moment to rub at her ankle. When she straightens and resumes walking, there is a white tendril sprouting from the back of her hand. Probably one on the ankle, too, though Manny can't see it.

Bronca's breath quickens. She rounds on the coming-soon poster and narrows her eyes. "*This* didn't just start when the city came to life," she growls, scanning the text in a rapid left-right scroll. "I don't care how many people they're paying off or mind-controlling, even eldritch abominations can't get a construction permit overnight in *this* city. Which means *Dr. White* has been planning her move for a lot longer than just the past two or three days."

"How can that be, though?" Manny's still peering through the window, though now that he knows the white tendrils are on the other side, he's keeping his feet well back from the bottom edge of the fence. "Did she know the city was about to be born?"

"No idea. Been so caught up in Raul's political bullshit..." Bronca's engrossed in the fine print, muttering as she does so. "Didn't notice what I should've noticed. The land here hasn't been healthy for a hundred years, but this is a new sickness, and *I should have noticed*. They're destroying everything that makes New York what it is, replacing it with generic *bullshit*." She swats the poster—

—and then she blinks, drawing back a little in surprise. "Better New York Foundation?"

The name sounds familiar. Manny leans in to see. Yes; tucked into the corner of the sign text is a little logo. It's a stylized letter *B* and the miniature skyline of New York—well, of Manhattan.

Then his skin prickles as he belatedly realizes *that's not the Manhattan skyline*. The longer he looks, the more anomalies he notices. There's a distinctive-looking structure in the middle of it that at first he thinks is something like Seattle's Space Needle: a long tapering column topped with something flatter and wider. Then he notices the odd lumps spaced irregularly along the column's length. Also, the structure at the top doesn't look like a restaurant or observation booth. It's more organic. Polyp-like, like some kind of deep-sea organism.

"Better New York is the foundation that offered us the fucked-up donation I told you about," Bronca says. Her anger seems gone now, replaced by confusion and not a little unease. "The one 'Dr. White' said she worked for."

The familiarity pings then. "It's also the same foundation that's claimed ownership of Brooklyn's brownstone," Manny says.

"What?"

"Brooklyn got an eviction notice yesterday on two buildings that her family has owned for years," Manny explains. "Her lawyer says there's some kind of city program that's meant to reclaim distressed or abandoned properties. They give them to nonprofits that rehabilitate them and sell them off. But the program has gone wrong. They've been eminent-domaining properties that *aren't* distressed, in some cases over paperwork errors or minor tax bills that aren't in arrears. Or nothing at all—like in Brooklyn's case."

Bronca raises her eyebrows and whistles a little. "Oh, so *that's* what's wrong with her. Apart from being Brooklyn."

Manny nods. Brooklyn is more connected than most, and she's already gotten some kind of injunction against the eviction notice, putting everything on pause while an investigation takes place. But the situation still has her on edge, understandably.

And—"The nonprofit that's been given ownership of her brown-stones is this Better New York thing."

Bronca turns to him; she looks as horrified as she is angry, her eyes wide. "My God. She's been *waiting* for this."

Veneza pulls back from where she's been peering through the window. "What?"

"This is a trap. White's been setting up little traps like this, all over the city. It was inevitable that the city would come to life someday, and she had all this in place here, *just in case.*"

"Or, maybe, setting little traps all over the world," Veneza says grimly. When they turn to her, she sighs. "Squigglebitch is a planner, right? So . . . why would she only plan here? If most big cities eventually come alive, then she's probably everywhere, yeah? Maybe all the cool tentacles from Planet X are on that real estate tip."

Bronca and Manny look at each other.

Manny grabs his phone and quickly plugs in the website for the Better New York Foundation, reading it off the poster. Just before he's about to hit "go," however, Veneza grabs his hand. "Oh my God, what is wrong with you, do not go right to their site! What if it gives you *phone tentacles* instead of malware? Look, just see if there's a news article or something."

So Manny instead does this. "Wikipedia says that the founda-tion has been around since the 1990s," he says. "Holdings in New York, Chicago, Miami, Havana, Rio, Sydney, Nairobi, Beijing, Istanbul—"

"They *are* everywhere," Veneza says, clearly horrified to find her theory correct.

Manny backs out of the Wikipedia entry and scans some other news items for a few moments. "It looks like they didn't do most of this, the property acquisitions and policy proposals I mean, until recently. Like, just the last five years or so. Before that, the foundation existed, but was pretty much dormant."

"Well, something woke that shit up." Veneza crowds in to look at his phone. At once she gasps and pokes a finger at something Manny was about to scroll past. It's a business news site link reading BETTER NY PARENT COMPANY TMW HONORED AT VC GALA. "Parent company TMW?"

"I guess there would be an overarching corporation running things, if they're this widespread," Manny says, clicking on the link. "Can't roll into Boston as Better New York."

Bronca finally leans in, too, though she makes a little disgruntled sound as she squints at the phone's text. Manny, trying to be helpful, enlarges it for her. She glares at him, though it's obviously easier for her to see. "I guess they really did have millions of dollars, huh. Probably chump change, all things cons—"

She stops. Manny flinches. Veneza's mouth falls open. They've all seen it at once. The parent company's name.

TOTAL MULTIVERSAL WAR, LLC.

There's no need to go around the block anymore. They've figured out what's really wrong.

Night has fallen. Behind the Center's shutters, they've gathered in Murrow Hall, beneath the self-portrait of the primary. Being here makes Manny feel better, despite the implicit threat of the primary's image. He's fairly certain it's not comforting to anyone else, but he doesn't really care what they think as long as they keep it to themselves.

No one seems inclined to talk about the primary anymore, however. After they've explained everything about Better New

York to Hong, Paulo, Padmini, and Brooklyn, Hong actually looks alarmed for the first time since Manny's met him. Brooklyn, meanwhile, is incandescent.

"They stole *my property*," she snarls, getting up and starting to pace; her politician voice is gone entirely, and once again Manny hears MC Free in her anger. "My father *bled* for them buildings, and these multiversal motherfuckers stole my goddamn *house*. What do you know about this?" Now she rounds on Hong.

"It isn't something we—the other cities, and I—have noticed elsewhere," he says slowly.

Padmini stares at him, incredulous. "Have you even been *looking*?"

Paulo sighs heavily. There's a whiff of *I told you so* in it, but less than there probably should be; Paulo is too clearly exhausted for proper schadenfreude. Hong scowls at him, then shakes his head and says to all of them, "Before a city is born, it's nothing. Just buildings, people, and possibility. We've focused on actualities."

"So while you and the other cities have been doing business as usual, *reacting*, this thing has been planning preemptive strikes everywhere," Bronca says. She's pacing on one side of the main gallery. On the other side of it, Brooklyn is nearly her mirror, pacing as well, though faster and with her arms crossed. Bronca pokes at points on an imaginary map. "Little corporate traps in every city, in case it comes to life. Infusions of cash here and there to weaken cities before they're born—maybe keeping them from being born?" She shakes her head as both Hong and Paulo stiffen. Clearly that possibility hadn't occurred to them. "Either way, as soon as a city *is* born, the Enemy has a foothold already."

Manny's leaning on the wall next to the primary's portrait. Veneza and Padmini have huddled together on one of the viewing benches, using Padmini's laptop to learn more of their enemy's corporate structure. It's branched and extensive—almost tentacular—but they're tracking it down. Everyone's let Paulo have the lone chair, rolled in from the reception desk, because he's looking only a little better, even though he's appropriated the rest of Veneza's brigadeiros and is chewing on them now and again, meditatively, as he listens. (Veneza sighs, resigned to the sacrifice.)

"And the Enemy has probably been waiting particularly for something like *this* city," Brooklyn says. She's still furious as she eyes Hong, but her anger has cooled a little, and Politician Voice is back. Manny suspects she is a terror in city council meetings. "You said most cities are either nothing—completely vulnerable, but of no value. Or else they're alive, and the Enemy wants them, but they're too tough to crack. We're stuck in between. The perfect target, valuable *and* vulnerable."

Paulo nods slowly. "I told the Summit that the Enemy's behavior had changed. I had no idea it had taken on a human shape, or that it could *talk*; that's new. But even without that, it's been smarter, more subtle, more malevolent. The last two cities to awaken before you, New Orleans and Port-au-Prince, were stillbirths—and neither should have happened. But the elder cities, and more than a few of the younger ones, didn't believe me. They implied that we young cities of the Americas might simply be awakening prematurely, before we have the strength to survive the process." His lip curls as he says this.

Hong shakes his head, restlessly and angrily. The exchange has the feel of an old argument, to Manny. "The process has not changed for centuries. Millennia! Longer than recorded human history! Why would it change *now*?"

"I don't know. Maybe something's happening that we don't

know about. Something beyond this world, some catalyst which has spurred the Enemy to evolve. But we *should* have started investigating this before now." Paulo's hand has become a fist on his knee; his jaw is tight. "I should have done it myself, if you weren't going to. But I let you talk me into joining your complacency."

Hong glares at him for a moment, a muscle flexing in his jaw. "I just wanted you to be safe," he says finally. Softly. Manny blinks in surprise at the shift in his tone. For a moment, Hong sounded almost human. But is that . . . ?

Paulo smiles bitterly and spreads his arms. His meaning is clear, although his arms have healed and he's looking much better than when they first met him. He will not leave New York unscathed.

"What we are," he says to Hong, with the same softness, "is not a safe thing. No city is—even we whole ones. We can be sacked and set ablaze, drowned when a new dam is built, bombed into craters. We live for as long as our cities, and we have great power . . . but you were the one who told me to study history. And I did. I saw that very few cities have died *peacefully*." Hong winces. Paulo presses on, relentless. "And I, for one, will not live with my back to the wall, ruled by fear of death. *Or* of that creature."

Hong just glares at him, but. There's an undercurrent. Manny finds himself exchanging a sidelong glance with Bronca. *Is this what I think it is?* Bronca raises her eyebrows and purses her lips. *It sure as fuck ain't what we thought it* was.

When Hong does not reply, Paulo lets out a long, steadying sigh. Then he gets to his feet. He seems stronger, but he's still holding a hand to his lower ribs—where Padmini shoved him earlier. She notices this, Manny sees, but sets her jaw and lifts her chin; not sorry.

"Blame Hong and me for your misfortune," Paulo says to them. "Blame the other cities, too, if that comforts you. But unlike all of you, I've seen a living city die. I don't want to see it again."

"New Orleans?" Manny guesses. He's been wondering about Hurricane Katrina.

Hong is the one to shake his head. "I handled that one. There are often complications with smaller cities, so the Summit was *concerned* enough to send someone more experienced in that case." He looks pointedly at Paulo. Then he sobers. "So much went wrong there, however. Its avatar was shot in an attempted robbery. *Before* the birth; indeed, before I even arrived. Pure bad luck, I thought—but then the hospital mishandled her chart and nearly killed her in surgery, and then they turned her out before she was fully recuperated because she was indigent..." He shakes his head, muttering in Cantonese about barbaric American health care for a moment before resuming English. "I gave her a place to stay, but she had no strength when the city tried to rise, and the Enemy came. The levees broke after she died, and rather than help, your media and incompetent leadership compounded the catastrophe at every turn." Then his frown deepens. "But if the Enemy was at work there, interfering somehow even before the city chose its champion..." He trails off, visibly troubled.

Paulo looks bleak. "Port-au-Prince was mine to oversee."

Manny winces despite himself. "The earthquake." The one that killed a quarter of a million people, then thousands more from cholera and mismanagement and foreign interference.

Paulo nods, but does not elaborate. Then he lifts his chin. "New York is much bigger than Port-au-Prince. It's surrounded on nearly every side by satellite cities and massive exurbs. This Woman is *looking* for him, the primary—and, having infested so many citizens with her essence, acting as her eyes and ears, she will eventually find him. If you haven't awakened him by then..."

He shakes his head, and none of them speak for a moment. It's hard to argue with the tight-jawed tragedy in his face.

"Look," Brooklyn says. She sighs and leans against a wall. "Without Staten Island...You can't ask us to sacrifice ourselves if we don't even know that it's going to work. If it takes dying to make her safe, I can pay that price. In a heartbeat. But I'm not going to leave my daughter motherless for *nothing*."

"What if you go find Staten Island?" Veneza's voice is hesitant; when they turn to her, she is sitting against the far wall of the room, knees drawn up and arms wrapped around them, looking tired and unhappy. Manny can guess why. He hasn't quite sussed out the relationship between Bronca and Veneza—surrogate-mother-and-daughter, superhero-sidekick, or maybe just odd-couple best friends. Love is love, however, and it probably bothers Veneza a lot to know that she's going to lose Bronca if they see this through. "What if all of you go to her, and convince her to help? It's the one thing you haven't tried, but it seems...I don't know. The obvious next step."

It's true. Yet Manny finds himself disliking the idea, and for a moment he is flustered as to why. He's never been to Staten Island. What is this reluctance to go there? Is he afraid of an avatar who is clearly violent and might be crazy? That basically applies to all of them—himself more than most. Or is he somehow being affected by Manhattanites' collective distaste for the littlest, least-loved borough?

"It's worth a try," Brooklyn says, at last. She sounds reluctant, too. All of them look reluctant, which backs up Manny's theory. But no one objects.

Hong rubs his eyes. "None of you seem to realize how urgent a matter this is. While we waste time with endless chatter, what's happening in this city is *escalating*, rapidly. Each person infected infects others. Each new structure that grows unchecked infects *many*. It's clear that the Enemy is building toward some goal, and I don't know what it is, but you need to stop it. Now, before it gets worse."

"We *are* being urgent," Padmini snaps. "A few days ago I was doing coursework, today I'm actually standing here and not leaving while strangers try to convince me to kill myself. This is as fast as I get."

"If we go to City Hall," Manny begins. Padmini groans, and he glares at her, annoyed. "If we go now, and can't wake the primary, we'll have wasted a lot of time. I think we should split up. Some of us go get Staten Island. The rest see if we can do anything at City Hall—or just keep the primary avatar safe, if not."

Padmini blinks. Bronca looks duly impressed. "Agreed. Surprised to hear it from you, but agreed."

Manny lets out a slow breath, attempting patience. "I want the primary to live. I haven't made any secret of that, but I can't see why you wouldn't, too, given what's at stake."

Bronca snorts. "You're the one who's in love with him, Mannahatta."

"Not *suicidally*," Manny snaps, although he's also blushing. "What good does it do me to save his life and then die at his feet? I want . . . more than that." Jesus. He's going to blow some blood vessels. But it's the truth. "I'm going to fight for more than that."

"That's almost sweet," Brooklyn says. She's smiling, albeit with a hint of sadness. "I hope you get what you want. I hope we all do."

Bronca lets out a little tired sigh and shakes her head. To Manny, she says, "I take it you're Team City Hall?"

"Of course."

She eyes Padmini. "You?"

"I don't want to go anywhere near City Hall," Padmini declares.

"Team Staten Island, then," Hong drawls. "Since São Paulo should not return to that borough, he'll obviously have to—"

He tenses, midsentence. Paulo, too, frowns and turns, his eyes unfocusing. Manny's trying to figure out what's the matter—and then it hits all of them, too. A sinking sensation. A strange gravitic dip, which is all the stranger because it does not exist in the real world, where there is light and time and space and they all stand upon a floor. Something in the other place. Close, whatever it is.

"What is—" Padmini begins. Paulo shakes his head, frowning.

"Nothing I've ever felt," Hong says.

Bronca groans softly, bending and grinding a fist into her midriff as if she's got heartburn. "Urgh. I feel like I'm going to be sick."

Manny doesn't feel sickness, but he definitely feels something. An offness, a wrongness. An…imminence. He looks down, his perception caught half in and half out of the real world, and frowns at a whispery rustle at the edges of his hearing. "Why does it sound like there's something moving underneath us?" And why is there something familiar about the sound?

Bronca looks at the floor, too—and all of a sudden, her eyes widen. "Because there is. *Rising toward us.*" She grabs Veneza and hauls the girl to her feet. "Everybody out! Now!"

"What? Why?" asks Brooklyn. But she's moving.

Then they can all feel it. Something is growing underneath the Center—a layer of wrongness between them and the city's bedrock, interfering with the bond they should feel by simply standing on their home ground.

Manny curses and grabs Paulo, since he's nearest. Paulo does not protest, though he stumbles a little, shaky on his feet. Veneza comes up on Paulo's other side, however, and between the two of them they're able to keep up as the rest pelt for the door. Bronca swings a little right as they're hurrying down a corridor so that she can yank on a fire alarm panel. An old-fashioned clanging bell starts to go off. Manny remembers her mentioning that there are artists who sometimes spend the night in the Center, upstairs. But even as the alarm goes off, the building's lights flicker.

They begin to hear a sound. A whispering susurrus. A many-layered slither, rising into a growl beneath them. And they're not running nearly fast enough.

Manny tries to think, tries not to be afraid—and then for some reason, he finds himself thinking about his one experience of being on a subway. That rush between express stops, hurtling through the dark in the belly of a gleaming metal sheath. That sense of endless, perilous, chaotic speed—

It isn't much. He's not in his home borough. Still, abruptly there is a stir of city-energy, and the ghostly shape of a subway car shimmers into visibility around them as they run. Manny's feet seem to lift off the ground and he zooms forward, fast as a train's acceleration; Padmini yelps and Bronca curses as they're all swept along. Then the world rushes past with a whiff of rat droppings and the blare of an industrial horn, and suddenly they have shot *through* the front windows of the Center and its shutters, too, their bodies briefly as intangible as the ghost-train—

Then they are on the sidewalk across the street from the Center, stumbling and crying out as the train screeches to a halt there. "Holy shit," Veneza blurts. "That was wilder than the Cyclone!"

But as the phantom subway fades away and they turn back to the Bronx Art Center, a column of white erupts from the ground around the building and flings itself skyward. It is not completely here, not quite in this world; for a moment they can still see the Center within the rising mass, and the building itself seems undisturbed. But the column rises to quickly become *thousands* of white tendrils, each more massive than the flare that Manny once battled in an FDR fast lane. They interlock as they grow, enveloping the entire block in seconds. Manny can only stare, reverberating with the same stunned horror as the others, while the tangled wall of white rises before them. Fifty feet high. Sixty, and the tendrils have begun to tighten their weave and solidify together into a singular mass. Eighty feet high.

A tower.

"Oh, no, no, no," Bronca breathes as they crane their necks, watching the thing form. It will be as high or higher than the strange arch over at Hunts Point, it's already clear. "The keyholders. I don't think any of them could have...I have to get them out!" And she actually starts back across the street, before Brooklyn and Veneza both drag her back.

"You can't," says Hong. It's softer than Hong usually speaks, but no less brutally true, for that. Bronca shudders all over and groans, anguished.

"We should go." Padmini is shaking visibly, her eyes wide and distraught. "We shouldn't be this close."

Manny heartily agrees. Traffic on the street in front of the Center is a wreck—cars veering away and stopping in the middle of the street, others speeding up and getting the hell out of Dodge. None of the drivers can see the tower, but they're all reacting to it regardless, sensing the presence of an interloper.

Out of this chaos, however, a familiar yellow shape suddenly makes a U-turn and comes rapidly hurtling down the street before screeching to a halt in front of them. It's a Checker cab. Someone's put a sign in the passenger window with prominent handwritten letters: NOT A REAL CAB. DO NOT HAIL. The sign falls into the cab, however, as a woman leans across the passenger seat to hand-crank the window down. She stares at Manny, and Manny stares back. "Oh, I fucking *knew* it," says Madison.

It's unbelievable. Well, no, it's not. It's the city. In spite of everything, Manny can't help grinning, though he suspects he looks a little hysterical. "Small world?"

"Is it?" She scrunches her face. Today she's wearing a T-shirt that reads I'M NOT PERFECT BUT I'M FROM NEW YORK AND THAT'S KINDA THE SAME THING. "Are you gonna do the whole ride-'em-cowboy thing again? Because you probably should." She jabs a thumb toward the Center.

"No." There's only one reason for the city to have sent them a ride. "Can you take us to City Hall Station?"

Madison rolls her eyes. "I'm not even going to ask how you knew I was headed that way anyway. Get in, damn it."

"Okay, hang on." Manny straightens. "Do we have another car, for the Staten Island group?"

Bronca tears her eyes from the awful thing that has enveloped her Center, and then rummages through her pockets. Her movements are shaky, her expression shocky, and Manny doesn't blame her. But she sighs in relief and pulls a set of keys from one pocket. There's an electronic key fob on it. "Yeah. Mine."

"I'll go with you to Staten Island, then," Brooklyn says to her. She looks at the Checker oddly. "Uh, you guys got a ride, I guess?"

"Yeah," Manny says. It is a need now, the pull toward City Hall that sits in his breast. Everything in him that understands strategy, violence, warfare, is certain that this tower, this direct attack, is a sign. The Woman in White has abandoned pretense; she's making her move, and they aren't ready. Manny's going to City Hall even if none of the others want to go with him.

Paulo says to Manny, as if hearing this thought, "I'll go with you." He's still not looking great, but he moves with tolerable speed to climb through the cab's rear passenger door, nodding politely to Madison inside.

With a sudden gasp that makes all of them jump, Veneza slaps at her pockets, then groans in relief as she finds her car keys, too. "Oh my God, thought I was gonna be walking home. I can also carry—"

Bronca makes a growling sound. "The only place you're going is home!"

They all jump again, except Brooklyn. It was a mom-voice, sharp and incontrovertible. Brooklyn just nods grimly, and takes out her phone.

Veneza stares at Bronca like she's crazy. "Old B, come on, you're going to need all the—"

"Shut the fuck up!" Then Bronca gestures at what used to be the Bronx Art Center. The tower is still growing, although not as quickly as before. It's going to be taller than anything else in the Bronx, as far as Manny can tell. And it is *breathing*, he sees, in fitful, arrhythmic heaves; or pulsing, or maybe that's its malleable, tendril-flecked surface just randomly twitching. The sound of it is poorly maintained nails on a cracked chalkboard; he finds himself humming tunelessly in a futile effort to drown it out. He can't look at it for long, either, which makes Bronca's next words painfully ironic. "Look at that shit! Do you know what it would do to me if *you* were in there?"

Veneza blinks at her for a startled moment, then wilts a little. "Yeah. Yeah, okay. I just..." She sighs. "Wanted to help."

Bronca lets out a shaky breath and goes to her, gripping the younger woman's shoulders. "*You can't help us.* And right now, you're just something else I have to worry about."

She thinks they're going to fail, Manny realizes. Bronca believes they will be killed by the Enemy, and that the city will then be struck by some catastrophe. She's sending Veneza away so that the girl will survive whatever happens.

Veneza looks hurt by Bronca's words for a moment—and then she scowls. "No, you did not just try the whole reverse-psychology thing on me. Do I look stupid? If you want me to go that bad, just say it outright, don't pretend you don't want me around—"

"I want you to go," Bronca says. Her voice is flint.

Veneza falters and falls silent, then grimaces. "Well. Shit. Okay." After a moment, she begins backing toward her own car, though she's clearly not happy about it. "B, if you get killed, or eaten, or...squiggleized, or whateverthefuck, I'm gonna kill you," she says. "I'm gonna follow you to the happy hunting ground and slap the shit out of you." But then she turns and runs toward her car, which seems to be a good ways down the block.

Bronca looks torn between sorrow at Veneza's leaving and relief that the girl doesn't think less of her for the attempt at harshness. "We talked about those stereotypes, didn't we," Bronca calls after her. "Didn't we!" Veneza lifts a middle finger in farewell.

Bronca gazes after her for a moment, smiling a little, though her lips are tight. Then she takes a deep breath and beckons to Brooklyn and the rest. "Gonna be a tight squeeze in my car," she says. "And somebody else is going to have to pay the Verrazano toll, I don't have any cash—"

"That's all electronic now," Brooklyn says, though she's distracted. Manny can see that her phone is dialing someone. "They snap your license on cameras, send you a bill later."

"Well, whoop-de-do for the surveillance state. I'm right here." She uses the key fob to unlock a Jeep a few cars down.

The others follow her. Padmini has been furiously texting someone; a moment later the phone rings, and they all hear Aishwarya's voice shouting in rapid Tamil while Padmini winces and tries to explain that the family needs to get out of town. Brooklyn says, "Yeah, Dad. Like we talked about. My aide will be there to pick you up in thirty minutes. Tell him to drive like you know an earthquake is coming." Pause. "I love you, too."

She hangs up, and then she alone glances back at Manny. There's so much guarded fear in her expression that it makes him ache inside. She isn't afraid for any of them, of course; they are nothing to each other, the boon companions of less than three days. Still, on their collective success or failure does her family's fate now rest. Words like *goodbye* or *good luck* would just feel too final.

In token of which, Brooklyn finally just turns away and hurries after the others to Bronca's car.

Manny stares after her for a moment longer, registering only belatedly that he, alone among them, has no family or loved ones to worry about. Except New York itself. Himself.

He gets in the cab with Paulo, and Madison pulls away from the curb quickly, as eager to get away from the tower as any of them. Now Manny can focus, at last.

"On my way," he murmurs very softly to the air. Paulo glances at him, but says nothing. He knows exactly who Manny's talking to. "See you soon."

And as Veneza anxiously drives away from the others and tries to convince herself that surprising her asshole father down in Philly really is a better choice than staying to face an interdimensional apocalypse—

—something in her back seat gulps, very softly,

Da-dump.

CHAPTER FOURTEEN

The Gauntlet of Second Avenue

It starts as soon as they're in the car. Bronca takes out her phone so that she can use navigation. She squints at the thing as she always does, laboriously pecking out letters and numbers with one finger until Queens says, "I'll do it," and reaches up from the back seat to take the phone from her. "Just start heading for Staten Island."

It's no worse than what she's put up with from Veneza, but Queens isn't Veneza. "Ask before you take things from people, heathen."

"I'm just trying to be efficient! I need a destination address." Her fingers fly across the keyboard with the uncanny speed of anyone younger than thirty. Bronca starts driving. Since Brooklyn's on the phone in the front passenger seat, Queens looks at Hong.

"I'm Hong Kong," he snaps.

"Oh, yes. I guess you wouldn't know." Queens opens out the map as Bronca starts driving. "But can you at least point to where you found Paulo? She's probably somewhere near there."

While she and Hong haggle over the approximate last known

location of the Staten Island avatar, Brooklyn gets off the phone again. She's been talking more quietly this time, and Bronca hasn't bothered her because she recognized that tone and pitch of voice. That's how parents sound when they're trying to say goodbye to their kids, possibly for the last time. It's what she probably should be saying to her own son... but Mettshish is in his thirties and lives in California, and frankly that's likely to turn into an argument, which she doesn't have the strength for at the moment. And orphaning a grown man is an entirely different thing from doing it to a fourteen-year-old girl. If anything, Bronca wishes she could say farewell to her grandchild, due to be born in three months or so... but maybe it's best that she be only a mystery to the child, and not a tragedy, when they tell stories of her.

In the wake of her phone call, Brooklyn gazes out the window for a while, brooding, and Bronca lets her. Not much that can be said in a moment like this. But eventually she tries. "Sending her to her dad?"

Brooklyn snorts with such bitterness that Bronca immediately knows it was the wrong thing to ask. "Her father's dead, so I hope not."

Ouch. "Drugs?"

Brooklyn turns to glare at her. "*Cancer.*"

Ah, shit. Bronca sighs. "Look, I didn't mean—I just used to listen to your music, sometimes, and you always talked about getting with guys who were dealers or bangers or... you know."

"Yeah. A lot of dudes like that are just doing what they have to do to take care of people they care about, which makes them more decent than your average nice upstanding predatory lender or whatever. But regardless, what I talked about in my music wasn't always what I was doing in real life. Shit, I thought only white people believe everything they hear in rap is real." She shakes her head and stares at the road.

Bronca feels herself getting heated. It's the wrong place and the wrong time and the wrong target, and she's old enough to know that she's only sniping at Brooklyn because this is something she can control, unlike the rest of their whole awful situation. But even knowing all this . . . well, Bronca's never going to be a very good wise elder, if she even makes it that far.

"Yeah? It's not real?" She keeps her eyes on the road, but her hands have tightened on the steering wheel. "I remember some of your lyrics that were pretty fucking real. 'And if a bitch tries to hit it, I'll gut her with my gat,' you remember that one?"

Brooklyn is groaning and angry-laughing at once. "Oh, here we go. I *apologized* for those lyrics, years ago, publicly. And I donated a thousand dollars to the Ali Forney Center—"

"You think that makes up for it? You know how many queer kids get stabbed or shot to death—" She takes a corner to get them lined up for the Bruckner Expressway and slews a little, forcing her to cross-control the wheel more than usual to get them back on track.

"Please, please, get into a catastrophic car accident," Hong sighs from the back seat. "Destroy half the city in a single collision, do all the Enemy's work for her. Then I can go home."

Bronca sets her jaw, fuming. But in the silence, Brooklyn lets out a long, slow breath.

"I know an apology don't make up for it," she says. She's slipped back into her old-school Brooklyn accent, dropping the politician voice, and somehow this eases a little of Bronca's temper. Neither Brooklyn is false, but this one feels a little truer to MC Free, and that's the part of her Bronca's got beef with. "I know it don't, okay?

I damn sure got called a dyke enough myself just for stepping into a ring that dude rappers thought was theirs by default. Mother-fuckers tried to rape me, all because I didn't fit into what they thought a woman should be—and I passed that shit on. I know I did. But I *got better*. I had some friends slap sense into me, and I listened when they did. And I figured out that the dudes were fucked in the head, so maybe it wasn't the best idea to imitate them. Shit, back then, most of us were just..." She gestures in frustration, then sighs heavily. "Bullshitting, right? High on the hype. Cooning for a record deal and suburban white-boy dollars. I just..." She sighs. "Fuck. It's done."

Bronca looks at her, reading the deep weariness and sorrow of her. And sincerity. So she drives on in silence for a while, letting the aethers settle, before she finally says, "Sorry about the 'drugs.' That was, uh, racist. Technically *prejudiced* because the power dynamics are basically flat, but..." She grins in an attempt to ease the awkwardness. "I have Black friends? Also aunties and grandmothers."

She can almost hear Brooklyn roll her eyes. Still, after a moment, quietly: "I did lose a lot of friends to drugs, so I'm a little..."

Touchy. Yeah. "Me, too." She snorts. "I *am* the Bronx."

An answering snort, followed by a tired, dry, "And I am Brooklyn."

"You fight crime!" says Queens, beaming. Brooklyn turns and looks at her until she sits back and shuts up.

They're taking a route that should get them there fastest, even though it means paying a pirate's ransom in tolls. But right before they're supposed to transfer from the Bruckner to FDR, Bronca's phone bleeps a warning. "Uh, there's an accident or something on FDR," Queens says, frowning as she leans forward to peer at it. She reaches forward and taps something. "There's an alternate route through the city that seems clear."

"Fine," Bronca says, and follows the directions issued by the bland computer-lady voice of the navigation app.

"Through the city is actually faster than the FDR?" Brooklyn asks. "Huh. Must be a hell of an accident."

"I don't think—" Bronca's been half listening to the radio; it's just on for noise. But the DJ mentions the FDR, so Bronca turns the radio up.

"—have actually shut down the FDR Drive," the guy is saying, sounding incredulous. "Police are describing this as a spontaneous demonstration because apparently there are no permits on file, but news agencies in the city have received a statement from the group, sent several hours before the protest began. They call themselves the Proud Men of NYC. Not to be confused with NYC Pride, this group is right-wing and has been linked to violent incidents such as—"

The report goes on for a bit, and then there is a brief audio clip. Bronca hears many voices—all of them male, as far as she can tell—chanting indistinctly, with police sirens in the background. "We're here to let New York know!" says one young man's voice, shaky with movement and adrenaline. "We took over Greenpoint and Williamsburg and now it's time for Manhattan to see that the men—" Someone jostles him. "Dude, come on, these shoes are new. The men of New York City aren't going to take—" There's a jumble of words that Bronca doesn't get. Something about being replaced. "—and feminist liberal nonsense! It's okay to be a white man! We're not gonna feel guilty about our white dicks, and you're gonna learn how it feels to get f—"

The clip cuts off abruptly, back to the DJ who is now chuckling with palpable unease. "We-he-hell, hopefully we didn't just earn ourselves an FCC violation there. Anyway, folks, stay away from FDR Drive for now, unless you want to park and look at the view." The station's music resumes.

Brooklyn stares at the console. "Are you kidding me? A what, a racist white dude march? In New York? At almost *midnight*? What are they trying to do? They're not even going to disrupt the city's traffic much."

"Well, they're disrupting *us* pretty fucking well," Bronca mutters, turning onto Second Avenue. "Bet NYPD isn't even going to stop them. Or else they'll arrest any counter-protestors or people these guys pull out of their cars for a beatdown."

"But a march of angry white men, though," Queens says worriedly. "That's never good."

It most definitely is not. And Bronca muses that it's damned strange for New York—which has its share of racists, God knows; the city's special in a lot of ways, but not that one. Generally, however, the ones in the city are content to live and let live, as one must in any major city, especially if one doesn't want to get knocked the fuck out on the subway.

"Like New Orleans," Hong murmurs, so softly that Bronca almost doesn't hear him.

"What?"

In the rearview mirror, his stone face has gotten stonier. "What killed New Orleans was bad luck," he said. "A series of terrible coincidences—institutions breaking down, old hatreds taking new form, subcultures choosing just the wrong moment to make a drastic change. So I thought at the time."

Then Bronca gets it. "You think this march is, what, bankrolled by Better New York? To force us onto a different route?"

"I have no idea. But city avatars are generally quite fortunate. Helpful coincidences fall into our laps with great frequency. It's part of what we are, how our cities help us. Your city is weak." Bronca sees him shake his head in the rearview. "Or perhaps something else is working even harder, to counter its efforts."

There's nothing they can say to that. Dread works best in complete silence.

They hit Second Avenue at Spanish Harlem. Working-class neighborhood, late on a weeknight; Bronca's unsurprised to see that the streets are mostly empty. Only the bodegas stand open, sentinels of The City That Never Sleeps And Occasionally Needs Milk At Two A.M. Gentrification here has taken the form of endless coffee shops. For the last few blocks these have been indie places, proudly touting their locally roasted pour-overs, all with different decor and sign fonts. Then comes the proof that it's all over for the neighborhood's original character: they pass a Starbucks on the corner. Bronca thinks. She can't be sure. Because it is so covered in white tendrils and stiffer projections that she can barely see its logo or facade.

It's like some kind of animal. The overlapping, moving layers of white tendrils have given it a kind of brindle-furred appearance, blurring the building's overall boxy shape. It's a typical New York multiuse building: ground-floor business, apartments above. The apartment portion has a few tendrils on each level, but nothing like the monster down below.

And when that monster abruptly ripples all over like water, and *forms a huge, inhuman, vast-mouthed face—*

Bronca swerves. It's reflex. There aren't many other cars on the street, but two taxis and an Uber immediately honk, because sudden swerves do not mesh well with Manhattan traffic patterns at speed. When they've passed the Starbucks, Bronca looks at it in her rearview while Brooklyn slews around in her seat to stare, and Queens does the same. "What the fuck," Queens says. She's hyperventilating a little. Then her phone rings; she answers it. They all hear Aishwarya again, calmer than before but still sounding tense as she asks some question. "I can't talk right now, I'm so sorry," Queens murmurs before hanging up on her.

Hong mutters something in Chinese. Then: "You need to ready a construct. If you have to fight—"

"Oh, fuck!" Bronca cries, and this time she has to not only swerve, but lunge into the bike lane—as on the right side of the street, another Starbucks that is covered in glittering white feathers suddenly hops a little out onto Second Avenue. At them. The building attached to it lurches a little, but Bronca can see that it's happening but not happening: something of the building, its solidity, is still there, even as in the other world it becomes a monster and comes at them. This particular Starbucks must have late open hours. Bronca can see human figures through the skin of the creature, blank-eyed as they sit at its window bar to sip their drinks, unperturbed by its lumbering attack.

And two blocks farther down, Bronca can see another building, this one vaning colossal white porcupine spikes as it readies itself to pounce.

The car that Bronca just cut off in order to escape the bird-Starbucks is leaning on its horn, the driver furious. Bronca doesn't blame him. She pulls ahead to the next block and then stops at the curb, shaking as she grips the wheel and catches her breath. (She keeps an eye on the bird-Starbucks in the rearview, but the thing seems unable to go more than a few feet from its foundations. After glaring at Bronca in the mirror and snapping its glass-door beak at her once or twice, it drools foul-looking coffee-ground sludge before grudgingly backing into its former position.) The furious driver pulls around her, gesturing out the window and yelling something in the universal language of Fuck You Learn To Drive, before heading off.

"It's every Starbucks," Brooklyn says, squinting down the street.

"Not just them, look." Queens points at a Dunkin' Donuts that is heavily overgrown with corkscrewing wirelike stuff; from a distance it looks like a massive white 'fro. Across the street is some kind of café that has developed a silky white chin curtain, which scraggles over the sidewalk. "That Au Bon Pain there looks like it's going to start telling jokes at open mic improv any minute now."

"Those aren't actively *chasing us down the street* like the damn Starbucks, though." Bronca shakes her head, peering down the length of Second Avenue. "I could try Lex or Park, but the real problem is that there's one of those things on every other corner—especially near Grand Central and the other tourist spots." Fleetingly she finds herself wishing that they'd brought Manhattan with them. Maybe he could've somehow secured the route against this.

"This doesn't make sense!" Queens cranes her neck to see the porcupine thing on the next block. It's very still, but Bronca doesn't trust it. It's also one of the newer buildings on the block and might be more flexible than the older, unrenovated bird-Starbucks. "Starbucks has been in the city for years! It has to be part of New York by now."

"Starbucks is everywhere," Hong rumbles. "All over my city, too. Big chain stores make a city less unique, more like every other place. We do not have *time* for your breakdown, Bronx."

Bronca freezes, then turns around in her seat. "Disrespect me again," she snaps. "You will be walking back to JFK from that corner right there. Hope nothing eats you on the way."

There must be enough true fury in her voice; he looks away and takes a deep breath. With brittle, exaggerated politeness, he says, "Apologies. Do you have an alternate plan?"

She's not really mollified, but they've got other problems. In answer to his question, she sets her jaw and pulls the car away from the curb.

"What are you going to—" Queens begins.

"I'm gonna drive like a motherfucking New Yorker, is what I'm going to do," Bronca snarls. And then she cuts off a truck and accelerates to fifty.

Queens cries out, and Bronca hears her scrambling for the seat belt that she should've already had on. The truck blats an air horn at Bronca. "Honking's illegal! You're gonna get a ticket!" she shouts—but she's grinning, in spite of herself. It's been a shitty few days. So at full speed she rockets down Second Avenue, cutting neat zigzags across the traffic, threading the needle between two Land Rovers, shooting through an intersection just as its light turns red. Hong curses Cantonese behind her. A right-lane car pass. An impatient swerve around a slow-moving pedestrian. There's a police speed monitor on one side of the road down by Twenty-third, reminding drivers that the speed limit in the city is twenty-five, and it blinks a baleful red seventy as she blasts past.

But the Starbucks monsters can't touch them. After ten blocks, silvery flickers of light have begun to appear around Bronca's Jeep, licking at the edges of her vision. After fifteen, it's not a peripheral thing anymore; a sheath of white light surrounds them. A snake-like Starbucks lunges out of the lobby of a chain hotel, its ghostly, stretched-wide mouth open, and just past its translucent white gullet, a tired-looking barista slumps on his knees, scrubbing up a spilled iced something. But the snake's spectral teeth bounce off Bronca's car as if it's tried to bite a rock. And Bronca blazes on.

The cops don't stop her, or even seem to see her. Hong and Queens have sat back, gripping the armrests and making sure their seat belts are buckled. Brooklyn, bless her, helps by shouting out the window at any car that looks as if it's about to impede their route. "Are you blind, motherfucker?" and so on. Adding to the construct, Bronca now realizes, blending the power of their two boroughs into one massive, preemptive wave of Get The Fuck Out The Way. Now the sheath of energy is bullet-shaped, and long enough that it physically shunts aside cars that are going too slow or about to cut them off. Bronca's grinning like a clown. Brooklyn's laughing, too, giddy with it. It's beautiful.

Second Avenue ends at Houston, so the GPS starts directing them on a more zigzagging route toward Brooklyn. Now they're in the Lower East Side. The only Starbucks in the area is a tired old fishlike thing on Delancey, which can't even make it past its own curb when it tries to flop at them. Bronca does the speed limit past that one, just as an extra unspoken fuck-you.

The Williamsburg Bridge is gone, long may it rest. There's something in the water past all of the warnings and roadblocks and memorial photo walls, something white and heaving and organic that seems to fill the entirety of the East River, and enormous enough to tower over the lone support pylon that remains standing in the bridge's wake. As they pass Delancey, the white thing slowly undulates, even as they watch. It radiates a sickly greenish-white light that hurts Bronca's eyes, and she swerves off Delancey sooner than she might have, because of it.

"Oh no," Queens murmurs in a soft, horrified voice. "That's the thing that broke the bridge. It's real, but I didn't think it would *still be there*." No one answers her, mostly because there's nothing to say.

Instead, Brooklyn taps Bronca's phone. "I'm adjusting the route to take us over the Brooklyn Bridge. No chain stores on the BQE."

"Yeah, okay," Bronca says. Then she pulls over to the curb again, while they're on one of the smaller streets where this is still possible.

"What—"

"I hate driving in Brooklyn," she says, unbuckling her seat belt. "Handle your own damn borough."

Brooklyn laughs in spite of herself, and gets out to switch places with her. "You want to drive once we get to Staten Island?" she asks Queens, while they buckle in.

"I don't drive, remember?" Queens looks sheepish.

"Oh, right, forgot."

"How can you not know how to drive?" Hong asks, scowling.

"Because *usually*, New Yorkers don't need to," Bronca snaps at him. Not that she's any big fan of Queens, either, but it's habit to defend other women when men start ragging on them, and the fact that Queens is New York and Hong Kong is an out-of-towner just adds impetus. "Now shut up again. I was starting to not hate you."

The rest of the ride to the island is uneventful. Still, they all see them as they crest the Verrazano, which gives them a good view of the island: more towers. Two of them, at least, though there's also a humped, nodule-covered thing in the distance that is either a really ugly stadium or yet another weird structure.

Brooklyn slows down in Staten Island—not just because the streets here are narrower and there are a lot of cops around, but also because they can *sense* the avatar of Staten Island, now that they've entered her domain. It's a strange feeling, but not altogether different from that new deep awareness they all have of the primary, which has lingered in them since they did their little group-vision thing. It is as if there is a lodestone in their heads, sort of, with one end that points toward City Hall instead of north. The other points toward somewhere in the middle of Staten Island—an area that Hong pointed out to them on Google Maps, which is called Heartland Village.

To get there, they must drive through a sprawling, hilly woodland, which that night is full of strange shadows. They're tense the whole way, watching the spaces between the trees, ready for anything. Nothing happens, but the unease lingers—getting worse, Bronca notes, as they move deeper into the island's territory. Before long, they've pulled onto a neat little street where all the houses are cute two-story single-families interspersed with semi-attached double houses. They are eerily similar in frame, these homes, though they've all got different paint jobs and siding and hedges. It's the suburbs, where conformity trumps comfort. Bronca's never liked places like this.

Here they stop, however. Because growing from the lawn of the house that probably belongs to their target, there is another white tower. That's a bad sign in itself, Bronca thinks—but as they start toward the house, white curling vine-like things appear out of nowhere, erupting from the soil and spinning down from the nearby tower and thickening and drawing together and solidifying, forming a human-sized tangle ... until the Woman in White stands before them, arms folded, legs braced apart, and feet planted solidly on the lawn.

This time she has a mane of white hair that is long and raggedly straight. Very Seventies chic, which matches the pointed, narrow, sloe-eyed face that she currently wears. Incongruously, she's wearing booty shorts and a loose tank top. She looks like an evil midcareer Joni Mitchell.

And this time, she isn't alone. Looming out of the hedges behind her and from the neighbors' lawns, Bronca can see huge, attenuated, spindly shadows—which had at first seemed like just ordinary castings from the streetlamps. It quickly becomes clear that they are something more when they begin to sway and move. There are sounds accompanying this movement: a lilting series of hoots, dry crackings like the breaking of tree limbs, faint low vibrations as something heavy, but mostly unseen, humps across the lawn sods. No pretty paint people here. Bronca almost misses them, after she gets a not-good look at a few of the shadow things.

"I can't see anything well," Queens says, in a hushed tone. "Why can't I see them? I have to look off to the side. When I look at them directly—"

"Yeah," Bronca says. "I'm getting the sense that she's got new tricks every time she shows up." Something to her left is swaying from side to side, though occasionally it stops and jerks upward in an awkward, vaguely amphibianesque movement. It's not close, hiding amid the hedges of one of the neighboring houses, but she really doesn't like that movement for some reason. It feels like the thing is practicing for a jump.

"*None* of this is how it should be," Hong says. He's got a hand inside his suit jacket, grasping something out of sight. "She has always been enormous, monstrous, attacking when a city is new-born and weak. Not human in shape. Not *speaking*. Never this."

"When you assume," says the Woman in White, "you make an ass of u and me."

And all of a sudden, all four of them are yanked into the other place, where time and space have no meaning and all of them bristle and vane with cranes and rusting girders and blurry Beaux Arts glass. Massive Hong Kong looms at their backs, but this is not his city; Bronca can see Manhattan's skyscrapers better, even though he's a little apart from them as well. Staten Island is here, too, somehow apart from the rest of them and more subdued in size and shine, even though they stand within her borders.

But between her and the rest of them stands something else. *Another* city, positioned as if to protect Staten Island.

It's not any part of New York. It's enormous, bigger than all of them combined, and everything about it feels so wrong that its very close-ness makes Bronca flinch back, raising construction scaffolds in auto-matic defense. The new city is precisely circular in its footprint. Its towers gleam, its neighborhoods sprawl, its parks teem with animals and trees, but all of it is wrong. *Those aren't towers*, Bronca thinks in ris-ing horror. They're breathing. *Those aren't buildings. I don't know what the fuck*— She can't think. It's too close. Just the sight of it hurts.

And every skew-angled building, precisely marked street, and suppurating organism of this city gleams in brilliant, perfect, unnaturally bright white.

They snap back into peoplespace, are *thrown* back, and there every one of them stands stunned by the awful, nauseating real-ization that the Woman in White *is a city, another city, a monstrous city from nowhere in or even close to this universe, whose very streets are inimical to their entire universe.*

"Welcome, avatars of New York," says the Woman in White as they stand frozen in the night-shadow of her tower. Her eyes—acid yellow this time, not even pretending to be a human color—flick at Hong and away dismissively. "And Hong Kong. Is it time for the final confrontation, then? Shall we play some exciting music? Should I deliver a villainous monologue?" She laughs abruptly. It is an utterly delighted laugh that sends chilly fingers dancing down Bronca's spine. That's the laugh of someone who's pretty sure they've already won.

Hong is breathing hard, Bronca notices, and there is a deeply shaken note in his voice as he speaks. He is a city of deep history and tradition, underneath its bright modern trappings and rebel reputation. It's clear he does not take well to things that defy his understanding of the world. "This can't be," he murmurs. "We've fought you since the beginning. How can you be . . . I don't understand."

"Obviously." The Woman in White rolls her eyes and shifts to stand akimbo, leaning on one leg with her hand on her hip. "Well, smart amoebas are still just amoebas, aren't they?"

Bronca is still trying to reconcile Crazy Daisy Duke with the prim, sophisticated Dr. White—even though every newfound instinct within her affirms that *they are the same person*. Who isn't a person at all. "What the hell are you, then?" she demands, hoping that her voice doesn't shake. "Really."

"Really?" The Woman in White grins, delighted, as if she has waited whole ages of the world to be asked this question. "Really *really*. Oh, yes, no more need to whisper, now that the foundations have connected, and as my transplants choose themselves. Thank you for asking, fragment of Lenapehoking, or avatar of the Bronx, or whatever you prefer to be called. My name is *R'lyeh*. Can you say it?"

It's a shivery-sounding name—one that makes Bronca's inner ears twitch and the roots of every hair follicle crawl. But while the name is otherwise meaningless to her, she sees from the corner of her eye that Queens' eyes widen as she mouths, *Oh fuck*.

Then the Woman in White giggles suddenly and pantomimes holding something, like a broomstick, in front of herself. In a pretend-gruff voice, she says, "Youshallnotpass. Always wanted to say that! And you shan't, you disgusting creatures, pieces of this monstrous murdering city, pieces of shit. Staten Island has chosen to do what is right, and I will not let you interfere with her decision. So let's rumble, boroughs of New York, soul of Hong Kong! Isn't that what you call it? A rumble?" Somewhere beneath them, there is a deep, reverberating roil of sound, like a thunderstorm far belowground. Bronca catches her breath, thinking of the Bronx Art Center and the tower that consumed it, but nothing rises beneath them. It's just a sound, for now. Just a rumble.

And before them, grinning so widely that they can see nearly all of her teeth, the living embodiment of the city of R'lyeh spreads her long-fingered, long-nailed, elegant white hands in open invitation. "Come, then, City That Never Sleeps. Let me show you what lurks in the empty spaces where nightmares dare not tread."

CHAPTER FIFTEEN

"And lo, the Beast looked upon the face of Beauty"

The cab ride is smooth and uneventful the whole way. Even Madison remarks on it: "Huh, I'd heard there was some kind of protest on FDR—it's always the FDR, right?—forcing people to make all kinds of detours. But I haven't seen a single 'alternate route' sign. Even feels like the traffic is getting out of our way."

Manny, who has noticed the faint aura limning the windows and visible exterior of the cab, glances at Paulo, who nods. "Well, you said your cab liked me," Manny says. "Thanks for giving us a ride, by the way."

"Yeah, yeah," Madison says. She sounds amused rather than annoyed. "Only reason I'm headed this way is because the mayor wants to do some kind of old New York–new New York photo shoot tomorrow. You're lucky as hell, dude."

Paulo nods again. Cities make their own luck, apparently.

Getting into the old City Hall Station is almost too easy once Madison has dropped them off at the vaulted, colonnaded entrance to the Brooklyn Bridge/City Hall subway stop. There are cops clustered all around it, and Manny sets his jaw, ready for unpleasantness as he and Paulo approach; three of the cops have visible white tendrils jutting from necks or shoulders.

Two of the ones who don't, however, move to intercept the tendriled ones when they make noises at Manny about not letting anyone into the station due to an apparent bomb threat. "Let 'em through," says a woman who seems to outrank all the rest. She's in plain clothes, and seems to be barely paying attention to anything, instead flipping through a sheaf of papers on a clipboard. "They're here to fix things."

"Uh, these guys don't look like Con Ed engineers," says one of the intercepting cops. The tendril that juts from his left cheekbone is thick as an electrical cable.

The plainclothes woman fixes him with a glare. "There some reason why I have to tell you things twice, Martenberg?"

"No, I just—"

"Did I ask for your opinion, Martenberg?" He protests again, and she tells him off again, eventually lowering the clipboard and squaring off to establish her dominance. While the two cops' companions watch the combatants, Manny and Paulo walk into the station unmolested.

"Want to tell me what just happened there?" Manny asks as they walk. "Because we really don't look like Con Ed."

"Those who would help protect the city see what they need to see."

Well, alrighty then.

The 6 trains aren't running, shut down due to police investigation. They pass a few more cops, MTA engineers, some uniformed people who might be Homeland Security, and some actual Con Ed engineers, but no one else stops them, or even seems to see

394 • N. K. Jemisin

them. These people thin out as Manny and Paulo descend to the train platform, but the tunnels amplify their laughter and jokes. It's clear they're not worried about any bomb. Manny can't see any signs of construction. Someone in authority has simply shut the station down for no clear reason.

On the platform, an empty train sits with doors open and no conductor inside. "Do we just wait?" Manny says, stepping into the lead car. Paulo sits down opposite the conductor's booth, but Manny can hear that there's no one in it. He stands at the train's forward window, peering into the dark that awaits down a curving, downward-angled tunnel corridor.

"If you wait, will it go?" Paulo asks. It seems a sincere and not sardonic question, so Manny doesn't bristle. In fact, it belatedly occurs to him that Paulo is trying to teach him something. And after a moment, as he feels the powerful nearby tug of the primary, he gets it.

So he takes a deep breath and puts his hands on the smooth metal that surrounds the window. He's only ridden a subway once before, but he makes himself remember that sensation now, as he did at the Bronx Art Center. The power of unseen, relentless engines driven by the mysterious and deadly third rail. The rocking, hectic speed. The driving needs of hundreds of people riding within—to get to important places for important reasons, to have a warm place to sleep, to keep them safe along the way.

Safe, he thinks at the primary, and at the train that surrounds them. *Yes. I'm coming to keep you safe. Now.*

"Stand clear of the closing doors, please," he whispers. In the reflection of the glass, behind him, he sees Paulo smile.

The PA system utters a little "ding-dong" tone, and then the train's doors slide shut. There's a faint hum from the undercarriage as the train turns on and its engines warm. In the tunnel up ahead, a signal switches from red to green. Then, slowly, the train jolts into motion.

Manny's half expecting someone to come running onto the platform to try to stop them, but it's New York; if any of the personnel in the station hear the train start moving, they dismiss it as normal background noise, more familiar than the strange silence of before. So Manny's 6 glides unmolested into the tunnel—and then, surprisingly quickly, they are at the old City Hall Station platform. Manny turns to the door as the train slows and then stops of its own volition. It knows where it needs to go better than he does.

When the doors slide open, the platform beyond is pitch-dark; the defunct station has no power. Manny can make out glass skylights on the ceiling here and there—the same pattern of Beaux Arts ironwork that he saw in Bronca's books—and a bit of moonlight coming through them. The light from the train car helps, but even this fades as they walk away from the train and into the bowels of the station. Manny fumbles in his pocket for his phone and turns on its flashlight. It's barely enough to illuminate more than a foot-wide circle on the stone floor ahead of them; he hasn't charged it since Inwood and the battery's getting low. Better than nothing.

When they're a couple of feet past the subway train's circles of illumination, the train's lights suddenly go out with a loud electrical snap. In spite of himself, Manny jumps. But he doesn't need his eyes to know where to go, not anymore. He can feel it. "This way," he says.

He feels Paulo latch on to the back of his jacket, letting Manny take the lead. "We must be careful," Paulo says. "It was necessary that we come here, but the Enemy has seen us." Manny grimaces, thinking of the tendriled cops. "It will know now that its target is here."

Manny sets his jaw. "Roger that."

There's a set of steps after about twenty paces. Shining the flashlight around, Manny finds that it leads into an arched stairwell. A sign on the arch, etched in green tile, proclaims that they stand within the station of CITY HALL. The ceiling of the arch is covered in marching, elegant white Guastavino tile patterns.

Manny follows the stairs up, barely noticing as Paulo barks his toes on a step and mutters some imprecation in Portuguese. The sound of their footsteps and breathing whispers back at him from the arches of the ceiling. In his mind, the whisper forms words: *here here here* and *at last at last at last*. And then he turns the corner.

It is both like, and unlike, his vision. There is the bed of old bundled newspapers. Its occupant lies amid a pool of pale moonlight, still and curled, his breathing so slow that it's barely visible. Just a too-thin young Black man in worn cheap clothing, sleeping on trash like a homeless person. And yet...he radiates power. Manny shivers as waves of it ripple along his skin, feeding something within him that had begun to starve. Here, at last: the most special person in the whole city.

Without thinking, Manny moves closer and puts out a hand to shake him awake. He needs to touch him. But a few feet from the primary avatar's shoulder, Manny's hand halts in the air. Something resists the gesture, as if his hand pushes against a sponge that he can't see or feel. He tries again, harder, and makes a frustrated sound when, after a little give, the unseen resistance goes as hard as concrete. He cannot touch the primary.

"So eager to be eaten?" Paulo's soft voice startles Manny into turning sharply. He'd actually forgotten Paulo was there, for a moment. And then he twitches with the reminder.

"I...didn't think about the eating thing," he admits. It makes him want to touch the primary a little less, but only a little.

Paulo's not much more than an etching in the dark, illuminated more by reflected moonlight than Manny's phone light. He's watching Manny, though, and his sadness is visible.

"I'm his," Manny blurts. It's defensive, but he's feeling a little raw right now. "He's mine."

Paulo inclines his head in acceptance. "I will admit some envy," he says gently. "To be part of a *group* going through this together is astonishing to me, and wonderful in many ways. I went through my own rebirth alone, like most cities."

It's a perspective shift that Manny wasn't expecting. "You knew him, then? Before..." He gestures at the bed of newsprint.

"Of course. That's how it usually works. The youngest city sees to the next." Paulo sighs a little, into the dark. "It should have been Port-au-Prince. But I was happy to see this one make it through... until he fell into my arms, and then vanished."

Manny considers this as he gazes down at the sleeping figure. He tries to imagine the primary awake, vibrant, able to laugh and dance and run, and it's easy. He's so vibrant now, even asleep. But then Manny imagines his vibrancy muted, voice undergirded with the same loneliness that all of them have noticed in São Paulo, and it hurts to think of it. Even though it means Manny's death, he can't help thinking: *I'm sorry we'll leave you so alone.*

"What is he like?" Manny finds himself whispering. In the close, quiet confines of the alcove, even this carries.

He can actually hear Paulo smile. "Arrogant. Angry. Frightened, but unwilling to let his fear restrict him." After a moment,

Paulo moves around the bed of papers, to the primary's other side. He's smiling down at the boy, with unmistakable fondness. "He pretends to be less special than he is, because the world has punished him for loving himself. And yet he does. He knows he's more than whatever superficialities strangers see and dismiss."

Is that what the city of New York is like? Manny's been here three days, but it feels right so far. He sighs. It's a shame. He really wanted to make a life here.

He looks up at Paulo. "I need the others, to touch him."

"Yes, I can see that. We must rely on your comrades and Hong, then."

Manny's lip curls. "I'll rely on my comrades. Hong can go to hell."

Paulo laughs once. "Don't be too hard on him," he says, to Manny's surprise. "Before he was a city, he lived through the Opium Wars. He's watched so many die—cities as well as ordinary people—that his attitude is understandable. If infuriating."

Manny frowns, trying to remember what he can of Chinese history. "Jesus, that's . . . Hong is almost two hundred years old? What, are we immortal?" *Unless we're eaten.*

"No. But we live as long as our cities do, provided we don't go picking fights with our fellow city entities." He grimaces, putting a hand to his ribs, though he lowers it just as quickly. "Healed at last. If I were home, the bones would have knit in moments."

"Just other cities? The Enemy can't harm you anymore?"

"Oh, I imagine it can, now that it has taken this more virulent, *intent* form." Paulo shakes his head. "The process has been wrong since at least New Orleans. Probably longer. Maybe now the others will finally listen, and do something—and I pray it is not too late already."

Something Paulo has said troubles Manny. "Have a lot of cities been killed in the process of being born?"

"Countless numbers, over the millennia. More lately." When Manny's eyes narrow, Paulo half smiles and then begins rummaging in his pockets for a cigarette. "Yes, it is exactly as you think: the deaths are accelerating. I suppose that follows, if the Enemy has been weakening new cities even before they quicken. What a horrifying development."

"It wasn't like that for you?"

Finding his cigarette and lighting up, Paulo regards him over the faint orange glow before exhaling smoke. "No. There was unrest in my city, certainly. The military dictatorship that had taken over the country—most likely backed by your country's government, thank you for that—decided to clean up the favelas by destroying them, evacuated or not. As I was from one such favela, I objected. So did São Paulo, which chose me to become its voice and champion." Manny sees the memory warm his eyes for a moment. Then Manny recalls that the military coup Paulo just mentioned was sometime in the 1960s. Paulo looks great for a seventy- or eighty-year-old.

"When the Enemy came," Paulo continues, after another long, appreciative drag on his cigarette, "it tested my resolve as was traditional. I and my city met it in the rubble of a shattered marketplace, where I blew its harbingers to hell with a rocket launcher I had stolen from the soldiers." Manny laughs, startled. Paulo so often has a genteel air—ah, but there beneath the stylish professional veneer, Manny can see a cold brutality to match his own. He strongly suspects that Paulo did his own share of hurting people, back before he became a multidimensional entity.

Did you choose to be different? Manny wants to ask. *Is that why the city claimed you for itself?*

But just as he opens his mouth, a loud *clack* echoes throughout the empty old station. It's a familiar clack, Manny realizes; the same thing they heard when the subway train's lights went out. It's followed by more clacks, faint metallic groans, pops like sprung rivets. He's not too troubled by the sound—some kind of electrical shutdown procedure, probably—until he realizes it's getting louder. Speeding up, rather than slowing down: clack clack *clack clack* CLACK CLACK **CLACK KRIIDONK**.

Silence for a moment. Then Manny hears something new and awful: a low, grindingly slow, distressed-metal screech. There is a tinkle of cracked, falling glass. He tries to think of what else that sound might be, but only one conclusion feels possible: The train is moving. With no one aboard, and while powered down. The train is moving in a way that no train is meant to move.

Behind them. On the platform they just vacated.

Paulo throws him a wild-eyed look. Manny knows. He must prepare a construct to channel the city's power. Think of some quintessentially New Yorkish thing, a habit or a gesture or a symbol, then wield it as a weapon. They stand in Manhattan, upon the concrete and beneath the dirt of his own borough. Manny should be nearly invincible here.

But as the clacks and metallic screeching grow deafening, and the thing that has come for the primary avatar crawls crunching and ravening up the steps, Manny finds that amid his sheer and absolute terror, his mind has gone completely blank.

Aislyn jerks awake to the sound of shouting, right outside the house. Then the whole house shudders, as if with an earthquake.

Startled, she fumbles first for the knife under her pillow—

though Conall is not home, she knows. He and her father are out for the night, her father on shift, Conall God knows (or cares) where. Only her mother is home, and Aislyn knows from experience that on nights like this, when she is left to her own devices, Kendra Houlihan will be deep in a bottle of gin. Aislyn doesn't know if it counts as alcoholism when you only drink yourself into a stupor once a week or so, but... well. Aislyn is effectively alone in the house.

So she gets up. She's in pajamas again, but this time she takes the time to put on a heavy terry cloth bathrobe, even though it's hot. While she does this, bright light flashes outside, nearly blinding even through the curtains. Someone—a young woman, sounds like—screams in a voice that is high-pitched and revolted and more than a little hysterical. Someone else with a deeper voice shouts—rhythmically but breathlessly, like she's reciting poetry while running—"But once on the scene / we start killing kings!" There is another of those house-jolting thuds as Aislyn finally runs out of her room, and the bright light beyond the blinds fizzles out. Something—huge and inhuman, with a voice like a high-pitched bus horn—shrieks, and the sound of this is enough to make Aislyn cry out and cover her ears as she stumbles against the wall hard enough to dislodge an old family portrait. (Her and Mom and Dad, and a teddy bear to represent Conall.)

Sudden silence. Everything outside has gone still. Her mouth dry with fear, Aislyn hurries to the front door and eases it open.

In the front yard are four women and an older man. The man, who is maybe Japanese, is picking himself up off the ground. In one of his hands is a strange, bright red envelope covered in gold foreign characters, which he's holding like a shuriken from one of the anime shows Aislyn used to watch. His glasses are spider-webbed on one side. Of the women, the stocky short-haired Mexican-looking one stands with her feet planted, crouched low like she's about to do a wrestling move, even though she's old enough to be Aislyn's grandmother. She's also wearing the biggest, ugliest old boots Aislyn's ever seen. The tall, stately Black lady is vaguely familiar, though Aislyn can't place her face. She's in a skirt suit that is covered in dirt all along one side, and she's barefoot. On the curb nearby, neatly positioned next to her sensible heels, is a pair of small gold-loop earrings. The third woman, who sits shaking on the ground, is Indian and plump and young enough to be Aislyn's own age. She seems all right despite the shakes, but she's brushing at her own arms as if frantically trying to wipe something away.

And above them all *floats* the Woman in White, who glows as if a white sun shines through her skin. There are other things in the front yard, too, moving at the edges of Aislyn's vision, other things that— She shudders and resolutely does not look at them again.

The Woman beams over her shoulder as Aislyn steps outside. "Lyn, my dear! Sorry that we woke you. Did you sleep well?"

"What the hell?" Aislyn stares at the strangers in front of her house. They're mostly in the driveway and on the lawn, though keeping well away from the big white tower. But all at once, Aislyn *recognizes* them—even though she's never met a single one of them before, she feels certain. She knows them without sight or name, as well as she knows herself. The big Black woman? Can't be anyone but *Brooklyn*. The mean-looking old lady, *The Bronx*. The nervous-looking Indian girl. *Queens*. They are her, and she is them. "We are New York," she murmurs, and then flinches. No.

They're missing one, because the old Japanese guy definitely isn't Manhattan, though Aislyn senses at once that he, too, is a city. Another substitute. Who's standing, or trying to remain standing since he seems unsteady on his feet, in the flower bed. In *Aislyn's* flower bed, where she grows herbs and chamomile for her tea. She can see his filthy, foreign foot planted square on the dill.

The anger comes on faster than Aislyn's ever gotten angry in her life. It is as if Conall has broken a dam within her, and now every bit of fury she has ever suppressed over thirty years just needs the barest hair trigger to explode forth. She steps out of the house and onto the walkway, and there is shimmering, terrible light around her as she summons forth every drop of belonging that her island can give her, which is a whole heaping lot. The foreigner and her other selves all turn to stare at her, eyes widening at the manifestation of her power. They are *awed* by her and it's delicious. She bares her teeth.

"Get off my lawn," she says.

What happens next is instantaneous. One moment, they're trampling Aislyn's herbs and the grass that her dad works so hard to keep neat. Next moment, all four of them have been picked up and flung backward by some invisible force, hurtling them away from the grass and driveway onto the street. The Woman in White, who isn't technically standing on Aislyn's lawn, remains where she is; the rest of them land on the asphalt of the street with cries or groans or curses. The Woman claps in delight when she sees what Aislyn's done.

The other avatars look shocked, except the Japanese guy, whose expression is unreadable as he picks himself up. Queens, grimacing and stumbling a little, helps up the one who is the Bronx. The Bronx rubs her hip, then picks up each of her booted feet and then puts them down, carefully, as if she cannot believe they have been moved without her volition.

"That's what you did to Paulo," says the Queens girl, sounding both astonished and horrified. "My God, why are you attacking *us*?"

"Because I don't know you," Aislyn snaps, "and you were standing on my lawn."

"You know who we are," says Brooklyn. She's frowning, and favoring her right wrist. "You have to, by now. And you know what *that* is." She nods toward the Woman in White.

"Yeah," Aislyn says, offended now. "That's *my friend*."

"You're crazy." The Queens girl is shaking her head in disbelief. "Oh my God, you really are batshit crazy. You know what she's going to do to you? To the whole city, if she can?"

Aislyn hates being called crazy. Her father says it all the time; all women are crazy, as far as he is concerned. She loves him, so she does not protest when he says it, but these are strangers, so now she feels free to hate.

"She doesn't want to," Aislyn says coldly. "She has to. Sometimes people—" Aislyn's father. Her mother. *Herself.* She flinches with this thought, then sets her jaw. "Sometimes people do bad things because they have to. That's just life." Aislyn folds her arms. "And there can't be anything there, in her world, that doesn't already exist here. It's just that there, people *try* to be decent. So maybe..."

She falters at the looks on their faces. They're just staring at her as if they don't understand. As if she's *wrong*. Who the hell are they to judge her, though? Yes, maybe they're the destiny she's spent her whole life yearning for, but it has shown up on her front lawn and trampled her herbs and slapped her in the face with insults and disrespect, and now that it's here she's pretty sure she does not *want* this destiny. Destiny is rude and ugly, and maybe—

"Maybe I don't want the rest of the city to be okay," Aislyn snarls. "Maybe it *should* all go to hell."

Eyes widen; there are gasps. The Japanese guy's mouth has set in a hard, resigned line. Then the Black lady's face contorts with anger, and she starts forward. "Now, see, what you're not gonna do is leave my daughter to die because you're a selfish xenophobic little heifer. Come the fuck on here." The Bronx, obviously having reached the same conclusion, also strides toward Aislyn. Both of them plainly intend to force her to go with them.

Aislyn stumbles back. "You can't— You're going to *kidnap* me? My dad's a cop, I'll—"

"Uh uh uh," says the Woman in White. The two older women stop as the Woman in White moves between them and Aislyn, while Aislyn presses back against her house's front door, panting a little with an incipient panic attack. But the Woman in White is smiling—as she turns and opens a door in the air.

Through an arched entryway is a small cavern lined with black, glittering walls. On the floor of this cavern, Aislyn can see another young woman, this one chubby and brown-skinned, with loose curly hair. She's lying on the ground in this place, and she appears to be unconscious. She's also covered in gross-looking sticky wetness of some kind.

"Oh no," groans the Bronx-woman, going still with shock. "Veneza?"

"Always check your back seat," says the now-grinning Woman in White. "I used to think that was a euphemism for making sure your ass was on straight! But no, it literally means check your back car seat; you people never make jokes when I expect them." She

406 • N. K. JEMISIN

sobers. "If you want her back with her shape and sanity intact, you'll leave. And leave me with *my friend* here." She turns a winning smile on Aislyn.

"And then you'll destroy the city," says the Japanese guy.

"Naturally. But I'll at least make sure it's quick and painless, all right? We've never wanted to cause suffering. That's your people's way." She lifts her chin a little. "We can be civilized. You stand down. I bring my city into this world and use it to begin erasing this universe and all of its antecedents and offshoots. If you like, I can create a temporary pocket universe where some members of your species will survive the collapse, though of course without the support of nearby universal branches or a city's power, it will eventually succumb to entropy. But it should last long enough for your brief, unidirectional lives to end naturally. Peacefully. We all win." She beams.

The Japanese man scrunches his face in confusion and rapidly growing denial. "*What?*"

But the old woman, the Bronx, shakes her head. Her lips are pressed tight together. "That's not how this fucking works," she says. "You don't get to do this. You don't roll up in here and threaten to kill everything we love, and claim to be *civilized* while you do it."

"Oh my God," says Queens. She's staring at the girl in the cavern, and her face is distorted with disgust. When Aislyn looks into the cavern to try to understand what Queens is so horrified by, she realizes belatedly that the cavern walls have begun to flex in a strange, arrhythmic way. When one of the walls shifts in an odd way, Aislyn glimpses something hard and ridged slide out from behind it. *A comb?* she wonders. She thinks it's a comb. It's black, like a comb meant for men or Black people. The comb's teeth are irregular, and needle-sharp at the tips, and they curve a little. Inward, toward the young woman, almost like

teeth they are teeth not a comb teeth teeth teeth

And the place that the girl lies within isn't a cavern at all.

A fold of the glittering (glistening, Aislyn realizes, her gorge rising; it is glistening with *saliva*) cavern wall shifts aside a little, to bare a narrow, vertically oriented throat that vibrates for an instant. The sound that emerges is not a voice, but a dead, flat throbbing tone. *Ump*. It flexes again. *Dad. Ump*.

It's the Ding Ho. A Ding Ho has that poor girl in its open mouth, threatening to swallow her alive.

"You're the most horrible thing in the world," Queens says. She's crying, but her fists are clenched. "Veneza isn't even one of us. She's just ordinary! Why would you hurt her?" She raises those plump fists, ready to fight. All three of the other parts of New York are tensing, crouching, preparing themselves to fight the Woman in White. To fight Aislyn's only friend.

Aislyn clutches and shakes her head. It's too much. She just wants it to be over already. So she shuts her eyes and clenches her fists, and wishes with all her might that every one of these dangerous strangers would just *go away*.

Everything then happens very quickly.

The thing emerges from the stairway tunnel slowly, more of a *bulging forward* than an active movement. Fast glacial. Ghostly in its shifting, fluttering white shapelessness. It's easy to see the bones of the subway train that it used to be, underneath what it is now: a living, flexible, snakelike thing covered in a proliferation of white tendrils so thick as to resemble fur. That fur ripples back in waves, pressing against the tiled stone, easing the passage of the train through the narrow archway mouth in the same way that cilia move things through the small intestine. As Manny and Paulo watch, the elongated nose of the train oozes to the side, turning and questing about like a living thing on the hunt, reshaping itself by the moment... and finally focusing on Manny, Paulo, and the sleeping primary.

Paulo holds his cigarette the way Manny remembers holding a knife. He blows a hard puff of smoke at the train-beast, and despite a gap of yards, the thing flinches, its unearthly light flickering momentarily as the tendrils covering its nose die away. Underneath is the metal and wire of the former front train car, now horribly distorted into a bullet-like shape—but after a moment, tendrils from the unaffected portion of the car grow rapidly forward again. New ones sprout on the denuded nose, and within seconds the whole thing is as it was before.

Then a line seems to peel its way down the length of the thing, and it splits apart from the tip. Two halves of a whole. A *mouth*. And at their core, a black throat lined with jagged, broken-off subway seats.

Paulo curses softly, stepping back. There is fear on his face. Manny flexes his fists, stepping forward as fear for the primary eclipses any fear for himself. He still hasn't thought of a construct, but there is a growl in his chest; all has faded into a red haze of instinct. "He's mine," he snarls. His voice has deepened, reverberating; Paulo throws him a startled glance. "Mine! You can't have him!"

The train monster hisses like sliding doors, and splits further. Now it's a mouth in four parts, wormlike and wrong. The lower mouths end in molars formed from the train's metal wheels, now razor-sharp and spinning with manic, devouring speed. There's even a tiny uvula back there, dangling above the wheels: a red pull-knob on a chain, behind which a cracked sign reads EMER-GENCY BRAKE.

And, horror of horrors, it is *talking*. "S-staaaaand...c-c-clear," it purrs, in a distorted, singsong electronic voice. "Closssssing... d-d-d-dooooooooors..."

But Manny does not stand clear. He stands to fight. And he is changing, too. He is bigger, suddenly, taller; he feels his button-down pop loose and his jeans rip as all at once his head and shoulders brush the ceiling. He clenches his fists and bares his teeth and no longer cares about pretending to be the good-looking, friendly creature others see. All that matters is the primary. All Manny wants, all that he is built to do, is protect him.

And as black fur and shimmering city-power sheaths Manny's limbs, and as his shoulders broaden and grow heavy with super-humanly strong muscle, he has one last fleeting thought before he becomes in sum total the beast he has always been within:

I'm really going to have to watch some better movies about New York.

Then King Kong pounds the floor, and charges forward, fists raised, to do battle.

The world ripples around Aislyn's house. "Go away!" Aislyn screams. "Leave me alone! *None of you belong here!*"

And because *belonging* is as quintessential to Staten Island–ness as *toughness* is to the Bronx and *starting over* is to Queens and *weathering change* is to Brooklyn, and because they stand upon Aislyn's ground where *she is Staten Island* and her will becomes supernatural law—

Her voice echoes and the wave of city-energy that ripples along the grass and leaves and air and asphalt is like a thousand-clarion hurricane blast—

And then they are gone. Their car is gone. All of the awful, spindly creatures that have been drawing closer around Aislyn, their movements too illogical and jittery to contemplate and their voices rising and falling in soft inhuman jibbers, are gone—even the one that held the unconscious girl in its mouth. When it vanishes, there is a faint, startled *ump?* But then Aislyn's front yard is quiet and empty again, at last.

Only the Woman still floats nearby, because Aislyn didn't mean her.

Aislyn stands trembling in the wake of all this, her hands loose, her head swimming. She's tired. Exhausted, suddenly. It takes a lot, she realizes, to drive away so many parts of herself. But sometimes, to survive, that's just what you have to do.

She folds herself down into a crouch and covers her head with her hands and sits there on her house's doorstep, shaking and rocking back and forth. After a moment, the Woman lands with a light tap of feet on the concrete beside her. Then a hand touches Aislyn's shoulder, gentle and warm.

"Friends," says the Woman. "Right? Facing the big, scary multiverse together."

It's surprisingly comforting. "Yeah," Aislyn murmurs softly, not lifting her head, although some of her shakes ease off. "Friends."

She feels that sudden sharp sting again, high on her shoulder, near the back of her neck. The pain of it fades quickly, however—and in its wake, as the Woman in White takes her hand away and sighs in satisfaction at last, Aislyn feels warmer. Safer. No longer confused at all.

She lifts her head and smiles up at the Woman in White, who smiles back in warmth and welcome. And for the first time in perhaps Aislyn's whole life, she no longer feels alone. A whole city cares about her! So what if that city is not New York.

Quietly, all over Staten Island, more towers and oddities begin to grow. It is the infrastructure of a different city, laying the foundations of a different world. And now, only one thing can possibly stop it.

CHAPTER SIXTEEN

New York Is **Who?**

They reappear in front of the *Charging Bull* of Wall Street, collapsing in a pile beneath its bronze nose. Tourists do stuff like this all the time for selfies, so neither the super-early-morning joggers—it's nearly dawn—nor the cluster of nuns on their way to morning prayers pay them much attention. There lie the unremarked-upon avatars of New York, or three out of the five at least, panting and dazed and trying to get their bearings after suffering a colossal defeat.

Bronca's still a little out of it when she struggles up enough to check on Veneza, who appeared with them. Young B's seen better days. Her brown skin is more sallow than it should be, and her hair is lank and still wet with ... something ... that stinks. It's an utterly alien stink. The waste products of incomprehensible metabolic processes from a completely different evolutionary pathway, bad breath from beyond. But as Bronca ignores the stink and checks to make sure Veneza is still breathing, Veneza's face scrunches and her eyes crack open. Even then Bronca is worried. She can't see any of those white things growing on Veneza anywhere, but the poor girl was in Squigglebitch's hands ... mouth ... for a while.

As soon as Veneza sees Bronca, however, she groans. "I was headed out of town. I *was*. Don't start with me."

The complaint eases a lot of Bronca's fears at once, and she lets out a weak laugh. "I wasn't going to. Just glad you're alive."

"Yeah. Eu também." Veneza sits up, rubbing her eyes. "God, *fuck*, I thought I was gonna die. Just *looking* at some of those things . . . I felt like everything in me was just ready to shut down. They shouldn't exist. That place shouldn't exist."

"What?" That's Brooklyn, who is climbing to her feet and ineffectually trying to hide the giant split torn into her skirt. It's nothing indecent, but she's the type.

"Nice legs," Bronca says, just to fuck with her. Brooklyn grimaces back.

"That place. Where Squigglebitch is from." When Veneza lowers her hand, her expression is haunted, and that's when Bronca sees the strain. She's playing it off well, but there's deep, atavistic fear in her face. "It wasn't actually where she was from. She didn't take me *there*, thank God, because I don't think . . . It was more like a halfway point, where things from both places could exist. That's where she hangs out when she's not here. Except it's wrong all in itself, yeah? Nothing's supposed to work that way. I just don't understand how buildings could be *built* like that."

"Like what?" Queens asks, before Bronca can mom-look her silent. Bronca reaches up to check Veneza's forehead and press the back of her hand against Veneza's cheeks. She's chilled rather than warm, and shaking with more than the chill. Her voice skirls higher and louder when she answers.

"Like things that shouldn't *exist*, damn it! All skewy, and . . ." She scrunches her eyes shut. She's trembling so hard that it shakes her voice. *"The angles were fucked up, Old B. They were all wrong."*

If she had delivered this in her usual snarky tone, Bronca still would've been unnerved. That Veneza instead drops it in a high-pitched stage whisper makes every little hair on Bronca's skin stand on end.

"Oh-kay, no," she says, taking hold of Veneza's shoulders and shaking her, gently, until she lowers her hands and stares at Bronca. "Stop thinking about that shit," she says. "Some thoughts are poison. You can think them, but only when you've got the strength—or therapy, whichever floats your boat. 'Til then? Right now? Close it off. Focus on right here and now."

"I, I don't . . ." But Veneza swallows and takes a deep breath. "Okay. I'm going to try." Abruptly she grimaces, looking around. "Why the fuck am I sitting on the ground? Gross. And—" She sniffs at herself, then makes a horrified face.

"Yeah, you're very rank," Queens says, though she's grinning, relieved to see Veneza's all right. "When this is all over, I'll go home and get you some of that good incense. My aunty will probably send you a million idlis, too, once I tell her you ate all of mine." Veneza giggles, and Bronca feels her relax.

But then it's Queens' turn for a haunted look, as she blinks and sobers. "But it *is* all over. Isn't it? Without Staten Island . . ."

"I can't believe she did that." Brooklyn's frowning as she extends a hand to help each of them to their feet. To her shame, Bronca actually needs the help. She's exhausted, and her hip hurts, and her back has twinged something awful. "I don't even know what she did. Like, that was *Star Trek* shit. We didn't go fast like when Manny carried us out of the Center, we just *went*. She didn't even put us on the ferry. Straight-up teleportation."

Bronca rubs at the small of her back. "Well, now we know what her super-special power is, I guess: magic xenophobia." She looks around, then looks around again. Her stomach clenches. "Hong."

They all look. Hong is nowhere to be seen.

"Maybe he's gone back to his city?" Queens grimaces. "He did keep saying that he wanted to. Maybe he recovered first and..."

"I'm going to hope so," Brooklyn says grimly. "I'm actually going to hope he's just that much of an asshole, abandoning us while we were out of it."

Because the alternative is that the strange, impossible, and instantaneous transit from Staten Island somehow left Hong... elsewhere. In limbo, maybe. Or nowhere at all.

That's too much for Bronca to contemplate, so she doesn't, focusing instead on practical matters. "And where's my fucking— oh." Her old Jeep, none the worse for having been teleported across New York Harbor, is sitting next to the bull. There's already a parking ticket stuck under one of the wipers. Well, at least it wasn't towed. She sighs. "Come on, then. I'll drive us to City Hall."

She starts forward, then stops as Queens grabs her arm. "You're not listening to me," Queens snaps. "This is *pointless*. We can't wake up the primary, not without the fifth borough. What are we going to do, go there and let him eat us for nothing?"

"*Yes*," Brooklyn says, glaring at her and moving around them to go to the car. "Either that or we go back to Staten Island to knock that little dumb-ass in the head and bring her along anyway. But that'll probably take another hour, and somehow I don't feel like we've got that much time left anymore. Going to see the primary is the next best thing." She slaps at her clothing, finds her phone in a back pocket of the skirt, and then grimaces. "I don't have Manhattan's number. Why the hell didn't we exchange numbers?"

"He's underground, anyway, so reception would be iffy," Bronca replies. She finds her key fob and unlocks the doors.

"Do you just want to die, then?" Queens, not following them, looks from one to the other in disbelief. "Are *all* of you crazy?"

"Yeah, we are," Bronca says with a single weary laugh. "We're New York, remember; we're all fucked in the head. Can't talk too much shit about Manhattan, really."

"I'm not giving up," Brooklyn says to Queens. She puts a hand on her hip; her expression is implacable. "Don't you dare try to make it sound like that, young lady. Giving up is what *you're* doing. So go on, run back to Jackson Heights and hide, and hope that woman and her monster things don't get you. Or leave town, and we'll all hope the next Queens steps up to try and save people—"

At this, Queens flinches. "I want to save people! You think I don't? But we don't even know if this will work..." And then she trails off, wincing; her shoulders sag in defeat. "But...ah, shit."

Bronca has managed to get her hip to stop hurting, which feels like a victory. "What."

Veneza has peeled off the light sweater she had on—last night, a lifetime ago, she'd been complaining that the Center's air-conditioning was too much. The sweater is now smeared with God knows what, so she leaves it on the ground under the bull's nose. "Sniff that, capitalism." Then she, too, heads for Bronca's car.

"I was just thinking that you've run the numbers." Queens is looking at them sadly, and smiling. "I guess I should've run them, too, but all of this has been...too much. It's there in the probabilities, though, right? Running means we have zero chance to save the city. Trying to talk sense into Staten Island, nonzero chance, but so small as to be meaningless. Trying to wake up the primary, even with just the four of us . . . is the best chance we have." She shakes her head, then finally sighs and starts toward Bronca's car. "I hate that there's no ninetieth-percentile scenario, though."

"Yeah, sucks, don't it?" Bronca claps Queens on the shoulder, and they all get in.

Brooklyn's phone is down to a sniff of power, but it warns that there's been some kind of police incident at the Brooklyn Bridge/ City Hall Station. She calls one of her magical aides and makes arrangements. "Someone from the Transit Museum's going to meet us," she says as she hangs up, then tosses her phone onto the floor. "They can let us into the old station."

"I do have a car charger," Bronca says, pursing her lips at the dying phone.

"Leave it," Brooklyn says, turning to look out the window. "I'd only call my daughter again."

Bronca sighs and thinks, *I really hope they don't name my grand-child something corny.*

At City Hall, parking is a nightmare. It takes half an hour to get there, even though it's not far; they might have walked faster, even if they'd stopped on every corner to watch the sunrise. The traffic has likely been caused by the weird white structures that seem to be sprouting all over the city now, at a rapidly accelerating rate. Bronca drives past a gnarled treelike thing with yawning distorted faces in lieu of boles, which has webbed up the little park between two financial services' corporate headquarters. There's another small one on the south lawn of City Hall Park, like a white humped frog without legs or eyes. Just a mouth and warts, rooted to the ground and shivering as if it's cold.

Worse than the structures are the people. More and more

of the financial and political warriors Bronca sees have tendrils growing somewhere on them. Some have just one or two, but a few are covered in the things, like albino Sasquatches strolling along in Manolo Blahniks.

"Getting worse," Veneza says unnecessarily.

"Yeah, noticed," Bronca replies.

She feels Veneza turn to stare at her. "You know she's like you, right? A city. Just not from this world."

Bronca sighs, questing briefly for a parking spot before finally grabbing a narrow slot that's very likely going to get her towed. Fuck it. "Yep. Noticed that, too."

"And you know she wants to *come* here? That's what those white things all over the city are about. She called them 'connector pylons.' " Veneza grimace-smiles. "She's trying to connect *herself* to *us*. Bring her city here—right on top of New York."

"What? How?" asks Brooklyn. Bronca shuts the car off, so thrown that she forgets to put it in park first; the engine chugs to a halt with an aggrieved sound.

"I don't know how. But have you noticed the shadow?"

Bronca stares at her. Brooklyn frowns—then abruptly gets out of the car, looking up at the sky. She swears. Bronca does the same, aware of Queens scrambling to follow.

There's nothing to see, she thinks at first, except unoccluded blueness; it's a typical June morning, with the sun almost seeming to leap above the horizon now that dawn has broken. Except... Bronca frowns around, noticing at last that the ground is shady. The trees and people cast shadows, but these are thin, almost blended in with the general lack of light. It's a bright morning, or it should be. There isn't a single cloud in the sky. The sun's light should be saturating this area, turning all the shadows stark. It isn't, though.

And Bronca suddenly suspects that, if she could get up high, she would see the whole city shadowed. As if there is something floating above it—something vast and terrible, but thus far observable only via its effects on the world. Soon, though . . .

Veneza has gotten out of the car. She's resolutely not looking up, Bronca notices. Afraid of seeing something else that she shouldn't. "Yeah, so," she says, her voice tight. "You guys should do everything you can. Um, fast."

Yeah. Bronca's getting that impression.

They find the entrance to the old station, an unobtrusive green-painted thing incongruously labeled BROAD STREET SUBWAY, EXIT ONLY, and locked with a pull-down shutter. There's a harried-looking young man waiting there. He's barely pubescent to Bronca's eyes, which makes her figure him for the summer intern. "Ah, Council Member Thomason," he says as they arrive, smiling and stepping forward to shake her hand. "Thank you, we got your message. Will you be needing a tour guide? We don't have any of our usual guides on hand, I'm afraid, but I can—"

"There's no need, Director," Brooklyn says smoothly. "Thank you. I've been on the tour before, I can handle it. We didn't bring a flashlight, however."

"Oh, take mine." He—the director, to Bronca's astonishment, damn children everywhere these days—hands Brooklyn his flashlight. It's one of those survivalist dealies that needs to be cranked instead of having batteries, but this one's fully charged. "And how long will you be?"

"Not long. I'll be sure to return the keys by tomorrow morning." Brooklyn extends a hand.

The director blinks. "You— I didn't realize—" Now he looks around at the rest of them. Wondering, Bronca guesses, why a city council member has shown up with a bunch of raggedy, dirty, tired-looking people, to go exploring a defunct train station. "Um."

"I'll make sure my friend on the Brooklyn Museum board knows how helpful and professional you are," Brooklyn says, with a perfect shit-eating smile. Bronca almost admires her for it. And the director, who apparently wants a better job, is helpless against it. He sighs as he hands over the keys. They exchange a few more lines of friendly small talk, which are aggravating to hear while the city grows steadily dimmer. Now Bronca can't tell her own shadow from the general gloom. Finally, though, the child-bureaucrat leaves, and Brooklyn starts wrestling with the shutter lock. After a moment, they're inside. Down some steps and around a corner—and then they all stop, in shock.

Strewn across the curving platform, beneath an arch lined with gorgeous Guastavino tilework, lies the scattered, twisted corpse of a biomechanoid monster. The bulk of it hangs off the subway platform—and as Bronca stares, she belatedly realizes that the back end of the thing is an unadulterated subway train, the last car of which still sits on its track. All the cars ahead of it, however, have jumped the track. The foremost cars have actually come up on the platform and transformed into something more like an annelid than an inanimate vehicle. It has tiny, stumpy legs, made of twisted engine parts. It's also covered in white, glowing strands that have grown as thickly as dense fur . . . but all of the white strands are dead, Bronca sees with some relief, crumbling away to nothingness even as she watches. She gives the strands a wide berth anyway while they pick their way around the train's remnants.

In fact, Bronca sees that the thing hasn't just died; it has been *killed*. Ripped apart, in fact. Part of the first car lies crumpled on the other side of the platform, flung against the wall by some incomprehensibly powerful force. The rest is jammed halfway up a side tunnel of the station. But just beyond the jammed-in bit, Bronca can hear someone panting.

"Hello?" she calls.

There's a curse in Portuguese, and abruptly Paulo appears in the narrow gap of the torn-out conductor's cab. "Thank God," he says, his eyes widening with relief. "Is Staten Island with you?"

They start climbing over the debris. Bronca's ashamed to need a hand from Queens, but she makes it. "No," Brooklyn says. "She didn't like us any better than she did you. The Woman in White had already..."

She trails off. Bronca gets through the torn-up piece of subway monster and follows her gaze to see Manny slumped against the wall. He's the one who's panting, plus visibly exhausted and bloodied all over. He's also completely naked, although Paulo's jacket covers his lap.

"What," Bronca says, dazed.

"Train monster," Manny replies.

"Uh, yeah, what I mean is—"

"*Staten Island,*" Paulo snaps. He's shaking his head in disbelief. "You're saying she's thrown in with the Enemy? Completely? Does she understand—"

"She understands." Queens has gone over to help Manny up. On his feet, he looks like Bronca feels, bent over and holding himself gingerly against the pain of any possible movement. He's clutching the jacket over his dangly bits, so Bronca figures Paulo's not going to want that one back. "And then she threw us off the island. We, uh. We don't know where Hong is, by the way."

Paulo stares at all of them, speechless in his horror. Manny sighs, then turns and stumbles toward something in an alcove beyond them. "We'll have to do what we can, then."

"And if it isn't enough?" That's Brooklyn.

"It'll have to be enough." Manny's so obviously hurting that Bronca goes over to try to help him. Her back seizes up the instant she bends, though, and she has to quit. Veneza shakes her head and runs over to both of them, glaring at Bronca 'til she backs off. Veneza slides a shoulder under Manny's arm.

"Will we at least be able to protect our boroughs?" Brooklyn smiles in a pained sort of way that makes it clear she knows exactly how fucked up the question is. Bronca doesn't blame her, though.

"How should I know?" But then, so that she doesn't sound completely heartless, Bronca adds, more softly, "Did they get out? Your father and your girl?"

"I hope so." Brooklyn turns away then, and heads toward the alcove, moving more briskly than is strictly necessary.

Bronca limps into the alcove as well, to behold the primary just as the portrait depicted him: too slim, too young, and entirely too vulnerable here within the fading light of the city. "Doesn't look big enough to eat more than a couple of mouthfuls of each of us," Bronca quips. No one laughs.

Paulo comes over and takes Veneza's arm, pulling her back, much to Bronca's relief.

Then it's just them and the primary. Four out of five stars, good but not great. Bronca takes a deep breath, waiting, trying not to be afraid. She finds herself watching Manny, though, who seems to get this part of it better than the rest of them.

Manny, however, just looks troubled as he gazes down at the primary. "Nothing's different," he says. He reaches out toward the shaved side of the primary's head, but stops a few inches away, as if he is afraid to follow through on the gesture. His expression tightens in frustration, and Bronca abruptly sees the scene a different way. His hand *has been stopped*. By something that she cannot see.

"What..." There's only one way to know. Bronca steels herself. *Let me die as Tundeewi Loosoxkweew,* she thinks. *As Fire Burns Woman, as Turtle Clan. As the warrior Chris always called me.* And then she reaches for the boy's head, too.

Something stops her hand. It doesn't feel like anything at first, just a progressive slowness, until her hand grows still and will go no farther. Queens starts, then stretches out a shaking hand. Hers stops, too. They all look at Brooklyn, whose expression has gone bleak. She knows it's pointless. But because they need her to, she reaches out. Her hand stops on the same invisible barrier.

Above them, through the skylight, the daylight fades more. It's like an eclipse, Bronca recalls, thinking of that strange, eerie twilight she's seen a handful of times over the course of her life. *R'lyeh draws near,* she thinks, and flinches at the welt this whips across her thoughts.

"It's coming," Paulo says unnecessarily. He's looking up. They're all looking up. His expression is grim.

"So she's really going to do it," Queens says, her voice now full of despair. "She's going to—to put a city from *that place,* here. On top of this one. What does that even mean?"

"That a lot of people are going to die," Brooklyn says. "You heard her. Bringing that city here will somehow cause this whole *universe* to collapse."

"How can that be? I don't understand any of this." Queens groans, rubbing a hand over her hair.

"You should've gone, too," Bronca says to Paulo. It's useless, but she's never been able to keep herself from saying, *I told you so.* Probably the biggest reason why she's single now.

Paulo takes a deep breath. "There's a not-insubstantial chance that whatever happens will simply push me back home to my city. Until the universe ends, in any case."

"Do you think Hong, then—?"

"Uh. Old B?"

They all turn, startled. That's because Veneza sounds dazed. When she looks up, she's breathing harder, her face all over sweat. But she doesn't look ill or faint, which Bronca is glad to see, because she doesn't want to think about what it means if that awful creature stung her or bit her or poisoned her in some unearthly way. Maybe it's foolish to fret so over one person's life when the entire city is about to get cosmically curb-stomped, but that's how the human heart works sometimes.

So she goes over to Veneza. "Yeah, kid? What—"

And then she stops. Veneza abruptly backs up a step. Bronca stops, too. They stare at each other, eyes widening.

She is a dirty, tired little thing—struggling in the shadow of greatness, but proud of what she has. Potential is what she's got, in spades, and she stretches out stubby little piers and puffs a sunken chest of long-vanished industry and tosses her crown of new, gaudy skyscrapers as if to say, **Come at me, I don't care how big you are, I'm just as badass as you—**

"No," Bronca breathes, stunned.

"Um," Veneza says. She's shaking a little. But she's also grinning. "Man, what the fuck."

"What?" Manny looks from Veneza to the rest of them and back. Queens is just as visibly confused.

"Nothing that matters," Brooklyn murmurs. Her head is bowed; she's already mourning her family.

Paulo, however, is staring at Veneza, his eyes wide with realization. A strange look comes over his face. He scrambles around the newspaper pile, fast, and grabs Veneza by the arm so hard that she yelps. Bronca reacts immediately, grabbing his arm in turn. "Hey, what the hell are you—"

"Living cities aren't defined by politics," he says. It's almost a shout, so urgently does he speak. "Not by city limits or county lines. *They're made of whatever the people who live in and around them believe.* And there is no other reason for her to have instantiated, here, now, than—" He gives up on words and yanks Veneza again, toward the newspaper pile. Bronca gets it this time. Her hand has gone numb. She lets him go, then hurries to follow.

The little room has begun to darken. Part of that is because the museum director's flashlight is starting to run down, but it's also because the sunlight is gone, completely gone. When Bronca looks up, she can see blue sky, but it's a dark blue, as if the stars are about to come out. And when she squints, she sees that something is solidifying out of nothingness, an unearthly foundation forming in the air high above New York—

Veneza resists Paulo, looking wildly back at Bronca. "B! B, this is freaking me out, what—"

Bronca bats at Paulo until he lets go, then she pulls Veneza into the circle around the primary avatar. "Every single person I've ever met from Jersey City says they're from New York," she says,

426 • N. K. JEMISIN

speaking with low urgency. "Not to New Yorkers, because we're assholes about it, but to everybody else. And the whole world *accepts* that. Right? Because to most people with sense, a city that's in spitting distance of Manhattan, closer even than Staten Island, *might as well be New York*. Right?"

There is a sound building around them, above them, throughout the city. A rumble would come from the earth; this is a low, howling siren, like a choir of ten thousand voices screaming at once. Or—no. Like wind howling as it is displaced, shoved aside so fast that the air grows hot. Bronca has not heard anything like it since Hurricane Sandy's freight-train blasts of destruction, and this is much worse. R'lyeh comes.

But the others get it now. Even Veneza, who's staring at all of them. Tears have welled in her eyes. She's grinning, elated— because, Bronca realizes very belatedly, this is what she's hoped for. She's been with them since the beginning, after all, watching and wanting to help. Understanding enough to envy, perhaps. And the city of New York, which gobbles up any newcomers foolish enough to want in, has reacted accordingly.

It's impossible not to smile, too, even here at the end of the world. Joy is joy. Bronca takes one of her hands, letting her love show; they are family now. Manny takes the other, his expression intent.

"What are you, Young B?" Bronca asks her. She's grinning.

Veneza laughs, tilting her head back like she's drunk. "I'm *Jersey City*, goddamn it!"

Manny's expression clears finally. He exhales in relief as strange mechanisms within his psyche shift and bring into focus the path forward. They all feel this. "And who are *we*?" he asks them, just as the little chamber goes dark.

All of it, that is, except for the light that surrounds the primary on his bed of tabloid tales and buried ledes. He's *glowing*, they see at last. The light never came from anywhere else.

And as they watch, he inhales, stretches, rolls onto his back, and opens his eyes.

"We're New York," he says. And grins. "Aw, yeah."

They are New York.

They are the single titanic concussion of sound from every sub-woofer and every steel drum circle that has ever annoyed elderly neighbors and woken babies while secretly giving everyone else an excuse to smile and dance. It is this sound, a violent wave of pure percussive force pouring from a thousand nightclub doors and orchestra pits, that slams upward and outward from the city. If it were happening in peoplespace, there would be a lot of hearing impairments in its wake. It happens in the place where cities dwell—and where rude R'lyeh has actually dared to try to usurp New York's seat upon the world. *Oh no the hell you don't*, they snarl, and shove the interloper away.

They are methane-green sewer fire that races through the streets, unreal and yet extradimensionally hot, tracing out grid-lines and curbs—and searing away every atom of alien universe that has made its unwelcome home on the city's asphalt. Every tower and white structure freezes, then crumbles into nothingness. Office workers who've spent the morning covered in tendrils stop midwalk, blinking, as suddenly they are blasted clean. It doesn't hurt. At worst their skin prickles a little. Some of them sigh and put on eczema cream, then go on about their day.

But *they* have become hunting packs of many-limbed, faceless stockbrokers, as hot on the scent as they are on an insider tip, who crawl along the city's walls and leap across its flat rooftops, grinning with feral teeth. *They* are stick-figure stick-up kids, scarecrows dressed in knockoff Burberry, who lurk in the shadows to ambush their prey. *They* stoop out of the sun as screeching PTA helicopter parents, brandishing standardized tests in one hand and razor claws on the other.

Their prey is the Woman in White as she runs through the city. There are dozens of her, they see at last; many bodies, infinite shapes, one entity, all of her working together and wholly dedicated to the war she was built to fight. But she is a city, in the end—fair R'lyeh where the streets are always straight and the buildings all curve, risen from the brine-dark deep well between universes. And no living city can remain within the boundary of another while it is unwelcome.

As each iteration of the Woman in White is caught and rent apart into the featureless, undifferentiated ur-matter of which she is made, R'lyeh quails in fear. She is caught now, helpless between realms, too committed to the invasion to return to the buffer dimension. The towers were both adaptors and guide-rails for what parts of its substance have already transferred, and as the cleansing wave of New York energy roils outward from Manhattan toward Westchester and Coney Island and Long Island, not a single tower remains standing. Anchorless, R'lyeh will be lost in the formless aethers outside of existence itself, if she does not find and claim some kind of foothold. Anything will do. She flails, desperate to survive. Any chance—

There.

It's so tiny, though. Not nearly enough to contain the entirety of a massive city . . . but perhaps the whole borough can act as a singular sort of anchor all by itself. R'lyeh cannot come through, but with Staten Island's help, she can *hold*. She can anchor her substance in this new exurb of itself, and establish a commerce of citizens and resources that will keep her alive, for now at least. And in the process, this small angry part of New York that has chafed to be free for so long now gets its wish.

But *they*? New York's remaining embodiments, plus the now-honorary borough of Jersey City? *They* are just fine.

We are all fine, thanks for asking. We're New York. Welcome to the party.

CODA

I live the city. Fucking city.

Never liked Coney Island. Too many damn people, in the summer. Too cold, any other time of year. Nothing to do if you don't have money and don't know how to swim. Still. I'm standing on the boardwalk, feeling wood vibrate under my feet with the kinetic energy of thousands of walking adults and running kids and bounding dogs, and feeling something more intrinsic to my being reverberate in concert with five other souls. My soul's in there, too. We're conjoined now, a spiritual freak show more than fit for Coney Island; that was what that whole "devouring" business meant, see. If you can't eat 'em, join 'em.

I'm enjoying myself in spite of everything. Today is July 9th. Not July 4th. This is a day that means something to *us*, since New York declared its independence from England on the ninth of July in 1776. Fashionably late as usual. We've decided that it commemorates almost three weeks since we turned into cities, so it's time for a celebration. Still alive, woop woop, pass the blunt.

Paulo gets off the phone and comes over to where I stand at the railing, and we both relax there for a while. Beyond us, out on the sand, Brooklyn's daughter, Jojo, is playing Marco Polo in the water with Queens and Jersey. She's kicking their ass, because she's fast and clever like her mama. Queens is having too much fun letting herself get caught, and Jersey's too scared of the water—can't swim, thinks every warm current is somebody's piss and every blop of seaweed is a Portuguese man-of-war—to really do much. Up on the assemblage of blankets, Queens' aunty is cooing to her baby while her husband, a small man with an enormous moustache, crouches over a portable hibachi nearby, making something that smells amazing. Bronca is half-asleep in the full sun, a broad bronze lump spread out across the cloth. She's wearing a bikini. I don't know where old girl found a bikini that big, but she's got maximum Don't Give A Fuck mode engaged, and I'm surfing on her bitch wave. (No idea why so much of me is apparently female, but I'm down with it. It's so me. And I am them.)

Manhattan sits on the blankets, too. He's been swimming, but has mostly dried out by now and is just watching the others, vicariously enjoying their pleasure. Part of him is still so much the newbie, amazed to find this place of sand and sun stuck onto the ass end of the greatest city in the world, but the rest of him has relaxed into acceptance already. He's Zen like that.

Then I see the muscles in his back tense just a little as he senses my attention. Most people would ignore it, but not this guy. He twists around to look at me, and I'm the one who looks away, unable to meet the intensity of his gaze. I never asked for a knight? An enforcer? Whatever the fuck he is. But of them all, I know that he is the one meant to . . . serve me. Which sounds way too damn BDSM for my ass, and I don't know what to make of it. He will kill for me. He'll love me, too, if I let him. Jury's still out on that because I never wanted a fuckshit-crazy light-skinned Ivy League boyfriend. Like, I mean, he's nice to look at? But the rest . . . There's reasons I haven't done the rest for a while, except as pretend.

His eyes lower a bit. They all know me, we all know each other, but he's the one who's most sensitive to my moods. He gets that he makes me nervous. (He also gets that I don't like admitting that it's nervousness.) So he backs off, for now. He'll wait 'til I'm more comfortable with the whole thing. Then, somehow, we'll figure it out.

I sigh and rub my eyes. Paulo lets out a breath of amusement. "It could be worse."

Yeah, we could all be getting gnawed to pieces by non-Euclidean Ding Hos, I get that. Still. "This is some what the fuck, man."

"It's you. Whether you like that or not." He sighs, watching the others, looking entirely too smug with himself. He's better now that I've purged the part of myself that didn't want him; it means that he's no longer unwelcome in New York. He's got serious shit to talk about, though. "The other cities of the Summit are astonished. Everyone thought you would be like the tragedy of London, but perhaps that was foolish on its face. I cannot think of two cities more different than this one and that one."

"Yeah, I get it, yo." He still talks too much. I straighten and stretch a little. (Manny looks again, his gaze hungry, before he turns away. Such a gentleman.) "Your boy in China okay?"

"Hong is not my boy. But yes. When he recovered from suddenly finding himself back in his home city, he called the others to meet in Paris. New York as well, now that you have become a full-fledged city. The Summit will need to speak with all of you, and discuss . . ." He sighs and gestures around at the beach, the sky, the high-rises behind us. And then he looks across the water.

This isn't the touristy part of Coney Island, so even though it's a gorgeous summer day, it's not too crowded. Technically we're in Brighton Beach, except the beach part is still called Coney Island, which makes about as much sense as keeping that name when Coney hasn't been an actual Island for a hundred years. Anyway. We're at this end of Coney Island for a reason, see. From here, you can see a long stretch of Staten Island. There's not much to it—mostly flat on this side, trees and elevated houses, the island's low profile interrupted by the occasional industrial crane or cell signal tower. Pretty. Boring.

All of this, however, sits in a deep well of gloom. There are no clouds overhead. No satellites, no eclipses. No one's reported on it in the news, though we've seen a few people commenting on it in social media, as a curiosity more than anything else. Only we can see it easily, us and those others throughout the city who have been granted the gift/curse of its sight. No big deal. Just a huge, perfectly circular—Brooklyn took a helicopter ride across the harbor and told us that part—shadow over Staten Island.

Yeah. It's like that. She has betrayed us more completely than we ever believed she could.

Paulo straightens away from the railing. "My flight leaves in a few hours. I'd best head to the airport."

It's out of nowhere. I knew it was coming, of course; he only came here to see me through the change, the next-youngest city helping the newbie, and now his duty is done. Still. I bite the inside of my cheek and try not to show how hurt I am.

"My sublet is paid through the end of the month," he continues, "if you want to remain there. Just leave the keys and close the door when you go. Try not to make a mess."

I sigh. "And after that." Back out on the street. At least it's summer.

"After that," he says, looking meaningfully from me to the people sitting on the beach before us, "you have five other selves to take care of you, instead of me."

It's gentle. I've had worse breakups. This probably doesn't even count as a breakup. Still. I fold my arms on the railing and prop my chin on them, trying not to resent my other selves. Take care of me, Paulo said.

"They need you," Paulo says. This, too, is gentle.

"To live."

He shakes his head. "To be great. I'll see you in Paris."

Then he takes out a cigarette, lights it up, and walks away. Just like that.

I gaze after him and *don't* miss him, and then I gaze at the others and *don't* want to be with them. But we're all New York. New York is so full of shit sometimes, and nobody knows that better than New York.

So Queens comes over first, laughing and dripping from the sea, to grab my arm and complain that I must be too cool to walk on sand like everyone else, until I finally give up and let her pull me off the boardwalk. And then Jersey City—she prefers Veneza, so we use that name, but she's also Jersey City—runs over and hands me a foil-wrapped sandwich of some kind, because, she says, "I'm sick of feeling how hungry you are. You need to eat more." She pulls me across the sand to the blankets. (The sandwich is good. Chicken kebab. I'm not supposed to get hungry anymore, Paulo said, but New York is always hungry.) When Jojo flops down and sprinkles all of us with water, Brooklyn wryly hands me a paper towel to wipe my face. Then Bronca tells me to lie the fuck down because I'm shadowing the sun, and she's trying to soak up enough light and warmth to get her through next winter even though that's like six months off. When I sit down, Manny moves aside to make room for me—but he stays bodyguard-close. Also near enough to touch, if I want. When I'm ready.

"Welcome back," he says, handing me a Snapple from the cooler. Pink lemonade. Probably just chance that it's my favorite flavor.

"No place in the world that can compare," I say, and we all smile with the magic of this truth.

Acknowledgments

It's been a surprise to me—and perhaps it shouldn't have been—
that writing a story set in a real place, even a real place that I know
well, has required more research than all the other fantasy novels
I've written, combined. Most of this is because real worlds feature
real peoples, and therefore it's important that I not depict them in
ways that disrespect or cause harm. Also, though, I know a lot of
these people, and they'd rag on me mercilessly if I described, say,
Shorakkopoch wrong. Leave me alone, y'all. New York is fucking
huge. I did the best I could.

Unfortunately, for various reasons including real-world events,
I was unable to visit Hong Kong or São Paulo during the writing of this book. I based both men's personalities and abilities on
what little information I could glean from books and articles and
some friends who'd been there, but end of day, I took substantial
creative license with both. I hope to "meet" both cities (and their
people!) someday, but I don't know if that will happen before I've
finished this trilogy. That said, I hope residents of both cities will
accept my long-distance admiration in lieu of a visit, for now.

Now for the credits, which are substantial. In addition to the
usual assistance provided by my editor and agent (thanks!), I
needed a small army of advisors and inspirers for this book. First
but not most, let me credit fellow writer John Scalzi for the phrase

"racist sexist homophobic dipshit." So useful, that one. Thanks to creative genius Jean Grae for the lyrics Brooklyn uses during her literal battle rap; I wrote them, she fixed them. Particular thanks also to my sensitivity reader for Lenape language and cultural tidbits (and Bronca's Lenape name!), who prefers not to be listed here, and to the Nanticoke Lenni-Lenape tribal nation for excellent website references (sorry I missed the pow-wow though). Thanks for general advice and guidance to another Indigenous consultant, who also prefers not to be named, and who helped me find my Lenape consultant. Many thanks to fellow writers Mary Anne Mohanraj for sensitivity reading re Padmini's Tamil heritage and Mimi Mondal for sensitivity reading re Padmini's Dalit caste markers and nuances, as well as to former Orbit intern Stuti Telidevera for general review and guidance. Continuous thanks to Danielle Friedman for context re survivors of the Shoah. Passive thanks to the Crash Override Network for its tips on maximizing cybersecurity, especially in circumstances that warrant a lockdown; I've unfortunately had to use such techniques to guard my own life for years now. Also thanks to accuracy readers Kevin Whyte for checking my math, Ananda Ferrari Ossanai for general Brazil notes and omg delicious brigadeiro, and Orbit UK editor Jenni Hill for assistance with Bel's Britishisms and helping make this story more comprehensible to people unfamiliar with NYC. Major thanks to fellow writer Genevieve Valentine for overall editing and story direction advice, and for hip-checking some of my more egregious New Yorkisms. Long-ago thanks to writing group mate K. Tempest Bradford for introducing me to Inwood Hill Park and Inwood in general. More recent thanks to Orbit's art director Lauren Panepinto for puncturing some of my assumptions and clarifying the many myths about Staten Island. Lifelong thanks to my father, Noah Jemisin, for exposing me to NYC's art world, and its many politics and wonders.

Also, personal thanks to New York itself. I consider myself to be roughly 50 percent New Yorker. I spent most of my formative years in Alabama—but every summer and break in Brooklyn, and of course I have now lived in the city full-time since 2007. Much of who I am as a person comes from those earlier, fragmentary chunks of New York life. I have walked over a layer of crack vials, run into Double Dutch jump ropes (got smacked in the face like 75 percent of the time, but during that successful 25 percent, I felt like a goddess), ridden the Cyclone until they wouldn't let me on it anymore, run through the spray from a popped water plug, sweated through heat waves without AC, adopted a street cat, kicked a street rat when it came at me. I love hip-hop and fear cops because of New York. I learned courage and adventurousness from New York. I have fantastic problem-solving skills because of New York.

I have hated this city. I have loved this city. I will fight for this city until it won't have me anymore. This is my homage to the city. Hope I got it right.

extras

orbitbooks.net

about the author

N. K. Jemisin is a Brooklyn-based author and the winner of three Hugo Awards for her novels *The Fifth Season*, *The Obelisk Gate* and *The Stone Sky*. She previously won the Locus Award for her first novel, *The Hundred Thousand Kingdoms*, and her short fiction and novels have been nominated multiple times for Hugo, World Fantasy and Nebula awards, and shortlisted for the Crawford and the James Tiptree, Jr Awards. She is a science fiction and fantasy reviewer for the *New York Times*, and you can find her online at nkjemisin.com.

Find out more about N. K. Jemisin and other Orbit authors by registering for the free monthly newsletter at orbitbooks.net.

reading group guide

1. In *The City We Became*, the avatars draw their power not just from the city itself but also from representations of the city in popular culture and from stereotypes. How does the novel both utilize and undermine those stereotypes?

2. If your hometown had an avatar, what kind of person would represent it? What kind of magic would give them their power?

3. *The City We Became* is set in a real place and deals with real, serious themes, but also has magic. How do the supernatural elements enhance these themes? Could the same story have been written without the magical influences?

4. Manny is the only character who doesn't remember anything about who he was before he became an avatar. What do you think this means about him, his borough, and his role in the story?

5. Reviews have called the novel a metaphor for gentrification. Do you agree or disagree? Why?

6. The Woman in White is an active antagonist while Staten Island is more passive, allowing destruction to happen to the rest of New York without intervening. Do you think their roles are comparable? Which has the greater impact:

the one causing the destruction, or the one with power to stop it who stands aside?

7. The Woman in White justifies her actions by explaining that she is trying to save her own parallel universe from destruction. How does that complicate her role as the antagonist and the role of the heroes?

8. This book was published in 2020 around the beginning of the COVID-19 pandemic in the US and during a time of widespread protests against police brutality. How does the timing affect your reading of the novel?

if you enjoyed

THE CITY WE BECAME

look out for

THE BONE SHARD DAUGHTER

The Drowning Empire: Book One

by

Andrea Stewart

The Sukai Dynasty has ruled the Phoenix Empire for over a century, their mastery of bone shard magic powering the monstrous constructs that maintain law and order. But now the Emperor's rule is failing, and revolution is sweeping across the Empire's many islands.

Lin is the Emperor's daughter, but a mysterious illness has stolen her childhood memories and her status as heir to the empire. Trapped in a palace of locked doors and old secrets, Lin vows to reclaim her birthright by mastering the forbidden art of bone shard magic.

But the mysteries behind such power are dark and deep, and wielding her family's magic carries a great cost. When the revolution reaches the gates of the palace itself, Lin must decide how far she is willing to go to claim her throne — and save her people.

1

Lin

Imperial Island

Father told me I'm broken.

He didn't speak this disappointment when I answered his question. But he said it with narrowed eyes, the way he sucked on his already hollow cheeks, the way the left side of his lips twitched a little bit down, the movement almost hidden by his beard.

He taught me how to read a person's thoughts on their face.

And he knew that I knew how to read these signs. So between us, it was as though he had spoken out loud.

The question: "Who was your closest childhood friend?"

My answer: "I don't know."

I could run as quickly as the sparrow flies, I was as skilled with an abacus as the Empire's best accountants, and I could name all the known islands in the time it took for tea to finish steeping. But I could not remember my past before the sickness. Sometimes I thought I never would – that the girl from before was lost to me.

Father's chair creaked as he shifted, and he let out a long breath. In his fingers he held a brass key, which he tapped on the table's surface. "How can I trust you with my secrets? How can I trust you as my heir if you do not know who you are?"

I knew who I was. I was Lin. I was the Emperor's daughter. I shouted the words in my head, but I didn't say them. Unlike my father, I kept my face neutral, my thoughts hidden. Sometimes he liked it when I stood up for myself, but this was not one of those times. It never was, when it came to my past.

I did my best not to stare at the key.

"Ask me another question," I said. The wind lashed at the shutters, bringing with it the salt-seaweed smell of the ocean. The breeze licked at my neck, and I suppressed a shiver. I kept his gaze, hoping he saw the steel in my soul and not the fear. I could taste the scent of rebellion on the winds as clearly as I could the fish fermentation vats. It was that obvious, that thick. I could set things right, if only I had the means. If only he'd let me prove it.

Tap.

"Very well," Father said. The teak pillars behind him framed his withered countenance, making him look more like a foreboding portrait than a man. "You're afraid of sea serpents. Why?"

"I was bit by one when I was a child," I said.

He studied my face. I held my breath. I stopped holding my breath. I twined my fingers together and then forced them to relax. If I were a mountain, he would be following the taproots of cloud junipers, chipping away the stone, searching for the white, chalky core.

And finding it.

"Don't lie to me, girl," he snarled. "Don't make guesses. You may be my flesh and blood, but I can name my foster son to the crown. It doesn't have to be you."

I wished I did remember. Was there a time when this man

stroked my hair and kissed my forehead? Had he loved me before I'd forgotten, when I'd been whole and unbroken? I wished there was someone I could ask. Or at least, someone who could give me answers. "Forgive me." I bowed my head. My black hair formed a curtain over my eyes, and I stole a glance at the key.

Most of the doors in the palace were locked. He hobbled from room to room, using his bone shard magic to create miracles. A magic I needed if I was to rule. I'd earned six keys. My father's foster, Bayan, had seven. Sometimes it felt as if my entire life was a test.

"Fine," Father said. He eased back into his chair. "You may go."

I rose to leave, but hesitated. "When will you teach me your bone shard magic?" I didn't wait for his response. "You say you can name Bayan as your heir, but you haven't. I am still your heir, and I need to know how to control the constructs. I'm twentythree, and you—" I stopped, because I didn't know how old he was. There were liver spots on the backs of his hands, and his hair was steely gray. I didn't know how much longer he would live. All I could imagine was a future where he died and left me with no knowledge. No way to protect the Empire from the Alanga. No memories of a father who cared.

He coughed, muffling the sound with his sleeve. His gaze flicked to the key, and his voice went soft. "When you are a whole person," he said.

I didn't understand him. But I recognized the vulnerability. "Please," I said, "what if I am never a whole person?"

He looked at me, and the sadness in his gaze scraped at my heart like teeth. I had five years of memories; before that was a fog. I'd lost something precious; if only I knew what it was. "Father, I—"

A knock sounded at the door, and he was cold as stone once more.

Bayan slipped inside without waiting for a response, and I wanted to curse him. He hunched his shoulders as he walked, his footfalls silent. If he were anyone else, I'd think his step hesitant. But Bayan had the look of a cat about him – deliberate, predatory. He wore a leather apron over his tunic, and blood stained his hands.

"I've completed the modification," Bayan said. "You asked me to see you right away when I'd finished."

A construct hobbled behind him, tiny hooves clicking against the floor. It looked like a deer, except for the fangs protruding from its mouth and the curling monkey's tail. Two small wings sprouted from its shoulders, blood staining the fur around them.

Father turned in his chair and placed a hand on the creature's back. It looked up at him with wide, wet eyes. "Sloppy," he says. "How many shards did you use to embed the follow command?"

"Two," Bayan said. "One to get the construct to follow me, and another to get it to stop."

"It should be one," Father said. "It goes where you do unless you tell it not to. The language is in the first book I gave you." He seized one of the wings and pulled it. When he let it go, it settled slowly back at the construct's side. "Your construction, however, is excellent."

Bayan's eyes slid to the side, and I held his gaze. Neither of us looked away. Always a competition. Bayan's irises were blacker even than mine, and when his lip curled, it only accentuated the full curve of his mouth. I supposed he was prettier than I would ever be, but I was convinced I was smarter, and that's what really mattered. Bayan never cared to hide his feelings. He carried his contempt for me like a child's favorite seashell.

"Try again with a new construct," Father said, and Bayan broke his gaze from mine. Ah, I'd won this small contest.

Father reached his fingers into the beast. I held my breath. I'd only seen him do this twice. Twice I could remember, at least. The creature only blinked placidly as Father's hand disappeared to the wrist. And then he pulled away and the construct froze, still as a statue. In his hand were two small shards of bone.

No blood stained his fingers. He dropped the bones into Bayan's hand. "Now go. Both of you."

I was quicker to the door than Bayan, whom I suspected was hoping for more than just harsh words. But I was used to harsh words, and I'd things to do. I slipped out the door and held it for Bayan to pass so he needn't bloody the door with his hands. Father prized cleanliness.

Bayan glared at me as he passed, the breeze in his wake smelling of copper and incense. Bayan was just the son of a small isle's governor, lucky enough to have caught Father's eye and to be taken in as a foster. He'd brought the sickness with him, some exotic disease Imperial didn't know. I was told I got sick with it soon after he arrived, and recovered a little while after Bayan did. But he hadn't lost as much of his memory as I had, and he'd gotten some of it back.

As soon as he disappeared around the corner, I whirled and ran for the end of the hallway. The shutters threatened to blow against the walls when I unlatched them. The tile roofs looked like the slopes of mountains. I stepped outside and shut the window.

The world opened up before me. From atop the roof, I could see the city and the harbor. I could even see the boats in the ocean fishing for squid, their lanterns shining in the distance like earthbound stars. The wind tugged at my tunic, finding its way beneath the cloth, biting at my skin.

I had to be quick. By now, the construct servant would have removed the body of the deer. I half-ran, half-skidded down the slope of the roof toward the side of the palace where my father's bedroom was. He never brought his chain of keys into the questioning room. He didn't bring his construct guards with him. I'd read the small signs on his face. He might bark at me and scold me, but when we were alone – he feared me.

The tiles clicked below my feet. On the ramparts of the palace walls, shadows lurked – more constructs. Their instructions were simple. Watch for intruders. Sound an alarm. None of them paid me any mind, no matter that I wasn't where I was supposed to be. I wasn't an intruder.

The Construct of Bureaucracy would now be handing over the reports. I'd watched him sorting them earlier in the day, hairy lips fumbling over his teeth as he read them silently. There would be quite a lot. Shipments delayed due to skirmishes, the Ioph Carn stealing and smuggling witstone, citizens shirking their duty to the Empire.

I swung onto my father's balcony. The door to his room was cracked open. The room was usually empty, but this time it was not. A growl emanated from within. I froze. A black nose nudged into the space between door and wall, widening the gap. Yellow eyes peered at me and tufted ears flicked back. Claws scraped against wood as the creature strode toward me. Bing Tai, one of my father's oldest constructs. Gray speckled his jowls, but he had all his teeth. Each incisor was as long as my thumb.

His lip curled, the hackles on his back standing on end. He was a creature of nightmares, an amalgamation of large predators, with black, shaggy fur that faded into the darkness. He took another step closer.

Maybe it wasn't Bayan that was stupid; maybe I was the stupid one. Maybe this was how Father would find me after his tea – torn to bloody pieces on his balcony. It was too far to the ground, and I was too short to reach the roof gutters. The only way out from these rooms was into the hallway. "Bing Tai," I said, and my voice was steadier than I felt. "It is me, Lin."

I could almost feel my father's two commands battling in the construct's head. One: protect my rooms. Two: protect my family. Which command was stronger? I'd bet on the second one, but now I wasn't so sure.

I held my ground and tried not to let my fear show. I shoved my hand toward Bing Tai's nose. He could see me, he could hear me, perhaps he needed to smell me.

He *could* choose to taste me, though I did my best not to think about that.

His wet, cold nose touched my fingers, a growl still deep in his throat. I was not Bayan, who wrestled with the constructs like they were his brothers. I could not forget what they were. My throat constricted until I could barely breathe, my chest tight and painful.

And then Bing Tai settled on his haunches, his ears pricking, his lips covering his teeth. "Good Bing Tai," I said. My voice trembled. I had to hurry.

Grief lay heavy in the room, thick as the dust on what used to be my mother's wardrobe. Her jewelry on the dresser lay untouched; her slippers still awaited her next to the bed. What bothered me more than the questions my father asked me, than not knowing if he loved and cared for me as a child, was not remembering my mother.

I'd heard the remaining servants whispering. He burned all her portraits on the day she died. He forbade mention of her name. He put all her handmaidens to the sword. He guarded the memories of her jealously, as if he was the only one allowed to have them.

Focus.

I didn't know where he kept the copies he distributed to Bayan and me. He always pulled these from his sash pocket, and I didn't dare try to filch them from there. But the original chain of keys lay on the bed. So many doors. So many keys. I didn't know which was which, so I selected one at random – a golden key with a jade piece in the bow – and pocketed it.

I escaped into the hallway and wedged a thin piece of wood between door and frame so the door didn't latch. Now the tea would be steeping. Father would be reading through the reports, asking questions. I hoped they would keep him occupied.

My feet scuffed against the floorboards as I ran. The grand hallways of the palace were empty, lamplight glinting off the red-painted beams above. In the entryway, teak pillars rose from floor to ceiling, framing the faded mural on the second-floor wall. I took the steps down to the palace doors two at a time. Each step felt like a miniature betrayal.

I could have waited, one part of my mind told me. I could have been obedient; I could have done my best to answer my father's questions, to heal my memories. But the other part of my mind was cold and sharp. It cut through the guilt to find a hard truth. I could never be what he wanted if I did not take what I wanted. I hadn't been able to remember, no matter how hard I'd tried. He'd not left me with any other choice than to show him I was worthy in a different way.

I slipped through the palace doors and into the silent yard. The front gates were closed, but I was small and strong, and if Father wouldn't teach me his magic, well, there were other things I'd taught myself in the times he was locked in a secret room with Bayan. Like climbing.

The walls were clean but in disrepair. The plaster had broken away in places, leaving the stone beneath exposed. It was easy enough to climb. The monkey-shaped construct atop the wall just glanced at me before turning its limpid gaze back to the city. A thrill rushed through me when I touched down on the other side. I'd been into the city on foot before – *I must have* – but for me, it was like the first time. The streets stank of fish and hot oil, and the remnants of dinners cooked and eaten. The stones beneath my slippers were dark and slippery with washwater. Pots clanged and a breeze carried the sound of lilting, subdued voices. The first two storefronts I saw were closed, wooden shutters locked shut.

Too late? I'd seen the blacksmith's storefront from the palace walls, and this was what first gave me the idea. I held my breath as I dashed down a narrow alley.

He was there. He was pulling the door closed, a pack slung over one shoulder.

"Wait," I said. "Please, just one more order."

"We're closed," he huffed out. "Come back tomorrow."

I stifled the desperation clawing up my throat. "I'll pay you twice your regular price if you can start it tonight. Just one key copy."

He looked at me then, and his gaze trailed over my embroidered silk tunic. His lips pressed together. He was thinking about lying about how much he charged. But then he just sighed. "Two silver. One is my regular price." He was a good man, fair.

Relief flooded me as I dug the coins from my sash pocket and pressed them into his calloused palm. "Here. I need it quickly."

Wrong thing to say. Annoyance flashed across his face. But he still opened the door again and let me into his shop. The man was built like an iron – broad and squat. His shoulders seemed to take up half the space. Metal tools hung from the walls and ceiling. He picked up his tinderbox and re-lit the lamps. And then he turned back to face me. "It won't be ready until tomorrow morning at the earliest."

"But do you need to keep the key?"

He shook his head. "I can make a mold of it tonight. The key will be ready tomorrow."

I wished there weren't so many chances to turn back, so many chances for my courage to falter. I forced myself to drop my father's key into the blacksmith's hand. The man took it and turned, fishing a block of clay from a stone trough. He pressed the key into it. And then he froze, his breath stopping in his throat.

I moved for the key before I could think. I saw what he did as soon as I took one step closer. At the base of the bow, just before the stem, was the tiny figure of a phoenix embossed into the metal.

When the blacksmith looked at me, his face was as round and pale as the moon. "Who are you? What are you doing with one of the Emperor's keys?"

I should have grabbed the key and run. I was swifter than he was. I could snatch it away and be gone before he took his next breath. All he'd have left was a story – one that no one would believe.

But if I did, I wouldn't have my key copy. I wouldn't have any more answers. I'd be stuck where I was at the start of the day, my memory a haze, the answers I gave Father always inadequate. Always just out of reach. Always broken. And this man – he was a good man. Father taught me the kind of thing to say to good men.

I chose my words carefully. "Do you have any children?"

A measure of color came back into his face. "Two." He

answered. His brows knit together as he wondered if he should have responded.

"I am Lin," I said, laying myself bare. "I am the Emperor's heir. He hasn't been the same since my mother's death. He isolates himself, he keeps few servants, he does not meet with the island governors. Rebellion is brewing. Already the Shardless Few have taken Khalute. They'll seek to expand their hold. And there are the Alanga. Some may not believe they're coming back, but my family has kept them from returning.

"Do you want soldiers marching in the streets? Do you want war on your doorstep?" I touched his shoulder gently, and he did not flinch. "On your children's doorstep?"

He reached reflexively behind his right ear for the scar each citizen had. The place where a shard of bone was removed and taken for the Emperor's vault.

"Is my shard powering a construct?" he asked.

"I don't know," I said. I don't know, I don't know – there was so *little* that I did know. "But if I get into my father's vault, I will look for yours and I will bring it back to you. I can't promise you anything. I wish I could. But I will try."

He licked his lips. "My children?"

"I can see what I can do." It was all I could say. No one was exempt from the islands' Tithing Festivals.

Sweat shone on his forehead. "I'll do it."

Father would be setting the reports aside now. He would take up his cup of tea and sip from it, looking out the window at the lights of the city below. Sweat prickled between my shoulderblades. I needed to get the key back before he discovered me.

I watched through a haze as the blacksmith finished making the mold. When he handed the key back, I turned to run.

"Lin," he said.

I stopped.

"My name is Numeen. The year of my ritual was 1508. We need an Emperor who cares about us."

What could I say to that? So I just ran. Out the door, down the alleyway, back to climbing the wall. Now Father would be finishing up his tea, his fingers wrapped around the still-warm cup. A stone came loose beneath my fingertips. I let it fall to the ground. The *crack* made me cringe.

He'd be putting his cup down, he'd be looking at the city. How long did he look at the city? The climb down was faster than the climb up. I couldn't smell the city anymore. All I could smell was my own breath. The walls of the outer buildings passed in a blur as I ran to the palace – the servants' quarters, the Hall of Everlasting Peace, the Hall of Earthly Wisdom, the wall surrounding the palace garden. Everything was cold and dark, empty.

I took the servants' entrance into the palace, bounding up the stairs two at a time. The narrow passageway opened into the main hallway. The main hallway wrapped around the palace's second floor, and my father's bedroom was nearly on the other side from the servants' entrance. I wished my legs were longer. I wished my mind were stronger.

Floorboards squeaked beneath my feet as I ran, the noise making me wince. At last, I made it back and slipped into my father's room. Bing Tai lay on the rug at the foot of the bed, stretched out like an old cat. I had to reach over him to get to the chain of keys. He smelled musty, like a mix between a bear construct and a closet full of moth-ridden clothes.

It took three tries for me to hook the key back onto the chain. My fingers felt like eels – flailing and slippery.

I knelt to retrieve the door wedge on my way out, my breath ragged in my throat. The brightness of the light in the hallway made me blink. I'd have to find my way into the city tomorrow to retrieve the new key. But it was done, the wedge for the door safely in my sash pocket. I let out the breath I hadn't known I'd been holding.

"Lin."

Bayan. My limbs felt made of stone. What had he seen? I turned to face him – his brow was furrowed, his hands clasped behind his back. I willed my heart to calm, my face to blankness.

"What are you doing outside the Emperor's room?"

2

Jovis

Deerhead Island

I hoped this was one of my smaller mistakes. I tugged at the hem of the jacket. The sleeves were too short, the waist too roomy, the shoulders just a bit too broad. I sniffed the collar. The musky, star anise perfume went straight up my nose, making me cough. "If you're trying to attract a partner with that, best try a little less," I said. It was a good piece of advice, but the soldier at my feet didn't respond.

Is it still talking to oneself if the other person is unconscious?

Well, the uniform fit enough, and "enough" is what I could hope for most days. I had two full, standard boxes of witstone on my boat. Enough to pay my debts, enough to eat well for three months, enough to get my boat from one end of the Phoenix Empire to the other. But "enough" would never get me what I truly needed. I'd heard a rumor at the docks, a whisper of a disappearance similar to my Emahla's, and I'd be cursing myself the rest of my life if I didn't suss out the origins.

I slipped from the alleyway, resisting the urge to tug at the jacket hem one more time. Nodded to another soldier when I passed her in the street. Let out my breath when she nodded back and turned away. I'd not checked the yearly Tithing Festival schedule before stopping. And because luck rarely worked out in my favor, this meant, of course, the Festival was here.

Deerhead Island was swarming with the Emperor's soldiers. And here I was – a trader without an Imperial contract, who'd had more than one run-in with the Empire's soldiers. I held the edge of my sleeve in my fingers as I navigated the streets. I'd gotten the rabbit tattoo when I'd passed the navigational exams. It was less pride and more practicality. How else would they identify my swollen and bloated body if I washed ashore? But now, as a smuggler, the tattoo was a liability. That and my face. They'd gotten the jawline wrong on the posters, the eyes were too close together and I'd cut my curling hair short since then, but aye, it was a likeness. I'd been paying gutter orphans to take them down, but then five days later I'd see some damned construct putting another one back up.

It was a shame that Imperial uniforms didn't come with hats.

I should have taken my witstone and fled, but Emahla was a string in my heart that fate couldn't seem to stop tugging. So I set my feet one in front of the other and did my best to appear as bland and blank as possible. The man at the docks had said the disappearance was recent, so the trail was still fresh. I didn't have much time. The soldier hadn't seen me before I'd clobbered him, but he'd patched a section of the left elbow and he'd recognize his uniform.

The street narrowed ahead, sunlight filtering down through gaps between the buildings and laundry hung to dry. Someone inside called out, "Don't keep me waiting! How long does it take to put on a pair of shoes?" I wasn't far from the ocean, so the air still smelled like seaweed, mingled with cooking meat and hot oil. They'd be preparing their children for the Festival, and preparing the Festival meal for when their children returned. Good food couldn't heal wounds of body and soul, but it could soothe them. My mother had prepared a feast for my trepanning day. Roasted duck with crisped skin, grilled vegetables, fragrant and spiced rice, fish with the sauce still bubbling. I'd had to dry my tears before eating it.

But that was a time long past for me – the scar behind my right ear long since healed. I ducked beneath a shirt hung too low and still damp, and found the drinking hall the man at the docks had described.

The door creaked as I opened it, scraping a well-worn path along the wooden floorboards. This early in the morning, it should have been empty. Instead, Imperial guards lurked in dusty corners, dried fish hanging from the ceiling. I made my way to the back, my shoulder against the wall, my wrist hidden by my thigh, my head down. If I'd been a better planner, I'd have wrapped the tattoo. Ah well. My face was the bigger problem, and I couldn't wrap that.

A woman stood behind the counter, her broad back to me, hair tied up in a handkerchief with a few loose strands stuck to her neck. She hunched over a wooden cutting board, her fingers nimbly pleating dumplings.

"Auntie," I said to her, deferential.

She didn't turn around. "Don't call me that," she said. "I'm not old enough to be anyone's auntie except to children." She wiped her floured hands on her apron, sighed. "What can I get for you?"

"I wanted to talk," I said.

She turned around then and gave my uniform a long look. I don't think she even glanced at my face. "I sent my nephew along to the square already. The census takers would have marked him by now. Is that what you're here for?"

"You're Danila, right? I have questions about your foster daughter," I said.

Her face closed up. "I've reported everything I know."

I knew the reception she'd received upon her report, because Emahla's parents had gotten the same – the shrugged shoulders, the annoyed expressions. Young women ran away sometimes, didn't they? And besides, what did they expect the Emperor to do about it?

"Just leave me in peace," she said before turning back to her dumplings.

That soldier in the alleyway might be waking up right now with a splitting headache and a good many questions on his lips. But – Emahla. Her name chased itself around my head, spurring me to action. I slid around the end of the counter and joined Danila at the cutting board.

Without waiting for any sort of approval, I picked up the wrappings and the filling and began to pleat. After a startled moment, she began again. Behind us, two soldiers bet on their game of cards.

"You're good," she begrudged me. "Very neat, very quick."

"My mother. She was – *is* – a cook." I shook my head with a rueful smile. It had been so long since I'd been home. Another life, almost. "Makes the best dumplings in all the isles. I ran about a lot, sailing and studying for the navigational exams, but I always liked to help her. Even after I passed."

"If you passed the navigational exams, why are you a soldier?"

I weighed my options. I was a good liar – the best. It was the only reason I still had a head on my shoulders. But this woman reminded me of my mother, gruff but kindhearted, and I had a missing wife to find. "I'm not." I slid my sleeve up enough to show the rabbit tattoo.

Danila looked at the tattoo, and then at my face. Her eyes narrowed, then widened. "Jovis," she said in a whisper. "You're that smuggler."

"I'd prefer 'most successful smuggler in the last one hundred years', but I'll settle for 'that smuggler'."

She snorted. "Depends on how you define success. Your mother wouldn't think so, I'd guess."

"You're probably right," I said lightly. It would deeply pain her to know how far I'd fallen. Danila relaxed, her shoulder now touching mine, her expression softer. She wouldn't give me away. Just wasn't the sort. "I need to ask about your foster daughter. How she disappeared."

"There isn't much to tell," she said. "She was here one day and then gone the next, nineteen silver coins left on her bedspread – as though a silver phoenix was all a year of her life was worth. It was two days ago. I keep thinking she'll walk back in the door."

She wouldn't. I knew, because I'd thought the same for a year. I could still see the nineteen silver coins scattered across Emahla's bed. Could still feel my heart pounding, my stomach twisting – caught in that moment of both knowing she was gone and not being able to believe it.

"Soshi was a bright young woman," Danila said, a quaver in her voice. She struck the tears from her eyes before they could reach her cheeks. "Her mother died in a mining accident and she didn't know her father. I never married, never had any children of my own. I took her in. I needed someone to help."

"Was . . . ?" The word thudded from my mouth; I couldn't form the question.

Danila picked up another wrap and studied my face. "I may not be old enough to be your auntie, but to me you are still a boy. If the Empire had anything to do with her disappearance, she's already dead."

I have never been in love. We never met as children, we never became friends. I never took the chance, never kissed her. I never came back from Imperial Island. I told myself the lie, over and over. Even so, my mind layered on top her teasing smile, how she rolled her eyes when I made up a particularly silly story, the way she leaned her head onto my shoulder and sighed after a long day. But I needed to believe the lie. Because every time I thought about living the rest of my life without her, panic fluttered up my chest and wrapped itself around my throat. I swallowed. "Did you look for her? Did you find any trace?"

"Of course I looked," she said. "I asked around. One of the fishermen said they saw a boat leave early that morning. Not from the docks but from a nearby cove. It was small, dark and had blue sails. It went east. That's all I know."

It was the boat I'd seen the morning Emahla had disappeared, rounding the edge of the island, the mist so thick I wasn't sure I'd seen it at all. In seven years, this was the best lead I had. If I was quick, I might be able to catch it.

One of the soldiers in the hall laughed, another groaned and cards hit the table. Chairs scraped against the floor as they rose. "It was a good game." A beam of sunlight warmed the back of my neck as they opened the door. "Hey you. You coming with us? The captain will bite your head off if you're late."

No one answered, and I remembered the soldier's jacket I wore. He was talking to me.

Danila seized my wrist. The one with the tattoo. Both her voice and her grip were intractable as tree roots. "I've done you a favor, Jovis. Now I need a favor of you."

Oh no. "Favors? We didn't speak of favors."

She talked over me, and I heard footsteps approaching from

behind. "I have a nephew. He lives on a small isle just east of here. If I have it right, you'll be headed in that direction anyways. Take him before the ritual. Get him back to his parents. He's their only child."

"I'm not one of the Shardless Few. I don't smuggle children," I hissed. "It's not ethical. Or profitable." I tried her grip and found her strength greater than mine.

"Do it."

By the sound of the footsteps behind me, there was only one soldier. I could handle him. I could lie my way out of this. But after all these years, I still remembered the trickle of blood from my scalp, running down my neck. The cold touch of the chisel against my skin. The wound felt like fire. The Emperor says that the Tithing Festival is a small price to pay for the safety of us all. It didn't feel like so small a price when it was your head bowed and your knees digging into the ground.

I am hardened to the suffering of others. Another lie I told myself because I couldn't save everyone; I hadn't been able to even save my own brother. If I thought too much on all the suffering, all the people I couldn't help, I felt like I was drowning in the Endless Sea itself. I couldn't carry that weight.

Mostly this worked. But not today. Today I thought of my mother, her hands on each side of my face: "But what is the *truth*, Jovis?"

The truth was that someone had saved me. Sometimes one is enough. "I'll take him," I said.

I was a fool.

Danila let go of my wrist. "He owes me for a mug of wine. He'll be along shortly," she told the soldier.

The man's footsteps retreated.

"My nephew's name is Alon," Danila told me. "He's dressed in a red shirt with white flowers embroidered on the hem. His mother is a cobbler on Phalar. She's the only one on the isle."

I brushed the flour from my hands. "Red shirt. Flowers. Cobbler. Got it."

"You should hurry."

I'd have snapped at her if her grief wasn't so obvious. She'd lost a daughter. I'd lost a wife. I could be kind. "If I find out what happened to your foster daughter, I'll figure out a way to let you know."

She wiped at her eyes again, nodded and turned back to pleating dumplings with the ferocity of a warrior on a battlefield. It seemed the lie she told herself was that these dumplings were the most important thing in the world right now.

I turned to go and the earth moved beneath me. Mugs rattled in their cupboards, Danila's rolling pin fell to the floor, and the dried fish swayed on their strings. I put my hands out, unsure of where to steady them. Everything moved. And then, just as quickly, it settled.

"Just a quake," Danila said, though I knew already. She said it more to soothe herself than me. "Some people think it's the witstone mine causing them – it runs deep. It's nothing to worry about. They've been going on for the past few months."

A lie she tells herself? Quakes happened sometimes, but it had been a long time since I'd felt one. I took an experimental step and found the ground steady. "I should go. May the winds be favorable."

"And the skies clear," she responded.

Spiriting a child away from the Tithing Festival wasn't going to be easy. The census takers made sure that all children who had turned eight years old attended, so I'd need to find a way to strike his name from the list. But I'd dealt with census takers before, and Imperial soldiers, and even the Emperor's constructs.

I smoothed the front of the uniform jacket and went to the door. I should have drawn aside the curtains, or cracked the door to look beforehand. But the quake had unsettled my nerves, and I was close to finding the boat that had taken Emahla. I was close to an answer. So instead, I stepped back into the narrow street, the sunlight hot on my face, wide-eyed and unsteady as a newborn lamb.

And found myself in the midst of a phalanx of Imperial soldiers.